The

One for the Money

Dave Harker was born in Cleveland in 1946, and grew up in the declining ironstone mining villages of that district of the old North Riding. He went to the local grammar school, and then to Cambridge. For the last seven years he has taught at Manchester Polytechnic, and now specializes in courses for adult trade unionists.

One for the Money

Politics and popular song

Dave Harker

Hutchinson

London Melbourne Sydney Auckland Johannesburg

Hutchinson & Co. (Publishers) Ltd

An imprint of the Hutchinson Publishing Group

24 Highbury Crescent, London N5 1RX

Hutchinson Group (Australia) Pty Ltd
30-32 Cremorne Street, Richmond South, Victoria 3121
PO Box 151, Broadway, New South Wales 2007

Hutchinson Group (NZ) Ltd
32-34 View Road, PO Box 40-086, Glenfield, Auckland 10

Hutchinson Group (SA) (Pty) Ltd
PO Box 337, Bergvlei 2012, South Africa

First published 1980

Set in IBM Press Roman by Donald Typesetting, Bristol

Printed in Great Britain by The Anchor Press Ltd
and bound by Wm Brendon & Son Ltd,
both of Tiptree, Essex

British Library Cataloguing in Publication Data

Harker, David
    One for the Money.
    1. Music, Popular (Songs, etc.) — Great Britain
    — History and criticism
    2. Music, Popular (Songs, etc.) — United States
    — History and criticism
    I. Title
    784'.0941   ML3650

ISBN 0 09 140730 3 cased
        0 09 140731 1 paper

I don't want to die and leave a few sad
songs and a hump in the ground as my
only monument.

GEORGE JACKSON, *Soledad Brother*

Let me just leave you with this plain in your head
That I've never heard nobody yet get a whole room full
Of friends and enemies both
To sing and to ring the plaster down singing out a novel.

WOODY GUTHRIE, *Born to Win*

(Gleason)   In a lot of your songs you are hard on
             people . . . . Do you do this because you want
             to change their lives, or do you want to
             point out to them the error of their ways?
(Dylan)   I want to needle them

Rolling Stone Interviews, Vol. 2.

Well it's one for the money
Two for the show
Three to get ready
Now go cat go
But don't you
Step on my blue suede shoes
You can do anything
But lay off my blue suede shoes

CARL PERKINS, *Blue Suede Shoes*

Acknowledgements

Thanks to: Eddie Barnes
Les Berry
Ian Birchall
Theresa Calder
David Craig
Ian Dobson
Terry Eagleton
Alex Glasgow
Paul Graney
Trevor Haines
Maureen Harker
Marilyn Jeffcoat
Rowland Jones
Claire L'Enfant
Don Limon
Gill Prest
Bill Robb
Ian Rogerson
Tony Stimson
Stephen Struthers
Paul Willis
Ian Winship
Linda Zuck

and all the students and friends I've learned from

Contents

Why what follows follows

Who needs a book on 'popular song'? Isn't that one area where we are all of us experts? Won't a book like this degenerate into a spiritual autobiography; or won't it try to lay claim to yet another area of social life for trendy academics?

The dangers are obviously there. But on the other hand, where can the reader turn for an analysis of *why* popular song is such an important part of our lives? Where is the book which attempts to *explain* the production, dissemination and reception of what we know as 'popular song' in such a way that this sensitive area of our culture isn't patronized or blown up out of all proportion? We have hundreds of 'pop' biographies and autobiographies, dozens of partial accounts of the music industry, and even the occasional learned article about particular periods in the development of popular song. But there is no attempt to systematize what is valuable in these accounts, no serious effort to break out of the ego trip syndrome. We still lack a book which seeks to clarify the key elements in the development of popular song in a self-consistent way, from a particular point of view.

Of course, it's not possible in a book of this length to attempt an exhaustive historical survey even of post-war popular song in Britain and the USA. Not that such an enterprise is impossible, or unnecessary; but it would need a team of researchers and several volumes to do the subject justice. This is why the analyses which follow have had to be carefully selected. Some selected themselves. For example, there had to be discussion of the technological and institutional basis on which popular song has developed. We need to be aware that the applications of electricity helped transform the music industry and the market for certain kinds of music; and we must recognize that changing patterns of use produced part of the impetus for further transforming musical institutions, even for developing further technological innovations. In other words, the ganglion of institutions which make up the popular song industry may *try* to control their market — us, the consumers, and our ways of using music and musical products — but our role is by no means a passive one. On the other hand, the industry does not 'give the public what it wants'. Instead, it gives the public what the industry wants, by and large; but we are always in a position to refuse to consume, or to consume and appropriate even commercial products in genuinely creative ways.

We will examine this key relationship when we discuss terms like 'popular' and 'culture' later on; but even from this brief analysis it is clear that criteria for popularity can vary quite significantly. Of course, we must deal with those musical products, the hit singles, which have proven popular according to *market criteria*, not least because they must have some purchase on the lives of millions of people to have been sold in such large numbers. Secondly, we have to take account of the largely indirect popularity of influential singers, songwriters and musicians. Whether we like it (or him) or not, Bob Dylan's work has permeated a large sector of the song industry during the past twenty years, perhaps more thoroughly than any other individual artist. So, what I have tried to do is to show the 'production' of Bob Dylan up to the end of the 1960s, chiefly in terms of his developing *repertoire* as represented by his available recordings. Thirdly, and in order to illustrate the way in which the industry's concept of popularity has narrowed the category of 'popular song' in a strictly irrational manner, I have attempted an analysis of a series of songs composed around a particular *theme* — coal-mining — over a period of 200 years. By so doing, I hope to show more clearly that alternative criteria exist for popularity — popularity of origin, transmission and reception. Inevitably, this apparently idiosyncratic excursion has involved me in some limited discussion of the term 'folksong', and of the 'folksong revival' which sprang up in Britain in the later 1950s.

To supplement these case studies, the third part of the book deals with two important themes in the study of song. In the chapter, 'Song and history', I try to show how songs can be used as a form of historical evidence. Choosing a fairly well-known set of pieces — all from the north-west of England, and all to do with the industrialization of the cotton industry — I point out the chief problems and possibilities in using songs as evidence, say, of class consciousness. In the final chapter, 'Commitment', I explore the problems faced (and very rarely solved) by songwriters and singers who wish to use their talents in order to intervene in working-class culture, or in political movements. The contradictions of the commercial artist's role are set out briefly in terms of analyses of particular songs; and some attempt is made to tie this argument back into the central concern of the book, as expressed in the chapter title, 'Their music or ours?'

Finally, by way of a brief reminder of work yet to be done, I include a series of particular research projects crying out for academic commitments. This is intended to dovetail into the bibliography, which is itself meant to save people unnecessary labour by the use of a rating system, and by the inclusion of occasional comments. I could wish no harder task on anyone than to read the acres of garbage that have been published on songs, singers and musicians. Doubtless, we will eventually have our academic accounts of that garbage in its own terms; but for the researcher seriously interested in learning about popular song, perhaps 80 per cent of the texts in the bibliography will not be required reading.

A final word of warning: I have not tried to please everybody. There will be those, without doubt, who would expect to see more time spent on, say, the Beatles. Others will find my analyses of songs rather strange, and perhaps even preposterous, especially on first reading. More seriously, some readers will miss musical analysis (in the formal sense); while others will find my use of theory either too difficult or too easy. But I am convinced that all these criticisms are an inevitable product of my trying to achieve the aims set out above in a book of this length for the audiences I am concerned to reach. I am only too aware that there are 'holes', and that experienced readers will find the text uneven. If they can do better, well and good: I hope the weaknesses of this book spur them on to do research, just as I hope the book as a whole provokes a wider readership than students, performers and teachers into rethinking their ideas about 'popular song' in particular, and working-class culture in general.

Introduction

Kill or cure?

Much of the analysis which follows may come across as a form of pathology. Popular song — the songs we all know and love — will seem to be a *problem*, a symptom of a deep-seated disease in Western capitalist society. Were this the case, we wouldn't need a book of this kind. But we all know the kind of account, too often from so-called socialists, which holds up its hand to cover its nose in the face of commercialism, professionalism, and suchlike bogies. The reader is left high and dry, wondering *why* (s)he enjoyed commercial popular song, feeling a bit guilty and defensive, and being even more pessimistic about ever changing those parts of the system which are obviously wrong.

Pessimism is easy: it is also irrational. What we have to remember, right through the uncomfortable and most grating parts of this book, is that working men and women *have* survived the commercialization of 'folk-song', the co-opting of Bob Dylan, the degeneration of one musical 'alternative' after another. We none of us give in, whatever we may say. Partly, of course, we refuse to give in because we fervently believe that *our* favourite singer or musician really *is* different. He or she has not sold out, really. We tend to react aggressively when that belief is challenged, because to many of us that faith is tied in closely with our sense of identity. Our conception of John Lennon, say, is unique; and when it comes down to it, John Lennon doesn't have very much to do with it.

In part, this situation is a product of the way in which we are encouraged to try and separate work and leisure. Work, in a capitalist or state-capitalist society, is largely out of our control. (By state-capitalist, we understand an economy where control of industry is vested in the rulers of a state, but where production is carried on in a largely capitalist manner.) We can't (or shouldn't) hope to enjoy that part of life. So we tend to overvalue leisure, often in the teeth of rational argument. At one level, for example, we might try to deny the significance of lyrics, and make a tactical retreat to the safer ground of music. We may even accept that 'popular' song is a commercial

product like any other, but then deny (quite correctly) that we consume it in the same way as corn flakes. Then again, we may choose
to personalize any criticism of 'our' music by interpreting it as an
attack on the little leisure 'space' we have left. We can accuse the critic
of judging people rather than songs. In extremity, we can glory in the
inadequacies of lyrics and the eccentricities of style, holding up formal
illiteracy as the songs' 'greatest value'.[1] *

Such responses are entirely understandable. Critics — and especially
academics — have usually been hostile to working-class culture. A good
rule of thumb is not to trust a word they say. *We* know that we use
commercial song differently, that it signifies more to us than any
textual analysis can hope to elucidate; and so we sometimes use it as a
stick with which to beat the values and assumptions that have been
stuffed down our throats at school, the values of 'Eng Lit'[2] or 'musical
appreciation'. At other times we use popular song as a catalyst for
hedonism, nostalgia and sentiment. We wallow in its very privatized
status, knowing full well that it is our way of using commercial songs
which gives them their validity, not the antics of the performer, or the
stamp of approval given by some self-appointed critic. Of course, we
are a little paranoid because we are so thoroughly alienated.[3] Anyone
who seeks to analyse our private behaviour is an invader, a cultural
imperialist. They want us to believe what they believe; and to do this
they try to destroy what we're clinging on to, the little 'space' that we
feel we have left for individual initiative and creativity. And it is one of
the characteristics of popular songs that they tend to get associated with
events, times, places and relationships often of the most intimate significance. Not only nostalgia and sentiment — potent though they are in
their own right — but more fundamental attitudes, values and behaviours
are triggered by particular songs, singers or even individual records. Any
meaningful discussion of popular song has to take such factors into
account, and do so in a sensitive way, if it is to have any analytical
validity at all.

All forms and modes of cultural practice have their own validity.
If irrationality is built into our economic system, we shouldn't be
surprised to find contradictions in social life. The point is not so much
to attack certain forms of behaviour for the sake of showing how clever
we are, or think we are, but to try to explain the ways in which those
forms of behaviour come about, and to show how society can be
changed to modify or eliminate them. For example, it isn't enough to

---

* References are collected in a section beginning on page 231. No additional
information is given there.

describe the National Front as Nazis, though that does have the effect
of sensitizing people to certain dangers. Fascism has certain material
roots — is, in fact, an irrational response to the irrationality of the
economic system at times of crisis — and it is those roots which must
be laid bare. What's more, in order not to leave people high and dry,
we have to outline a meaningful alternative to the recurrent crises of
the system — in this case, a political alternative.[4]

This leads us to a more general difficulty — the impossibility of
keeping politics, or economics for that matter, out of the discussion of
culture. (There will be times when the book reads like social history;
others when it will be almost literary criticism, and so on.) Whether
we like it or not, songs do have ideological tendencies, even our favourites. Those tendencies might not manifest themselves openly in the
lyrics; but the politics will be built in. It is the job of the cultural
critic (and of the historian) to tease them out; because to try to ignore
them is itself a highly *political* act. Of course, we face an immediate
difficulty. Most writing and teaching of literature, music and history is
done from precisely this position. It is riddled with internal contradictions, what the Russians term 'obyektivism'. Indeed, it would be
quite possible to 'decode' the work of the key figures in the history of
song-criticism in terms of the way in which their ideology forced them
to mediate their material, as the present writer has done with Cecil
Sharp, amongst others, in the area of 'folksong'.[5] The problem is that
we lack this kind of decoding work in the area of popular song.
So, while we may be in no doubt where a George Tremlett, an Emperor
Rosko,[6] let alone a Rod Stewart or an Eric Clapton, may stand, we just
don't have any systematic analyses which explain how and why this is
the case.

There is an even greater difficulty, however, in the way in which our
so-called liberal democracies have tended to encourage the mystifi-
cation of working-class history and culture, as part of the general drive
to fit people to operate efficiently, in a subordinate and alienated
capacity, in the capitalist mode of production. It is vital to remember
that at the same time as we are evaluating and analysing commercial
popular song, we are simultaneously reconstructing an alternative
account of working-class history and culture. So, we cannot simply
stick to the songs, or even the repertoire, of any given artists, because
those songs and those persons were produced in a particular culture.
On the other hand, it is not yet possible to reconstruct the full history
of that culture, precisely because we don't have the detailed accounts
available. Any attempt to produce an analysis of, say, the rise of 'rock

'n' roll, will therefore be a highly mediated account in its own right. Its value will depend on its self-consistency, and on its ability to explain the function of particular songs in a particular social setting at a particular time. Inevitably, such an account will be written from a particular perspective: there is no interpretation, no description, which is politically innocent. All that can be expected of a researcher and a writer is transparency and self-consistency. This is why the accounts which follow have a partizan flavour. Even people who disagree violently with my perspective will still be able to use the factual material; and they will be better able to define their own positions, as it were, 'against' my own.

Us and them

What most people do with their lives — the activities they pursue, the choices they make and have made for them, their achievements and failures — these are now held to be self-evidently important in any discussion of culture and history. It wasn't always so. In Britain, before Richard Hoggart's *The Uses of Literacy* (1957) and Raymond Williams's *Culture and Society* (1958) and *The Long Revolution* (1961), such an assumption, in academic circles, would have seemed positively idiosyncratic.

Thanks in large measure to the work of these men, literary study has been significantly broadened and deepened; and what were once 'common sense' values and assumptions in academia now stand out for the class-based special pleading that they are. Of course, the battle is not over. Williams is still doing battle with the battered corpse of 'lit-rat-cha'; and Hoggart's book now reads more like an autobiographical novel than a sociological treatise. Politically, the early work of both men bears the marks of liberal radicalism. Unsurprisingly so, given what passed for marxism in the 1940s and 1950s was often riddled with the contradictions of Communist parties dominated by Stalin and his heirs.[7]

On the basis of these men's achievements there has now sprung up a whole range of courses in cultural and communication studies, many of which, like those at Hoggart's Centre for Contemporary Cultural Studies at Birmingham University, have developed significant marxist tendencies, especially under the directorship of Stuart Hall. Williams's own work has also developed, albeit cautiously, into a full-blooded form of marxism (in terms of *theory*, at any rate); and we now have a situation in which marxist theory has become positively trendy in literary circles.

There is, however, a third man whose influence on the development of marxist cultural study cannot be underestimated — Edward Thompson. Thompson's great book, *The Making of the English Working Class*, has permeated historical studies so thoroughly, that liberal and reactionary historians now tend to define their positions *against* it. They have to, because Thompson's work is so overwhelmingly convincing and self-consistent that it must be challenged *in toto*. After Thompson, there can be no more 'innocent' history. His reconstruction of the making of the English working class is profoundly partisan. It is also transparent. In his own discipline, then, Thompson too has shifted the terrain of debate, and so helped transform historical study to a point at which it is barely disassociable from cultural studies.

It would be possible (and in its own way, interesting) to illustrate this repoliticization of cultural and historical studies in terms of the history of the New Left in post-war Britain, above all in their academic journal, *New Left Review*. This isn't the place for such an analysis, but it is important to note one or two key elements. Above all, revolutionary socialists in post-war Britain and America had nowhere meaningful to go in party political terms. The British Labour Party, for example, was by this time wholly controlled by liberal social democrats at national level. The leadership of the British Communist Party was rigidly Stalinist. (Incidentally, Williams left the Communist Party in 1940, at the time of the Hitler–Stalin pact; and Thompson left with 10,000 others after the Russian invasion of Hungary in 1956.) Almost inevitably, there followed a retreat from fully active politics — all serious intervention in the class struggle — and a simultaneous development of activity on an academic plane.

The contradictions of this embattled position, in Britain and the USA, have taken some of the combatants a long time to live through. One or two still haven't made it:

One aspect of the collapse of the old 'New Left' . . . has been the disappearance of the political discussion of popular culture. The New Left's approach was open to criticism on two counts. First, they tended to make cultural questions central to their strategy, a symptom of their retreat from class issues in industry and politics. Second, their attitude often wavered between an elitist desire to propagate the standards of bourgeois culture, and a reactionary nostalgia for the art-forms of an earlier, less assertive working class.[8]

We can recognize this attitude clearly in Hoggart's main book, and in the fact that Williams is forced to rely on conservative radicals for his historical criticism of *laissez-faire* capitalism, in *Culture and Society*. What's more, the undiluted elitism of F.R. Leavis has done its work even amongst his most consistent critics. Williams, for example, has done no work at all on proletarian culture, other than in a brief account of the work of some artisan poets.[9] His position, even now, is fundamentally literary. One irony is that *his* chief critic, Terry Eagleton — one of the pillars of the *New Left Review* after the palace revolution that unseated Edward Thompson and others — is also innocent of any serious work on working-class culture. He, too, is tied firmly to the concept of a 'great tradition' in literature, which he is proceeding to give a marxist gloss. The privileged status of literature — and therefore, of literary criticism — is merely asserted, not argued for. Eagleton's practical criticism, if you like, is a form of left wing pathology of 'lit-rat-cha'.[10]

What has all this to do with popular song? Well, because such theoretical contradictions are still present in transformed literary and historical study, they reappear in even the most innovatory and progressive of courses. What start out as history workshops, for example, come dangerously close to becoming history factories. Their sheer size has led to a crucial change in the educational mode of production. Courses in Communications and Cultural Studies tend to be assimilated into mainstream academic life. They are all too often fossilized as degrees and diplomas, following the habitual institutional pattern of syllabus, essay and exam, with perhaps a token project tossed in for good measure. The same old academic structures underpin these developments, deforming them, just as, at a wider level, the Byzantine structures of our universities have been assimilated as a whole by the polytechnics. So, while the 'disciplines' and domains of literary and historical study will continue to interpenetrate, during the 1980s and 1990s, and though elements of sociology and philosophy, of economics and politics, will be drawn in too, there is a great danger that the resulting academic fusion will be thwarted by the carrying over of reactionary institutional structures and methods.

How would this matter to working-class people, even if it did happen? Quite a lot. Apart from the fact that students from working-class homes now have more chances of getting some higher education than ever before, the declining birth-rate of the later 1960s will mean that existing higher education institutions will be forced either to accommodate themselves to more working-class entrants, or to contract significantly. After the 1982 bulge in student numbers, the Department of

Education and Science envisages cut-backs in higher education pro-
vision. On the other hand pressure is now building up amongst teachers
and other interested parties to see the 'excess' capacity not as a
problem, but as an opportunity. The case is being put that more courses
must be put on for the benefit of the educationally underprivileged —
children from working-class backgrounds, and mature students in
general. Of course, given that the present educational structures cope
quite well with individuals who wish to 'get on', the opportunity of
the 1980s is to develop courses and resources which cater explicitly
for workers at leisure. Such people will, inevitably, demand to know
about the history and culture of their own class. They will want to
learn how to understand the mechanisms of contemporary society,
the better to be able to change them, so that they work in the interest
of the majority, and not of the few. It is for these people, for their
precursors and their future teachers, that this book has been written.

Why theory is important

Theory *is* important. It helps us understand general problems, and
so helps us to overcome them. But theory without practice is sterile.
No matter how much professional theorists may insist that theo-
rizing is a kind of political practice, and proclaim that they are
marxists, they are not. Marxism involves the combination of theory
and practice — it involves commitment of an active kind, with all the
problems and compromises that brings. So, while the politically
active reader may choose to skip the new few pages, and begin reading
about the commercial music industry, perhaps coming back to this
point after the end of the book, others may decide to enter into the
technical discussion and debate straight away.

Basically, there are three major areas of difficulty — that of the
problem of *mediation*, that of the meaning of *key terms*, and that of
method. All three are interconnected. In fact, they are indissoluble;
and we can separate them for the purpose of theoretical discussion only
if we recall that interdependence continuously.

Mediation refers to the ways in which accounts dealing in ideas and
analyses are never 'innocent', but always bear the marks of a particular
ideology, a particular methodology. At the simplest level, mediation
can refer to problems associated with scholarship — the accurate
transmission of texts. At the most common level, particularly in liberal
democracies, mediation refers to the way in which theories and
methods derived from one form of study get applied to other areas of

cultural practice, wholesale. For example, the theory and practice of literary criticism often gets used in the evaluation of popular culture, even though the latter does not operate according to the same rules as 'literature'. The result is a systematic (if often unconscious) misinterpretation or distortion.

Thirdly, we have the *mediation* which is not only misinterpretation, but deliberate falsification. A more or less fully conscious ideology is imposed on to cultural activity, and, by systematic omission and selection, plus some judicious over-emphasis or under-emphasis, a wholly inaccurate 'analysis' can be produced.

Put like this, I might seem to be implying that there is such a thing as an unmediated account. Of course, there isn't. There is no 'true essence' of working-class culture, waiting to be magically revealed, no matter how thoroughly we decode the mediations of the key mediators. What I term the *reconstruction* of working-class culture is precisely that; and there will be many occasions when building materials cannot be found, because they are not present even in mediated form. On the other hand, I would stress the need for demystifying and decoding what we do have left to us of mediated working-class culture. This, of course, is the only available method for past workers' culture, even up to the beginning of this century.

The key terms in any cultural analysis of this kind are crucial. In order to decode the writer's mediations, the reader has to know what is meant by terms such as 'culture', 'class', and, in this case, 'popular'. The problem is that it would be possible to argue for particular conceptions of these terms for the rest of this book. All that can be reasonably expected here is a brief statement of what the present writer understands by these terms; and because this text is written from a marxist standpoint, it is necessary to begin with a discussion of the term 'class'.

Class is a process, not a thing. Nobody can flash a class card. Nobody has impeccable class credentials, because class is only *there* in particular historical relationships, between real people at a particular time and place. In other words, I agree with Edward Thompson when he writes:

Like any other relationship it is a fluency which evades analysis if we attempt to stop it dead at any given moment and anatomize its structure. The finest-meshed sociological net cannot give us a pure specimen of class, any more than it can give us one of deference or of love. The relationship must always be embodied in real people and in a real context. Moreover, we cannot have two distinct classes, each with an independent being, and then bring them *into* relationship with each other. We cannot have love without lovers, nor deference without squires and labourers. And class happens when some men, as a result of common experiences (inherited or shared) feel and articulate the identity of their interests as between themselves, and as against other men whose interests are different to (and usually opposed to) theirs. The class experience is largely determined by the productive relations into which men are born — or enter involuntarily. Class-consciousness is the way in which these experiences are handled in cultural terms: embodied in traditions, value-systems, ideas, and institutional forms. If the experience appears as determined, class-consciousness does not.[11]

In other words, there is no *mechanical* connection between the relations of men and women to the means of production in their society, and the way they think, feel and act.

Of course, Thompson's formulation draws heavily on Marx's analyses:

In the social production which men carry on they enter into definite relations that are indispensable and independent of their will. These relations of production correspond to a definite stage of development of their material forces of production. The sum total of these relations of production constitutes the economic structure of society — the real foundation, on which rises a legal and political superstructure and to which correspond definite forms of social consciousness. The mode of production in material life determines the social, political and intellectual life processes in general. It is not the consciousness of men that determines their being, but on the contrary, their social being that determines their consciousness.[12]

People can be in particular class relations without realizing it. They can realize their position, and still not act to change it. Only when the forces of production are developed to such a point that the relations of production act wholly as a clog to progress will social revolution become inevitable. Before that crisis, and even after it, it is still the case that if history makes men, men make history.

Culture, like class, is not a thing but a process. You can't eat it. At its most general level, culture is the process through which men make their history; and this involves not only choices about modes of behaviour, patterns of relationships, and the use of material objects, but also, in a class society, the *struggle* to keep those choices open and to develop them in the face of opposition. Central to this struggle is the cultural practice of work. A loss of control, of choice, here is particularly clear in a class society — so much so, that we are encouraged by the dominant ideology to separate work and leisure, even work and life.

So, we have to remind ourselves that work *is* a form of cultural practice. Books are printed, bound and sold: sewers are planned, dug and lined; songs are constructed, published and recorded. But these material objects can be taken up in our own or other people's cultural practice, and put to differing uses. Books may be read, used to keep doors open, or burnt. Sewers may be blocked or under-used. Songs may be sung or listened to or read. To speak of the culture of a group of people, then, is bound to involve substantial generalization. We may have to speak of the cultural practices common to the majority, and leave to one side alternative patterns of cultural practice. When we get to larger groupings — communities and nations, say — this problem becomes almost beyond solution. We have to find some way of expressing differences in patterns of cultural practice; and, in a class society, we have to speak of *class culture*.[13]

The value of the term, culture, is the way it indicates those activities which hold people together, which help characterize them as a group. Equally importantly, this definition of culture reminds us that, no matter how totalitarian the regime, it is not possible to legislate particular forms of cultural practice into existence. Certain kinds of thought, ideas, activities and relationships survive. The most that can be done is to attempt to outlaw them (literally), and to restrict access to their sources. Even in concentration camps it was possible to record the horrors in words, pictures and memories. Better than that, more open forms of resistance were possible (if dangerous), including the use of ambivalent songs — for example, *The Peat-Bog Soldiers*.[14] Culture embodies this notion of relative autonomy.

In past societies, attempts at cultural control have taken the form of laws, codes of ethics, religions and troops. In our own, the relatively subtle logic of the market economy prescribes its own notion of appropriate cultural practice, and inflicts its own forms of sanctions. Of course, the market mechanism is no impersonal force. It is operated by and on behalf of particular people, whose interests are different from (and usually opposed to) those of the majority population. Inevitably, this dominant economic and political grouping requires an equally dominant ideology to justify itself, to legitimize its dominance. The market, and capitalism are offered as 'natural' — as 'inevitable', even — in much the same way as feudalism was once justified. Unhappily for capitalism, the material justifications for the system, and for the inequality and alienation it involves for most people, are undermined by its very success. Once it becomes materially and technologically possible to transform production, and to progress beyond the productive relations that correspond to that mode of production, the legitimacy of the old system begins to crumble.

The irony is that what always delays the transformation of capitalism into socialism is precisely that relative autonomy of cultural practice which we value as 'free space' in a class society. People may be part of an oppressed class, and may even be conscious of the fact, but there is no inevitability in their going on from there to act decisively to transform society. If there was an inevitable connection, then we would not need Marx, or the Bolsheviks, or any of today's revolutionary socialist parties. It would already have happened. To take this point further, there is no guarantee — no automatic mechanism — which will ensure that the winning of state power by a revolutionary socialist party will lead directly to socialism. The victims of Stalin's Russia are evidence of this unfortunate fact. So, consciousness and the cultural practice which it forms (and is formed by) cannot be 'read off' from a particular dominant mode of production. On the contrary, people have to 'feel and articulate the identity of their interests as between themselves' right through the transition from capitalism to socialism, until the productive relations have been transformed. And this, in turn, implies transformation on a world-wide scale; for otherwise international capitalism will continue to pose a political and economic threat that can only be countered by stopping the transformation at state capitalism, with all the problems inherent in that kind of system, including the continuance of capitalist relations of production. Here, too, Russia testifies to the contradiction of the ideology of 'socialism in one country'.

Lastly, if culture in a class society is a whole way of struggle, what is non-culture? Thompson equates these two 'poles' of a dialectical interrelation with Marx's notions of 'social consciousness' and 'social being'; and goes on to stress that, in a class society, Marx held that 'social being' determines 'social consciousness'.[15] In other words, non-culture determines culture. A whole way of struggle is determined by the real class relations in which people find themselves, which in turn are determined (in the last instance) by the relations of people to the means of production in society. So, the transition from non-culture to culture is the transition from a whole way of oppression and passivity, if you like, to a whole way of struggle. The development of class-consciousness and of class-controlled political activity, or revolutionary culture, is as much a product of the demystification of the class interests which underpin the dominant ideology, as the learning of the possibility of an alternative economic and ideological form of practice and of the forms of cultural practice in a class society which will bring such a system closer.

So, if class is the process which separates those who largely control the economic and social system from those who are, within limits, controlled by it; and if culture, in such a class society, describes those practices, values and ideas which characterize people in particular classes, what does *popular* mean?

Popular can mean 'liked by' or 'suited to' a particular person or a group. In a market economy, 'liking' is usually reduced to a commercial transaction, and the 'suiting' derives from that nexus, without much thought being given to the problem of the range of possible choices. Very often, the use of *popular* tells us more about its user than what it seeks to describe. To a considerable extent, in a mass consumer market, popular is a euphemism for working-class. And nowhere is this more obvious than in the use of the term, *popular culture*.

We have already noted that to suggest that a pattern of cultural practice is liked by or suited to a group of people is meaningless. People's cultural practices include things which aren't likeable, such as most work; and the notion that a set of cultural practices can be suited to a group of people, more or less at will, has proved to be nonsense even in Hitler's Germany. So, the use of *popular culture* tells us more about its users than about workers' culture, not least because it implies non-popular/unpopular/elite/ruling-class culture as being quite different from what is, at heart, *working-class culture*. And usually, those who speak of *popular* culture do so precisely from the standpoint of *ruling-class* culture.

Of course, *popular* has similar overtones to that unhistorical concept, *folk*. Its connections, ideologically, are with just the same nationalistic, sentimental falsification of class culture and pre-industrial workers' culture.[16] The analysis of this cultural practice is, however, properly the concern of the pathologists of bourgeois and ruling-class culture.

Fortunately, *popular* has a further range of meaning. It can signify 'of, or by, the populace'. In a class society, there can be no homogeneous culture of the people at large; but *populace* is customarily used to signify the 'common people', the 'general mass of the population', above all by those who consider themselves to be *un*common people, and part of a particular *minority* of that same population. These are the kind of people who have systematically mediated and falsified pre-industrial workers' culture, and above all working-class culture, on behalf of the dominant ideology. That mediation deserves separate treatment, elsewhere, especially in the area of 'folksong'; but it is possible and necessary, here, to set out the key problems in the analysis of popularity in terms of the cultural practice of pre-industrial workers and the industrial working class, as regards songs.

Briefly, there are the twin problems of *intention* and *reception*. By *intention* I mean to indicate the production of those songs which were written by 'outsiders' (non-workers) with a view to their becoming popular amongst working communities, and those written by 'insiders' for the same purpose. By *reception* I refer to the taking up of those songs, whether made by insiders or outsiders, intended for other purposes – or even for other classes – which have in some way been appropriated (and occasionally transformed) by workers, or perhaps by members of another class. The problem of *method* is how to differentiate between songs of these kinds, and then how to generalize out from particularly well-detailed instances of *intention* and *reception.*

Some of the problems of *method* for this book are implicit in what has already been written about mediation and the key terms. Where necessary, scholarly standards will have to be introduced on the question of accurate texts. Misinterpretation and falsification will have to be analysed in terms of the ideology of the mediator, however briefly. And some attempt will have to be made to situate particular texts in terms of their culture of origin or transmission (or both). Questions of intention and reception will have to be pursued, so far as evidence allows. For the post-industrial period, working-class/ bourgeois/ruling-class culture will be designated as such. Where confusion arises with the term 'popular', in quoted material, for example, the reader is asked to recall that the use of the term tells us most about its user.

There are, of course, other methodological problems, notably that of using songs as historical evidence at all, and, if we do, that of how far it is possible to generalize from evidence of this kind. We are not helped in this difficulty either by a developed marxist musicology, or even by empirical research into working-class culture in general, especially in a historical context. To take the last point first: there is a startling lack of research and publications on working-class culture even in this century. Whole institutions are without their historians, let alone the more detailed variations in cultural practice in particular regions and communities. We are even without an up-to-date people's history of England, not least because of the inadequacy of area studies, institutional studies, and so on, on which to build a reconstructed workers' history. Instead, we have the magnificent example of Thompson's major work, and a handful of books and articles of varying degrees of usefulness.

I have already explained why any account of working-class culture has to be partisan. What has to be stressed, here, is that that partisanship must not be based on theoretically naive empiricism (indeed, it couldn't be), or upon the incestuous jargon peculiar to certain contemporary professional theorists. History and cultural criticism have to be intelligible, and they have to be rigorously self-consistent, openly aware that what is being produced is a reconstruction of workers' culture on the basis of a particular political perspective.

This much, I hope, is now clear. But when we come to examine the available marxist theoretical literature on contemporary commercial music and song, we find only T.W. Adorno with any kind of valuable suggestions, and even his attempt at constructing a marxist musicology is riddled with contradictions.[17] However, it is worthwhile spelling out the problems with Adorno's methods, if only to justify the basic methodology outlined above.

Adorno starts from the position that there is 'serious' music and 'non-serious' music (which he terms 'popular', significantly). 'Serious' music is good, apparently, because it is complicated and sophisticated. 'Popular' music is bad because it is simple and 'standardized'; and it is standardized because of the way in which it is produced and disseminated by the commercial music industry. (Evidently, though 'serious' music is disseminated and packaged by that same industry, it survives the mediation infinitely better!)

There is an assumption throughout Adorno's major article, 'On popular music', that people have no autonomy *vis-à-vis* the commercial products. They 'consume' musical products as the industry wishes them to do, and the usual characteristics of 'built-in obsolescence' and 'pseudo-individuation' apply. This, of course, is determinism of the most vulgar kind; but there are historical reasons why Adorno should have thought in this crude way. To be blunt, he was writing in 1941, at a time when the American music industry was at its most brutally instrumental. The production-line techniques of music publishers were in full swing; and, at a more general level, marxists were in full retreat from both Hitler *and* Stalin. It is ironic, then, that Adorno should carry over the vulgarities of a Stalinist marxism into his denunciation of 'popular music'; and even more ironic that he should argue that denunciation in terms of the values and the products of bourgeois culture. What is missing from Adorno's anaylsis, is any systematic *dialectical* argument.

That this is the case comes across most strongly in the way he downgrades the innovations that even this brutal industry needed to survive. On the one hand he argues that the logic of the process of standardization is, ultimately, to 'synthesization'; and on the other he recognizes that innovation is a factor, even in the most 'popular' of music. In general terms, then, Adorno imports a critical apparatus from the study of bourgeois music, applies it to the products of the commercial music industry, and finds them (unsurprisingly) wanting. He proceeds to assume that the ways in which people appropriate and transform even commercial songs, in their own cultural practice, are unimportant. He is therefore led to the idea that 'popular music' is 'predigested' 'social cement', which triggers only a 'conditioned reflex' in the relatively passive consumer audience. Fatalism and pessimism pervade his texts; and in general this work has very little in common with marxist analysis other than that certain marxist *terms* are periodically invoked. Of the dialectical marxist *method*, however, we have precious little evidence. Adorno's value is in helping us understand the isolation and pessimism of socialists in the most powerful capitalist nation in the world, at a time when marxism in general had been internationally discredited by Stalinism to such a point that it could colourably be linked to fascism. About 'popular' music, however, his work tells us very little indeed. About working-class music and song, he can tell us nothing.

Part One
The industry

1 Electricity

Electricity and electronic engineering are so obviously important in the recording and transmission of song and music in our society that we tend to forget about the changes their use has wreaked. The introduction (and the subsequent mass production) of the microphone, amplifier, speaker, record turntable and tape recorder, made possible the transformation of the social role of singer, musician, songwriter and audience, not least by helping give access to recorded music and song to almost everybody, all day and every day.[1] The account which follows seeks to outline a few of the key 'moments' in this process.

Before 1925, singers and musicians usually recorded their material by performing at a hole in a wall, or a screen, behind which was an acoustic recording machine. The problems of balanced sound level, sound clarity and sound variety (given the constraints of studio size) will be self-evident; let alone the hit-or-miss nature of 'field' recording, using the old wax cylinders. When the microphone was introduced, singers took some time to adapt to it. Indeed, some of the old acoustic recording techniques and singing styles were actually carried over. For example, because big band singers had had to use a megaphone in order to be heard, they sang in a 'curious deadpan and emotionless manner'. In front of a microphone, this same style came to be known as 'crooning', notably as performed by Bing Crosby until he had mastered the techniques of singing close to the instrument.[2]

Singers soon came to realize that the mike and the amplifier enabled them to produce *more* noise than an unamplified band. With a mike, you could accompany yourself with a guitar, and subtle differences in tone and volume could still be heard. In the final analysis, you could fill a football stadium with noise on your own. Once understood and applied, this last fact helped make sudden structural changes in the music industry, above all in the USA. Big bands came to be economic albatrosses, and were undercut by small groups and solo artists. In fact, we can date the rise of the solo performer in North America from the early 1940s.[3] Yet while the changeover was to some extent helped by the adoption of Frank Sinatra by one of the first nationally networked radio shows, 'Your Hit Parade', and by a protracted musician's strike, the tenuousness of the process is underlined by the way in which Sinatra took his own PA system from booking to booking, so as to ensure a reasonable standard of sound reproduction, rather than prejudice the public's acceptance of the 'new' phenomenon.[4]

At just this same period, the electric guitar was coming into *general* use in the USA. Initially, its use was largely confined to bluesmen and country musicians:

as the jukebox became a firm fixture in roadside taverns, some of the honky-tonk operators complained to Decca that it was difficult to hear Ernest Tubb records after business picked up at night.[5]

In order to oblige, Tubb introduced the fuller sound of the amplified electric guitar into his band, and is now credited with being the first 'country' band leader to do so on a regular basis. In the Chicago blues clubs, Muddy Waters began using amplified guitar simply to be heard; and as early as 1941, Sonny Boy Williamson pioneered the use of electrified blues on the radio KFFN 'King Biscuit Show' – whence the man's nickname, the biscuits being made from Sonny Boy flour. Williamson's lively recordings began to sell in the previously segregated white market, as more and more young whites tuned into the show, thus making possible ever greater cultural integration. Aiming to exploit the consequent commercial demand, KFFN encouraged the development of independent (so-called 'indie') record companies, by giving air-play to their 'race' record product. In this way, the foundations for the 'integrated' audience and music of the 1950s were gradually laid, well before Alan Freed latched on to the 'new' music he promoted as rock 'n' roll.[6]

The application of electricity worked like a catalyst and a solvent in other areas of musical activity. Just as with the relatively crude wax-cylinder recording machines, it was soon recognized that the use of more sophisticated tape recorders

made it possible to record music almost any place in the United States, whereas in the 1940s music could only be recorded in elaborate studios, and by the use of extensive recording equipment, which was available in only a few localities.[7]

After tape had been developed, the musician did not have to go to the advanced technology: it could come to him. Yet this technology brought with it certain problems into the transformed transmission and reception of music. Johnny Otis and other black musicians had a hard time convincing Los Angeles recording engineers that the twangy guitar effect they wanted was not a violation of taste:

The engineer would make the drum prominent and slap the afterbeat for us or he wouldn't. Usually they'd refuse, they didn't like the idea, it wasn't up to standard, they thought it was distorted ... there were times when we tried other studios and left in despair. Most engineers were a very snobbish lot in those days because they were used to recording Jack Benny, Bing Crosby whoever and we'd come in. We were black and we had these raggedy little instruments and we presumed to tell them what we wanted and it turned out disastrously.[8]

Ironically, the industry's built-in conservatism tended to *provoke* innovation. Though drums were taboo in 'hillbilly' ('country') music in the 1940s, Hank Williams discovered that he could simulate that effect by turning down the amplifier on his electric guitar.[9] Further experiments followed, notably the twangy, growling effect produced by Duane Eddy's addition of a tremelo to his guitar's lower strings.[10] But the conservatism stayed even into the 1960s, when American Decca thought that the Who's use of feedback was a fault in the recording![11]

Conservatism was not the sole preserve of engineers or record company directors, however. What musicians saw as an opportunity, others saw as a problem. Amongst blues men in the USA, it was accepted that

The transition from gutbucket to string bass to electric bass and the effects of these shifts on ensemble timbre are but one example among many of material causation at work.[12]

Yet British jazz 'purist' Ken Colyer was.horrified when Muddy Waters took to playing an electric guitar on his 1957 British tour. We shall meet what Charles Keil guys as 'the moldy fig mentality' in other areas. With minor modification, his definition could easily apply to some American and British folklorists:

The criteria for a real blues singer, implicit or explicit, are the following. Old age: the performer should preferably be more than sixty years old, blind, arthritic and toothless (as Lonnie Johnson put it, when first approached for an interview, 'Are you another one of those guys who wants to put crutches under my ass?') Obscurity: the blues singer should not have performed in public or have made a recording in the last twenty years; among deceased bluesmen, the best seem to be those who appeared in a big city one day in the 1920s, made from four to six recordings, and then disappeared into the countryside forever. Correct tutelage: the player should have played with or been taught by some legendary figure. Agrarian milieu: a bluesman should have lived the bulk of his life as a sharecropper, coaxing mules and picking cotton, uncontaminated by city influences.[13]

It is ironic that Colyer's fetishizing of 'authenticity' (like so many other such attempts, notably with 'folksong') should have ignored the technological and material basis of the culture from which the 'pure' music sprang. It now seems more likely that what Colyer knew as blues had been distorted by artistic submission to technological determinants. Only four blues stanzas could be squeezed on to a ten-inch 78 r.p.m. shellac disc,[14] and 'pure' bands' like the Original Dixieland Jazz Band quickened their customary playing tempo to fit those constraints (as players have done with the ragtime music of Scott Joplin, until very recently). A third conservative factor, this time culturally determined, is the way in which music like 'jazz', 'blues' and 'folk' are usually analysed and described in terms derived from the study of west European 'classical' music. Thus, most books on jazz are written by whites, and

generally describe the blues as a sequence of chords, such as the tonic, subdominant and dominant seventh. Such a definition, however, is like putting the cart before the horse. There are definite patterns of chords which have been evolved to support the blues, but these do not define the blues, and the blues can exist as a melody perfectly recognizable as blues without them. Neither are the blues simply a use of the major scale with the 'third' and 'seventh' slightly blued or flattened. The fact is that both this explanation, and the chord explanation, are attempts to explain one musical system in terms of another; to describe a non-diatonic music in diatonic terms.[15]

Bearing all this in mind, especially at the key cultural moment of the mid to late 1940s, the arrogance of Johnny Otis's recording engineer and of Ken Colyer come more closely into focus.

On the credit side, the applications of electricity to musical production did help liberate artists and the industry from the stranglehold of the major band leaders, the 'musical Fuhrers' as they have been termed.[16] And not only were the relations of musical production transformed: the role of the engineer in the process of artistic creation became potentially a positive (rather than a passive, or even conservative) one. Artistic innovation even reacted back on to technological development:

Long before most studios had a VFO (variable frequency oscillator) which can change the speed of things as it turned, we had speeded a wrap. On the spindle that the tape runs against we could take a piece of editing tape and wind it around the capstan . . . . The human voice . . . could be moulded, distorted, electronically tampered with, almost computed. A bass voice could be slowed down to such an extent that it came across with just the right touch of indolence while natural flaws could be ironed out, perhaps by cutting tape to remove consonants like 'S' from the ends of words.[17]

Similarly, Leiber and Stoller's rudimentary over-dubbing (taking the tape back and forth between two mono machines) undoubtedly encouraged the development of stereo and eight-track machines in the later 1950s.[18]

One of the long-term consequences of technologically sophisticated recording was the relative demise of the live performance group during the later 1960s and early 1970s. Those same technological developments which, helped in Britain by hire purchase, led to a significant democratization of music making, also led to the eventual removal of the commercially successful groups from live performance altogether. The Beatles' first LP cost £400 to produce. By the time of *Revolver*, however, their exploitation of the new electronics in the studio made reproducing the same sound on stage all but impossible. After *Sergeant Pepper*, which took four months and £25,000 to make, live performances were totally impossible outside the most sophisticated studios. So, if technology allowed the Beatles to free themselves from the mangling of rickety PA systems in the world's stadiums, it also allowed them to be free of the vital feedback gained by playing for live audiences. In turn, while audiences were able to listen to significantly more complex music on record, they were simultaneously forced back into what was almost a totally privatized experience, symbolized by the alienation involved in using hi-fi stereo earphones. In this situation, the appeal of the live US west coast groups, of skinhead music, and even the glitter artists of the early 1970s — not to mention the punks of the later 1970s — is obvious enough. Yet the tendency to withdraw further into the electronic womb is still evident in some quarters. If making money from tours (especially in the USA) is said to be almost impossible, given that ticket prices are to be kept within reasonable bounds, many performers have turned to other electronic media — notably film, and especially video — in order to try to transmit more than the music to their audience.[19]

It was very difficult to dance to *Penny Lane* or *Strawberry Fields*, or even to participate in them.[20] Amongst other factors — notably economic ones — the further application of electronics to the production of popular music has led to greater experiment and innovation, and in turn to the development of the LP as the major channel. Some artists now produce an LP before they produce a single; and, on the other hand, some produce only singles, or LPs of previous singles. This latter phenomenon has been encouraged by the proliferation of that French invention, the discothèque, since the early 1960s — an innovation itself made possible by the previous development of the role of the disc jockey on 'one-lung' US radio stations, who wished to 'simulate network grandeur' but couldn't afford to employ live bands. (In turn, the logic of this process has now led to the automation of the DJ's job, using pre-recorded tapes.) In Britain, Jimmy Saville's Teen and Twenty Club in Manchester was one of the first to play records in between live bands;[21] but the dominant trend since then has been to exclude live artists from discothèques, and to employ ever more sophisticated technology — light shows, stereo, and suchlike — in purpose-built clubs. In turn, this has meant the employment opportunities for new, live bands have withered. Either they take a risk, and invest in high-cost equipment, so as to break in to the posher clubs, or they continue to play at a loss in pub back rooms, or as support groups at concerts. Mostly they continue as part-timers.[22] Here again, with the rise of the punks during 1977, and the politicization of many of them during 1978, we can note what artistic results such technological and economic pressure can help to produce.

Not all developments associated with the application of electricity to music have been detrimental. There is no mechanical connection between electronics and aesthetic atrophy. People still play for pleasure, after all. But we have to be continuously aware that popular song, like all other aspects of culture, can be only relatively autonomous *vis-à-vis* economic and technological change. After all, even war, prostitution and puritanism have played their part in the development of musical styles. Take New Orleans:

At the turn of the century, Brass Bands, concert and marching, fraternal, funeral and fire-house, multiplied rapidly, as the short-lived Spanish-American War left pawnshops stocked with second-hand instruments.[23]

When these Western-style instruments made their way into the hands of working-class musicians, their use effected certain changes in timbre, tonality and ensemble amongst people accustomed to more rudimentary (sometimes home-made) instruments. New Orleans, being an embarkation point for US troops, had certain facilities — notably for drinking and fornicating — which had arisen to meet the demand, in the true spirit of commercial enterprise. Of course, the US government sought to disassociate itself from such necessary institutions, and had military laws enacted prohibiting drinking houses and brothels within so many miles of any army installation; but it took the non-combatant upholders of moral purity to shut down the red light district. Storyville was shut down by 1916: public dance halls had been under close scrutiny since 1910; and by 1920 the anti-saloon movement had succeeded in getting alcohol temporarily prohibited.[24] These legal and social manoeuvres blocked off employment opportunities for some New Orleans musicians, but much more important were the underlying trends in America's wartime economy. Heavy industry — above all, munitions and motor transport — flourished, while immigration was stopped. As early as 1914, Henry Ford was offering five dollars a day for assembly-line workers, irrespective of a man's colour; and once war was declared with Germany, the demand for labour in the northern manufacturing industries hit the roof. Agriculture was fast coming to be a mechanized industry: the black and poor white southern workers were available, and the migration got underway. These people took their culture with them, into the speakeasies of Chicago, for the professional musicians, and for the others on to the streets of the emerging black communities of Washington, Detroit, New York and Philadelphia. In turn, the relative affluence of the migrants made it economically — as well as culturally — possible to establish black-owned record companies and radio stations; so it is no surprise that much of the musical innovation of twentieth century America has come from these new communities.[25] After all, the applications of electricity to manufacturing in general were having a significant effect on other areas of the economy, and on US culture, too, notably in radio, recording, play-back technology and television, each of which deserves a fuller analysis.

2 The average popular song

As early as 1922 there were some 200 commercial radio stations in the USA. By 1926, there were 694.[1] Currently, there are between 5000 and 6000. Radio ownership was equally early and widespread: three million sets in 1922, fifteen million in 1931, fifty-one million in 1939. But this apparent diversity covered an amazing degree of concentrated ownership. In the 1930s, the National Broadcasting Corporation (NBC) and the Columbia Broadcasting System (CBS) owned, together, some 88 per cent of all US transmitting power.[2] RCA bought Victor records in 1929; and from about this period the music industry began to conglomerate noticeably.[3] This incipient monopoly gave institutions like NBC enormous power. In 1928, the network banned the words of over 200 songs.[4] In turn, this unelected and non-responsible censorship led songwriters to produce work according to NBC's specifications, or to accept commercial failure. They mostly succumbed. In their 1939 manual, Silver and Bruce gave the following disingenuous advice:

Direct allusions to love-making, or the use of such words as 'necking', 'petting' and 'passion' must be avoided. Love, in popular songs, is a beautiful and delicate emotion, and marriage is a noble institution . . . . Profanity should never be used in a popular song . . . . Direct references to drinking, and songs that have to do with labor and national and political propaganda are also prohibited on the air . . . .[5]

In *How to Write and Sell a Hit Song*, then, Silver and Bruce were simply articulating the values of the dominant ideology. A popular song was in large measure known before it was written, let alone sold to a music publisher or broadcast on the radio. So, Cole Porter's *I Get a Kick out of You* had to have 'champagne' substituted for 'cocaine' on American radio; and Hank Williams's *My Bucket's Got a Hole in It* had to have 'milk' substituted for 'beer' on the 'Grand Ol' Opry' radio show so late as the 1940s.[6]

Apart from these forms of irrational suppression, the most far-reaching and numbing effect of censorship was on the structure of popular song:

in the average popular song, the chorus is thirty-two bars long ...
divided into four sections of eight measures each. The average line of
poetry comprising eight or ten words will usually take four measures,
so that, as a general rule, two lines of poetry will be equal to one eight-
measure phrase .... The general *song-form*, which eight out of ten
popular numbers follow, is called the *AABA* pattern ....[7]

With song content rendered anodyne, and song structure prescribed, all
that remained was to drill the songwriters in the production methods
of Henry Ford:

In the 1950s, most pop songs were written in music publishers' offices
in New York (hit factories) by a task force of writers, who were
generally treated like assembly line workers.

Which is precisely what they were. Jammed into cubicles with a piano
and a deadline, set against the person in the next cubicle, liable to be
fired at a moment's notice, and, in general, treated as callously as
battery hens, the songwriters inevitably produced large quantities of
hack-work. (Carole King had this apprenticeship: and 10CC experienced
similar problems even at their own Strawberry Studios, in the late
1960s.)[8] Equally inevitably, the stranglehold exercised by the like of
NBC and CBS also fostered innovation in other, 'freer', areas of
musical culture, above all amongst the semi-professional musicians and
singers in the cities.

Blacks had been economically exploited and culturally expropriated
for centuries in the USA; and racial prejudice had had vital structural
consequences on the development of American popular song at least
since the time of Stephen Foster. No US radio band had a black musician
until 1942; no Negro appeared on the 'Grand Ol' Opry' show until
Bobby Hebb in 1953; and Negro artists suffered systematic indignities,
having to enter clubs, hotels and theatres by the back door. What
happened to Billie Holiday may stand here as symbolic. Because of the
paleness of her complexion, several theatre managers

told Basie I was too yellow to sing with all the black men in his band.
Someone might think I was white if the light didn't hit me just right.
So they got special dark grease paint and told me to put it on.[9]

The startling mindlessness of this prejudice gave rise to an even less
rational attempt to segregate the radio audience. While blacks set up
so-called black radio stations, which were financed by firms having
goods or services they wished to sell to the black community, notably

hair treatment and foodstuffs, and while a station like WLAC continued to play only what whites sensitively termed 'race' music well into the later 1940s, conservatives and racists could not well counteract the cultural consequences of 15,000 watts beamed non-directionally over twenty-two states, from Chicago to Florida. White and black alike could listen to music not predigested for them by CBS, NBC or New York publishers; and a glance at biographies of artists as diverse as Presley, Dylan and Buddy Holly indicates the importance of the 'black' radio stations in the creation of 'white' popular song since the mid 1950s.[10]

Symptomatically, the white-owned, white-controlled song institutions were loth to admit that black people's music was *there*. Only the hard cash in the pockets of the white radio audience made them rethink their business practices. The people Billie Holiday called the 'plantation owners', the impressarios of New York's Fifty-Second Street music businesses, found that they 'couldn't hold the line against Negroes forever':

They found they could make money off Negro artists and they couldn't afford their old prejudices. So the barriers went down, and it gave jobs to a lot of great musicians.[11]

Of course, the jobs were given on the white man's terms:

Black hit songs were usually covered and castrated for the white market . . . and even multi-million R & B sellers like Joe Turner, Ruth Brown and Bo Diddley never made the pop Charts . . . it was quite possible for someone like Eddy Arnold, say, to sell fifty million records and still mean hardly anything on the national charts.[12]

US charts are in part based on the amount of air-play a record gets; so when by chance a black singer's record made those charts, the major record companies and radio stations swung into action in support of a white cover version:

the Orioles' version of 'Crying in the Chapel' stayed several weeks on the best-selling lists and sold over a million copies . . . [but] the disc jockeys did not play it enough to put it on the list of twenty most-played records; . . . [while] they did play the other three best-selling versions, all recorded for major companies, enough times to get them on the lists.[13]

So, the black-owned companies and their black artists were in an invidious position. Either they accepted the theft of their material, and the consequent suppression of their songs in the white market, or they came to an arrangement with the white-owned companies and sold them songs, masters or singers' contracts. Of course, the small white-owned companies were in a similar position. The independence of the so-called 'indie' record companies was minimal, outside their home ground. Both provided the test-bed for the Majors, who took none of the risks which are supposed to justify capitalist ventures, and both had their successes ripped off.

Just as radio and record companies shook up the music publishing business during the 1910s and 1920s, so Hollywood shook up radio in the next two decades. Once Al Jolson had broken into song on one reel of *The Jazz Singer*, in 1927,

Tin Pan Alley was tottering. Hollywood now stepped in and took over many publishers. Warner had the cream. Their Music Publishers' Holding Corporation held the copyrights to most of the songs of Victor Herbert, Jerome Kern, Cole Porter, Noel Coward, George Gershwin, Sigmund Romberg, and Rodgers and Hart. As a result Warner Bros. controlled a majority of ASCAP's governing board . . . so that when radio defied ASCAP in 1939 it was really defying Hollywood.[14]

ASCAP was the music publishers' body which negotiated music broad-casting fees with radio companies. Warners simply bought a controlling share of that body, when shares were low, and thereby hog-tied the entire industry. In 1939, ASCAP demanded that the radio licence fee be doubled. The radio stations refused to submit; and a blackout of all ASCAP material followed during 1940. This left the radio industry (itself dominated by CBS and NBC) with no alternative but to con-struct its own copyright corporation, Broadcast Music Inc. (BMI), from the miscellaneous small music publishers not affiliated to ASCAP, who in turn had links with the 'independent' recording com-panies. This struggle, combined with the effects of a twenty-seven month American Musicians' Union strike up to November 1944, technological innovation, and an American economy boosted by war work and post-war boom conditions, brought about structural changes not only in the American recording industry, but also in the form of popular song.[15] But before we examine this key *moment* it is important to understand what kind of product was commercially successful under the ASCAP regime.

We have seen how the dominant form of the musical mode of pro-duction tended to standardize musical forms in the 1930s and 1940s almost enough to justify Adorno's contemporary paranoia. But when we shift our attention to the mode of consumption of such songs now, two generations later, we have to recognize that the audience's relative autonomy plays a significantly greater part than it probably did when the songs were first published. Then, however, we must be aware that songs were still to a large extent 'consumed' from sheet music — literally *re*-created — and that the standardizing effects of recording were only just beginning to wreak changes in this area of cultural activity, via film and radio rather than by phonograph for the majority audience. Failing sufficient research, we cannot properly re-conjecturalize the 'moments' of the songs which follow: that will have to be done elsewhere. But what we can do is to try to tease out the ideological structures of the key songs.

According to crude market criteria, Irving Berlin's *White Christmas* is the most popular song ever recorded in the English language. Within a year of its first appearance in the film *Holiday Inn*, in 1942, it had won an Academy Award, and it had sold over a million copies in versions by both Freddie Martin and Frank Sinatra. Bing Crosby, who sang the piece in the film, had to wait until 1946 before his recorded version sold a million copies, however; and it wasn't until he sang it on film again in 1954, this time in a film named after it, that Crosby's success was fully assured. In 1955, Berlin earned over a million dollars in royalties from this one song; and by 1963 it had sold over 45,000,000 records, in one version or another. By 1975 — even before the upsurge occasioned by Crosby's death, and the calculated re-release of his version of the song — *White Christmas* had sold over 135,000,000 records, almost one-quarter of which were of Crosby's rendition (see Appendix 1, page 221). If we are seriously trying to understand the nature of popularity, and whatever we might think about this particular song, we have to cope with the fact that over 135,000,000 men and women deliberately went into a shop and paid cash for *White Christmas*. Similarly, we have to try to understand what it is about *Rudolph the Red-Nosed Reindeer* which caused over 110,000,000 people to buy it, and how *Winter Wonderland* has found over 45,000,000 willing customers. At the same time, we must remember that pieces like Hoagy Carmichael's *Stardust*, W.C. Handy's *St Louis Blues*, Lennon and McCartney's *Yesterday* and Levin and Brown's *Tie a Yellow Ribbon* are said to have been recorded by over a thousand different artists, itself an indication of popularity amongst that obviously important section of the music industry; and we have to recognize the impor-tance of the performer as well as the song, bearing in mind that the best-selling version of *Rudolph*, that by Gene Autry, sold *only* 8,000,000 copies, or just over 7 per cent of the total sales of the song.[16] Clearly, even the market criteria for popularity are not straight-forward; and we must be very careful when we are attempting to discover what sales figures of 100,000,000 *mean*, culturally.

Some generalizations are evident enough. It is surely significant, for example, that Christmas (and all it stands for in Western culture) is at the heart of these three best-selling recorded songs. What, though, is Christmas about? On the one hand, it retains a vestigial religious significance; but this element cannot be held to be important in a culture which, like Britain's, has seen a decline in religious observance since at least 1851 (when the first census question on the subject was included). On the other hand, Christmas hasn't yet been fully absorbed into the mainstream of holidays pure and simple. There remains sufficient official religiosity in the media and in certain areas of commerce to prop up key elements of the festival, so as to prevent its becoming wholly secular; though this is less the case in Scotland, for example, where New Year (Hogmanay) retains a large measure of its pre-Christian significance, and dwarfs 25 December altogether. In any case, it is the former importance of 26 December, Boxing Day, which dwarfs the day before, even though the customs of Boxing Day have now been eased back twenty-four hours, and in some cases to Christmas Eve.

Christmas, in our culture, is primarily about spending money, and not working. Presents are given and received, parties are held, camaraderie (real or feigned) usually predominates in the family (which, in turn, the ritual helps sustain) and in public. More basically, the holiday functions as a break in the long grind of winter work, the temporary release from the wet, the tedium, the insecurities of societies increasingly seen to be in crisis at shorter and shorter intervals. Conversely, to those many who have no real economic security − to the millions out of work or below the poverty line − Christmas serves to underline their relative deprivation. To an important extent then, Christmas highlights many of the contradictions of capitalist societies, and it would be surprising if songs like *White Christmas*, *Rudolph* and *Winter Wonderland* did *not* articulate some of the key values (directly or indirectly) of the dominant ideology.

Every line of *White Christmas* (unfortunately, we have been refused permission to print the lyrics) could fit inside a Christmas card. The second verse (as we know the song, without the introduction) even mentions those curious objects. Every line is, and is meant to be, evocative of those fantasy pictures on the front of Christmas cards −

glistening tree tops, attentive, angelic children (usually boys, and more often than not, choir boys), elaborately wrapped parcels, and, of course, the superbly irrational reindeer and sleighs with bells and Santa. But when we think for a moment, it is clear that for these images to have any purchase on reality, there has to be an underlying assumption about a generally high level of material comfort in society. Only then could snow be seen, unequivocally, as attractive and welcome. To put the point baldly, how is snow perceived by the 100,000 or so old people in Britain who are at risk from hypothermia each winter? Then again, we have to suspend disbelief not only in the reindeer and all, but we must also ignore the relative infrequency of a Christmas Eve snowfall in most of the English-speaking world! But Christmas is *about* irrationality just as much as it is about sentimentality. It's about substituting the purchase of commodities for the effort of the year round affection and care. It's about throwing out anxieties and sympathy along with the wrapping paper and the heat-distorted, token cards. And it's about adding insult to injury, by twisting the emotional arms of those many who cannot really afford to indulge in the sentimentalities, but who are still driven to buy fripperies rather than food or heat. This is certainly the case in Britain; but perhaps it is less true in the affluent USA. Of course, this is not to put the finger on Irving Berlin for multiple crimes against humanity; but perhaps we can better understand how a song like *White Christmas* has lent itself so easily to parody, like many another commercially successful piece. What fitter subject for ironic inversion, overstatement, or hamming?[17]

It's not Irving Berlin's fault, or Crosby's, if we choose to buy their work. What is important is the extent to which this song has been able to penetrate even working-class culture, as part of the general ideological success of capitalism's ruling class. Then again, it would be quite silly to accuse Berlin and Crosby of being part of some devious plot, and to place the onus for the song's success on the cleverness of our rulers. What we have to confront in songs like this is our own weakness, our own susceptibilities. For all Crosby's trite stutters, and in spite of the amazingly crude choirs of 'angels' who we *know* are on piece-work, it is the case that *White Christmas* has permeated English-speaking cultures, perhaps permanently, over almost two generations. In analysing the song's appeal, then, we must of course bear in mind that Western working-class culture has to a large extent embraced the dominant capitalist ideology since the 1940s; but we must also beware of the conspiracy theory that workers have been unconsciously bamboozled into swallowing that ideology whole, uncritically, and in the prescribed manner.

It is no accident, for example, that the song was first sung, by Crosby, to US troops in the Philippines in 1942. As Berlin was well aware, by writing 'a peace song in wartime' and by having it included in a film which would be guaranteed to reach millions of people in the armed forces overseas, he was well on the way to commercial success. No doubt this is why in the film, *White Christmas*, Crosby is pictured singing the title song on just such an occasion, near the front line, to a captive audience of army personnel (almost all of whom were men). Lovers apart is perhaps the dominant theme of most successful Western songs in any case, and what more poignant than separation by war? The answer to that question, of course, is just such a song set at Christmas time.[18] If it were simply a question of these elements, suitably wrapped up by Berlin, the conspiracy theory might have some credibility; but, of course, the reality of being in the army and having a good time at Christmas are two activities which do not fit neatly into what our 'betters' would regard as appropriate working-class behaviour.

Christmas, in a working-class community, is by no means dictated by authority — by the state, by employers, or by commerce, let alone by the church or chapel. In practice, once the kids have got their presents — which are often bought at considerable economic sacrifice on the part of the parents, and which form a significant part of the yearly 'leisure' budget — Christmas is primarily about rest, food, drink and companionship. What differentiates working-class Christmases from those experienced by their 'betters', however, is the *public* character of much of the celebration. In spite of the fact that workers know the whole enterprise is horribly commercialized, and that their part in the business is to help keep cash registers tinkling by eating, drinking and buying strictly unnecessary products, they are still determined to enjoy themselves, not least because the return to 'normal' life is as inevitable as it is unwelcome. The apparent irrationality of over-eating and over-drinking, which leads 'sophisticated' commentators to recall the understandably all-but-paranoid pagan festivities during the crisis of the winter solstice, is socially *necessary*. So the irrationality of *White Christmas* is to a large extent also a *necessary* irrationality. It is by now almost a traditional element in both the official and the unofficial Christmases, those quite different events — the former being what is publicly offered by those who control the major channels of transmission, and the other being how the official Christmas is *appropriated, and transformed*, by working-class people worldwide.

So, we can sleep easy. No propaganda expert could have produced a song such as this to keep the masses in the approved state of mindlessness. Fortunately, our leaders aren't that clever. What is true is that the Christmas evoked by Berlin's sparsely worded song and sentimental music does, indeed, have a fair degree of 'fit' with the dominant ideology; but what is also true is that those key elements of working-class culture which can so easily be trivialized, the compassion, the caring and the collectivity, are actively reinforced in the way in which the song is 'consumed'. It doesn't matter, then, though it is intriguing, that Berlin was once forced to admit 'I like sunny Christmases,' as he left for Florida.[19] It doesn't matter, because it's not Berlin's fault or his responsibility how people behave in the market-place for music and song. If his song is manipulative — if it does effectively reinforce the values and assumptions of the ideology of capitalist individualism, taken straight — the point to remember is that *White Christmas* is *never* taken straight. Even in the lyrics, Berlin recognizes that his song operates at the level of wish fulfilling fantasy: the best that can be hoped is that days *may* be merry and bright, and that Christmas *may* be white.

Compared to *White Christmas, Rudolph* (again, we have not been allowed to print the lyrics) is crude. It is also rather a nasty little song. It was written by Johnny Marks, and had its live debut at Madison Square Gardens in 1949, when it was sung by Hollywood cowboy, Gene Autry. His version went on to become the best-selling US record of 1949-50; and by 1964 the 300 recorded versions of the song had sold an aggregate of over 40,000,000 copies. The figure is now over 110,000,000.[20] (Amongst others, Perry Como and Pinky and Perky have produced records of the piece,[21] but it is perhaps in Autry's version that the song is best remembered, especially in Britain, where that version was most fequently used in radio broadcasts for children.)

Aimed as it is at children, the song's story line is simple enough. In fact, in Britain at any rate, it came across quite clearly as a Christmas version of that other 'Children's Hour' regular, the versified version of Hans Christian Andersen's tale, *The Ugly Duckling*. (At least, comic-grotesque was a change from wholehearted sentimentality.) But the assumptions on which both stories are based, and the bland manner in which quite extraordinary events are passed off as normal, deserve more than token analysis. Though it would in certain ways be comforting, and though we continually run the risk of becoming over-earnest, there's no escaping that what *Rudolph* sets out to validate are peculiarly brutal examples of behaviour. So, while on the one hand it *is* a sad little story for kids, with the usual 'happy ending', on the other hand it offers itself as an account of 'human nature', thinly disguised as 'reindeer nature'.[22]

Leaving aside the grand irrationality of the whole setting, for the moment, what can we learn of the social structure of Lapland/ Greenland/the North Pole? We start with the isolated figure, Rudolph, who was a little out of the ordinary. The whole tone of the song suggests that, after all, its hero was *deformed*; and this is allowed to 'explain' why all of the other reindeer 'used to laugh and call him names'. So, while we are encouraged to sympathize with the deformed one, we are also invited to understand why Rudolph is treated vindictively by his fellows, even though (as verse two reveals) the whole reindeer community is equally subject to one authority figure, Santa. But it is surely disingenuous to believe that by transposing the scene to the fantasy world of Christmas, all moral distinctions are automatically invalid. Children *do* learn from a song that this kind of behaviour is allowed to go on — is, almost, acceptable — because it's allegedly 'reindeer nature'. And part of the potency of the song is the way in which all this is implied, never fully articulated. The 'absences', if you like, are more articulate than the lyrics.

The second verse reveals the social structure more fully. There is a single (human) authority figure who exercises a form of benevolent despotism over the remaining (non-human) reindeer population. But this is no *1984* scenario. Rather than see dissension in the ranks, Santa, the benevolent dictator, goes out of his way to find a practical use for Rudolph's 'deformity'. Ironically, by bringing this-worldly problems into an allegedly fantasy setting, Marks undermines the fantasy itself. After all, at the most obvious level, if we can imagine speaking reindeer, why should fog present any problems to Santa! Then comes the most crucial revelation. Immediately official approval is given, the four-faced reindeer bow, scrape and suck up to Rudolph (who, presumably, responds with a certain arrogance, now). Sycophancy, and implicit obedience, are as socially acceptable in this kind of society as is hypocrisy — '*then* how the reindeer *loved* him' indeed! Of course, the song offers no comment on this dramatic reversal of behaviour amongst the servile reindeer, let alone on the power of Santa. After all, it isn't meant to be a sociological treatise. But that's precisely the point: what *do* real, live human children make of this curious sequence of events? Do they learn that fickleness is part of reindeer (*read*, human) nature? Do they learn that truckling to individuals in authority — no matter how they came to be there, or whatever their behaviour – is not only acceptable, but necessary? Does the inculcation of servility – though I do not suggest for a moment that this was either Mark's or Autry's intention – in any case seem appropriate in societies where most children will remain in the working majority, the 'herd'? Or is this simply a happy little song for kids?

At least *Winter Wonderland* (lyrics on page 49) is transparent. It was written by Felix Bernard and Dick Smith in 1934, and sold over a million copies in the version recorded by Guy Lombardo and his Royal Canadians with the Andrews Sisters. Amongst others, Ted Weems and his Orchestra, Perry Como, and the Ray Charles Singers have had successful recordings of the song; but it is probably the version produced by Johnny Mathis in the 1950s that is most familiar now, particularly to a British audience.[23] (Though it is interesting that Mathis' version could reach only number seventeen in the British singles charts in 1958.)[24] The scene is already familiar: sleigh bells, glistening snow, picturesque lanes and all; yet the courtship which is enacted in the song in terms of this fantasy landscape is notably revealing. It is not wholly preposterous to claim that *Winter Wonderland* articulates the key fantasies not only about the Christmas period (though the festival is not referred to directly) but, crucially, about the pattern of sexual relations felt to be most appropriate for a particular social order.

We begin deep into fantasy, being asked to hear sleigh bells (which, of course, can be simulated on record); and then we're introduced into what is literally 'wonderland'. After all, the point about the situation is precisely that 'we're happy tonight', so there must clearly be something extraordinary going on! What could be more natural (or extraordinary, depending on your point of view) than to build a snowman – snow being a suitably chaste symbol, perhaps, until the thaw back to reality turns it to grey slush – and to pretend he is the parson? After the 'snowman' has asked an impertinent question, what more polite than to answer encouragingly, accepting his right not only to interfere, but also to perform the rites necessary to legalize the relationship? It goes without saying, in this 'wonderland', that courtship inevitably leads to marriage. But then look what happens. Once the couple return to their fireside, a little nearer the real world, they have to '*conspire*' to '*face unafraid*' the plans that they made in the first flush of their relationship. It's as though what had seemed like an opportunity, 'outside', had turned a little sour back 'inside'. So, whereas exuberance was possible – almost, demanded – in the 'wonderland', in

Winter Wonderland

Sleigh bells ring are you list'nin'
In the lane snow is glist'nin'
A beautiful sight, we're happy tonight
Walkin' in a winter wonderland

Gone away is the blue bird
Here to stay is a new bird
He sings a love song as we go along
Walkin' in a winter wonderland

In the meadow we can build a snowman
Then pretend that he is parson Brown
He'll say 'Are you married?' – we'll say 'No man
But you can do the job when you're in town'

Later on we'll conspire
As we dream by the fire
To face unafraid the plans that we made
Walkin' in a winter wonderland, sleigh bells land

the reality of marriage they recognize that a 'dream' is necessary to enable them to cope with their responsibilities. The relationship becomes the problem, not the opportunity it had once seemed. The heads go down, the brows furrow, and the possibility of a full and free relationship seems to recede rapidly, making the fantasy world of 'wonderland' ever more attractive as an intellectual bolt-hole. Ironically, it is 'sleigh bells land' which can seem more real than reality.

Getting married in a capitalist society is, indeed, a form of escape from the pressures of independence, and at the same time, more or less a deeper entry into the sentimental ideology favoured by that form of society. This is its basic contradiction, in the West. At its heart, of course, marriage is essentially a property relation; but it was usually seen (certainly in the 1930s and 1940s) as not only 'natural' but inevitable, almost as a precondition of adulthood.[25] This is no longer the case, of course; but there is a residual irrationality in the notion that marriages or equivalent relationships *are* somehow 'made in heaven', or 'wonderland', or whatever. What remains genuinely extraordinary is the way in which marriage is seen as 'normal' – as, of course, is the family – even to the point where not being married can often be taken as evidence of abnormality. The reasons for capitalist ideology's support of marriage and the family (as we know it) are transparent enough. Marriages tend to produce children, more often than not. Children are needed so as to increase the labour market, and thereby compete with each other as orthodox individualists. Without a surplus of potential producers, how could unemployment be a threat? And without that threat – without the divisions it fosters as part of the general antagonisms politely termed the 'market mechanism' – how could this form of society continue to exist? If the competitive individualistic system broke down, some half a million rich people in Britain alone would be worse off, and we can't have that, can we?

Yet, here again, there's no point in blaming Bernard and Smith for articulating elements of the dominant ideology in their song. It's hardly their fault if the song-buying public responds overwhelmingly to fantasy, any more than a capitalist ruling class can be blamed (in its terms, that is) for seeking to continue its dominance. If blame is appropriate, perhaps it ought first to be directed at the weakness in all of us which encourages us to wallow periodically in sentiment and nostalgia, rather than setting about changing a society in which such refuges are necessary.

3 Thank God for Elvis Presley?

Charlie Gillett believes that

audiences or creators can determine the content of a popular art communicated through the mass media. The businessmen who mediate between the audience and the creator can be forced by either to accept a new style. The rise of rock and roll is proof.[1]

As it happens, the rise and fall of rock 'n' roll is proof of something completely different. What we see in parts of the USA, after about 1940, is the formulation of a 'new' musical style, right enough; but we also see up to about 1960, its rapid encapsulation in the wider music industry. And when we examine the institutional and cultural origins of that 'new' style, we have to admit that the formulation of the style was itself in large part determined by crises and conflicts within the music industry itself.

'Rock' was a term used in the early 1920s. Joe Haymes recorded a jazz orchestra piece called *Rock and Roll* in 1935; and Billy Matthews and the Balladeers had a record with the same title in 1949.[2] The claim that Alan Freed invented the term is therefore spurious. What fostered the development of the *style* was a combination of artistic innovation (of a curious sort), and of the conservatism of the US music industry:

The 'majors' had dabbled heavily in blues before 1940, but during World War II, they marked time and, as raw materials became scarce, they economized on all but the most popular product.[3]

As a direct consequence,

the majors more or less ignored the small-scale live entertainment in clubs and dance halls, which was what the indies began to record in increasing numbers from 1945 onwards.[4]

What the majors cared about was sustained profit. They were umbilically connected to the ASCAP publishing houses, and to the radio corporations; and they were structurally wedded to conditions of production which were 'antagonistic to base-level change in taste and style of popular music'.[5] Their standard contract was for five years.

Because they controlled the white market for song, their mode of operation 'relied on and tended to produce a system of gentle change in musical styles':[6]

for most record companies what's important is to produce and sell an *act*, an image and not just a record — in the long run it's easier to run a star with assured sales than to have to work on a series of one-offs.[7]

Of course, when the 'raw material' or 'machine tools' weren't to hand, the majors were able to buy into musical 'products' already road tested by the indies. Some blues artists, for example, were kept on contract for an annual pittance, simply to keep them off the market;[8] while people like Ellington (at the Cotton Club) and Fletcher Henderson (who worked for Benny Goodman) were gradually integrated into the white man's music. At one and the same time, then, such talented black artists were lost to the black communities in the northern industrial cities, and to the indies, who couldn't hope to outbid the majors for their services.

One and a quarter million blacks left the South to work in those cities between 1940 and 1950.[9] The potential indie market was enormous, and there was little competition from the majors, though at first the 'black' indies were run on a shoestring:

what was left to them was T-Bone Walker, Joe Liggins, Roy Milton, Charles Brown, Big Jay McNeely, things like that. They'd take people like ourselves into the studio and, for a couple of hundred bucks, the whole thing is done and the next day you have records.[10]

Economic pressure also affected what the likes of Johnny Otis's band could play. The same factors which brought about the dissolution of the big bands forced him

into a small band situation, but through my years with the big bands I'd realized that the thing that people really loved was what we loved too, the blues. We didn't need to get fancy just to do what comes naturally and effortlessly. It was the folk music with the driving beat and it differed from the old country thing because I just had to have some horns. We'd get a couple of saxes and a trumpet — we'd still have our horns but by coincidence it also made a very unique sound and I loved it. I suddenly realized that I didn't want four trumpets and five saxes, absolutely not. I wanted four horns with the baritone sticking out.[11]

The problem was that the maximum sale of any 'race' record in the black community was 500,000. To break through that barrier, black artists and black-owned record companies had to appeal to an audience which was only beginning to accustom itself to Rhythm and Blues via 'black' radio stations.[12] The more calculating black artists weren't above compromising their music a little in order to achieve that break-through, however:

When the white audience appeared and we saw it and we knew it was there, it didn't take us very long before we realized what they pre-ferred. We found that if we played a blues or a very bluesy thing, we lost them. But when we played very spirited R and B things, we cap-tured them. And when we did a *caricature* of rhythm and blues, we *really* got to them![13]

It was, therefore, a *caricatured* version of R & B that was made avail-able to, and taken up by, white artists, as part of the raw material of rock 'n' roll.

The other major musical and lyrical strand in rock 'n' roll was, of course, 'hillbilly' music. Before the 1940s, what we now term 'country' singers didn't figure as a national phenomenon in the USA. Even though a singer like Jimmie Rodgers could sell over twenty million records between 1927 and 1933, he could remain unknown in Oklahoma and Kansas, let alone in the northern cities.[14] As with R & B, what changed this situation was the northward migration of poor whites, as well as the ASCAP blackout of 1940 and the decline of the big bands. BMI had to turn to the largely unexploited hillbilly and R & B artists and songs, and to give people like the Carter family unprecedented access to a national radio audience, in order to stay in business. That audience obviously liked the alternatives to 'the average popular song'. By 1943 there were over 600 hillbilly radio stations, and jukebox operators as far north as Detroit were noting that hillbilly records were easily the most popular.[15] To give variety to this kind of music, Hank Williams produced an up-tempo band of country music which earned him eleven million-selling records between 1949 and 1953; while thirty-eight other country records reached that kind of market penetration.[16] Ernest Tubb's introduction of the electric guitar, and the leavening influence of the R & B music of the likes of 'Sonny Boy' Williamson, began to generate changes in instrumentation and line-up, and so in playing techniques and style, right across hillbilly music, resulting in a formula first known as 'rockabilly', and then, ever after, as 'rock 'n' roll'.

Carl Perkins's *Blue Suede Shoes* pioneered the first phase of rock-abilly, to become the first million-seller in that style; but it was Bill

Haley's *Crazy Man Crazy* which broke into the sanctum of the American music industry, *Billboard's* national charts.[17] Haley knew what he was doing:

> I felt that if I could take, say, a Dixieland tune and drop the first and third beats, and accentuate the second and fourth, and add a beat the listener could clap to as well as dance this would be what they were after. From that the rest was easy . . . take everyday sayings like 'Crazy Man Crazy' . . . and apply that to what I have just said.[18]

In other words, in the majority white market, it was the white musicians' version of caricatured R & B which triumphed. Perhaps the final indignity was the way in which Haley could rip off Joe Turner's version of Jesse Stone's *Shake Rattle and Roll* in late 1954. What before had been an open, adult, sexually explicit shouted blues became, in Haley's hands, an anodyne, mawkish, slightly hysterical stomp.[19] The same can be said of Haley's major success, *Rock around the Clock*. This song was originally part of the soundtrack for a film on classroom conflict, *The Blackboard Jungle*; but it took Haley's record over half a year to reach number 1 in the US charts. In January 1955, the song barely scraped into the British Top 20. In July it toppled Perez Prado's *Cherry Pink and Apple Blossom White* from number one in the USA, and eight weeks later it was replaced by Mitch Miller's *Yellow Rose of Texas*.[20] Rock 'n' roll did not take the music industry by storm. In fact, it was only when Haley and his Comets made a low-budget Hollywood quickie, costing $200,000, and named after their hit song, that large audiences could see the band in performance. Only then did this 'new' kind of music break out — the film grossed $1,000,000 in its first year.[21]

Other entrepreneurs were working towards the same kind of product. Sam Phillips, at Sun Records in Memphis, later claimed that he had worked out what he wanted down to a formula:

> If I could find a white man who had the Negro sound and the Negro feel, I could make a million dollars.[22]

If this wasn't simply hindsight, it's clear that (like Cinderella and the glass slipper) the slot was ready for a young Memphis truck driver to fit. Presley, of course, acknowledged the debt he owed to black singers and musicians. A man like T-Bone Walker had pioneered the use of electric guitars in 'jump combos' before Presley reached puberty, and had long used the guitar as a stage prop, 'sometimes for acrobatics' and 'sometimes for sexual provocation'.[23] One of Presley's early hits, *Hound Dog*, was reputed to have sold over half a million copies for Willie Mae 'Big Mama' Thornton, after August 1952;[24] and Perkins's version of his own *Blue Suede Shoes* sold over two million copies. (White-owned indies like Sun Records not only appropriated the work of black artists; they also weren't above exploiting that of white people.) Nor was Presley unique. There were a number of singers in Memphis alone who got involved in 'country rock', a style whose distinctive characteristic was, as Gillett coyly puts it,

> aggression, but curiously the target was enigmatically vague . . . it effected a release of violent feelings, not that any particular group was attacked.[25]

That release, of course, was the music's prime function, amongst whites. Blacks already had the blues as therapy for their frustrations. And though poor whites (particularly in the South) had used hillbilly music in much the same way, rockabilly and then rock 'n' roll effectively diverted the audience away from blues, via the rhythm of R & B and the lyrics of country rock, into a much safer direction. The openness, explicitness and general honesty of the adult blues were left well alone: the 'target' was left conveniently 'vague'.

To be fair, the South in July 1954 was not the most opportune place and time to launch a singer whose voice sounded 'integrated'. Two months previously the US Supreme Court had banned racial segregation in public schools and tension was already mounting.[26] Doubtless this general situation added a further touch of excitement for Presley's schoolroom audiences, just as his relatively brash sexuality would raise the hackles of emotionally insecure white males. Certainly, he got involved in plenty of fights. Yet a closer examination of Presley's trajectory, even in the early years, does little to support Gillett's thesis about consumer power. Like any other so-called independent record company, Sun Records survived by having a captive local market, by doing one-off recordings for individuals (such as the job which first brought Presley into the studio), and by selling masters of promising material to the majors. For most black artists, in the early 1950s,

> there was no place in the South they could go to record. The nearest place where they made so-called 'race' records . . . was Chicago, and most of them didn't have the money or the time to make the trip.[27]

They were, therefore, at the mercy of men like Sam Phillips, as indeed were the majority of hillbilly artists.

Before the Acuff–Rose publishing firm opened in 1942, there was no southern-based US music-publishing company.[28] Simply by being honest (but by no means generous), this firm prospered at the expense of the many shady dealers:

> It treated its writers as people, not as victims. 'They didn't pay better than the other publishers,' says Rule, 'but they always paid. Whatever your song made, you got your share'.[29]

In any case, by the 1940s the real hillbilly publishing agent was the radio programme, the 'Grand Ol' Opry'. Begun as 'a travelling road-show of the air' in 1925 the 'Opry' quickly became *the* showcase for any aspiring country singer or musician. By the early 1950s,

> the *Opry* was the thing and no one functioned much without reaching the *Opry* or being booked by the Artists Service Bureau, which was run by Jim Denny right there in the *Opry* office.[30]

When Presley had served his apprenticeship on the road, and had managed to get to the 'Opry', he was told by Denny that he ought to consider going back to truck driving. Thus did the employees of the National Life Insurance Company (which gave the 'Opry' financial backing) seek to dictate what should and should not be encouraged in music. But the process of encapsulation and accommodation was only beginning for Presley. Ed Sullivan refused to allow Presley's subversive hips to be shown on his nationally networked television show, and stipulated that he be filmed only from the waist up: Presley submitted. When Sam Phillips was offered $35,000 for Presley's contract by RCA-Victor, he was glad to take the cash, and Presley was delighted with his $5000. In the traditional manner of commodity-production, once the small-time capitalist had road-tested the product, the major company bought the machine tools. In any case, Sun couldn't afford to run the risk of a national promotion campaign, whereas RCA could with ease, given that one or two adjustments in the packaging and content of *their* Presley could be effected.[31]

What the majority record-buying audience got was not 'what they wanted', as Gillett romantically claims. They got what RCA-Victor offered; and, in Presley's case, what they offered was strikingly unlike the Presley of the Sun recordings, let alone the early live performances. Just as RCA hammered out and honed down their product, so the other majors winnowed the products of other indies, knocking off corners, proscribing, prescribing, and in general making rock 'n' roll bland enough for the most sheltered white adolescents (and their parents). *This* is what lies behind the gradual elimination of the - 'valuable complex of styles', and the production of a nationally recognizable style.[32] Whereas prior to 1955, rock 'n' roll had existed as a variety of local amalgams with varying line-ups and interpretations, in the later 1950s it was reduced to a formula:

its distinctive 'trademark' was a break two-thirds of the way through the record, in which a saxophone player produced a sound that was liable to tear paper off walls, a fast screech that emphasized almost every beat for several bars.[33]

In turn, the lyrical content was further restricted by the majors, who

narrowed the reference of songs to adolescence and simplified the complicated boogie rhythms to a simple 2/4 with the accent on the back beat . . . .[34]

Tin Pan Alley reasserted itself in the customary reactionary manner; and country or R & B artists had either to conform (and take the money), or resign themselves to a self-righteous obscurity, which in turn tended to attenuate to the 'moldy fig mentality':

Before Elvis a hit for Hank Snow sold maybe half a million copies, but now Hank and most others couldn't get half that. This caused a split in country ranks. In rejecting rock 'n' roll, some went even more 'country' than they had in the past. Others jumped aboard the rockabilly bandwagon rolling through town, so many that by 1957 the record charts were nearly dominated by good ol' country boys – Jerry Lee Lewis, Johnny Cash, Sonny James, Marty Robbins, George Hamilton IV, Conway Twitty and the Everly Brothers among them. In the meantime about a hundred country stations changed format and went rock.[35]

In spite of all this, it has to be said that the advent of rock 'n' roll had certain important progressive cultural consequences. R & B artists like Fats Domino were given a belated push into the white record market: by 1960 he'd sold upwards of fifty million records.[36] Other, lesser-known black artists were giving a national airing to undiluted R & B, and in turn helped fuel the white beat music of the 1960s and 1970s. Ray Charles was able to get an audience for his mixture of blues, jazz and gospel after 1954;[37] amd other innovators, including Chuck Berry and Little Richard, broke through the plantation owners' fences. Richard recalls that when he stopped working in a kitchen,

they wasn't playing no black artists on no Top 40 stations, I was the first to get played on the Top 40 stations – but it took people like

Elvis and Pat Boone, Gene Vincent to open the door for this kind of music, and I thank God for Elvis Presley.[38]

Ironically, going through that open door involved submitting to the mediation of the majors. Richard's original version of *Tutti Frutti* was held to be too ripe for white adolescents, and the lyrics were speedily rewritten into an onomatapoeic jumble by a young lady in the recording studio.[39] But if Richard submitted, Presley was beginning to grovel.

In his first two years at RCA, Elvis had the best-selling record for 55 out of the 104 weeks.[40] His first RCA single, *Heartbreak Hotel*, has now sold 11,000,000 copies.[41] Yet this same chart success was bought at the cost of considerable stylistic changes:

At Victor, under the supervision of Chet Atkins, Presley's records featured vocal groups, heavily electrified guitars, and drums, all of which were considered alien by both country and western audiences and by the audience for country rock.[42]

Of course, we can never know whether he would have made it, nationally, singing in the Sun style; but Presley had few qualms about conforming to the RCA pattern. His voice

became much more theatrical and self-conscious as he sought to contrive excitement and emotion which he had seemed to achieve on his Sun records without any evident forethought.[43]

Gradually, not only the delivery, but more importantly the tone and content of his records changed, becoming more and more like the songs of the 'all-round entertainer' and film star. The string of million-plus sellers which had stretched to eighteen before 1960 led inevitably to the final metamorphosis which took place in the Army. When he was drafted, Presley still had the aura of a *threat* to some aspects of the US dominant ideology. When he came out, after barely a whimper, with short hair, sergeant's stripes and a generally clean-cut demeanour, he was *safe*.

The period which stretched between *Rock around the Clock* and Presley's *It's Now or Never* was only six years, but it witnessed the succumbing of commercially oriented rock 'n' roll. Haley's song sold 22,000,000 copies, up to 1975, whereas Presley's sold 20,000,000; yet *Rock around the Clock* (lyrics on page 59), for all its now-evident triteness and slowness of rhythm, is by far the more adult song. True, it purports to be about dancing, and this is certainly the way in which it

Rock around the Clock

One two three o'clock four o'clock rock
Five six seven o'clock eight o'clock rock
Nine ten eleven o'clock twelve o'clock rock
We're gonna rock around the clock tonight

Put your glad rags on join me hon'
We'll have some fun when the clock strikes one
We're gonna rock around the clock tonight
We're gonna rock rock rock till broad daylight
Gonna rock gonna rock around the clock tonight

When the clock strikes two three and four
If the band slows down we'll yell for more
We're gonna rock around the clock tonight
We're gonna rock rock rock till broad daylight
Gonna rock gonna rock around the clock tonight

(Guitar break)

When the chimes ring five and six and seven
We'll be rockin' up in seventh heaven
We're gonna rock around the clock tonight
We're gonna rock rock rock till broad daylight
Gonna rock gonna rock around the clock tonight

When it's eight nine ten eleven too
I'll be going strong and so will you
We're gonna rock around the clock tonight
We're gonna rock rock rock till broad daylight
Gonna rock gonna rock around the clock tonight

(Saxophone break)

When the clock strikes twelve we'll cool off then,
Start a-rockin' round the clock again
We're gonna rock around the clock tonight
Gonna rock rock rock till broad daylight
Gonna rock gonna rock around the clock tonight

was taken outside the USA. But it was a commonplace in North American cities that the phrase, 'rock and roll' had other associations. 'Roll' in Negro (and, therefore, hip white) slang, meant 'fuck'; and while Haley's version does not use the phrase, it was generally heralded as the first major example of the 'new' style by white DJs, notably Alan Freed. If you listen to the song again, bearing in mind the alternative reading, the whole thing becomes a sustained celebration of sexual prowess, in which the female partner is accorded equal status, equal potency. Rocking (and rolling) around the clock gives new significance to phrases like 'seventh heaven', 'going strong' and 'have some fun'. And it's not just, as D.H. Lawrence once sourly remarked about another style of dancing, that rock 'n' roll was 'making love to music'. The dance hall was a fundamental part of British and American courtship, right into the 1960s; and so the real relations between dancing and sexual intercourse were generally (if tacitly) understood to be crucial, well before 'bop' had become rock 'n' roll. (ASCAP, and not BMI, held the rights to the song; so there was no campaign to get it banned from radio, as Ray's BMI hit *Such a Night* had been in the USA.)[44]

Rock around the Clock seems surprisingly slow, now, and the excitement of the guitar and sax breaks crudely produced. But compared to what else was readily available for the majority white audience, even the antics of a group of slightly balding, 30-year-old musicians were highly preferable. (Remember, even *I Saw Mommy Kissing Santa Claus* was held to be slightly *risqué* in 1953 Britain; and Gene Vincent's later *Be Bop a Lula* was actually banned by the BBC!) Of course, the fact that rock 'n' roll was denounced as unrespectable only helped its development, both sides of the Atlantic. Haley and his Comets were able to live off their major hit, and the various close copies, for some time to come. At least their brashness and vitality were genuine: when we get to Sergeant Presley, half a decade later, we can see the deterioration clearly. The audience that was 15 in 1955 was, by 1960, 20. Presley might be sure of their loyalty — and he had one of the best-organized fan clubs ever known — but he was far from sure that he could capture the new generation of 15-year-olds, the ones who had been brought up (or was it down?) on the 'high school' music of the late 1950s, when he was in the Army.[45] *It's Now or Never*, then, was a deliberate attempt to widen the potential Presley audience:

it was played on many more radio stations than were accustomed to playing Elvis records, a fact that must have been noticed by RCA and the Colonel, because the next single release was even further away from the rock 'n' roll beat.[46]

The next release was *Are you Lonesome Tonight*. That tendency, plus the immersion in a series of bad films, spelt the end of Presley's career as a rock 'n' roll singer. The step to cabaret was only a matter of time.

It's Now or Never (lyrics on page 62) is a rag-bag of musical clichés, lyrical clichés and overacting. It's a reworked version of *O Solé Mío*, with a springier tempo and a more liberal helping of sentimentality. None of this is remarkable, of course. But what is striking is the way in which the song expresses an attitude towards women, and to female sexuality, which is little short of vicious. The whole piece, once you've penetrated the forced eroticism and suchlike, is centred wholly on three words — 'I', 'me' and 'my'. The woman is systematically reduced to a sexual object, whose only choice is to submit to the man's sexual drive, or to get lost. There is a hint of a threat of auto-eroticism in that final crescendo, the hysterical if-you-won't-I'll-find-somebody-who-will-or-do-it-myself which is built-in to the title. Behind all this is the assumption that any old mish-mash of verbal and physical posturings will serve to satisfy the emotional and physical needs of the woman. That such a song sold 20,000,000 copies in Presley's version, up to 1975, fourth behind Crosby's version of *White Christmas* and *Silent Night*, and Haley's *Rock around the Clock*, tells us a good deal about the Western market for commercial musical products.[47]

Of course, the song was popular in a commercial context precisely because it did (and to some extent, still does) articulate certain key strands in the dominant ideology. The denial of female sexuality, the reduction of love to ejaculation, the inability to come out with emotion honestly, the habit of implying intercourse is a 'dirty little secret' (as Lawrence termed it), the acceptability of emotional blackmail on the part of the man, and so on, tell us a good deal about the paradigms of femininity in the late 1950s, *and* about the paradigms of masculinity, for all those men who had to try, presumably, to imitate Elvis Presley. Gratification could be equated with what was understood as fulfilment. The demand of one man's erection, of one man's physical release, was primary, and had to suffice for the woman too. We have only to ponder the changes brought about by the women's movement in the last two decades to recognize how oppressed they (and many men) were by the images and values promulgated and reinforced by such things as this.

It's Now or Never

Ooo-ooo-ooo-ooo
Ooo ooo ooo

It's now or never come hold me tight
Kiss me my darling be mine tonight
Tomorrow will be too late
It's now or never my love won't wait

When I first saw you with your smile so tender
My heart was captured my soul surrendered
I spent a lifetime waiting for the right time
Now that you're near the time is here at last

It's now or never come hold me tight
Kiss me my darling be mine tonight
Tomorrow will be too late
It's now or never my love won't wait

Just like a willow we would cry an ocean
If we lost true love and sweet devotion
Your lips excite me let your arms invite me
For who knows when we'll meet again this way

It's now or never come hold me tight
Kiss me my darling be mine tonight
Tomorrow will be too late
It's now or never my love won't wait
It's now or never my love won't wait
It's now or never my love won't wait
It's now or never my love won't wait

The period 1955-60 was in many ways the economic take-off point for the American recording industry. True, there had always been a lot of money to be made in music publishing; as early as 1892, Charles K. Harris's *After the Ball* was earning $25,000 a week, and within twenty years it had sold ove ten million copies.[48] But, after a boom in the immediate post-first world war years, the US record market didn't pick up again until after 1945. That year, 110 million records were sold for the first time since 1922: within twelve months, that figure had doubled; and for the period 1947-54, sales kept steadily around the $200 million mark. After that, the yearly sales figures speak for themselves: $213 million, $277 million, $377 million, $460 million, $511 million, $603 million (see Appendix 2, page 223). What caused this expansion? Obviously, the people were there to buy the records, and they had the money for play-back equipment. The American economy was enjoying the fruits of a post-war boom. Equally obvious is the fact that there were records which the American public wished to buy. Here we can see the commercial consequence of the early innovations of Haley, Presley and company. Finally, there is the unsung technological change which contributed significantly to the attractiveness of gramophone records, that from shellac to vinyl as the raw material for the recordings themselves.

The 45 r.p.m. records were not new in 1954:

they had been introduced by RCA in 1949 and their new vinyl composition had been developed during World War II when the federal government drastically monopolized the supply of shellac — the material which had previously been used in record manufacture.[49]

That motor for capitalist innovation, war, was sparked into life;[50] and at one point prospective record buyers had to trade in an old 78 as part of the conditions for buying a new one, so strict was the control. In the event, the changeover in record speed reinvigorated the industries associated with record manufacture and record play-back equipment. Old technology could be replaced by new (thereby stimulating the machine tools and electronics sectors of the economy), at a time when war-related contracts were running out; but of course, there were problems:

the 45 medium was not accepted immediately because radio stations and individual consumers were reluctant to purchase the new record-playing equipment which the 45 demanded. The situation gradually changed, however, particularly when RCA introduced a relatively low-priced record player, and when optional centres became standard, so that the new records could fit conventional spindles. In 1954, more-over, several of the major record companies, including RCA and Mercury, announced that they would send 45s instead of 78s to disc jockeys.[51]

The country was bounced, willy-nilly, into submitting to the demands of the industry. But when Columbia, RCA and Capitol tried to standardize all record speeds at 33 r.p.m. – the speed of the LP, first introduced by Columbia in 1948 – in 1960 and 1961, there was a determined resistance, above all from jukebox operators, who dominated the singles market.[52] (Jukeboxes had spread after the end of Prohibition, and by 1939 there were 225,000 of them, using some 13,000,000 records a year. By 1940, they accounted for about 44 per cent of all singles sold in the USA; and by 1956 the 500,000 boxes consumed some 40 per cent of the vastly increased singles production.)[53]

In any event, by 1957 the 45 was completely dominant in the USA. The last sector of the market to succumb, not surprisingly, was the poorest, that for R & B. Black-owned companies and their customers could least afford the capital investment required for the changeover, a point which was surely not lost on the majors who forced that change through. In this way the least affluent sector of the market was isolated, and the black-owned companies temporarily cut off from the richer *white* audience.[54] A significant amount of technological change had been effected *before* the rock 'n' roll boom of 1954-7. But in any case, the 45 possessed qualities which would have probably assured its commercial success over a longer period:

The lightness, ease of handling, and physical resilience of the 45 sharply distinguished it from the cumbersome 78. It was easily manufactured, due to the development of automatic injection and compression systems in record production which obviated the old hand compression molds still in use for many 78s in 1954. For distributors and manufacturers, the new records presented fewer shipping problems, because they could be sent by air or first class mail instead of by the slower fourth class rate necessitated by the protective packaging of the fragile 78s. The lightness of the 45s, coupled with their doughnut shape and the large spindle of the 45 players, also produced faster, easier listening. The 'search' for the small hole in the center of the 78 was eliminated, and the listener could quickly skim through a large group of records, playing and rejecting them at a moment's notice. The process of playing records therefore became more casual, and there was a more immediate relationship between the listener and the record than had been possible with the heavy and breakable 78s . . . .[55]

The transformations in the cultural practice of young people, above all, which this changeover stimulated, are indeed manifold; but those produced by the LP have proved to be even more far-reaching, in terms of record content, structure and use.

Though it was first introduced by Columbia in 1948, it wasn't until 1954 that the LP became commercially important in the USA.

Each ten-inch disc usually contained eight songs, four on each side, and it took over a decade until the medium was exploited for any more imaginative format. What the LP did was to provide an artist like Sinatra with a way of disassociating himself in some measure from the 'new' youth market for the 45s, and indeed that for singles in general once the 78 died out, while at the same time maintaining his audience among the grown-up bobby-soxers. Indeed, his early exploitation of this medium gave Sinatra a lead and a status in the then richer 'adult' market which remained unchallenged until Presley took a similar turn, and ensured his canonization in that market for all time.[56] The 45/33 divide was not simply a technological one, then, but in some measure a cultural one too. You could use LPs differently from singles – in some ways, you had to, notably because the larger format wasn't so easy to manipulate mechanically without the danger of causing damage – and so the LP got woven into the leisure-time patterns of notably different age groups and economic groups than did the 45, especially after the introduction of stereo in 1957.

A further consequence of this cultural/economic divide was the subdivision of the market category, 'popular song', and the development of a more specialized 'pop' sector of the music industry, with advertising, promotion, marketing and suchlike to match. This general process culminated in the establishment of such influential institutions as the first nationally networked 'pop' television show, 'American Bandstand'.[57] In turn, the expansion of Philadelphia WFIL-TV's show from limited transmission (beginning in 1952) to national transmission, in 1957, helped in the standardization of the commercially available cultural products. Just as networked radio had helped iron out previously differentiated local musical and vocal styles, so *Bandstand* extended the process into dance styles, and even styles of dress and behaviour. It was, of course, purely coincidental that Dick Clark, the programme's Master of Ceremonies, happened to own part of the local record company whose records were given national exposure on his show![58]

4 Taming jazz

In Britain, in 1925, there were two million radio sets in use, almost all of them tuned in to the BBC. (The state monopoly of the air waves had been cemented by the changeover from the British Broadcasting Company to the British Broadcasting Corporation, in 1927, because of the strategic importance of radio communication.)[1] By 1939, when the BBC's national Home Service was begun, nine out of ten British homes had a radio set. The second world war, and especially the Forces Programmes begun in 1940, mopped up most of the remainder — just as news of Crimean war dead had forced Queen Victoria's government to repeal the newspaper stamp, the last of the 'taxes on knowledge', and the publishing of 1914-18 casualty lists had made the daily press a truly national phenomenon. By 1950, the peak year, there were all but twelve million British radio licence holders.[2]

In the mid 1950s, 1,500,000 radio sets were produced in Britain each year. By 1961, with the advent of transistor technology, that rate had doubled, and the boom in sales lasted until 1964. By that time, valve radios were all but obsolete, and the home market for radios was saturated. Interestingly, the peak years for production were 1954-5 and 1960-4, both periods which *pre-date* important developments in popular song. The rise of rock 'n' roll, and of the pirate radio stations (and the groups), was made possible in part by virtue of the material basis that radio production and sales had already established.[3]

One of the other factors which led to these key 'moments' in British commercial song was the conservatism of the BBC. Recorded music had played only a small part in the Corporation's output in the 1920s and 1930s. Up to 1939, most of that had been band music, because the Musicians' Union had a 'needle time' agreement which limited record air-play, and so ensured work for its members. In 1937, the BBC insisted that only every third piece on the radio should be a vocal. Radio Luxembourg had no such agreements, but that station became of significance in Britain only after 1950, when it began to transmit its sponsored record shows in English on the medium wave band.[4]

Recorded music and song was the mainstay of the continental station: after all, records were far cheaper than musicians, and besides, air-time could be sold very profitably to the four main European recording companies. EMI, Decca, Pye and Phillips each bought as much as they could of the time available, using it straightforwardly as advertising space for their products.[5]

Even in this period, and apart from the impact of American musical films, the penetration of US commercial cultural products in Britain was considerable. The American Forces Network beamed real US music and songs — blues, jazz, gospel and big band, as well as ballads — across a large segment of Europe. American religious groups purchased large blocks of Luxembourg's air-time for sermons and hymns. No wonder that the BBC seemed staid. According to the official blurb, the Light Programme (itself an indication of the hierarchy's attitude) operated in the belief that its 'ideal listener' was

not going to listen for more than half an hour, that he prefers orchestral sounds to the purer music sound of a string quartet, and that he is essentially not a highbrow.[6]

This is how and why young people in the 1950s got their broadcast music and song via the 'Billy Cotton Band Show' and 'Two Way Family Favourites', two programmes which filled the Sunday lunchtime period as much as the smell of steeped peas and Yorkshire puddings.[7]

Given this general situation, it is no surprise that the most successful British recording artists in 1955 were Victor Sylvester and his band. He and they had by then sold 27,000,000 records. Sylvester's textbook on ballroom dancing had gone through fifty-five editions between 1928 and 1955; and what is culturally highly significant is that the first edition was produced as part of a campaign by the Imperial Society of Dance Teachers to *tame jazz*. Along with four other teachers, the son of the Vicar of Wembley successfully imposed a strict tempo on American dance music and dancing styles, and cut out most of the improvization. He was helped to this influential position by being a Professional Partner at Harrod's Tea Dances, and by becoming the 1922 World Ballroom Dancing Champion; and he went on to become conductor of Britain's most successful dance band.[8] Sylvester also managed to gain regular access to the BBC. How did this happen? Part of the answer lies in the fact that American bands were not allowed to tour Britain, and vice versa, until the mid 1950s, so competition from the real thing could come only in the record market, which was in any case relatively unimportant.[9] Sylvester was a product of monopoly:

when that monopoly was broken so was he.

The British record industry in the late 1940s and early 1950s was a very curious thing. It, too, was protected by the fact that most record buyers were not working class (*they* made their own music, or went dancing to live bands), and by the virtual monopoly of the big four companies:

It was like bringing out a regular monthly magazine. Each month a company like Parlophone brought out around ten new records, all planned about two months ahead, which they called their monthly supplements. They were always very strictly and fairly balanced. Out of the ten new records two would be classical, two jazz, two dance music — the Victor Sylvester sort of dance music — two would be male vocal and two would be female vocal. There was no such category as pop. 'We never talked about pop. All we had was classical, jazz, dance and vocal!'[10]

At this time, around 1950, a really big British record hit sold only 30,000 copies.[11] The big money was in stage performances and in sheet music, in the *live* part of commercial musical culture; and that part of the business was controlled by a network of London-based agents and publishers. In other words, the transformation which had begun in the USA some twenty years before had not yet taken place. Even the BBC was under the thumb of the major publishers and record companies:

They had long-term agreements with the BBC by which they paid fixed rates to get songs plugged. In return, the BBC ensured that at least half of every popular music programme was made up of songs that had been paid for.[12]

Luxembourg, of course, was completely dominated by the commercial giants. All the Big Four had to do was to threaten to withdraw 'sponsorship' whenever they wanted to get their own way.

The inevitable consequence of this situation was that, if you hadn't the five shillings to spend on a 78 record — and most people hadn't, judging from the low sales figures of even hit records — then you listened to radio, went dancing, went to a variety show or made your own musical entertainment.[13] But, as with radio sets, the early 1950s saw a sharp rise in the production figures for record-playing equipment. Between 1952 and 1955, those figures trebled (doubling in 1953-4 alone), thereby creating a sizeable new market for recorded music and song.[14] It was into this situation that Bill Haley's *Rock around the Clock* was launched, late in 1954; but it is an indication of the conservatism of the record market that this same song could re-enter the charts in October 1955, and stay there for seventeen weeks. In September 1956, it entered once more, and stayed for eleven weeks.[15] When we talk about the rise of rock 'n' roll and the creation of the pop scene in Britain, we have to realize that the process was a very long drawn-out one indeed.

For all that any white, un-hip British adolescent knew, *Rock around the Clock* was about dancing and for dancing. Even so, the song was lucky enough to raise the hackles of an important section of their elders and 'betters' — lucky, because it and the film which it generated became the focus for a cultural struggle that was amplified out of all recognition by Fleet Street:

the picture played 300 cinemas scattered around the country (including such tough cities as Glasgow and Sheffield) without any trouble. Then, after a performance at the Trocadero in South London, there was some good natured larking: a few hundred boys and girls danced and chanted 'Mambo Rock' on Tower Bridge, holding up traffic. Some cups and saucers were thrown about too. Later there were a few ten-shilling fines. One boy was fined £1 for accidentally kicking a policeman.

When the more paranoid hacks on the worst daily papers got hold of the news they

splashed the story as a riot. 2,000 were on the streets, claimed the *Daily Express*. More stories followed . . . .[16]

Subsequently, other interconnections were made, quite arbitrarily at first. What the press termed the Teddy Boy phenomenon was yoked to the 'new' music and the Haley film. Cinema managers over-reacted, calling in the police to stop dancing in their aisles; and Watch Committees banned the film completely from certain towns.[17] By this time, if not before, rock 'n' roll had been made into a cultural battleground. It was a handy symbol for people in authority, and for those adolescents who resisted and resented their power, through which to express their mutual contempt.

For the next few years, the British music industry simply could not cope. True, they had managed to encapsulate Lonnie Donegan, after his *Rock Island Line* had sold 300,000 copies following a few radio plays in its original form as an LP track.[18] But Haley, and then Presley, were problems of a different order. *Rock around the Clock* became the first single to sell over 1,000,000 copies in Britain;[19] and Presley's *Jailhouse Rock* shot straight to number 1 on its release in 1958. Granted Donegan's *My Old Man's a Dustman* managed the latter feat in 1960, but by that date American artists dominated the British singles market.[20] Presley's *It's Now or Never* went straight to number 1, and stayed there for eight weeks over Christmas that same year. And this in spite of the fact that the man refused to perform in Britain!

The first attempt to combat the commercial invasion of US records took the form of imitation. Tommy Steele, as a pop star, was prefabricated from start to finish by John Kennedy his manager; but it is an indication of the conservative power of the British industry that Steele had to be defined *against* the prevailing American style and the 'bad' British publicity:

I told him my plans. I said that rock 'n' roll music had got a bad name from Teddy Boy hooligans who wrecked cinemas and broke up cafes. But it was coming to Europe nonetheless. It would get bigger and anyone who went along with it would himself grow big on the crest of a wave.

But someone has got to lift it out of its Teddy Boy rut, give it class and get society as well as the thousands of ordinary decent kids singing and dancing it.[21]

Kennedy's methods were nothing if not simple. He (and a friend working on a national daily paper) paid £25 to arrange a 'debs' party, with Steele as guest singer. They also arranged a 'fight' as to which deb would take Tommy home, so as to grab the headlines.[22] Right through the publicity campaign, Kennedy never missed a trick:

I doubled the salary he was being paid, trebled the size of his fan-mail, said he owned a motor-car when in fact he could not drive, credited him with owning *two* motor-bikes, and if a thought came to me – like printing round visiting cards because he hated 'squares' – then I blandly announced it as an established fact. But on the other hand, I played more than fair with requests for 'stunts' from reporters . . . if it was humanly possible, we would never send a journalist away disappointed.[23]

The whole shabby business proved too much for Steele. His very life was no longer under his control:

I can't eat where I want to eat. I can't wear what I want to wear. I can't say what I want to say. And now you're telling me I can't have the girl I want to have.[24]

As a refuge he built his parents a mansion, inside which was a replica of their old terraced house living-room, where he and they spent most of their time. It was all but symbolic of the dehumanized product that he had become.[25]

On the other hand, neither radio nor television could afford to ignore that sector of the potential audience which had already indicated its interest in recorded song. Television was the first to adapt. In 1947, there were some 14,000 current licences: in 1950, there were about 450,000; and by 1956 there were 6,000,000. Most British people had access to television directly or indirectly (through a neighbour or relation) by the time of the Coronation in 1953. By 1958, the number of television licences had outpaced that for radio.[26] But before February 1957, television coverage of contemporary single records was almost non-existent. What allowed access to such material was a combination of government relaxation of broadcasting times, and a wish on the part of the BBC to economize. In February 1957 the BBC was allowed to show programmes between six o'clock and seven o'clock in the evenings for the first time. So as not to cut into the budgets for other parts of the schedule, the shows that went into this slot had to be cheap, easily put together, and use ready-made material as much as possible. One result was '6.5 Special', a programme using contemporary music and song, with a cheap resident band, and an audience of teenagers drawn from Greater London. The whole thing had an engaging air of amateurism and informality — cameras and microphones were allowed into shot! — and though many US songs were performed by sub-standard British artists, at least the thing represented a refreshing break from Billy Cotton and Alan Breeze.

The success of '6.5 Special' prompted BBC radio to aim at a similar audience, this time on Saturday mornings. 'Saturday Club', introduced by Brian Matthew, didn't follow the request format then in vogue, but was able (unlike the television) to use US recordings.[27] What was more, low budgets actually encouraged the use of relatively unknown British artists, and this in turn fostered the growth of amateur and semi-professional musical activity right round the country. Of course, ITV was obliged to follow suit, with 'Oh Boy', in September 1958. But even there, the dead weight of propriety and conservatism lay heavily on the programme. In order to be made into a star, Cliff Richard cheerfully submitted to Jack Good's ideas, having his hair cut, his sideboards trimmed, and his clothes prescribed for him.[28] Apart from these ventures, television audiences were offered that non-event, 'Juke Box Jury', in which 'celebrities' — out-of-work actors, professional pundits, and assorted media hangers-on — gave their notably jaded and uninformed views on a carefully selected series of single records. They were not even asked for their opinions of the quality of the records played. Instead, their limited critical intelligence was sacrificed in favour of the criteria of the market. They were asked, simply, whether a record would be a 'Hit' or a 'Miss' in commercial terms. Thus, even though David Jacobs's silly and patronizing programme survived into the early 1960s, the appearance on it of the Rolling Stones — and their marvellous lack of respect, behaving in a deliberately yobbish manner — sounded its death-knell.[29]

5 Happy little rockers

The period 1959-62 was the deadest phase of British and American recorded song since at least 1945.[1] In the USA, rock 'n' roll had been bought up, neutered and repackaged, as a large-scale commercial phenomenon at any rate. In Britain, some people turned to 'trad' jazz or to 'folk'; but the whole dreary time is symbolized by the fact that a contrived thing like *I Remember You* by Frank Ifield was successful in chart terms.[2] For adolescents, it was a *desert*. If you weren't 18 (or couldn't pass for something like that age, though it was easier for girls) you couldn't get into the bars of pubs. Coffee bars and cinemas were the only alternatives to the streets, for the youth clubs were mainly run on what felt like semi-military lines. Unless you lived in a major city, or by the coast, or had access to a fairground or amusement arcade — unless you played a musical instrument, or were one of the few with a record player *and* the money to buy records — musically, it was a *bloody desert*. Older brothers and sisters could, perhaps, go to a local jazz club. But, outside the major urban areas, this meant having access to transport. Going by bus usually meant leaving early: railway lines were being cut; and the ownership of private transport (even a motor bike) amongst most working-class families was rare indeed. So much had 'affluence' contributed to the material culture of the post-war working-class generation!

By this time, the mid fifties rock 'n' roll had withered close to the root. Most of the major exponents were either doing other things, or *hors de combat*. Buddy Holly was dead, Chuck Berry was in prison, Jerry Lee Lewis was under a cloud of moral indignation, Little Richard had gone religious, and so on.[3] As far as the commercial music world was concerned, in the USA at any rate, the blues and country roots weren't worth cultivating anew. Ironically, it was the British skiffle movement which went back to the old bluesmen and their music, and to the likes of Woody Guthrie:

The first ones to be brought over were the great folkies like Leadbelly and Big Bill Broonzy. Later the Chicago blues stars also got gigs: Muddy Waters, Howlin' Wolf and Sonny Boy Williamson.[4]

Ray Charles had a fairly large British following. Sonny Terry and Brownie McGhee could eat here. And, in general, it is important to note that the British audience got 'rockabilly without rednecks, and R & B without racism'.[5]

By 1958, even advertizing men were beginning to realize that there was a new market for consumer goods, 'youth'. In Britain, they discovered, there were five million single people aged between 15 and 24, or about 13 per cent of the population. Here was £900,000,000 worth of spending power, or about £4 per person per week. Unsurprisingly, it was found that these young people spent 1.7 per cent of their money, or £15,000,000 a year on records and record players, and formed well over 40 per cent of the market. Besides, given that the turnover in the age group was rapid, young people represented a self-replenishing market:

Of the current 5 million members, 450,000 or nearly 10% will marry in the next twelve months, abandon their teenage spending habits and transfer their spending to the very different adult market . . . for the entrepreneur engaged in this market the pace never slackens: the teenage market has none of the comfortable inertia common to many adult markets.[6]

But the crucial cultural factor was the discovery that

the teenage market is almost entirely working class. Its middle class members are either still at school or college or else only just beginning their careers. Not far short of all teenage spending is conditioned by working class tastes and values. The aesthetic of the teenage market is essentially a working class aesthetic and probably only entrepreneurs of working class origin will have a 'natural' understanding of the needs of this market.[7]

The assumption that any entreprenuer, however proletarian in origin, could understand the culture of late 1950s youth indicated the manipulative way in which capitalist leisure industry felt it was able to operate. As it happens, the cultural situation at this time shows graphically how entrepreneurs could fail to innovate, and how they had previously failed to nourish the growth points of mid fifties working-class culture.

As ever, if 'they' wouldn't produce the music that 'we' needed, 'we' had to do it ourselves. Otherwise, like the remnants of the Teds in the provinces and in certain London districts, we were driven back to the musical roots which had helped form Teddy Boy culture:

By 1958-9 the 'real' Teds were only to be found in the provinces. In London they had become a very much submerged minority.[8]

Outside the frenzied brains of journalists there never had been much mindless violence in the Teddy Boy era. And, in any case, by the later 1950s, new possibilities were opening up for gangs who had previously been economically restricted to self-made entertainment, from 'punch-up' to palais. The key factor was the never-never. If you were over 21 and male, you could buy motor bikes and guitars via hire purchase. When the Teds and their younger brothers (for this was very much a male-dominated strand in working-class culture) took hold of the means of artistic production, however, they did not imitate the high school slush emanating from the USA. If Buddy Holly was dead, his backing group the Crickets were very active, and available as a model. One boy playing not too well on his own sounded pretty weak, but four or five could make a noise which was acceptable enough to their friends. Besides, in a group you could learn from each other, share expenses, increase the number of contracts, widen the potential audience good-will, pool records, and so on. Hence, in part, the rise of the Shadows, and with them the concept of the self-contained guitar-oriented group, often writing its own material. The usual line-up of drums, bass, rhythm and lead guitars became the starting point for many of the British groups of the early 1960s; while the cultural resources that were drawn upon from across the Atlantic were precisely the roots of rock 'n' roll — rockabilly and both country and city blues.[9]

More research needs to be done on this important cultural 'moment'; but if the sociologist Colin Fletcher's experience on Merseyside was at all typical, we have to recognize that the commercially dead period around 1960 was one of the most potent and creative times for British adolescent working-class musical culture. Access to musical instruments helped to transform patterns of behaviour, and also *values*:

As the process of producing a group from within a gang's ranks was cumulative one could feel the decline in tension in other forms of competition. What mattered now was not how many boys a gang could muster for a Friday night fight but how well their group could play on Saturday night . . . . The Park Gang literally nursed its group. To enable the group to buy microphones and speakers a system of 'shares' was set up which were to be repaid from the group's earnings.

Any member of the group could buy any number of shares and in this way help the group to compete successfully with the groups of rival gangs. The trusted 'spiritual' boys became the director and manager respectively. An electrical apprentice acted as an on-the-spot repairer when the amplifiers or guitar pick-ups failed . . . . Girls, too, assumed a new role. They became the seamstresses . . . .[10]

Just as when trade unions became respectable, or when a working-class family joined a nonconformist church, so with the transformation of the street-centred culture of the gang to the Saturday night (indoor) leisure culture of the group we find that there was a simultaneous accommodation to the values of the dominant class, and the seeds of a more organized opposition.

If the 'lads' were down at the youth club, practising, they formed less of a threat than they had done on the street corner. That media construct, 'delinquency', had been a problem for those in authority well before rock 'n' roll;[11] but now it could be more effectively contained, or at least diverted. Aggression could be vented in and through music. Adolescents could be helped to 'socialize' themselves with the minimum of expenditure: they could be converted into customers, caught up by hire purchase in the fetishizing of commodities, and generally encouraged to channel their energy and their restlessness into socially acceptable activities – like getting on. Thus they could be made into 'adults' all the sooner, and that worrying period of adolescent independence could be smoothed over. The truth is, in Britain and the USA, that only

as a customer and, occasionally, as an athlete are adolescents favourably received. Otherwise they are treated as a problem and, potentially a threatening one. No other group except convicted criminals and certified lunatics are subjected to as much restriction.[12]

What was reassuring about Abrams' market research was the possibility of coping with the teenager and at the same time making a profit:

We ourselves see no cause for alarm, and not much for diagnosing novelty except in the new levels of spending and their commercial effects.[13]

The cultural problem was reduced to a marketing problem. It was assumed that novelty would be kept at a premium, and innovation frowned upon. Exploitation was, as ever, the key word.

We have noted the fruits of just this attitude in the degeneration of

Presley and the making of Tommy Steele. In terms of music, it is a commonplace that

The bankruptcy of the British pop scene (and the American for that matter) had driven people away from the 'big time' and into local clubs, where local bands played.[14]

But *what* did they play? What was the musical orientation of the clubs? With hindsight, it is always possible to stress the dominant commercial strand which emerged from the early 1960s, and to forget the commercial dead-ends and false starts, the minority tastes and the expressly non-commercial initiatives. The guitar-spreading effects of the skiffle movement did not only result in the beat groups, even at the commercial level, let alone in the cultural matrix on which commercialism feeds. We will examine the folk movement in some detail later on; but it is interesting to note here, how the interface between jazz and blues, above all in London, produced much of the musical and lyrical resources for the beat boom of the mid 1960s.

Chris Barber's contribution was to import the city bluesmen to Britain, and to take them on tours, spreading the blues like seed-corn on an audience ripe for any meaningful alternative to Tin Pan Alley pap. In London, Alexis Korner and Cyril Davis got together at the Roundhouse pub in 1957, and helped to foster R & B. The roll-call of their regular performers indicates how important this resource was to become. Long John Baldry joined what was then Blues Incorporated in 1961. Charlie Watts played drums for Korner's band. Keith Richard and Mick Jagger played with Korner at the Marquee, and later persuaded Watts to risk leaving Korner to form the Rolling Stones. John Mayall was catalysed by Korner into forming the Bluesbreakers in 1962; and in the same year Graham Bond graduated from playing alto saxophone to being a member of Blues Incorporated. These were the people who went to form the R & B matrix, once blues had weaned itself away from the jazz fraternity (and embryo industry). In fact, the cadre of 1960s and 1970s star performers served their apprenticeships within the Korner fold. Baldry joined Cyril Davis's All Stars in 1963, then left to form the Hoochie Coochie Men with, amongst others, Rod Stewart. In 1965 and 1966, Baldry toured with the Steampacket, along with Stewart, Mick Briggs, Brian Auger and Julie Driscoll, before lining up with Reg Dwight (Elton John) and Marsha Hunt as Bluesology. Mayall teamed up with Eric Clapton (from the Yardbirds) in 1965. Jack Bruce left the Bluesbreakers for Manfred Mann. Clapton also left, in 1966, and went on to form the Cream with Jack Bruce and Ginger

Baker (who had formed a trio with Graham Bond as early as 1963, and then, with John McLaughlin, a quartet). Peter Green replaced Clapton in the Bluesbreakers, and then left to form Fleetwood Mac in 1967. In turn, Green was replaced by Mick Taylor, who was to join the Stones in 1969. Dick Heckstall Smith joined what was then the Graham Bond Organisation, which disbanded in 1965, when he became part of the Bluesbreakers and then Collosseum. Once Cream folded, Bond signed up with Ginger Baker's Air Force. And so on . . . .[15]

This matrix was, of course, London based, and it was a pretty tight group. But all its members toured, first to form and then to cultivate a national audience, penetrating to such unlikely places as Redcar Jazz Club (which stopped presenting jazz before the mid 1960s), as well as to the major midland and northern cities. As a result, there was a thriving basement club R & B musical culture by 1962, which was as much a celebration of the strengths of American city blues as a rejection of contemporary commercial cultural products. The orthodoxy of the London-based recording industry — of the session musicians who couldn't grasp rock 'n' roll, the singers who still feigned mid Atlantic accents, and all the rigidities of the instrumental line-up — was being seriously undermined.[16] Besides, R & B had an aura of authenticity (even in Britain) which was also associated with the folk movement, but which was decisively lacking in the trad jazz antics of Acker Bilk.[17]

Inevitably, once the R & B trend became established, and developed its own audience, it came up against the vested interests. To some extent, then, the rise of R & B was effected in spite of commercial conservatism, and against the opposition of men like Harold Pendleton, who, because he

owned all these trad clubs and he . . . got a cut from these trad bands . . . couldn't bear to see them die. He couldn't afford it.[18]

What killed trad was the relatively raw R & B — not so much the solo singer, as the group, and not so much the purists as the people who could weld British lyrics on to an amalgam of rockabilly and R & B music, or who could adapt US songs so as to resonate in the culture of a British audience which had been offered Cliff Richard and Tommy Steele as follow-ups to Gene Vincent and the early Elvis Presley. The sheer size of the music-producing sector of the community can be gauged from the fact that there were said to be some 20,000 groups operating in Britain, in 1963 (400 in Liverpool, 600 in Newcastle).[19] A year later, London alone could boast twenty-eight clubs, with a membership of 100,000 young people, and an average weekly attendance of 10,000.[20] What was new about this phenomenon was that both the musical producers and their audiences were at one and the same time local and national. The whole matrix was held together by the networks of clubs, the gigging and touring of bands, and, above all, by the fact that *this* music had been fostered from the 'bottom' up, not imposed from the 'top' down.

There was another factor in the making of the beat boom — pirate radio. From 1961, the Dutch-owned Radio Veronica had broadcast English language pop music programmes, and by 1964 its advertising revenue stood at about £1,000,000 a year. Clearly, there was scope for a free enterprise British counterpart, which could break the monopoly of daytime BBC, compete with the evening programmes from Radio Luxembourg, and make a fat profit. This was why Radio Caroline was begun by Ronan O'Rahilly, the son of a wealthy Irish industrialist and property owner, who had recently bought an entire Irish port from British Railways. Of course, the freedom to invest £500,000 was restricted to a small group of people, as was the ability to get the backing of five City millionaires. Inevitably, Caroline's imitators tended to be owned by people like O'Rahilly. Radio Atlanta was backed by a company whose chairman was Oliver Smedley (vice president of the Liberal Party), and by the Bank of England. The former Conservative MP for Cleveland, Wilf Proudfoot, was a large shareholder in Radio 270 moored off Scarborough. And so on. What if broadcast licensing laws were broken — they were broken by the right sort of people![21]

The point was that pirate radio made money. In its first eighteen months, Radio Caroline had a gross of £750,000. Almost from the start, which was on Easter Saturday 1964, its jaunty form of petty capitalism was supported by advertising from the police, the National Coal Board, the Egg Marketing Board, Royal Ascot, and many other bastions of the establishment. The press railed, it is true, but not really because of the illegality of the station. Commercial radio posed a real threat to the life-blood of an ailing industry, advertising revenue. The major record companies were also unhappy. People didn't have to buy their musical wallpaper when it was available free on pirate radio. Besides, pirates wouldn't pay royalties. The Musicians' Union had a related beef, because pirates had no needle-time arrangements. (DJs were therefore blacklegging on former colleagues, a contributory factor, no doubt, to their being banned from MU membership). All in all, the pirates gave Conservative MPs and their friends in industry just the boost they needed to argue for commercial radio. What if the law of the land was being flouted: hadn't William the Conqueror cut his way to the English throne?[22]

The Labour government was in an invidious position. Making the pirates wholly illegal straight away would have made them unpopular with younger voters. So, when the pirates were eventually closed down, HM Government was forced to institute Radio One, a pale and emasculated version of an already deteriorating original, using former pirate personnel. By 1966, BBC had rejigged its Light Programme blurb so as to fit in more closely with the market identified by the pirates:

The Light Programme seeks to provide a friendly and companionable service for those who are in the mood for entertainment and relaxation.[23]

Eventually, the pressure to grant franchises for commercial radio stations became unstoppable. The major point — crude market criteria — had already been conceded. And when the franchises were distributed, as had happened with 'independent' television in the mid 1950s, the newspaper publishing groups quickly established a substantial shareholding by way of hedging their bets. Throughout the late 1960s and into the 1970s, Radio 1 has moved ever closer to the commercial matrix which sustains 'independent' radio. Even so late as 1969, only fifty hours of recorded music could be played on Radio One and Radio Two together in any one week.[24] By 1970, less than 2 per cent of all weekday BBC Radio 1 day-time pop music air-time was devoted to pieces which were outside the charts; and by this time, the leading charts were compiled directly for the BBC.[25]

We have charted the outlines of the cultural matrix in which the Beatles were nourished. In terms of the *material* basis for the pop phenomenon of the mid 1960s, and of the consequences of commercial trends, it is interesting to note that 1964 was the key year for the industry. The realignments which have been associated with the rise of the Beatles were, in fact, already well underway before *I Want to Hold Your Hand* broke into the US market. Take British production of record players and radiograms. Output remained fairly steady at around 600,000 a year throughout the 1960s, peaking in 1964, and then steadying out to around 750,000 after 1968, once the market was all but saturated. By 1973, about 70 per cent of British households had record playing equipment. Sales of single records in Britain had risen sharply in the middle and late 1950s, but levelled off between 1959 and 1962.[26]

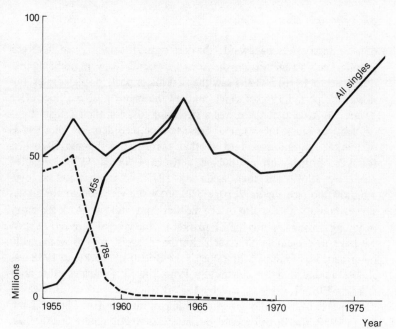

Figure 1   *Sales of singles in the United Kingdom, 1955-77*

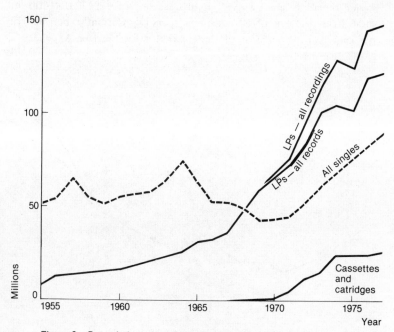

Figure 2   *Recorded music sales in the United Kingdom, 1955-77*

(The industry was backward: the last pop 78 single issued here was Brenda Lee's *Sweet Nuthins* in April 1960; and 78s went on being produced up to 1970).[27] 1957 saw the first major peak in singles sales, but it was the period 1963-5 which marked the major post-war boom (see Figure 1). After that there was a steadying off, and then a slight dip — probably as much the result of cassette tape recorders and 'pirating' as of market saturation — until another sharp rise in the mid 1970s. As for LPs, British output doubled between 1958 and 1965, doubled again by 1969, and then again by 1977, when it stood at over 120,000,000 (see Figure 2, page 81). So, while we *associate* the sixties singles boom with the rise of the Beatles, and while we mark the entry of young consumers into the LP market by the year of *Sergeant Pepper*, we have to remember that such shorthand oversimplifies what really happened. For example, the value of the British LP market in 1958 was almost double that for singles. By 1964, the LP to singles value ratio 5 :2; by 1967 it was 9 :2, and by 1977 it stood at 5 :1. And this was in the context of a steadily growing volume of business (see Figures 3 and 4). In 1953, the British record business was worth a mere £6,000,000. Within five years it *grossed* £27,000,000, or 0.25 per cent of all consumer spending and by 1977 it had reached over £272,000,000, or some 0.33 per cent of all consumer spending. Currently, between 75 per cent and 80 per cent of that market is for LPs (see Appendix 3, page 226).

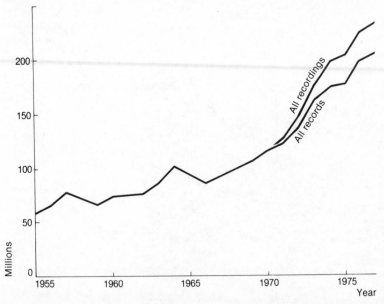

Figure 3   *Number of records and recordings in the United Kingdom, 1955-77*

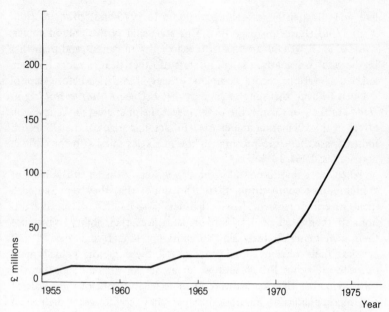

Figure 4   *Value (£) of the UK recording business at manufacturers' retail prices, 1955-75*

This information serves to remind us how small was the 1960s British singles market, and, coupled with the American dominance, how little was needed for a good British artist or group to become successful. What is culturally significant however, is the way in which the Beatles (and many of their contemporaries) were driven to the roots of rock 'n' roll, notably R & B and rockabilly, for their musical and lyrical inspiration. Of course, Liverpool youngsters were better placed than most to get access to genuine American music. Apart from the enormous American airbase at Burtonwood, the port of Liverpool was dominated by the Atlantic trade. As John Lennon was well aware,

it's where the sailors would come home with blues records from America in the ships. There is the biggest country and western following in England in Liverpool, besides London . . . .[28]

There were also the cultural resources of a nearer country, in this, the 'capital of Ireland'.

What did the Beatles make of these resources? Strangely enough, given the cultivated uncouthness of the group, the apparently hard and uncompromising Hamburg act, the irreverence in front of reporters, the hair and all, their largest-selling single up to 1975 was *I Want to Hold Your Hand* (lyrics on page 85). This song sold twelve million copies, worldwide. It was the group's fifth chart entry in Britain, and their first in the vital US charts, though masters of other Beatles songs had languished in various record company offices in America before Capitol decided to back this song in January 1964. Once *I Want to Hold Your Hand* 'broke', out came the other pieces, helping create a bandwagon effect in the US market and charts. (In fact, historians of the US record industry associate the precipitous rise in singles sales with the 'British invasion' of 1964-8.)[29]

When we come to consider the Beatles' early singles in the light of contemporary competition, there's no doubt that they represented a qualitative improvement. Their 'tightness' as a band, born out of eight-hour stints in front of live Hamburg audiences, their ability to produce their own material, their skill in imitating R & B and rock 'n' roll classics, their obvious intelligence — all these factors helped them outpace the other British groups, let alone the Frank Ifields and the Cliff Richards. The Beatles were in some measure out of the hands of the music-publishing mafiosa because they could write their own material. Yet when Brian Epstein finally got them a recording contract, and on to tours, these 'happy little rockers' accepted the uniforms, submitted to a stylised version of long hair, made sweeter music and became an even bigger commercial success. They became, in short, thoroughly *respectable*. Even *The Times* began reviewing their work, and parents learned to adapt to the new phenomenon almost as quickly as did the rag trade.

All this is a little less surprising once we take a closer look at their best-selling single. First of all, the song has nothing to do with *holding hands*. The repetition of the word, and its part in the build-up to the shrill chorus, would have been enough to convince the dimmest of pre-pubescent youth that some other activity was being hinted at. But the Beatles manage to convey the less-than-subtle hint, and to associate their lyrics and music with a beatier version of US High School songs, without directly offending the professional guardians of middle-class decency. In this lies the source of the Beatles' power. The whole record has a clean-cut sound. Even the shouts seem to have rounded aural edges. There's hardly a trace of unbridled spontaneity to encourage a listener to reinterpret the spoken shyness. 'Evil to him who evil thinks' is the keynote. As far as the lyrics and their delivery go, the object of the singers' affection *is* untouchable, virginal even, and the use of 'hand' is offered as a single-entendre.

I Want to Hold Your Hand

Oh yeh I'll tell you somethin'
I think you'll understand
When I'll say that somethin'
I wanna hold your hand
I wanna hold your ha-a-a-and
I wanna hold your hand

Oh please say to me
And let me be your man
And please say to me
You'll let me hold your hand
Now let me hold your ha-a-a-and
I wanna hold your hand

And when I touch you
I feel happy inside
It's such a feeling
That my love I can't hide
I can't hide
I can't hide

Yeh you got that somethin'
I think you'll understand
When I say that somethin'
I wanna hold your hand
I wanna hold your ha-a-a-and
I wanna hold your hand

And when I touch you
I feel happy inside
It's such a feeling
That my love I can't hide
I can't hide
I can't hide

Yeh you got that somethin'
I think you'll understand
When I say that somethin'
I wanna hold your hand

I wanna hold your ha-a-a-a-and
I wanna hold your hand
I wanna hold your ha-a-a-a-a-and

Verbally and emotionally the crassness of this song knows no bounds. Musically, as we've noted, it's High school with a dash of beat. Overall, it's thoroughly adolescent, whether by design or by default; and it makes *Twist and Shout*, or even *Love Me Do*, seem raw and spontaneous by comparison.[30] No longer is the girl invited to 'shake it'; no longer, evidently, does she oblige. Instead, we're back to that trite old musical formula of Crosby's, holding 'ha-a-a-a-ands' this time, instead of writing Christmas cards. So, when George Melly writes of this period as one in which 'revolt' was emasculated into mere 'style', we have to question whether there was any revolt in the first place, especially with the Beatles, or whether we're witnessing the transition from amateur style to commercially successful style. Certainly, there was never any revolt in their lyrics. Only — and it's a big only, mind — the music of their early singles retains any of its freshness after a decade and a half; and we're left wondering whether even that contribution would have seemed so epoch-making had not the commercial competition been so miserable as it was in the early 1960s. Nostalgia apart, I think not.[31]

6 Their music or ours?

The Beatles did not get their MBEs for charitable works. They got them for their considerable contribution to British exports. In the role of taxpayers, those pop stars who have not gone into tax exile are not insignificant. In 1972, the Business *Observer* reckoned that over fifty rock artists earned between $2,000,000 and $6,000,000. In 1975, the *Daily Mail* knew of over a hundred young men who made £100,000 and more from the British pop industry. Even in 1976, the rate of return on capital in British music companies was higher than in the majority of other firms. In the USA, by the mid 1970s, rock was 'supposed to be outselling both Hollywood and organized sport'.[1] Most writers on popular song ignore the economic structure of the leisure industry, and, while recognizing that the industry is guided by the profit motive, add disingenuously, 'why not?' *Why not* will be the purpose of this section to outline.[2]

In terms of the production and distribution of recorded music, the British leisure industry is becoming just as monopolistic as any other multinational-dominated sector of the economy. EMI cheerfully described its empire with the language of ITT, ICI or General Motors:

As the oldest and largest record organisation in the world, EMI covers every variety of music, classical and pop. Its current repertoire comprises at least 50,000 titles. It manufactures one in five of all records sold everywhere. It operates on every continent, through group companies in thirty-three overseas countries. Using hundreds of promotion men and thousands of salesmen it has the power to stimulate demand both in quantity and quality and to meet demand when sales accelerate.

Like any other multinational, EMI is fast absorbing businesses closest to its central interests, as well as others from its periphery:

[EMI owns] a seventy-one per cent shareholding in Capitol Industries Inc in America, an international network of music-publishing firms which includes the substantial KPM group and large investments in the leisure activity business. EMI has a substantial interest in Thames

Television, providers of London's weekday commercial television programmes. It owns EMI Film and Theatre Corporation, formerly the
Associated British Picture Corporation, which makes and distributes
films, manages cinemas, owns squash courts, public houses, bowling
alleys, and also the Blackpool Tower Company.

In 1979, EMI took over United Artists Records; yet within months
it had to try to sell half of its music and records business to Paramount
Pictures, part of the giant Gulf and Western conglomerate, in order to
stave off a £70,000,000 cash flow crisis because world recession had
overtaken it.[3] What are the technological (as opposed to institutional)
tentacles of this monster? EMI companies have marketed

Analogue and digital computers, data-processing equipment, machine
tool control equipment, guided weapons, radar and predictors, tele-
metric equipment, dynamic balancing machines, electronic printing
equipment, oscilloscope and electronic test equipment, stroboscopes,
hand and clothing nuclear health monitors, 'Rotobug' system of driver-
less trolleys; television transmission equipment (including cameras and
film channels, studio mixing and programme equipment), 'emitron'
camera tubes, microwave valves, instrument cathode ray tubes, photo-
electric and photo-conductive devices; internal loudspeaking telephone
systems, tape recording machines and sound control and distributing
equipment for professional purposes; radio and television broadcast
relay systems; sound amplification (public address) systems. High
quality capacitators and components . . . .
 . . . . Domestic radio and television receivers, domestic tape recorders,
gramophones, electrical reproducers, tape reproducers and accessories,
loudspeakers, motors, record-playing units. Emitape magnetic tape
(audio, video and computer). Emifilm magnetic film, Emidisc lacquer
recording discs. Ardente hearing aids, miniature and sub-miniature
electronic components, dry batteries.[4]

This selective list is worth reproducing simply to show how much
of the range of manufacture of contemporary electronic transmission is
in the hands of one company. Interestingly, one of the key factors in
the centralization process, and, indeed, in the survival of EMI as a company, was that favourite motor of the capitalist economy, war:

During the war, EMI was heavily engaged in electronics work, with
record production cut to an absolute minimum. Before the war the
company had never had a particularly successful financial history and
entered the post-war period with old and to some extent outmoded
factories.[5]

The shareholders brought in Joseph Lockwood, who promptly bought a ready-made chunk of the US record market. Clearly, a company which could pay $8,000,000 for control of Capitol Records was not exactly struggling.[6] Anyway, EMI was itself the result of a merger between the Gramophone Company (HMV) and the Columbia Graphophone Company, in 1931. The move across the Atlantic was simply the next logical step on the road to monopoly.[7]

The same kind of thing was, of course, happening in the USA. Columbia Broadcasting Systems had jointly dominated the US radio stations with NBC since the 1930s, and its progress along the EMI path has been equally noticeable. Around 1970 CBS owned

at least eleven labels in its Records Division. Fender guitars, basses and amplifiers are part of Columbia's Musical Instruments Division; Columbia also owns seven big radio stations (each with AM and FM) and has 237 affiliated stations around the country ... it is involved with multifarious operations around the world (about sixty of CBS's eighty subsidiaries are foreign), many of which are defense-related. In addition, by virtue of directors held in common, CBS can claim links with numerous multinational corporations, the Rockefeller Foundation, Atlantic Refining Corporation, the Council on Foreign Relations, the CIA and so forth.[8]

Now, before the days of ITT's involvement in 'destabilizing' the economy of Chile, which led to the bloody overthrow of a democratically elected government, this kind of industrial/military/governmental interpenetration could be offered as one of the successes of the 'free enterprise' system. After Chile, the dangers of non-accountable institutions linking up with 'defense' operations, getting involved in foreign policy, and even giving cover for CIA 'dirty tricks' experts, have become startlingly obvious.

What is the economic basis for this interpenetration, apart from the computerization and general electronic sophistication of modern weaponry? Writing in 1971, Shemel and Krasilovsky calculated that, in the USA,

The growth of the music industry in the past fifteen years has far outstripped the increase in the gross national product.[9]

In the late 1960s, the vice president of the Bank of California was confidently predicting that rock music and its associated industries would become the fourth most important sector of the San Francisco economy by the mid 1970s.[10] Far from being some sort of superstructural phenomenon, song and music and the associated electronics industries represent a significant sector of the USA's economic base:

Americans spend more money for the purchase of high fidelity equipment and concert music recordings than they do for all spectator sports combined . . . . The American public has a larger capital stake in the music industry than do all the phonograph and record companies, jukebox owners and music publishers. The public has invested in over 300 million radio sets and more than 85 million television sets. In 1970 over 80 per cent of electrically-wired American homes had record players. Over 57 million phonographs were in use at the end of the sixties and better than four out of five were stereo. Additionally, almost 12 million 8-track tape players and an equal number of cassette tape players had been purchased by the public by the end of 1970. Aggregate annual sales of musical instruments, accessories, and printed music passed the one billion dollar mark in 1970.[11]

The one billion dollar mark for US record sales was passed in 1967-8. By 1973, including pre-recorded tape sales, the cash value of that market was all but two billion dollars. We are speaking, then, of an industry which had a turnover of three billion dollars even before the 1973 oil crisis, before quadrophonics. By 1974, Simon Frith estimates that world sales of musical products was over four billion dollars.[12] By 1977, it was worth three and a half billion dollars. That sort of money represents a large slice of the disposable income of the richest nation on earth (see Appendix 2).

Surely this general process of concentration/monopolization/diversification/further monopolization is true only of one or two corporations? The CBSs and the EMIs must be the exception, rather than the rule. Regrettably, this is not the case. Paramount bought out DOT for $2,000,000 as early as 1957, and since that period the drive to takeover and to monopolization has worked through the music industry at all levels. Take, for example, what happened to Frank Sinatra's attempt to secure his financial interests. After years of exploitation by his former boss and his record company, Sinatra set up Reprise Records in 1961. In its first year, Reprise grossed $4,000,000. At the same time, Sinatra owned Essex Productions, four music publishing companies, a hotel-casino near Reno, Nevada, was co-partner with Danny Kaye in a string of radio stations in the Pacific north-west, and was vice-president and a major stockholder in the Sands Hotel, Las Vegas. Still, in multinational terms, this was relatively small fry. At this period, Sinatra's various enterprises were reckoned to gross about $20,000,000 a year.[13] By August 1963, however, the business of

Reprise was attractive enough to be bought into by Warner Brothers (who paid something between one and three million dollars for a two-thirds share). Warners already controlled a lot of US music publishing, apart from their film interests. In 1967, they bought up Atlantic Records.[14] But even bigger fish were now in the market, and in 1969 the Kinney Corporation (who already had huge investments in two other vital high-yield American institutions, car parking lots and funeral parlours) bought up Warner Brothers, lock, stock and barrel.[15]

But if this tendency is becoming more evident, surely the British Monopolies Commission or the US anti-trust laws would already have been invoked? Unfortunately, this rarely happens. Cynics point to the connections in terms of personnel as between governments, high finance and the multinationals, and ask what else we could reasonably expect from a group of people so tightly organized. Is nothing sacred? Well, take a closer look at that very silly British institution, the Royal Variety Show as it was around 1970:

The Royal Variety Show takes place in a theatre owned by Associated Television (ATV), which is run by Lew Grade — who just happens to be Bernard Delfont's brother. The proceeds from the show go to charity — presided over by Bernard Delfont. Mr Delfont is also a director of EMI, the largest record manufacturer in the world. Recently, EMI absorbed one of England's two big cinema circuits — Associated British Pictures — of which Bernard Delfont is also a director. Bernard Delfont is also deputy chairman and joint managing director of the Grade Organisation, which is owned by EMI (of which Mr Delfont is a director). Bernard Delfont thus owns himself — twice. So, if you read the *TV Times*, buy Pye, Marble Arch, Regal, Columbia, Parlophone, HMV, Pathe, Music for Pleasure, or Odeon Records; if you watch ATV or Thames Television, go to the Talk of the Town, the London Palladium, Victoria Palace, Hippodrome, Her Majesty's, Globe, Lyric, Apollo, or Prince of Wales Theatres; if you go to one of ABC's 270 cinemas or twelve bowling alleys or one of Ambassador's ten bowling alleys, then Bernard Delfont has an interest in what you're doing.

And this was the man, says a justly indignant Tony Palmer, who refused to bill any British pop group for the 1968 Royal Variety Show, because *he* felt there was 'no new good British pop'.[16] (Incidentally, in early 1979 Lord Grade's aptly named Associated Communications Corporation took over the Classic cinema chain, as part of a deal worth £12,800,000; and a decade before that ATV bought up Northern Songs, the Beatles' early publishing company.)

This is bad enough, but does the spider's web stop here?

One of the only outlets for pop on Independent Television used to be the Tony Blackburn Show. Blackburn's agent was Harold Davison. Also on Davison's books was Mike Mansfield, Blackburn's TV producer. One show starred Barry Ryan. He is now Harold Davison's step-son. And Marion Ryan — remember her? — was on the same night. She is now Harold Davison's wife. And the Harold Davison agency is owned by the Grade Organisation, of which the joint managing director is Bernard Delfont.[17]

Seedy and incestuous, you might think: but there are other curious links. Lew Grade was created a life peer by a Labour prime minister. The Queen (who is the real 'star' of the Variety Show) donates her services free, except that she too received half a million pounds and more a year even from a 'socialist' government. But what is really revealing is the way in which we find that a series of fifty-minute films on the history of pop song, called *All You Need Is Love*, were screened on London Weekend Television, financed by EMI (of which Bernard Delfont is a director), and written by that scourge of the music establishment, Mr Tony Palmer. Evidently the British music industry really is a very small business in terms of people,

numbering at its heart in successful musicians, writers, agents, publishers, managers, arrangers and publicists just a few hundred people, linked by contracts and friendship; a coterie as exclusive as any masonic lodge, operating world-wide almost as a separate kingdom . . .[18]

With this sort of coterie in control of the commercially significant sector of the music business, the only role expected of the majority audience is that of more or less passive consumer. We accept, or we reject. On, or off. Of course, in reality this is not what happens. People respond in a host of different ways to what is offered to them, adapting music to their needs, using television or radio as they think fit, rather than allow either to use them. But when sections of this majority audience do come into contact with the controllers and manipulators of the market, it is true that the latter remain pretty much in control. When 'Ready Steady Go' became the chief pop showcase on ITV, in the mid 1960s, it did so in ways which were fully in accord with the dominant values in British society. Perhaps nowhere is this better symbolized than in the note sent out to prospective members of the studio audience, each of whom

received a politely worded letter reminding him or her to dress stylishly, to dance his or her best, not to smoke, and generally to behave like a credit to British youth while on the show.[19]

The BBC's 'Top of the Pops' was heir to 'RSG' in this regard. Whereas in its early days the show would show the audience dancing quite frequently, now it is the artists who get all the air-time, plus the compère. The shots of real youngsters dancing have been replaced by elaborate sequences of dance by full-time professionals. When they do appear, the people in the audience are frequently herded into transparent cages, pushed up against the stage by bouncers, and generally organized in semi-military fashion. To make matters worse, girls are subjected to embraces from a distinctly ageing set of compères. The whole thing has become rather unpleasant, ersatz; and any attempt to turn back the clock to a relative liveness and spontaneity, as in ABC's 1978 late-night Saturday show, 'Revolver', has to face criticism from professional pundits for its apparent crudeness.

More and more, 'Top of the Pops' is becoming a 'dead' show. Singers mime to recordings made earlier in the day (so as to circumvent 'needle-time' agreements). Old video films are rehashed week after week. And, in general, the whole programme is a leading example of a withdrawal into an ever more mediated, second-hand entertainment. Perhaps the most efficient exponent of the new order is the Swedish group, ABBA. According to their proud management,

everything about ABBA projects what a pop group used not to stand for: conformity, efficiency, reliability, and a marked idea how to live in the harsh world away from love songs.[20]

That is bad enough, but what is interesting is that the 'ABBA sound' cannot be reproduced outside the studio. In concert, they try to disguise this fact by mere sound level, using 114 decibels as opposed to the legal limit in Sweden of 90.[21] For television purposes

They have supplied highly professional video films, arranged and produced by themselves, to television companies in more than twenty countries.[22]

So, what we get on 'Top of the Pops' is a television showing of a video tape using images of the singers performing to the studio-recorded version of their song. Even the studio audience is at two removes from the 'live' performance. We at home are at three removes! No wonder that ABBA's manager, Stikkan Andersson, resents the state-controlled Swedish media for their suggestion that the group could sometimes sing songs with some purchase on the problems of living in the real world. The real world is not ABBA's business: or, rather, ABBA's real world *is* business.

Of course, ABBA were the product of the Eurovision Song Contest, which has a huge audience. In 1970, 200,000,000 people across Europe failed to switch off when the show began; and in 1974, 500,000,000 failed to do so.[23] Ironically, the 'British' entry to this strange event is chosen from a list provided by the Music Publishers' Association. The singers are chosen by the BBC chiefs, and together they winnow the publishers' list. These songs are then presented to panels of viewers, also chosen by the BBC.[24] No wonder most of the songs are lousy! The Americans, of course, have gone further along this road. There, for over a decade, pre-digested, prefabricated records have been made for the singles market. Don Kirschner, who began his career working with Bobby Darin, Connie Francis, Neil Sedaka and Carole King, went on to manufacture the Monkees and the Archies, in 1966 and 1967. The Archies were not meant to appear live, but were simply a group of middle-aged session musicians and singers who were used to produce the musical background to a cartoon television series. All the same, because the Monkees' success in the singles charts had really surprised Screen Gems–Columbia, the Archies were constructed with that market firmly in mind. Of course, they couldn't go on tour to capitalize on their initial hit record – they were married, had children, and were without the youthfulness of the Monkees. Like the Monkees, the Archies couldn't perform what they liked: their contracts tied them down to doing what Kirschner ordained.[25] And though both groups were genuinely absurd, they do serve to remind us what is the logic of manufactured pop, that brink from which successive phases of real, raw music have so far managed to pull the commercial side of popular music.

Up to 1969, the British charts were a joke. *Melody Maker* began compiling the first one, in 1947, based on wholesale orders for sheet music, not on sales figures. (*Tennessee Waltz* is reputed to be the last song to sell over a million copies as sheet music, in 1950.) The *New Musical Express* produced the first chart (the top fourteen!) based on records in 1952. For almost twenty years these charts were the standard reference inside and outside the music industry for market popularity, but their laxness and built-in inadequacies were fabled. *NME* sent out questionnaires to 250 retail shops, and usually got half of them returned. They asked not for sales figures, but for something called 'the order of customer's preference'.[26] The scope for mistakes, not to mention deliberate distortion and manipulation, was enormous. If you wanted to push a record – if you were one of the full-time song-pluggers, say –

all you had to do was to discover fifty or so of the shops used by *NME*, and arrange for twenty copies of your record to be bought at each. At 1968 prices, this would have cost you around £450, and you could always recoup part of your 'investment' by selling the thousand records off cheap.[27] Such a sale would guarantee a place at the bottom end of the chart – even in 1970, 500 singles sold in any one day could get a record into the Top 50.[28] Once the record appeared in the chart, it inevitably attracted the attention of DJs and radio producers, and the owners of other retail shops. Given that the song was any good at all, you'd improved your chances of real market success no end.

Eventually, so great was the industry distrust of the accuracy of the *NME* charts that the BBC decided to sponsor its own. From 1969, the British Market Research Bureau began producing a new chart for the Corporation and *Music Week*. They choose 300 shops, and get returns from about 75 per cent each week. But two of the largest retailers, Boots and Smiths, refuse to cooperate. (Smiths have been Britain's largest record-sellers since 1963.)[29] So scrupulous are the BMRB that returns are vetted and cross-checked for signs of manipulation. By the time the charts are published the information they contain can be a fortnight out of date! In any case, these charts are subject to the same built-in distortions as the *NME* ones. The large difference in sales between a number 1 and a number 2 record draws attention away from the tiny differences between, say, number 30 and number 31, where the margin of error in the statistical sample could quite falsify the position of dozens of records. In turn, being outside the Top 20, Top 30 or Top 50 – or even the Top 100 – could mean disaster for a record, because of the way radio playlists are compiled. The charts *are* important, and they *are* incestuous, because the sheer power of the BBC playlist alone cuts across the 'scientific' pretensions of the BMRB survey: that playlist makes and breaks records.[30]

Each week, for BBC Radio One,

the four producers of the daily strip shows meet to put together a list of fifty-six records – a playlist for them all. Add one oldie of the week (to be played in every programme every day) and a record of the week for each DJ, and you get the sixty-one singles which take up about two-thirds of the fifty hours a week of day-time Radio One.[31]

How do they get the basic fifty-six?

every climber on the chart (they work with the Top Fifty) will be on the list, and every record that has dropped out of the Top Twenty won't be. Falling records in the Top Twenty are treated on their merits . . . . Gutted this way the charts yield 30-35 of the records on the play-list, and there'll also be five or six new releases a week which are chart certainties . . . . This leaves 15-20 records . . . [on which] the producers have to use other criteria of 'good programme material.' These are rarely explicit . . . .[32]

So, a record which moved from number 20 to number 21 will be out: falling records in the Top 20 stand a fair chance of being out; 'chart certainties' are, apparently, unmistakable, though the criteria are not made explicit, any more than are those for 'good programme material.' In other words, and apart from the built-in inadequacies of the BMRB chart, subjective evaluation is still the dominant method in use at the BBC. Ironically, this kind of process – and the general concept of Top Forty radio – was initially introduced in the USA to avoid bribery, notably after the 1959-60 scandals, when 225 out of 10,000 radio DJs were convicted of accepting bribes or inducements (so-called payola).

In the good old days of pirate radio, DJs played what they liked, or what they were encouraged to like. At the BBC, the old system of producers choosing their own playlist quite subjectively had to be dropped when it was found that some best-selling records were just not being chosen. This was represented by the industry as a case of the BBC not fulfilling its obligations to the public.[33] In other words, the general drive of the market was not being kotowed to. The new system does ensure that the favourite market criteria of built-in obsolescence and of bread-and-butter certainties are upheld. The record companies' investments are thereby assured by the public corporation. But compared to the policy of a station like Capital Radio, the BBC's methods are objectivity itself. At Capital, one man, Aidan Day, puts the play-list together on his own. Because Capital's power to 'break' records in London is widely acknowledged, and because 40 per cent of all singles sales take place in the capital, Mr Day's power to influence the contents of even the most scientifically based charts is second to none. Emperor Rosko, interestingly enough, advocates more of this kind of thing.[34]

There is no evidence to suggest that US charts like those in *Billboard* are more accurate though they do take radio play into account. However, the US payola scandals did establish two important facts. One was that even the biggest DJs were susceptible to bribery – Alan Freed, the self-appointed Big White Chief of rock 'n' roll , was convicted. The other was the way in which a DJ could willingly become enmeshed in the commercial side of the music industry. For example, Dick Clark was found to have significant financial interests in the music and media businesses, some of which clashed with those of his employers, ABC television.[35] But even after this kind of ritual purging, and for all the elaborate filtering mechanisms of the BMRB charts, can we feel confident that all producers and DJs are immune from the pressures of commerce?

In London there are daily invitations to lunch in the best restaurants at the expense of record companies. There are invitations to concerts, free tickets for big sporting events, free albums which in the main are sold by reviewers and others alike for fifty per cent of their face value, thus providing a lucrative additional income.[36]

In the USA, of course, this process is farther advanced. One DJ allegedly gets $10,000 of LPs from one major company alone, every year. This is all accepted, from the inside, as 'part of the record business'. DJ after DJ will insist that such perks do not (indeed, cannot) affect their judgement, because good records need no plugging, and bad ones won't make it anyway. A work like *Emperor Rosko's DJ Book* exudes such a matter-of-fact attitude, typifying the *real politik* passivity of many media performers in the face of commercialism in general. All power to the market, because the people are seen only as customers or as 'punters'. After all, goes this line of argument, if people were not inert, if they recognized that all the industry was giving them was the illusion of being a community, perhaps they might want to make a few changes![37]

By way of a postscript to this brief account of the music industry, it is amusing to examine the charts, if only to show what counts for popularity to the record companies. Of course, you could computerize, cross-refer and analyse the charts to your heart's content, and you still wouldn't know much about how songs get used in people's lives. The charts can tell us only about the commercial transaction – and they can't do that very accurately. About how many times a song is played at home, on radio or television (in Britain at any rate), used in a cinema, performed and adapted on football terraces, in the bath, in concert halls, pubs and clubs, the charts can tell us nothing. But even in their own terms what can the charts tell us?

Can we establish any correlation between the number of weeks a single record stays in the charts, and its sales performance? Sales figures are notoriously hard to come by – the industry is probably unwilling to show how few copies sold can get a record into the Top 10 – but we do have a rank order of the 100 best-selling single records for the period

1962-71. From this we discover that a record could have spent between nine and thirty-nine weeks in the charts, and stayed between two and eight weeks at number 1, to get into the best-selling list's Top Thirty (see Figure 5 below). Obviously, this depends on several factors: the size of the market, the number of record releases, the quality of the competition, and so on. We know, for example, that for every record that got into the British Top 20 in 1958, 440,000 records were sold in the market as a whole. In 1964, the ratio was 1:510,000. By 1969, it was down to 1:300,000; and in 1977 it was back up to 1:500,000. At the same dates, for every record that reached number 1, the industry shifted 4.2 million, 3.2 million, 2.6 million and 4.9 million discs overall. Then again, the total singles market in these years varied from 55 million to 73 million to 50 million to 83 million. A computer programme to take account of these variables would have to be a little more sophisticated.[39]

Other adjustments would also have to be made. *Can't Buy Me Love* sold over a million copies by the end of the first week of release. *Tears*

		Date of chart entry	No. of weeks in Top 20	No. of weeks as number 1
Beatles	She Loves You	Aug. 1963	14	4
Beatles	I Want to Hold Your Hand	Dec. 1963	13	5
Ken Dodd	Tears	Sept. 1965	21	5
Beatles	Can't Buy Me Love	March 1964	9	3
Beatles	I Feel Fine	Dec. 1964	10	5
Beatles	We Can Work it Out/Day Tripper	Dec. 1965	10	5
Engelbert Humperdinck	Release Me	Feb. 1967	15	6
Tom Jones	Green Grass of Home	Nov. 1966	15	7
Engelbert Humperdinck	The Last Waltz	Aug. 1965	21	5
Seekers	The Carnival is Over	Nov. 1965	14	3
Frank Ifield	I Remember You	July 1962	21	7
Acker Bilk	Stranger on the Shore	Nov. 1961	39	4
Cliff Richard	The Young Ones	Jan. 1962	15	5
Archies	Sugar Sugar	Oct. 1969	17	8
Ester & Abi Ofarim	Cinderella Rockafella	Feb. 1968	9	3
Searchers	Needles and Pins	Jan. 1964	9	3
Cliff Richard	Bachelor Boy/The Next Time	Dec. 1962	14	3
New Seekers	I'd Like to Teach the World to Sing	Dec. 1971	14	4
Rolf Harris	Two Little Boys	Nov. 1969	15	6
Tornadoes	Telstar	Sept. 1963	20	5
Dave Clark Five	Glad All Over	Nov. 1963	14	2
Beatles	Help	July 1965	10	3
Cilla Black	Anyone Who Had a Heart	Feb. 1964	11	3
Frank Ifield	Lovesick Blues	Oct. 1962	15	5
George Harrison	My Sweet Lord	Jan. 1971	12	4
Gerry & the Pacemakers	You'll Never Walk Alone	Oct. 1963	14	4
Beatles	Hey Jude	Sept. 1968	10	2
Beatles	Hello Goodbye	Dec. 1967	10	7
Beatles	Hard Day's Night	July 1964	11	2
Seekers	I'll Never Find Another You	Jan. 1965	11	2

Figure 5   *Best-selling British singles, 1962-71*

took five months to reach that figure; but *I Want to Hold Your Hand* had advance orders of 950,000, and so figured less well in the charts.[40] Cliff Richard got into the Top 20 more often than did the Beatles in this period (1962-71) because he issued more singles, and because the market for his records was modest but stable. Up to 1965, Richard never sold fewer than 240,000 copies of any single he made, but only 80 per cent of his records penetrated the Top 10.[41] His 1960s best-seller reached number 13 in Tony Blackburn's rank order, while the Beatles took five of the top six places, even though their career did not span the whole decade and Richard's did.[42] In terms of world sales, moreover, the Beatles are easily top with 575,000,000 units, and Cliff Richard does not appear in the Top 60 with his mere 30,000,000 units (see Appendix 4, page 227).

These and other factors lead to distortions over a longer period. Those artists already well established by 1962 will obviously tend to do better than latecomers, in chart terms. In terms of sales, however, it is interesting to note that none of the Top 30 best-sellers was released between 1968 and 1971. Of that Top 30, twenty-three were issued between 1962 and 1967, and over half between 1963 and 1965, the peak years of singles sales in the decade. Taking a twenty-year perspective, moreover, we find that only 117 singles entered the British Top 20 in 1957, while in 1974 there were 188. Similarly, there were only twelve number 1s in 1962, but twenty-four in 1965. The state of the industry and the market fostered a situation in which records tended to stay longer in the Top 20 before 1964 than after. Half the records which lasted twenty and more weeks in the charts in the period 1955-74 were issued before the end of 1956! The skewing of rankings in chart terms is therefore startling.[43]

When we look at the LP charts, the plot thickens even further. We have no adequate British sales figures, so the comparison has to be between world sales and British chart performance. Before the early 1960s, the British LP market was an adult domain. An LP cost five and six times the price of a single (not to speak of other, culturally determined, factors), and in any case the industry was not producing LPs directly for young people. This in part explains why *The Sound of Music* could stay in the British charts for all but seven years, selling over 17,000,000 copies worldwide, whereas *Sergeant Pepper* has shifted only 7,000,000 copies in eight years worldwide, and remained in the British charts for a mere forty-three weeks. Yet aggregate Beatles unit sales stood at over five times *The Sound of Music* units: and Mantovani, who sold two and a half times the number of units as *Sound of Music*, hardly appears in the various rankings of chart performance. Herb Alpert was the world's fourth most successful seller of records, and he fares little better than Mantovani in the charts; while Ferrante and Teicher, who sold over 20,000,000 records worldwide, and those mainly LPs, do not appear at all (see Appendix 4, page 227).

What can we learn from the various rankings of chart performance? Not a lot. Over half the LPs with most British chart stamina between 1962 and 1971 were of the stage/screen/television series/cabaret artist variety. Solo girl singers were markedly unsuccessful. Bob Dylan, Elvis Presley and even Cliff Richard were outstripped by the shmaltz of Rodgers and Hammerstein. Only when it comes to overall chart performance do the pop stars come into their own. The Beatles could not well do better than get all thirteen of their LPs into the number 1 position. Yet no chart can tell us how often mother plays her *South Pacific* album *now*, as compared to her daughter's use of *Led Zeppelin 2* or *Tapestry*. Only a detailed study could begin to provide such statistics, and even then we cannot quantify subjective factors such as involvement, enjoyment, or indeed pain! All we can say is that, in any family LP collection which spans the period 1962-71, we are as likely to find a Dylan LP as a copy of *The Sound of Music*, a Presley album as one by the Stones, a Sinatra LP as one by the Beach Boys.

In crude market terms, however, chart analyses seem to indicate that the same levelling-off that happened to singles sales in the mid 1960s will also happen to LP sales around 1980. After a sharp rise in LP chart entries between 1962 and 1966, from forty-nine to seventy-eight, entries remained around a hundred between 1969 and 1974. After the end of the Beatles' hegemony, in 1967-8, the average number of number 1 LPs jumped from four to fourteen a year, and has stayed at that kind of level and higher ever since. Never again will any one group or artists get three of the four number 1 LPs in one year, as the Beatles did in 1964. Other than these tentative conclusions, we have to recognize that there seems to be no significant correlation between chart performance and sales, even nationally. If we're interested in popularity — genuine popularity — we have to look elsewhere for our criteria.

Part Two
The 'alternatives'

7 Counter-culture

We found out, and it wasn't for years that we did, that all the bread we made for Decca was going into making little black boxes that go into American Air Force bombers to bomb fucking North Vietnam. They took the bread we made for them and put it into the radar section of their business. When we found that out, it blew our minds. That was it. Goddam, you find out you've helped kill God knows how many thousands of people without even knowing it.[1]

Keith Richard was very rich when he expressed these views, however sincerely held they might have been. But when we examine the Rolling Stones' record of social awareness, even outside (let alone inside) their songs, their inability to see social unpleasantness seems almost congenital. Whether it be the brutality of Seattle police,[2] or the orchestrated viciousness of Altamont, the Stones' public blindness has been all but total:

Dozens of people lay injured in the medical area, some with skull fractures, some on bad trips — there had been so many bad trips that the doctors ran out of Thorazine even though they didn't start using it until late in the day — but despite the battlefield look in the tent, it was practically dark inside: the Stones representatives refused to turn on the backstage lights so the medics could tend to the sick and injured. No lights until the Stones took the stage; to have the lights on before then would rob Jagger and his band of their entrance impact, so the injured will have to wait along with everyone else.[3]

Symptomatically, however, the Stones were quick enough to spot other people's rip-offs straight away:

Last time I was in L.A. I met the old lady that owns most of those head shops in the Strip, man. She's got a little home in Beverley Hills, she's rolling, you know. She's made a packet, man, and she gets those little hippies to work in there. And it's a front, man. It's all a fucking front.[4]

When we begin to look for alternatives to mainstream commercial music, we have to be fully aware that capitalism and the profit motive are able to absorb any challenge from people who play the game by the established rules. Nothing is sacred to promotions people. If it helps sell records or concert tickets, they'll use it, no matter what:

Columbia Records' 'revolutionaries' program . . . is being extended through April by field demand. The program's astounding success has forced the label to continue the campaign, which has been one of the most successful in Columbia's history and is even exceeding the success of Columbia's 'Rock Machine' promotion of last year.

The 'revolutionaries' campaign is an all-out merchandising program on Columbia's rock album product and has served as the launching pad for a number of outstanding contemporary artists who had debuted on Columbia in the past three months . . . .

The 'revolutionaries' campaign itself has been receiving tremendous rack-jobber response. The air-play on the product has been fabulous, and the sales have been pushing the albums up the charts . . . . There have been special 'Revolutionaries' display racks, window streamers and posters . . . .[5]

This sort of contradiction is familiar to British consumers, either in the form of a 'Marx Library' issued by Penguin Books, or in the 'Red Revolution' advertising campaign run by Watneys some years ago to promote their fizzy beer. But what is curious about much recent American writing on rock music is that this contradiction gets built into the critique of the music industry. At one and the same time, then, Eisen can subtitle *The Age of Rock* 'The Sounds of the American Cultural Revolution', and recognize that

there is no consensus in the industry other than to sell, and they will sell antiwar songs and good poetry just as easily as they will sell the schlock.[6]

Of course, this contradiction is further compounded by the appearance of that book from the Random House corporation, itself owned by RCA, who also own NBC, and other such giant subsidiaries. But we may 'solve' the problem by noting what the *Wall Street Journal* is quoted as saying in 1969, in *The Age of Rock 2*:

Record industry sales in the past several years have risen about 15% to 20% annually. Five years ago, Columbia Records, a 'complete label' offering everything from classical to pop, did about 15% of its business in rock. Today rock (using the term loosely) accounts for 60% or more of the vastly increased total.[7]

Rock music is 'product', 'business' and so on. It is so obviously the case that we tend to forget. Our favourite musicians and singers are, of course, immune to the debilitating effects of commerce. They can see through the exploitative system, even ridicule it in their work. There are, after all, some 'free' areas within the music industry. Or so we like to think. As it happens, this is not the case; and we will do well to note how little freedom from the profit motive, from monopolizing tendencies, and from cultural expropriation even the most radical-seeming institutions and individuals have won.

Take the indies in the USA, Charlie Gillett's favourite example of the ability of petty capitalism to innovate. Atlantic Records may have started as more or less the spare-time hobby of Ahmet Ertegun and Herb Abramson, but, as with Sun Records, the reality was that their company was only marginally less exploitative than its rivals:

The big companies – Decca, Columbia, RCA – hadn't been paying the black artists any royalties on sales. Black song writers were lucky if they ever got composer credits or song writing money; the publishers would usually cop that. Consequently the big companies often had trouble finding the artists when they wanted them for a recording session.

'By offering the black artists the same kind of terms that RCA would be offering to their top white artists, we were able to draw good performers.' This was Ahmet's recollection of Atlantic's early policy on contracts and royalties, but a music lawyer who represented performers in those years was skeptical. 'I wouldn't take my artists to Atlantic then. They might have honored their royalty agreements, but the rates were so low, it hardly made any difference. Other companies paid more in advance, which was what we were looking for.[8]

So, while we have to recognize that some majors were worse than others – Frank Sinatra kept only 6.66 per cent of the $11,000,000 he earned between 1941 and 1946, while Dorsey pocketed 33.3 per cent –their exploitation of black artists comes better into focus.[9] Even the Beatles got only 8 per cent of the profits from LP sales, as performers, while EMI got 40 per cent and the retailers 26 per cent. On singles, the artists earned only 2 per cent![10]

Ironically, not all 'plantation owners' were white, and not all wore sharp suits. Billie Holiday recalls that she made over 200 sides between 1933 and 1944 for R & B labels,

but I didn't get a cent of royalties on any of them. They paid me twenty-five, fifty, or a top of seventy-five bucks a side, and I was glad to get it. But the only royalties I get are on my records made after I signed with Decca.[11]

Chess Records of Chicago kept Muddy Waters with the company, without a contract, almost from its inception in the early 1940s; but they weren't prepared to pay the price ($150,000) to keep Chuck Berry from going to Mercury.[12] In 1963 they paid around $1,000,000 for the Chicago radio station WHFC; but Charles Keil was pretty sure that regular session men were 'kicking back some of their union scale wages to management in return for being called to the studio regularly.' People are evidently not a high priority, no matter how talented; and youngsters in Watts and Detroit recognize that black capitalism is no different from its white counterpart.[13]

To some extent, exploitation of artists by the indies was a consequence of the exploitation of those indies by the majors. But this was only part of the story, because there were other corner-cutting tendencies in the way the indies chose to operate. Southern musicians were cheaper than those in New York, who worked strictly to union rates, scales and terms. Hence what is described as the former's flexibility, and their preparedness to try out new ideas:

in New York it was best to have an arrangement ready before a session started, and to use musicians who could read music. After three hours, a producer would be inclined to settle for the best take he had made at that point, even if it did not represent what he had been hoping for. These conditions didn't lead to much spontaneous interplay between musicians . . . .[14]

This was the reason given by Jerry Wexler for using people from the South. But the fact is that by doing so he also saved an arranger's fee by stealing the ideas created by the 'spontaneous interplay' of the unorganized Southern musicians. Charles Keil reckoned that there was an inverse ratio between smallness and nastiness amongst the indies:

Generally the smaller the company is, the more unscrupulous, greedy, and desperate the management is likely to be.[15]

And in any case, after the 1950s, the possibility of starting a new indie became much more remote. Around 1960, it was possible to begin such a company for about $1000 because you paid no office rent, no warehouse charges, no advances to performers, and had no salaried staff.[16] But by the end of that decade, starting a new British indie was an expensive undertaking:

if you want to start something like Charisma or Track records . . . or any independent, fairly ambitious independent operation, you've got to be prepared to sink in at least £100,000 in the first twelve months.

Fifteen thousand dollars of that £100,000 was 'to establish yourself in the trade'.[17] Not many people have that kind of 'independence'.

But even before the 1960s and 1970s, the establishment of the US indies was definitely not undertaken in an altruistic spirit:

Most independent record firms started through a combination of accident, coincidence, and opportunism, often by people who owned record shops or a chain of jukeboxes, who saw that the audience wanted certain kinds of music that existing companies didn't know about or disdained dealing with.[18]

As early as 1945, Jack Gutshall had established a national distributive network for indie records. In order to compete with the majors, the indies had to reproduce the same conglomerative structures, albeit on a more modest scale.[19] We have already seen how these small companies exploited 'race' and 'hillbilly' music; and soon these fleas got their own bigger fleas, the companies set up specifically to exploit the rock 'n' roll boom, who sometimes 'earned more than most of the rhythm and blues companies earned in more than ten years'.[20]

At the same time, all the indies

shared a common attitude towards music: that it was a product whose artistic qualities were inconceivable or irrelevant.[21]

By 1961, there were over 6000 'independent' record companies in the USA.[22] What brought about a crisis in the majors, almost crippled the ambitious indie companies. The so-called British invasion of the mid 1960s left the larger companies high and dry, without the artists to adapt to the new tastes in the singles market. Such men as Calvin Carter at Vee-Jay Records already knew that the future was with the hit single, the million-seller. He and they also recognized that

Only one group buys that many records — the teenagers, the nine- to sixteen-year-old age group.[23]

So, remorselessly, the indies have been driven into the singles market, to compete with the majors;

the trend of the last few years of the sixties was for amalgamation, consolidation — or collapse. Several firms joined into conglomerates — Atlantic and Reprise with Warner Brothers, Stax with Dot and

Paramount, Liberty and Imperial with United Artists.[24]

And the direct consequence of this process is that whatever innovatory capacity there might once have been in some US indies has been snuffed out:

if a young B.B. King with talent to burn walked in here today I'd have to show him the door because there's no future in it.[25]

We could multiply examples of this general tendency, but it is probably not necessary. A handful of the grosser incidents will serve. Take your myth, and watch it explode before your eyes:

The Woodstock promoters — Joel Roseman, John Roberts, Michael Lang, and Artie Kornfield — claimed to be $1.3 million in debt at the end of the festival. Then they started trying to buy each other out, and it was reported that Albert Grossman, manager of Dylan, Janis Joplin, and The Band, among others, was offering $1 million for one-fourth of this business. Albert Grossman is the most successful money-maker in rock music; he doesn't make mistakes. Why, *Variety* asked, would Grossman offer $1 million to acquire a debt of $1.3 million.[26]

Could the film rights have had something to do with the offer? Was Grossman aware of the market potential of a full-length film on what was being talked about as the most spectacular example of the 'flower power generation'? Certainly, these same hard-pressed promoters were not at all bothered about allowing people into the festival free of charge towards the end, so clearly something had set their minds at rest.[27]

In Britain, the theme of 'love' proved equally successful in financial terms. 'Love-ins' were promoted, perhaps the most famous of which was the benefit for *IT*, the alternative paper, *International Times*. At the so-called 'Twenty-four-hour Technicolour Dream':

Seven thousand ravers at a guinea a head turned up to record their new found spontaneity for handy randy BBC cameras, yet only £1000 found its way into the *IT* coffers. With classical subterranean cool, no one ever asked what happened to the rest, but the following weeks saw a surprising number of new business ventures sprouting from the undergrowth.[28]

The counter-culture represented by such events, and by the kind of people who fed off them, had more to do with counters than with culture. But once the market had been opened up by the genuinely spontaneous elements in youth culture, the entrepreneurs moved in:

The Underground as a whole is a paying concern, with bank accounts, an efficient accountant (Michael Henshaw), and a penchant for forming companies as a protection against 'hustlers': the spivs of the Underground, who make their 'bread' from exploiting other people's ideas. The *International Times* is owned by Lovebooks Ltd (registered June 1965) whose directors are Hopkins, Miles, Henshaw, Haynes, Moore and McGrath. Art dealer John Dunbar, singer Peter Asher, and bookseller Christopher Hill are, with Miles, directors of Indica Books Ltd (registered September 1966). Hopkins and Henshaw are directors of U.F.O. Club Ltd (registered May 1967). And Miles and Henshaw are directors of E.S.P. Disk Ltd, registered last February (1967) to produce tape-recorders and tapes. Each company has a nominal capital of £100. There are ideas for a television consortium that would apply for a licence in five years' time. There is talk of at least one pirate radio station, and of an Underground Arts Council, to subsidise artists and writers ....[29]

Bernard Delfont would no doubt have felt quite at home amongst these modest imitations of his full-scale commercial ventures! What's more, those ventures which did survive, in Britain as in the USA, tended to become much more highly capitalized. Island Records may have started in 1962 with one hit song and £3000; but to survive in the 1970s it needed a turnover of £1,000,000 and its own factory (symbolically, for readers of *Private Eye*) in Neasden.

Wherever we look, the same basic structure and line of development present themselves. *Rolling Stone* started as an alternative paper, but its founder, Jann Wenner, was not only an ex-Berkeley student and the possessor of $7500, he was also close enough to Michael Lydon, the *New York Times* writer, and to Ralph Gleason, a rock journalist for a major California paper, to get them involved as co-partners.[30] This was in 1967: four years later, these young businessmen knew precisely where they were going:

By 1971 *Rolling Stone* was selling 250,000 in America and claiming 25,000 in England. The newspaper owned its own book-publishing company, Straight Arrow .... Wenner reckons that 'the average *Rolling Stone* reader is twenty-two years old. Seventy per cent of them are male. About fifty per cent are in college. They are quite wealthy. We reckon they account for half the record sales in America. They buy between four and five albums a month ....'[31]

With that kind of readership to sell to advertisers, the next step is obvious – you advertise in the *New York Times:*

If you are a corporate executive trying to understand what is happening to youth today, you cannot afford to be without *Rolling Stone*. If you are a student, a professor, a parent, this is your life because you already know that rock and roll is more than just music; it is the energy center of the new culture and youth revolution.[32]

After this, it comes as less of a surprise that it was the Diner's Club which funded *Cheetah* for a time, or that the Hearst organization helped *Eye* for a year, no doubt to help their corporate image with younger consumers, but also with a view to making a quick killing.[33] The fact is that *Rolling Stone* is being guided (or driven) by the logic of commercial orthodoxy into behaving like any other enterprise on the market place. It rehashed *Readers* under its own umbrella, and then used Warner Books to issue *Interviews* taken from its pages. Soon, no doubt, it will be driven into the arms of one or other conglomerate, just as in Britain, where IPC dominates the music-paper market (as well as other sectors of the periodical-publishing market). Bit by bit, whatever independence *Rolling Stone* might have had will be sapped, above all by lucrative advertising from record companies, until it becomes bland to the point of mindlessness.

One further example, before we discuss what can happen to even the hardest-nosed of artists. The thousands of US FM radio stations were heralded as the salvation of popular music. Consumers' freedom of choice, people were told, would force independent stations into giving them what they wanted. The Federal Communications Commission did manage to get these stations to vary their AM and FM programming; and people in New York did get to hear artists like Bob Dylan on a more regular basis.[34] But the development of the FM stations after 1967 did not signify the emergence of any radio counter-culture:

On the contrary, they are most often simply extensions of AM establishments, with all the reticence and commercialism of their parent stations . . . they are no more part of that [radical] community than the manufacturers of the clothing, pimple creams and records they tout on the air.[35]

All that the FCC can do in the public interest is to enforce anti-monopoly regulations, but even there it meets problems from the deviousness of record companies:

The Federal Communications Commission doesn't like to hear a record-company-controlled radio station devoting more than 10 per cent of its musical air time to company products; but this time can be used judiciously by the management, and it is always possible to 'buy' a certain amount of advertising time in which to plug a Chess record.[36]

If the indies can do this, what accounting tricks must there be available for a giant like CBS to bypass the minimal public control? Only a station like KMPX, the FM San Francisco broadcaster which cavalierly played album tracks, unissued tapes and test pressings, in the early stages of the West Coast boom, can make any sort of a dent in the monopolists' position. But such a protest is inevitably token, and ever liable to being bought out, sued or gobbled up.[37]

This is rather a depressing account. It had to be so, for fear of under-estimating the problems faced by consumers and artists alike. We have a situation in which people like John Lennon, Pete Townshend, Bob Dylan and 10 CC can have and control their own studios, but remain to some considerable extent at the mercy of pressers, distributors, marketers and retailers. The trajectory of the Beatles' Apple organization, well-financed though it was, graphically illustrates the size of the problem.[38] Under capitalism, it will remain the case that most artists (if not most of the audience) will have to be content to succumb to the commercial sausage-machine, and be compensated with cash. The power of the majors, the BBC and the Bernard Delfonts, will present insurmountable obstacles to all but the most determined, in the context of the music industry. Those who 'make it' will continue to be, by and large, the mindless, spineless creatures that pop stars have traditionally been. The analysis of this side of popular song will likely remain akin to pathology. But what of the genuinely innovatory aspects of popular working-class culture? What of the artists who try to take the industry on? These apparently marginal figures deserve more attention and respect than they are usually given by critics and students, let alone by the pop papers and the commercial media in general. They are, if you like, the yeast cells of a genuine counter-culture, deformed a little perhaps, but still possessing enough positive and innovatory properties to help germinate new generations of performers and audiences.

8 Which side can you be on?

Obliquely, the production of Bob Dylan tells us a good deal about the post-war music industry in America. Dylan's importance is not that of a Presley or a Little Richard — if anything, he is *more* central than they have ever been to the kernel of the problem of popular song culture. His apparent marginality belies the fact that Dylan has influenced more songwriters, singers, poets and musicians — not to mention more audiences — than almost any other living person. Dylan, in short, is an innovator. He uses the resources (or some of the resources) of American culture creatively. Only occasionally does he lapse into cultural parasitism. So, this account of Dylan's career up to the late 1960s starts from the assumption that his work *is* explicable as a phenomenon, both in its production and its reception (here, chiefly in Britain). In other words, I believe it is possible to penetrate the man's enigmatical pose, to comprehend the transformation of Robert Zimmerman into Bob Dylan.

Dylanologists (whose very existence indicate the power of the man's songs) usually seek to explain Dylan in psychological terms:

It seemed to most who knew Bob that he didn't like his father very much. Mr Zimmerman was a traditional kind of middle class American father; he believed in the American Dream: a man works hard at his business or career, becomes financially secure, sires a family, wins his neighbors' respect, and contributes something to the Gross National Product.[1]

Other strands in this photo-fit process draw crudely on Hollywood:

James Dean, the sinister adolescent, became a strong source of identity for Bob: resentful eyes, a mouth filled with scorn, face beat up, his mother dead, his father gone, friendless, a lone wolf.[2]

Now, nobody would deny that the American dream was stifling, or that Hollywood was good at providing stereotyped images of 'revolt'; but this kind of psychologizing skates over the heart of the matter, refuses to recognize the material and cultural factors which went to make Bob Dylan and his songs. In a sense, Dylan's own smoke-screen has enveloped the Michael Grays, the Anthony Scadutos and the Toby Thompsons, forcing them to emulate the deflective habits of the man they claim to describe.

If we want to speak in terms of revolt or of protest, we have to be clear what forms of oppositional consciousness were available in mid 1950s America. Take, first, the development of the socialist left in the USA. During the first world war, the American state took the opportunity to smash the chief political organization of working-class militants, the International Workers of the World. The 'Wobblies', as they were known, were literally beaten into the ground by vigilante groups like the American Legion, with the aid or tacit support of governmental agencies. In Dylan's home town, Hibbing, Minnesota, company police killed strikers and protected blacklegs from 1907 to 1916:

like company agents everywhere in those days, their assignment was to educate the miners about the glories of Eastern capitalism, and many heads were clubbed, imprinting the message.[3]

In the interests of Eastern capitalists, the whole village of Hibbing was moved, allowing the company to work the iron ore that lay under its soil.[4] During the war, the American state took the opportunity to decimate the Wobblies ranks. After the war, the IWW's political task became that much harder, not only because of the brutal treatment its members had received, but also because of the post-war economic boom. One group of members splintered to form the embryo Communist Party, while others left to take up economic cudgels in the labour movement. True, the crisis of the 1930s — and the organization of the socialists — managed to push the state in a mildly social-democratic direction, with the so-called 'New Deal'. But the second world war, and above all the post-war boom, meant that the little licence allowed to the American left up to the early 1940s could no longer be tolerated.

There has always been a singing element in the American socialist movement, since the days of the Wobblies and the songs of Joe Hill.[5] In the middle and later 1930s it was Woody Guthrie who carried on the tradition, not only in barns and union halls, but even on the radio. Guthrie accepted electronics as soon as they accepted him! WKVD in Los Angeles paid him a dollar a day for singing a few songs; and it was probably through this exposure that he came to the notice of Alan Lomax, in 1940. Lomax was employed to collect 'folksong' material for the archives of the Library of Congress, as part of the cultural spin-off of the New Deal Roosevelt programme; and he was also connected to a group of Greenwich Village (New York) radicals, many of whom wrote and sang songs. So, it was a natural enough progression for Guthrie to move to New York, and to form the Almanac Singers.[6]

Many of the singers, musicians and audiences at the Manhattan hootenanies were either in the American Communist Party, or were close to it; but the impotence of the CPUSA was such that it could be tolerated by the state in peace-time. This is why the Almanac's *Ballad of October 16th*, with its criticisms of Roosevelt, was ignored in 1941. But once America entered the war, the Almanacs were 'publicly sanctioned and discharged from the Office of War Information due in part to this song'.[7] Pete Seeger, one of the leading singers and songwriters, was banned from appearing on network radio. His brainchild, People's Songs Inc., originally intended to 'provide and perform propaganda songs for other social movements', was disbanded in 1949. It had achieved a peak membership of 2000, but once the governmental committees had attacked it, the Confederation of Industrial Organisations (CIO) withdrew support, allegedly because of a 'change in attitude in the CIO as to the type of tactics and organizers the labor movement desired to have.'[8] By this time, the largest capitalist economy in the world was booming (not least in its musical sectors), and the socialist and revolutionary left was in complete disarray:

The CIO was legitimized and institutionalized, the CPUSA and other Marxist groups had declined into political oblivion, and the IWW consisted of several small offices maintained by a handful of members, remnants of the 1910s.[9]

By 1953, one of the most popular singing groups of the late 1940s and early 1950s, Pete Seeger's Weavers, could not get a single booking.[10] With Stalinism still rife inside the CPUSA (even after the man's death in 1953), and with McCarthy rampant, American socialists and radicals of the pinkest hue had nowhere meaningful to go — except, perhaps, to Britain, or into intellectual exile in Greenwich Village. Guthrie was beginning his long decay at the hands of the little-known 'wasting' disease, Huntingdon's chorea, and the outlook for socialist singers must have been bleak indeed. For many of them, the only place to go was back, and this is what they did.

Pete Seeger and Alan Lomax went to England and took up with Ewan MacColl, a left-wing songwriter and singer. Freshened by the spiritual (if not the material) aspects of post-war Britain, Seeger returned to the USA in better heart, and fought the Weavers' case in front of congressional hearings. Of course, he was barred from network television;[11] but the radical overtones of his songs were quite adequate to rile the organizers of the Red Scare, and so appealed to many younger, liberal people in college campuses and coffee houses.[12] Guthrie's autobiography, *Bound for Glory*, was finally published, and his songs too were given a new lease of life. Then other Depression songs and singers were given a cautious airing; and, partly because the music industry wanted to junk the husk of rock 'n' roll and replace it with something even safer, other, blander, 'folky' performers and writers jumped on the bandwagon. Behind them, again, came the students and other youngsters, the ones who had always had access to guitars, to radio and to gramophones, for whom the mid and late 1950s presented a challenge and a problem that was new. By this period, the political situation was no longer so starkly polarized: 'one could be a rebel without being guilty of treason'.[13] Besides, the transformation of rock 'n' roll into high school left a musical vacuum in the culture of a generation who knew the demoralization of the war, and the obscenities of the McCarthy period only second-hand. Both musically, and in broader cultural terms — dress, lifestyle, whatever — the so-called folk revival of the late 1950s and early 1960s provided what seemed to be an authentic alternative.

Bob Zimmerman's development followed what was to become an almost archetypal path. As an adolescent he was not short of cash, and was therefore well able to indulge his musical tastes:

Bob bought most of the Hank Williams records available and had Crippa's order everything else it could get . . . Bob would spend hours listening to Gatemouth Page, a disc jockey on a Little Rock, Arkansas, radio station who played Muddy Waters and Howlin' Wolf and B.B. King and Jimmy Reed . . . .[14]

When *Rock around the Clock* was issued,

Bob's reaction to the song was almost explosive: 'Hey, that's our music!' a classmate remembers him shouting. 'That's written for us' . . . and it stunned Bob Zimmerman, Elvis Presley and Bill Haley and Buddy Holly really reached him. And especially Little Richard . . . . Little Richard became Bob's second idol.[15]

Hank Williams and Little Richard, electric hillbilly and electric city blues turned 'rock' — from the very first, electricity appealed to Bob Dylan, even to the point of his imitating Richard at a school concert, and having the headmaster pull out the plug because of the loudness of the band. But why this apparently strange mixture? Why was the music of poor country whites and poor city blacks so appealing to a white, middle-class, Midwestern adolescent? One explanation is that rock 'n' roll (and the musics from which it was derived) enabled such people to act out a symbolic revolt while at the same time they clung onto the benefits of consumer capitalism. It allowed them, psychologically (and to a limited extent, in terms of their lifestyle), to temporarily 'invert' their real material status, identifying with the less-well-off, without making any more overt political commitment. But in any case, as we've seen, genuinely oppositional forms of consciousness and of action were simply not available to most Americans. Only the negotiated forms of consciousness — of lifestyle, music — associated with Seeger and Guthrie on the one hand, and with Little Richard and Presley on the other, were possible.

In 1958-9, Bib Zimmerman had a group in Duluth, just when the very urban 'folk' music had begun to percolate out from Greenwich Village. The protest songs which had come to be accepted and taken over by northern urban singers were chiefly those of

Woody Guthrie and the Depression folk singers, Aunt Molly Jackson and her sister, Sarah Ogan Gunning, who wrote and sang about the bitter class feeling and labor violence in their region, the coalfields of Harlan County, Kentucky . . . .[16]

In Minneapolis, in 1960, Bob already sang

a few traditional songs, some country and hillbilly, a couple of Pete Seeger songs, and a lot of material then in vogue because of the popularity of slick, commercial folk interpreters such as Harry Belafonte and the Kingston Trio. He sounded like just another one of the thousands of college kids hooked on the folk revival that started in the mid-fifties.[17]

Then he came into contact with the real thing, Woody Guthrie:

Bound for Glory knocked Dylan out, and he was quickly caught up in the whole romantic hobo life that Guthrie had lived and written about. Dylan had been playing the role of Okie, telling some friends that he'd been born in Oklahoma, and others that he had lived there during his many runaway adventures. Guthrie was a ready-made identity for a young man in search of a strong image.[16]

After this, it was all but inevitable that Zimmerman should take on the role of a contemporary poet and become 'Dylan', that he should move to Greenwich Village. There, he quickly graduated to the Gleason household in New Jersey, where Pete and Toshi Seeger, Peter La Farge, Cisco

Houston, Jack Elliott (and, formerly, Guthrie himself) gathered to sing and to listen.[19] This group had its connections with MacColl and Bert Lloyd (a journalist who was then becoming a world expert on British folk song);[20] and it was in this milieu that Dylan was forged. Here, in East Orange and in Greenwich Village, the musical and political limitations that fettered Dylan's early songwriting were transmitted and learned:

Here was Guthrie, who from my youth was a very political figure, and Bob was singing from the *Little Red Song Book*, doing things from the Wobblies song book. He just seemed like a youngster who didn't have much that he felt sure of.[21]

The key point to remember is that you didn't have to be all that progressive to get branded as a 'radical' in mid 1950s America. The 'old left', the CPUSA and the Wobblies, were incapable of any meaningful intervention in trade unionism or conventional politics. The so-called New Left chose a *politically* softer option, and put its weight behind the civil rights movement, especially after 1954 and the de-segregation ruling. (This is not to say that the strategy involved personal cowardice – quite the reverse!) Campaign politics of this kind served two useful functions for the likes of the Greenwich Village intellectuals: it enabled them to feel that they could, after all, make some sort of dent in American capitalism, while on the other hand it 'freed' them from the responsibility of building up any rank-and-file socialist movement. Before and after Khruschev's speech denouncing the 'excesses' of the Stalin era, that organizational alternative was simply not open to any thinking socialist; but the corollary was that Left activity retreated further away from industrial into 'cultural politics'.[22] The logical step, for a youngster like Dylan, was to abandon the shell of symbolic disaffection that was commercial rock 'n' roll, and to move to the apparently meatier 'protest' music.[23] (In this sense, the move in the opposite direction, later into the 1960s, represents not so much a regression or a sell-out as a frantic attempt to draw once again on the vitality of rock 'n' roll.)

The Greenwich Village Left provided Dylan with just the right mixture of verbal workerism, radical chic and political impotence. It is unfair to blame Dylan for the failure: after all, he suffered too. The failure was there waiting for him:

They were tired, impotent and unsure of where they were going, or why they were going there . . . . The Left came to talk of the Negro, rather than the Negroes, of the Worker rather than workers, of the

Thirties rather than the fifties, and of the People rather than people.
. . . . Dylan had found his proper milieu. The corduroy cap, the dunga-
rees . . . .[24]

Later, many of those same lefties began to patronize Dylan, projecting
their own frustrations and impotence onto him, trying to make him
take the blame for their own failures:

'The only way to describe the feelings of people like Dave Morton and
Hugh Brown and the other Dylan friends is sort of Marxist-anarchists,
sort of predecessors of the New Left. Maybe a fusion of all these things,
along with a strong feeling of just *hating* the bastards. A feeling the
system doesn't work so throw it out, or maybe a little feeling that it
wasn't worth fighting it and you might just drop out.'

But it was the music most of all, for Dylan. Everything else was
tangential. 'He never read anything.' . . . . 'He never had any part in the
radical ideas . . . . He had contact with all the people, but he didn't
know about it at all.'[25]

There was *nowhere to go:* the 'radical ideas' were just *ideas*; there was
no 'it' to get involved with, at a practical level, outside the music, and
outside the protest movements association with anti-racialism and the
campaign against nuclear weapons. Dylan began attacking both problems
in his songs, all the while fighting shy of organizational commitments,
distrustful of the generalizations of the intellectual left, most of which
were in any case based on an impotence to cope with American capitalism
in full swing. All that could be meaningfully criticized, Dylan criticized.
He simply put his head down and got stuck into what was *obviously*
wrong.

After having rejected his father's store, and college life, Dylan began
making the rounds of the Village hootenanies, behind Van Ronk,
Len Chandler, Judy Collins, Tom Paxton, Cisco Houston, Jack Elliott,
Paul Clayton and Arlo Guthrie. He played professionally when he could
(as they did); and slowly there came to be a New York network, to be
followed by fairly regular tours of college campuses.[26] Above all, the
opening of Gerde's Folk City gave the singers a permanent rendezvous,
and Seeger's *Broadside* magazine (founded in 1961, and inspired by the
British folk club movement) gave the songwriters a means of publishing
their work. Dylan's song, *Blowin' in the Wind*, appeared in the sixth
issue, in April 1962; Joan Baez gave him a guest spot on her college
tours; and then Peter, Paul and Mary decided to record his song. In the
first two weeks it sold well over 300,000 copies, and became the
fastest-selling single in Warner Brothers' history. Even black R & B

radio stations in the South decided to give it air-play.[27] Played now, the song seems vacuous to the point of embarrassment: but in early 1960s America it really was a breath of fresh air. Ironically, Dylan's song made folk respectable. After all, it wasn't as gutsy as rock 'n' roll, and there *was* a distinct possibility of nuclear war. One by one, the radicals came in from the cold, many of them at the behest of John Hammond at Columbia. He, of course, had acquired a certain radical chic by working with Billie Holiday; but his motives, then as now, were almost completely commercial:

I was distressed at the fact that we weren't into too many kids . . . . The first thing I did was sign Pete Seeger, he was still under indictment for contempt of Congress, still being blacklisted by CBS our parent, but I felt he would give Columbia a better image with the kids. And we were willing to take a chance on a controversial artist because he was obviously a great artist. I was just waiting for somebody with a message for kids when I met Bob . . . .[28]

Dylan's first album cost Columbia $402, and took three or four sessions to record. By March 1963, it had sold 5000 copies, mostly (probably) to members of the newly founded SDS, Students for a Democratic Society. *Blowin' in the Wind* didn't enter the US charts until July of that year; so there was a short period during which Dylan could so easily have gone the whole socialist hog. After all, he had been catching up on his reading, consuming poetry from Rimbaud, Villon and Villiers, as well as work by Graves, Yevtushenko and Brecht, at the instigation of Suze Rotolo, his steady girl-friend; and there was SDS to turn to, itself

born in response to the failures of the old left, the liberals, the unions, and the other one-time radical groups at exactly the moment that Dylan's songs were becoming known.

This was in 1962; by the time of the Town Hall concert a year later, the SDS was in the vanguard of what had come to be known as the 'Movement'.[29]

Allegedly, Dylan's failure to make the commitment was partly the result of a talk with the motherly Mrs Smith;[30] but there were other pressures to conform. Perhaps CBS provided the final damper to Dylan's radicalism in 1963, when they refused to allow him to sing *Talkin' John Birch Society Blues* on their networked 'Ed Sullivan Show':

'We fought for the song. We pointed out that President Kennedy and his family are constantly kidded by TV comedians . . . . But the John

Birch Society — I said, I couldn't understand why they were being given such protection. But the network turned us down . . . .'

CBS's lawyers and officials discovered the song was scheduled to be included in Dylan's second album, and they ordered it taken off . . . .

During the height of the controversy over the record he had been running round the Village telling everyone 'They'll kill that song over my dead body. That song's going in the album.' But it was ripped out . . . .[31]

Again, it is meaningless to blame Dylan for truckling. Either he accepted censorship, and so got criticized for selling out to showbiz and to capitalism, or he lost access to the channel which guaranteed him an audience amongst those young people he wanted to reach, and resigned himself to almost total cultural impotence for the rest of his life. He faced the same decision as Johnny Otis, or as the hillbillies. So, the head went down.

Even after this brief attempt to situate Bob Dylan, we are better prepared to understand the development of his songwriting as it was experienced by most people, via the mediations of the gramophone record, the music press and the occasional live concert. The account which follows is necessarily subjective. What I want to show is something of how the work of an artist like Dylan was experienced — how it was discovered, what it meant (and came to mean), how it was used, what it contributed, where it failed and where it succeeded. What follows is meant as a contribution towards what Paul Willis wants to see done in the analysis of youth culture — in this case, 1960s provincial British youth culture — and not as an exercise in self-indulgence.[32] In trying to be specific, concrete and so on I have deliberately fought shy of producing a full-blown spiritual autobiography, as Cohn did in *Awopbopaloobopalopbamboom* or as Melly did in *Owning Up*. Not that there isn't a place for such enterprises — of course, there is — but they belong elsewhere.

In 1964, I was 17 — not old enough to go to pubs legally, or to go to any club which had a bar. Consequently, I was reduced to the BBC, to the early pirates, the local fairground (where the Waltzers played pop singles), and to the slender resources of my family's newly acquired record player and record collection. Because we weren't notably affluent, and I was still at school, I was dependent on my parents and elder brother for new records. Though some friends could afford the occasional single, I couldn't and this meant that I had the choice of my brother's Lonnie Donnegan and trad jazz collection, or of my father's 'Gunfighter Ballads' LPs. Music, in any case, was little more than an adjunct to my life, and politics hardly impinged so as to make me notice: I was barely moving towards Peter, Paul and Mary, and away from Donnegan's Glasgow–Appalachian whine, or from Frankie Laine's unregenerate male chauvinism. Then an accident happened. My father went to the nearest large town, Middlesbrough, and asked for 'something like Marty Robbins'. He was given Bob Dylan's *Freewheelin'* LP (*Bob Dylan* was not released in Britain until July 1964), and cheerfully brought it home without listening to it. When we did listen, we all thought it was just a joke played on us by the record shop assistant; though there *was* something about the raw earnestness of *Hard Rain* which struck some sort of chord. Soon after, I was given the LP, and promptly exchanged it for another with a friend. Amongst our group of adolescents, the record came to exercise a significant degree of influence. Doubtless, in part, there was the customary ego-tripping of those who felt that they'd latched onto something important well before anyone else in their respective classes at school. But there's no denying that the sheer power of the lyrics — Dylan's marvellous ability to juggle with words to form striking images and phrases — finally converted at least three of us, made us admirers ('fans' being too ignoble a status). In spite of the rudimentary musical frameworks, and in spite (perhaps, in part, because) of the raucous delivery, each new Dylan LP was eagerly awaited. Dylan had created in us expectations that only he was capable of fulfilling, and it was only much later that we came to rationalize how and why this happened.

What used to be termed 'lyrics' were, in Dylan's hands, transformed into statements. Sometimes he would be explicit, and at other times he would simply give a verbal framework — a run of images, say — into which any listener could try to fit his or her own experience. At the very least, Dylan

demolished the narrow line and lean stanzas that once dominated pop, replacing them with a more flexible organic structure. His rambling ballads killed the three-minute song and helped establish the album as a basic tool for communication in rock.[33]

But that wasn't all. As far as was possible, he drew on all the resources of British and North American music which seemed to him to speak out and to speak straight. True, those resources were mediated by MacColl and Lloyd, Lomax and Seeger: but even so what Dylan heard at the Gleason's house in East Orange represented far and away the best and widest range of 'traditional' and contemporary 'folk'-style music. Like Guthrie, however, Dylan was no doctrinaire folkie: as early as *Freewheelin'* he tried to get four electrically backed songs on to an album.[34] He failed, ironically, because the CBS marketing machine had him firmly in its 'folk' bag. But Dylan's biggest achievement is the fact that he made songs which could not be *consumed*. All the while, he shocked the listener into paying attention – by understatement, straight-faced humour, elliptical phraseology, crude delivery, and so on – and systematically refused to accept the responsibilities which insecure people have habitually foisted on to their favourite artists. You had, literally, to make over the significance of his songs in terms of your own experience. This in itself was an unaccustomed experience, a challenge. For Dylan is not his own man in his best songs: you have to *produce* these songs (and through them, your conception of the singer, if you want) *for yourself*.

Of course, not all of Dylan's early songs demanded this sort of attention. *Blowin' in the Wind* and *The Times They Are A Changin'* are simply didactic: they don't offer any solutions to the problems they raise, though they sound as if they're going to. Strictly, these songs are open to the point of looseness – a looseness which was sometimes later transformed, as in *Nashville Skyline*, to the merest of phrase-mongering.[35] Indeed, from the very first there is a tendency to lapse into shallowness or negativity when *action* is called for. It is as though Dylan can do no more than point fingers (*Masters of War*), lament (*Hard Rain*) or 'describe' (*Oxford Town*). Impassivity can sometimes feel like passivity: an unwillingness to advocate forms of action can communicate itself as a straightforward shying away from any kind of public commitment. All too often we find Dylan retreating into the private 'solution' in the face of the corporate state, which is no solution at all. But then, he recognized the political dilemma.

All these labor people, rich suburban cats telling their kids not to buy Bob Dylan records. All they want is songs from the Thirties, union hall songs, 'Which Side are you on?' That's such a waste. I mean, which side can you *be* on?[36]

So, simply to point up the contradiction in the American Dream is itself helpful and necessary, just as demystifying the notion of *With God on Our Side* is progressive. Fat cats eating large dinners and giving a Tom Paine Award to a young songwriter – this was no real alternative, and helps explain Dylan's withdrawal: 'Me, I don't want to write *for* people any more. You know, be a spokesman.'[37] So, from making public statements about public matters, Dylan began to write public statements about the most sensitive private matters, which, of course, were in part determined by those same public matters:

From now on I want to write from inside me . . . . They want me to handle their lives . . . . I got enough handling my own life.[38]

And we can trace this transformation in the songs.

First, the public statement about public matters. *Only a Pawn in Their Game* (lyrics on page 124) draws blood. Its chopped diction, the quietly sneering voice, the muscular compactness of the language, all give a cutting edge which would have been less keen in a more overtly sarcastic song:

A bullet from the back of a bush took Medgar Evers' blood
A finger fired the trigger to his name
A handle hid out in the dark
He hand-set the spark
Two eyes took the aim
Behind a man's brain
But he can't be blamed
He's only a pawn in their game

The musical economy — even the slight uncouthness of the guitar chords — plus the hint of a feigned Southern drawl, make the colloquial analysis and verdict all the more barbed. There is no retreat into sentimentality: the man is dead, shot by a person totally in the control of others, abjectly dependent to the point of surrendering identity. That separation of *finger* from *hand* from *brain* helps reinforce the idea of the killer's automaton-like behaviour, as does the idea that 'blame' is somehow not relevant in such a case, at least for the 'pawn'.

Then again, there's no need to name the 'South politician', because his identity is barely more differentiable than that of the 'pawn'. So dramatic is the language and performance of the song that you can almost *see* Dylan taking off the speaker, throwing his head back to preach to the poor, tub-thumping, venting vague threats, articulating irrational fears, and *explaining* not one thing. What Dylan shows in action is not one politician and one poor white so much as class politics in action. Only obliquely, or by implication, are we told of the divide and conquer politics adopted by careerist politicians, whose very existence (like that of their financial backers) depends on setting white against black, one poor section of the community against another. With such a system, blame for Evers's murderer is almost academic, as problematic as his own identity. The song links and explores these two points remorselessly.

Only a Pawn in Their Game

A bullet from the back of a bush took Medgar Evers' blood
A finger fired the trigger to his name
A handle hid out in the dark
He hand-set the spark
Two eyes took the aim
Behind a man's brain
But he can't be blamed
He's only a pawn in their game

A south politician preaches to the poor, white man
You got more than the blacks, don't complain
You're better than them, you been born with white skin, they explain
And the negro's named
Is used it is plain
For the politician's gain
As he rises to fame
And the poor white remains
On the caboose of the train
But it ain't him to blame
He's only a pawn in their game

The deputy sherriffs, the soldiers, the governors get paid
And the Marshals and cops get the same
But the poor white man's used in the hands of them all like a tool
He's taught in his school
From the start by the rule
That the laws are with him
To protect his white skin
To keep up his hate
So he never thinks straight
'Bout the shape that he's in
But it ain't him to blame
He's only a pawn in their game

From the poverty shacks he looks from the cracks to the tracks
And the hoof beats pound in his brain
And he's taught how to walk in a pack
Shoot in the back
With his fist in a clinch

To hang and to lynch
To hide 'neath the hood
To kill with no pain
Like a dog on a chain
He ain't got no name
But it ain't him to blame
He's only a pawn in their game

Today Medgar Evers was buried from the bullet he caught
They're lowerin' him down as a king
But when the shadowy sun sets on the one
That fired the gun
He'll see by his grave
On the stone that remains
Carved next to his name
His epitaph plain
Only a pawn in their game

Verse three repeats the pattern of verse two. First the dead-pan recounting voice, the homely colloquialism, the light touch upon the fact that the agents of the state, after all, *do* 'get paid' – by whom, to work in whose interest, are questions left hanging. Then the head goes back again, and we have Dylan coming out with more obvious irony, especially about the poor white's belief that it's 'his school' when in effect he has no control over it. This, of course, is the point. The impotence fostered by this social system leads to (and is part of) the lack of selfhood. In a real sense, the murderer is the victim well before he kills Medgar Evers, and his punishment is already given out – his namelessness, symbolized by the anonymity of the Ku Klux Klan hood, and by the ideological chains around his neck. On the other hand, Medgar Evers has a name, an identity, and fully deserves his kingly burial. He has control over his own life and consciousness, within the limits set by the State, its agents, and, of course, its 'pawns'. Not for him the nameless epitaph, the testament to his own political impotence. Even in death Medgar Evers has more dignity and more power than the perpetrator of pitiful, literally mindless violence.

Certainly, I wouldn't want to claim that Dylan's developing

When the Ship Comes In

Oh the time will come up
When the winds will stop
And the breeze will cease to be breathin'
Like the stillness in the wind
'Fore the hurricane begins
The hour when the ship comes in.

Oh the seas will split
And the ship will hit
And the shore line sands will be shaking
Then the tide will sound
And the waves will pound
And the morning will be breaking.

Oh the fishes will laugh
As they swim out of the path
And the seagulls they'll be smiling
And the rocks on the sand
Will proudly stand
The hour that the ship comes in.

And the words they use
For to get the ship confused
Will not be understood as they're spoken
For the chains of the sea
Will have busted in the night
And will be buried at the bottom of the ocean.

A song will lift
As the mainsail shifts
And the boat drifts on to the shore line
And the sun will respect
Every face on the deck
The hour when the ship comes in.

And the sands will roll
Out a carpet of gold
For your weary toes to be a touchin'
And the ship's wise men

Will remind you once again
That the whole wide world is watchin'.

Oh the foes will rise
With the sleep still in their eyes
And they'll jerk from their beds and think they're dreamin'
But they'll pinch themselves and squeal
And know that it's for real
The hour when the ship comes in.

Then they'll raise their hands
Sayin' we'll meet all your demands
But we'll shout from the bow your days are numbered
And like Pharaoh's tribe
They'll be drownded in the tide
And like Goliaths they'll be conquered.

repertoire increased regularly in quality. Compared to *Only a Pawn*, even so impressive sounding a piece as *When the Ship Comes In* (lyrics on page 126) comes over as mere flatulence. A flat, trying-to-be-defiant voice is audibly contradicted by what to Gray seems 'a quite unexceptionable moral cleanliness' (he was intending to praise), itself achieved by Dylan's intentional alienation from morality.[39] T.S. Eliot-fashion, he jumbles vaguely ironic phrases, thrusting all the responsibility on to the listener, and making the song *sound* much more impressive than its lyrics. Such a hurling together of interesting-sounding words, and an apparently happy ending was the looser, lighter side of Dylan that has appealed to his 'new' audience, that for *Nashville Skyline, New Morning* and *Planet Waves*. This is what sparked off people like Donovan, who parodied when they tried to imitate. With them, as with the Dylan of this song, we are not invited to consider the real world at all. The Ship is not the ship of state, it's the one from *Peter Pan*. What appears as 'moral cleanliness' is simply amorality dressed up in well-sounding phrases.[40]

The very weakest of Dylan's songs represented (and represents) a solider punch at the paunch of the dominant ideology than most of the commercially oriented competition. Thus, while the American might

She Loves You

She loves you yeah yeah yeah
She loves you yeah yeah yeah
She loves you yeah yeah yeah yeah

You think you've lost your love
Well I saw her yester da-i-ay
It's you she's thinkin' of
And she told me what to sa-i-ay
She said she loves you
And you know that can't be bad
Yes she loves you
And you know you should be glad

She said you hurt her so
She almost lost her mi-i-ind
But now she said she knows
You're not the hurtin' ki-i-ind
She said she loves you
And you know that can't be bad
Yes she loves you
And you know you should be glad
                              Ooooh

She loves you yeah yeah yeah
She loves you yeah yeah yeah
With a love like that
You know you should be glad

You know it's up to you
I think it's only fa-i-air
Pride can hurt you too
Apologise to he-e-er
Because she loves you
And you know that can't be bad
She loves you
And you know you should be glad
                              Ooooh

She loves you yeah yeah yeah
She loves you yeah yeah yeah
With a love like that
You know you should be gla-a-ad
With a love like that
You know you should be gla-a-ad
With a love like that
You know you sho-o-uld be gla-a-ad

Yeah Yeah Yeah
Yeah Yeah Yeah Yeah

Words and music by Lennon/McCartney. ©1963 Northern Songs Limited for the world. Reproduced by kind permission of ATV Music Limited.

be impressed at the market penetration of Beatles singles during early 1964, his only clear response to their music was *It Ain't Me Babe* (lyrics on page 130), an obvious enough parody of *She Loves You* (lyrics on page 128). A brief comparison will bring out the main differences. The Beatles' song drips with adolescent sentiment. It is structured around the persona of a go-between, and cheerfully reinforces the preferred mode of courtship in a capitalist society, using guilt-invoking mindlessness ('you know you should be glad', 'you know that can't be bad'), and generally relying on emotional blackmail at the shallowest of levels. To their inane 'Yeh, yeh, yeh' Dylan counterposed a full-throated 'No, no, no'. Instead of their emotional tinkering and patching up, Dylan insists on breaking the conventions of bourgeois courtship, refusing to accept anything less than full-hearted love. Instead of their fairy-godmother structure, Dylan offered a one-to-one confrontation, between equals. Instead of their magic 'solution', he reminded us that it's sometimes better to call it a day. While they denied individuality, he celebrated it — even in those forms with which he could not agree. While they underwrote the surface chatter of socially acceptable but emotionally stifling forms of interpersonal behaviour, Dylan raises a wry pair of fingers at the conventions, *not* at the woman. In fact, there's a sad slowness in the farewell that hints of another, less abrasive stage of the relationship. In the first recorded version, there's a hint at a possible reconciliation, even, but on *his* terms, and at a high level of maturity, for both their sakes.

It's not too much to say that *It Ain't Me Babe* is a conscious explosion

It Ain't Me Babe

Go away from my window
An' leave at your own chosen speed
I'm not the one you want babe
I'm not the one you need
You say you're lookin' for someone
Who's never weak but always strong
To protect you and defend you
Whether you are right or wrong
Someone to open each and every door
But it ain't me babe
No no no it ain't me babe
It ain't me you're lookin' for babe

Go lightly from the ledge babe
Go lightly on the ground
I'm not the one you want babe
I will only let you down
You say you're lookin' for someone
Who'll promise never to part
Someone to close his eyes for you
Someone to close his heart
Someone who will die for you and more
But it ain't me babe
No no no it ain't me babe
It ain't me you're lookin' for babe

Go melt back in the night
Everything inside is made of stone
There's nothing in here moving
An' anyway I'm not alone
You say you're lookin' for someone
Who'll pick you up each time you fall
To gather flowers constantly
And to come each time you call
A lover for your life and nothing more
But it ain't me babe
No no no it ain't me babe
It ain't me you're lookin' for babe

of stereotypes and stereotyping, a critique of bourgeois sensibility as it is usually offered to a working-class audience. That 'I will only let you down' is hardly ironic: in those situations, with such a set of expectations on the woman's part, Dylan *will* let her down. Accepting the situation and the expectations, on the other hand, will mean letting himself (he believes both of them) down, so why not reject the whole lot out of hand? In such ways are Dylan's songs – even his 'private' songs – genuinely cathartic. They open up the conventions of 'respectable' life to the light of rationality and plain feeling. Only when his honesty and his determination to do what he knows to be best are rejected does the knife go in. Let those who still cling to the small-change of conventional relationships 'melt back into the night', finally lose their identity, their individuality. Only then does Dylan turn sour, verbally kicking his former partner when she's down – 'An' anyway I'm not alone'. That's it, signals the final harmonica break, with its three clear blasts acting as musical evocations of the emotional full stops. The person is left in no doubt that she has failed herself, even more than him. This is the clue to Dylan's apparently glib response to the question

'In a lot of your songs you are hard on people . . . . Do you do this because you want to change their lives, or do you want to point out to them the error of their ways?'

Dylan replied: 'I want to needle them'.[41] Apart from the fact that he has long been the victim of pretentious-sounding questions (and of self-congratulatory or plain vapid explications), the kernel of this statement shows that Dylan early rejected the role of public executioner. In fact, he was one of the very first to bring the put-down of media men and hangers-on to the level of an art-form. The film, *Don't Look Back*, shows the needle being used to prick the bubble of unjustified self-esteem, self-assertion or even self-deprecation. It is as though, with the rejection of any overt political commitment, Dylan had to reject all the other usual songwriters' and singers' public roles one by one.

So, while the Beatles jigged further down the road to Pepperland, and made friends with the middle-class audience, Dylan cut himself down to writing about what he was sure of, his personal relationships. He took the opportunity to signal the break by electrifying the music he used, and by having a backing group. Of course, some dyed-in-the-wool folkies saw *this* as a sell-out. They need not detain us long; after all, country and blues artists had used amplification since the 1940s, Seeger and Guthrie sang on the radio and made records, and both had been part of a group. Dylan wasn't doing anything new in those ways.

Besides, most of the artists in the Newport Folk Festival audience would have gladly taken his place in the limelight. In a way, Dylan's folk influences were more authentic than those purists', being those of poor whites and poor blacks, hustling to get out of ghettos — the music of Williams and Presley, Little Richard and Chuck Berry.

Ironically, by breaking out of CBS's folk bag, Dylan was doing the opposite of selling out; and by disowning the 'prophet' status lumped on to him by those unable to handle their own lives (from which he got, understandably, a little paranoid), he also got back to his roots. Besides, for everyone who yelled 'Judas' at him, like the young man at the second Newcastle concert, two or more others made contact with Dylan all the more easily because of the new musical style. The pungency of the lyrics was if anything, heightened by the change. The fact was that Dylan's new audience was maturer than his old one had sometimes been, especially in Britain, where life-handling problems were reaching epidemic proportions amongst older school students and younger college students. Like Dylan, they too had to learn to cope with leaving home, going to the city, and confronting the rawer aspects of social life. For such people — and they were by no means all under-graduates, though they tended to be grammar school students — *Bringing it All Back Home* helped provide some sort of cultural framework in and through which they could come to terms with the break between school and work or college. The album was released in Britain in spring 1965. It was to become Dylan's first million-dollar seller,[42] and *Subterranean Homesick Blues* was its keynote.

It is best to be honest: it wasn't the lyrics of this song (see page 133) which gave me heart so much as their *tone*. Only later did I get round to thinking about what is said. The song is set firmly in American city streets. Its language, appropriately, is that of the many who live there, on the margins of economic (or emotional, or intellectual) security. It is written in the argot of the oppressed, the hip, the dis-possessed; and it speaks of the experience at the receiving end of the American Dream. What we have to remember is that that Dream pervaded Western European commercial youth culture too, during the 1950s and early 1960s. Though the experience of it was mediated by British culture, its values and assumptions had certainly penetrated daily life to a remarkable degree — enough to make *Subterranean Homesick Blues* intelligible:

Ah get born, keep warm
Short pants, romance, learn to dance
Get dressed, get blessed

Try to be a success
Please her, please him, buy gifts
Don't steal, don't lift
Twenty years of schoolin'
And they put you on the day shift . . . .

Phrases are deliberately hard to hear. The appraisal is sardonic, because, from this close to the gutter, starry-eyedness is positively dangerous:

Look out kid they keep it all hid
Better jump down a manhole
Light yourself a candle —

unless you want to fall victim to the cloying charms of American rectitude:

Don't wear sandals
Try to avoid the scandals
Don't wanna be a bum
You better chew gum
The pump don't work
'Cause the vandals took the handles.

Simply to play 'that noise' in a middle-class, or an aspiring working-class, living-room was itself a minor act of subversion, a symbolic defiance, because the voice that Dylan parodies is precisely that of a person imbued with the ideology of the Dream. The parents, in other words, are part of the problem, part of the situation which makes the home-leaver both homesick and determined to stay away. And of course, American youngsters had no monopoly on the physical (or the merely psychological) bolt to the street, the city, the road.

Throughout the song, the agencies of control and exploitation are intermixed. Their 'voices' — not just in the economic sphere, but the political, cultural and emotional ones too — are experienced as Them, collectively, as in life. To Us, then, Dylan offers street-brother advice, almost ventriloquized through smilelessly bared teeth: Get Out of Their Way. Gradually, he builds up a composite aural picture of the street, focusing on the conflicting pressures which puzzle or trouble the newcomer, the one who's homesick and yet without any umbilical connection to the gross national product (except in the form of relief, the dole or a student grant) to keep him or her on the dominant culture's straight and narrow. The picture rings true, not least because we know Dylan did live such a marginal life, especially after leaving home for college, and then leaving college for New York. But, true to form, the appropriate

Subterranean Homesick Blues

Johnny's in the basement
Mixing up the medicine
I'm on the pavement
Thinkin' 'bout the government
A man in a trenchcoat
Badge out, laid off
Says he's got a bad cough
Wants to get it paid off
Look out kid
It's somethin' you did
God knows when
But you're doin' it again
You better duck down the alley way
Lookin' for a new friend
A man in the coonskin cap
By the big pen
Wants eleven dollar bills
You only got ten.

Maggie comes fleet foot
Face full of black soot
Talkin' at the heat put
Plants in the bed but
The phone's tapped anyway
Maggie says that many say
They must bust in early May
Orders from the DA
Look out kid
Don't matter what you did
Walk on your tip toes
Don't try 'No Doz'
Better stay away from those
That carry around a fire hose
Keep a clean nose
Watch the plain clothes
You don't need a weather man
To know which way the wind blows

Oh, get sick, get well
Hang around the ink well
Hang bail, hard to tell
If anything is goin' to sell
Try hard, get barred
Get back, write braille
Get jailed, jump bail
Join the army, if you fail
Look out kid, you're gonna get hit
But losers, cheaters
Six time users
Hangin' around the theatres
Girl by the whirl pool
Is lookin' for a new fool
Don't follow leaders
Watch the parkin' meters

Ah, get born, keep warm
Short pants, romance, learn to dance
Get dressed, get blessed
Try to be a success
Please her, please him, buy gifts
Don't steal, don't lift
Twenty years of schoolin'
And they put you on the day shift
Look out kid, they keep it all hid
Better jump down a manhole
Light yourself a candle, don't wear sandals
Can't afford the scandal
Don't wanna be a bum
You better chew gum
The pump don't work
'Cause the vandals took the handle.

Words and music by Bob Dylan 1965. Reproduced by kind permission of Warner Brothers Music Limited.©M. Witmark & Sons.

survival attitude that Dylan offers is one of the siege mentality. All the while we're treated to a culturally defensive strategy in operation:

The phone's tapped *anyway*
Maggie says that many say
They must bust in early May
Orders from the DA . . . .

But if the word has got around (and it must have come from police sources) we have to notice how embroiled the DA and his minions have become in maintaining what is only a *surface* respectability. Ironically, when the time comes for such cosmetic action, the police's arbitrariness tends to be compounded:

Look out kid
Don't matter what you did . . .
Keep a clean nose
Watch the plain clothes
You don't need a weather man
To know which way the wind blows.

All this, delivered in the jaunty tones of a long-time survivor, and backed up with rock music that is shrill to the point of hysteria, represents a state of consciousness (if not of commitment or of organization) bordering on total opposition to the dominant ideology and its agents.

It was partly a rejection of the folk label, and partly the remarkable commercial success of the British groups in the USA, which combined to drive Dylan back to his rock 'n' roll musical roots. In 1965, he achieved his first number 1 single in some US charts with *Like a Rolling Stone*;[43] and this ever-growing audience was in turn attracted to his LPs, where picture painting was possible on a larger canvas. On the appropriately named *Highway 61 Revisited* LP we find Dylan's *Desolation Row* (lyrics on page 137), a song which follows through the analysis opened up in *Subterranean Homesick Blues*, but one which also begins to integrate the elements thrown up by the analysis into a more pungent critique of American city culture as a whole. The confusions, symbols and contradictions in street life are remorselessly exposed and satirized even from the first line, 'They're selling post-cards of the hanging.' But this time the tone of voice is decidedly pessimistic: the jaunty harmonica is replaced by a heavy organ accompaniment, and the outlook appears bleak indeed.

The contradictions of the American Dream had been analysed before, but never in such a sustained and imaginative way, let alone in the form

Desolation Row

They're selling post-cards of the hanging
They're painting the pass-ports brown
The beauty parlor is filled with sailors
The circus is in town
Here comes the blind commissioner
They've got him in a trance
One hand is tied to the tight-rope walker
The other is in his pants
And the riot squad they're restless
They need somewhere to go
As lady and I look out tonight from Desolation Row

Cinderella she seems so easy
It takes one to know one she smiles
And puts her hands in her back pocket
Bette Davis style
And in comes Romeo he's moaning
You belong to me I believe
Then someone says you're in the wrong place my friend
You'd better leave
And the only sound that's left
After the ambulances go
Is Cinderella sweeping up
On Desolation Row

Now the moon is almost hidden
The stars are beginning to hide
The fortune telling lady
Has even taken all her things inside
All except for Cain and Abel
And the hunchback of Notre Dame
Everybody is making love
Or else expecting rain
And the good samaritan he's dressing
He's getting ready for the show
He's going to the carnival
Tonight on Desolation Row

Ophelia she's 'neath the window
For her I feel so afraid
On her twenty-second birthday
She already is an old maid
To her death is quite romantic
She wears an iron vest
Her profession's her religion
Her sin is her lifelessness
And though her eyes are fixed upon
Noah's great rainbow
She spends her time peeking
Into Desolation Row

Einstein disguised as Robin Hood
With his memories in a trunk
Passed this way an hour ago
With his friend a jealous monk
Now he looked so immaculately frightful
As he bummed a cigarette
Then he went off sniffing drainpipes
And reciting the alphabet
You would not think to look at him
But he was famous long ago
For playing the electric violin
On Desolation Row

Doctor Filth he keeps his world
Inside of a leather cup
But all his sexless patients
They're trying to blow it up
Now his nurse some local loser
She's in charge of the cyanide hole
And she also keeps the cards that read
Have mercy on his soul
They all play on the penny whistle
You can hear them blow
If you lean your head out far enough
From Desolation Row

Across the street they've nailed the curtains
They're getting ready for the feast
The phantom of the opera
In a perfect image of a priest
They're spoon-feeding Casanova
To get him to feel more assured
Then they'll kill him with self-confidence
After poisoning him with words
And the phantom shouting to skinny girls
Get outta here if you don't know
Casanova is just being punished
For going to Desolation Row

At midnight all the agents
And the super human crew
Come out and round up every one
That knows more than they do
Then they bring them to the factory
Where their heart attack machine
Is strapped across their shoulders
And then the kerosene
Is brought down from the castles
By insurance men who go
To check to see that nobody is escaping
To Desolation Row

Praise be to Nero's Neptune
The Titanic sails at dawn
Everybody's shouting
Which side are you on?
And Ezra Pound and T S Eliot
Fighting in the captain's tower
While calypso singers laugh at them
And fishermen hold flowers
Between the windows of the sea
Where lovely mermaids flow
And nobody has to think too much
About Desolation Row

(Harmonica break, with guitar and drums)

Yes I received your letter yesterday
About the time the door knob broke
When you asked me how I was doing
Was that some kind of joke
All these people that you mention
Yes I know them they're quite lame
I had to rearrange their faces
And give them all another name
Right now I can't read too good
Don't send me no more letters no
Not unless you mail them from
Desolation Row

of a song. Like Guthrie, Dylan had used the song rather than the novel or the poem because it reached more people; but whereas Guthrie and the early Dylan had rested content with tackling one issue at a time, *Desolation Row* (and the whole LP) has to be considered as the 1960s equivalent of *The Grapes of Wrath*.[44] That sounds pretentious – to an English Literature specialist it might even sound preposterous – but it is the case. Of course, the song form imposes limitations. 'Characters' are presented more as in a *tableau vivant*, and each is little more than a caricature. But the point of Dylan's song is precisely that this is how people do appear to be: the structural limits actively reinforce his meaning, rather than deform or trivialize it. People do collide and pass, do stick labels on themselves and each other, much as in a Dickens novel.[45] They act out symbolic roles consciously, even outside fancy-dress parties, be their costumes and poses those derived from literature or film. And though Dylan is not offering any broad solutions, he does give us an incisive description of what is unmistakably The Problem.[46] It is fatuous to claim that this is a song celebrating bourgeois individualism – that Dylan wants to tell us that 'all *any* individual can do is to hold on to some integrity of personal perspective'[47] – because merely to show us Desolation Row is to have us recognize the fact that real people have built and maintained the society in which the Row has come to exist, and that there is the possibility of change. And to do that is to commit a conscious political act.

What is Desolation Row? Who lives there? Why does it exist at all? These are the questions which we are forced to raise, and which Dylan encourages us to answer. Evidently the Row is some kind of refuge for people with a dilemma — the dilemma of knowing what is wrong with the forces and agencies which impinge on the embattled community, and yet have no organizational means of effecting social and political change. On the other hand, the more people who escape to the Row make the chances of creating opposition all the greater. The song does not represent a retreat into paranoia in the face of overwhelming odds, even though the pressure is clearly communicated in and through the song. In fact Dylan satirizes the Ophelia 'solution' to a personal crisis, the wearing of 'iron vests' and walking near deep water. Suicide won't solve anything: the problems have to be faced, however unhopeful a real solution might seem to be. (After all, Dylan has gone on writing and singing for years when he had no need of the cash.) Then again, well-heeled middle-class American 'labour people' are no solution either. Those Good Samaritan white liberals are part of the problem, not the answer to it.[48] One by one, Dylan scrapes through to the real faces of the poseurs, behind the make-up and the fancy dress, rejecting them all as they stand, but not rejecting the possibility of a solution. He still *wants* to know which side he *can* be on, believes that such a side could exist. But not yet. Hence the need for the Row, for the spiritual and intellectual equivalent of the real ghettos, because only there is it possible to face the unhappiness of seeing contradictions clearly. *They* remain to be fought against, or at least fended off, and the Row provides a respite and a little support, however uncomfortable it may be.

Before you can fight, you have to know what the opposition looks like — how it behaves, what its powers and weaknesses are. You have to recognize the conscious and unconscious agents of a system and a state which produce the Row, and *depend* on it, no matter what their pretensions or their disguises. From insurance man to elitist poet, from Hollywood star to fairy-tale heroine, they have to be known. This is one of the preconditions of effective political action, not the capitulation to the agents and crews of the corporate state. Hence, in part, the 'straight' voice, more often sad than sardonic. Hence, too, the solemn pace of the song, and the measured delivery, punctuated by restrained guitar phrases. What Dylan wants to do is to show us not the surface appearance of the Row and all it stands for, but the reality of it; and he has no wish to allow the style of presentation to mar the central theme. Instead we have the whole pantomime/charade/fancy-dress party of a society which blandly celebrates capitalistic endeavour and enterprise, and cares nothing for the victims. 'The Titanic' sails at dawn', no doubt, but like the real ship it does so without any lifeboats for third-class passengers. This is the kind of viciousness which underpins the society that makes Desolation Row necessary; and by alternating between symptoms and cause, appearance and reality, Dylan confronts us with the inescapable truth that such contradictions are *built-in*, structurally determined. Whatever the mystifying mythology — be it Hollywood or 'lit-rat-cha' — Dylan ties it back to its ideological root. So, while capitalism would want us to believe that its preferred way of seeing the world is self-consistent, is 'common sense', Dylan decisively rejects any such notion, showing up all and every contradiction, and portraying the sheer insanity of a system amidst which Desolation Row offers to be a refuge.

Of course, the problem remains after the song has been heard. Unless you wish to languish in the ghetto, you have one basic choice — either to leave it behind, and join the insane, or fight to change it. For Dylan, this choice represented an impasse. After all, he was one of the contradictions he was criticising — a 'protest' singer who made money out of the system he protested at. Characteristically, he found a way of evading (or at least postponing) the choice. He had used drugs for years, for pleasure and to keep going on tours, as had large numbers of young Americans (and some British people), notably performers of one kind or another, or students. By the mid to late 1960s, however, the use of soft drugs was almost a respectable pastime, above all in places like Greenwich Village and San Francisco. Of course, the culture of which those drugs formed a part was easily penetrated (and then bought up, and marketed as 'flower power') by commercial interests. And this cultural appropriation undoubtedly took its toll of Dylan, too, notably in *Blonde on Blonde*, which represents all but total self-indulgence, and came as a nasty let-down after *Highway 61*, for all its superficial musical attraction. At this conjecture, conveniently for his reputation, Dylan 'broke his neck'.

When he was well, and had begun writing again, it was clear that Dylan had allowed himself to be driven even further into the Dream, into the myths supportive of it, in order to try to cope with his experience. His first new LP, *John Wesley Harding*, rejected the studio-based, high technology of *Sergeant Pepper*, and it also rejected the never-never land that the Beatles were marketing as the new mythology. Instead, after he had 'pulled out the plug'[49] (or at least some of the plugs), Dylan went headlong into the intellectual redneck country, to the country component of rock 'n' roll, pedal steel guitar and all. He had become a better singer and a better songwriter, judging by conventional standards — even a better musician — but his work suffered from what Gray terms a 'corresponding lack of what may be called "moral centre" '.[50] This was compounded by the man's practised arrogance: Dylan told an interviewer that if he said that the outlaw's name ended with a 'g', then it ended with a 'g', history notwithstanding. But even more revealing was Dylan's way of celebrating the hero of the title. 'Harding' was 'never known to make a foolish move', or to 'hurt an honest man'. Nothing positive: no affirmations (except by implication); and even the crass imitation of the country-rock idiom goes well over the bounds of mere parody: 'with a gun in every hand', 'sta-und', 'To lend a-uh helping hand' and all. Clearly the man was lost, grasping at straws, running full tilt away from the Problem and hiding behind any tree, however stunted.

Ironically, there is a centre to the songs on this LP, an *a*moral one. The values which are celebrated are existential ones — characteristically those used by bandits, fugitives, and outlaws in order to survive in a hostile world. But in the attempt to construct (even by negation) a credible position, Dylan was forced to celebrate survival for its own sake — 'There was no one around who could track or chain him down' — as though that were enough. This is no longer the openness of surface-breaking, reality-creating analysis, but the loose rhetoric of a man in despair. The whole LP is a systematic attempt to deny responsibility, to slough off any role as spokesman, to fend off answering the question: survive for what? Instead, we are asked to believe that any plain-speaking must be either hypocritical or self-defeating. St Augustine is portrayed as 'searching for the very souls whom already have been sold', and, anyway, he wears a 'coat of solid gold'. Tom Paine gets ensnared by the American counterpart of the Whore of Babylon; and a whole succession of drifters, immigrants and outlaws barely escape one or other kind of martyrdom.

In the end, Dylan is reduced to guying the very anger and frustration which his own 'escape' from commitment simply reinforces, as in *All along the Watchtower* (lyrics on page 144):

There must be some way out of here
Said the Joker to the Thief
There's too much confusion
I can't get no relief.

But at the same time, the refusal to differentiate between Joker and

All Along the Watchtower

'There must be some way out of here'
Said the Joker to the Thief
'There's too much confusion
I can't get no relief
Businessmen they drink my wine
Ploughmen dig my earth
None of them along the line
Know what any of it is worth'

'No reason to get excited'
The Thief he kindly spoke
'There are many here among us
Who feel that life is but a joke
But you and I we've been through that
And this is not our fate
So let us talk falsely now
The hour is getting late'

All along the watchtower
Princes kept the view
While all the women came and went
Bare-foot servants too
Outside in the distance
A wild-cat did growl
Two riders were approaching
The wind began to howl

Thief condemns Dylan to elite status in his own eyes:

Businessmen they drink my wine
Ploughmen dig my earth
None of them along the line
Know what any of it is worth.

Except, of course, the one whose wine and earth it is! It's all too neat, too mechanically defeatist, to ring true. Dylan the Holy Outsider, the great Uncommitted, the one who's 'been through that' no matter what it is, is in the end unconvincing because he is unconvinced. He hits the sitting ducks, and leaves the vultures unmolested. Gone the Dylan who, in Richard Goldstein's fine phrase, 'approaches a cliche like a butcher eyes a chicken'.[51] Instead, we get echoes of the Beatles, a musical and lyrical flabbiness:

Love is all there is
It makes the world go round
Love and only love, it can't be deni-i-i-ied
No matter what you think about it
You just won't be able to do without it
Take a tip from one who's tri-ied.

Only this time the element of self-parody is accidental rather than intentional.

It isn't simply that Dylan had made it. It's not simply that he's putting his audience on. He had been 'bigger n' Elvis' some time before, especially in the LP market. But when we find him sentimentalizing the family, legalized sex, and the home, in ways wholly supportive of the dominant ideology, we have to say that he is now still a bit of a Jester, but a *licensed* one. You can, if you feel sourly enough, reconstruct his earlier work in the light of what happened after 1967. You can denounce him as simply a pressure valve built into commercial culture, the better to control the head of steam built up by the insanities of the system. You can claim him back to liberalism, as Michael Gray tries to do; or you can recall the pressures that led to the construction of Desolation Row, the 'neck breaking' and all, and think more kindly about the man. After all, before he collapsed into the banalities we were used to hearing from people like Presley or the Beatles, before the 'sound' came to be more important to him (and his second 'new' audience) than the words, he'd managed to fend off many of the attempts to wrap him up and sell him wholesale. If Dylan *was* gobbled up – if he was eventually got at – it's hardly surprising. They had to get him: he was really dangerous. And even so, the old Dylan occasionally surfaces, notably in the acoustic version of *George Jackson* or in *Hurricane*, as he lets off a few rounds before getting sucked under again. Besides, the earlier songs remain even though it has become fashionable to downgrade their moral earnestness. They have had their formative effect on a generation and a half of adolescents, many of whom have gone off to write and to sing their own songs based on what they learned from him: *that* Dylan will never succumb as long as we don't.

9 Fakesong

We have spent some time examining the songs and music produced by the commercial music industry, the product which has been successful in market terms, or which has been influential in changing the characteristics of 'the average popular song'. But when we come to the other main definitions of the term, 'popular', that which is made and used by the populace, the people at large, we are met with two related problems. Firstly, music and song have been made chiefly by specialists, amateur or professional, for centuries in British culture; and, secondly, as a consequence, in public and now often in private, the majority of British people have been in the position of musical consumers. So, if we want to look at the music and song which has been popular in origin − in the sense of being made by people whose relationship with the majority of their community has been, largely, one of equality − or if we want to look at the music and song which have been popular in terms of reception by the same majority in the community or country at large − then we are faced with a further set of problems. We have to ask, Who made this song? Who used it, when, where and for what reasons? We need to know how a song circulated, whether it was in any way changed in the process of circulation, in terms of its function or content. Ideally, we would need sets of versions of a given song, over time, and a full knowledge of the characteristics of the communities in which it had currency. And so on: the list of possible questions is enormous.

The problem is that a certain group of people have clouded these specific historical and cultural issues, under the general heading of 'folklore' and 'folksong', to the point where theoretical debate is all but impossible. Mediators of working-class culture have been notoriously shy of arguing from fundamentals. Some evidently believe that their own position is clear. Others prefer one form or another of mysticism, and do not 'trust' theoretical discussion. Others again have had less than ingenuous motives. Consequently, as with all other accounts of non-scientific matters, our first task is to *situate* those mediators, to try and decode their mediations, in terms of their known predispositions, values, and assumptions, in terms of their *ideological* position, before we can properly assess and use their findings. This is why we have to give some considerations, here, to the terms 'folk' and 'folksong'. Though it will take a full-scale book to tease out and reconstruct the points of view of even the major British and American 'folklorists',[1] we can at least begin to map in the major problems here.

In terms of strict theory, there's no such thing as 'folksong', in Britain at any rate, because there were no 'folk'. At least, this is the case if we think of folk in anything like the same way as Cecil Sharp, founding father of the English folksong revival, whose assumptions have permeated the thought and activity of even the most historically aware contemporary writers and collectors.[2] What Sharp and his coadjutors did was impose on to the living culture of English working people (few of whom were agricultural labourers), in some parts of some predominantly rural counties in the south-west, notions of history and of culture which owe more to romance than to reality. But because people like Sharp had access to print, and so to the opinion-forming bourgeois 'public', and thus to educational institutions, generations of British schoolchildren have been obliged to swallow (if not to digest) his kind of 'folksongs' – what are, in fact, patched-up, bowdlerized, arbitrarily selected pieces, in no way representative of the repertoires even of those carefully chosen people from whom Sharp collected songs.[3] From the start, the revival was a thoroughly bourgeois movement; and its success in that milieu indicates just how supportive Sharp's notions were of the dominant ideology.

Briefly, the story of Sharp's work is this. He was a Cambridge graduate turned professional music teacher, and came from a London merchant family. After various adventures in Australia, he settled in England, and in 1903 he was introduced to the singing of a vicarage gardener, the appropriately named John England. The vicar was a Fabian socialist, as was Sharp, but the latter was also a member of the imperialist Navy League. From England's repertoire of a hundred songs, Sharp chose one, 'his only jewel'. This he labelled a 'folksong' and set about finding others like it, ignoring hundreds of songs which were actually current amongst working people in south-west England, even among his 'folksingers'. He proceeded by rejection: no songs from towns of any size, factory workers, or music halls. Instead, he chose suitably remote villages, suitably ancient people (following suitably non-industrial occupations), from whom he selected pieces which fitted his — not their — idea of what constituted a folksong. The 'folk', evidently, were not to be the judges of what was their song culture and what was not! Sharp would descend on a village, armed with the local vicar or squire, and wheedle old men and women into parting with their songs. From this idiosyncratically selected body of 'raw material' (Sharp's term), he and his friend edited out collections of texts and music for publication, adding piano accompaniments, collating versions, and eliminating anything which might offend polite ears. Sometimes, indeed, whole song texts were mangled, whole verses made up, even if the tunes were usually transmitted accurately. All this was bad enough; but so long as 'folksong' was kept within bourgeois culture, not much damage could be done to the live culture from which Sharp had taken his 'raw material'. Unfortunately, Sharp did not stop there: as early as 1907 he produced a book of what he termed 'theory', *English Folk-Song: Some Conclusions*, and set about trying to use this highly mediated folksong as 'an instrument of great value' which would 'tend to arouse that love of country and pride of race the absence of which we now deplore':

Flood the streets therefore with folk-tunes, and those who now vulgarize themselves and others by singing coarse music-hall songs will soon drop them in favour of the equally attractive but far better tunes of the folk. This will make the streets a pleasanter place for those who have sensitive ears, and will do incalculable good in civilizing the masses.[4]

Since Sharp's days, there has been a conspiracy of silence about the man and his work, especially about those aspects which are no longer fashionable even in bourgeois circles. For example, the original 1907 text of *Conclusions* has been doctored by Miss Maud Karpeles (his amanuensis-cum-secretary of later years) who has also effectively suppressed Sharp's American diaries. The motives are not hard to seek: like many of his contemporaries Sharp was an imperialist, and a racist, and he simply could not comprehend either British music hall or the music of black America. From a pirated version of his 1918 American diary, we find that Sharp felt Charleston to be 'a noisy place and the air impregnated with tobacco, molasses and nigger'. He was obviously surpised when an American friend 'resented my dubbing the negroes as of a lower race'; and he and Maud were obliged to flee from their lodgings in another town, because 'the squalling children and negro music were so disturbing'. The point is not to denigrate Sharp — after all, he was a product of his time and his class culture[5] — but to indicate why and how the ideas of such a man have been disabling in the second folksong revival, for all its populist — even socialist — rhetoric. Sharp's chauvinism, mysticism, racialism and fundamental conservatism have vitiated not only his own 'theory' but also that of those many others who have taken up where he left off. It is as irrelevant to blame Sharp as it is to blame Bob Dylan: the point is to be aware of how they came to be what they were, and to learn to understand how and why they acted the way they did. Not Sharp, but the Sharpites, are the targets of the following critique.

Perhaps the most serious contender for an alternative to the products of the music industry, in Britain at any rate, has been the second folksong revival, and above all the folk club movement. (In the USA, the situation is notably different.) By 1945, if not before, the English Folk Dance and Song Society (EFDSS) had withered to the point of being moribund. Within a matter of years, Princess Margaret could become involved with its doings, so well had it been integrated into bourgeois and ruling-class culture, at least at the London headquarters. Ironically, the folk movement — and especially the dance element — was seen by most working-class people as fit only for music hall jokes. Other than that, it was a question of largely petit-bourgeois music teachers forcing children to perform inane versions of *Bobby Shaftoe* or *The Miller of Dundee*. In a real sense, the second folksong revival was a rescue operation, an attempt to win back this form of genuinely popular song for the people as a whole. From the first, this revival had distinct political overtones; and its success owed much to the Labourist ideology of post-war Britain, as well as to an elitist attempt to reject commercial popular song — this tendency, at least, it shared with Sharp's revival.

It will take a full book to analyse the second folksong revival; but it is possible, here to point out some of the key tendencies, and to begin to situate the key personnel. For example, it has to be said that the milieu which gave rise to the revival was decidedly unproletarian, chiefly London-based (or London-oriented), and dominated by intellectuals who were of a radical frame of mind. Many of the key people, especially in the 1950s, were members of the Communist Party, of the Young Communist League, or of the various cultural organizations sponsored or supported by the CPGB. A glance at the pages of the early 'folk' magazines — *Sing*, above all, which was founded in May 1954 and had fraternal links with the US *Sing Out* — will show how striking was the political commitment of what was still a fairly small band of individuals. It's not simply that *Sing* was founded by the London Youth Choir, and run from Cambridge (and then Hampstead), or that it would take up the cases of Paul Robeson and Pete Seeger in their struggles with McCarthyism. The editors were perfectly open about their commitment to the CP-run World Federation of Democratic Youth, and were pleased to announce that one of their number was leaving (in 1957) to work as a freelance radio journalist in Hungary. Looking back now at copies of *Sing*, it is remarkable to note how the CP commitment to the revival has somehow been downgraded, or even forgotten.

Chief amongst the 1950s 'folk' *aficionados* were Bert Lloyd and Ewan MacColl. Lloyd was born in Wales, but has lived in London most of his life. In the 1930s he was out of work, but his dole office was convenient for the British Museum, and he spent a lot of time there, delving into folksong and folklore materials. Before the war, he took various jobs — a few weeks on a British whaler, a longer stay in Australia, and so on — but by 1944 he found himself in England, on a tank gunnery course. In between whiles, he wrote what was to become the first serious account of English workers' songs, published in 1944 as *The Singing Englishman*, by the Workers' Music Association, itself supported by left-wing musicians and singers. The book was, of course, hailed as another distortion of history by reactionaries; but for a generation of young performers it represented the beginning of an attempt to reconstruct the decaying 'folk' movement of the English Folk Dance and Song Society (Princess Margaret and all) into something which had at least some bearing on the lives and histories of working-class people. On the strength of his book, no doubt, Lloyd was asked by the newly nationalized Coal Board to edit a collection of pit songs as part of the NCB contribution to the 1951 Festival of Britain. *Come All Ye Bold Miners* has many faults, looked at from our present knowledge of pit-village culture, but in the early 1950s it was to many a revelation. By showing the depth and breadth of the songs produced in the British coalfields — and above all, in the north-east of England — Lloyd's compilation inspired young performers to seek fresh songs from their communities, and to produce new material in a similar idiom.

Jimmy Miller (stage name, Ewan MacColl) was born in 1915, the son of a Scottish union militant father, and a mother with a treasury of songs. Miller senior was forced from pillar to post, down through England; but the family spent most time in Salford, and that is where Jimmy learned to sing and to get involved in socialist politics. He became a member of a street theatre group, the Red Megaphones, and wrote the *Manchester Rambler* song in support of the Kinder Scout 'trespass' in the later 1930s. During the war, MacColl seems to have been less active, but at this period he wrote several plays for Joan Littlewood's company; and in 1945 he helped found the experimental Theatre Workshop, where he stayed for seven years. By 1951, he had teamed up with Bert Lloyd, the American folksong collector Alan Lomax, and the ex-public-schoolboy jazz musician, Humphrey Lyttleton, to work for the BBC. Together, they produced a radio series entitled *Ballads and Blues*, using the already well-established jazz 'revival' to give folksong a platform and an audience. (No doubt, also, the connections between the staff of *Picture Post*, for which Lloyd had worked, and that of the post-war BBC, helped smooth the way for the series). In fact, many of the personnel involved in Ken Colyer's revival of what he thought was 'pure' New Orleans jazz were also left-wingers, even if they were imbued with a romanticism about workers and the working-class based on what Geoff Nuttall terms 'a patronising idolisation of the lumpen proletariat that only the repressed children of the middle class could have contrived'. At least Lloyd and MacColl were originally from working-class families, even if they did share the 'workerism' — the 'Worker as Hero'-ism — which was most characteristic of CP members and fellow travellers at the period, as we shall see in the analysis of *The Big Hewer* (pages 180-5).

So, the intervention of the Communist Party and its fraternal organizations was absolutely crucial in the second folksong revival, and to a lesser extent in the blues revival which was to follow. Almost symbolically, the line-up for a concert in aid of the ailing *Daily Worker* in the mid 1950s included Colyer's Jazzmen, MacColl, and the Scots 'traditional' singer, Jeannie Robertson. Almost equally important was the connection of many 'folk' enthusiasts with the radical-to-socialist Greenwich Village fraternity in New York. Visas permitting (as they were for Pete Seeger to come to Britain in 1961, but were not for MacColl to go in the other direction), fairly regular visits were exchanged between the London and New York 'folk' personnel. MacColl's Ramblers Skiffle Group, for example, contained not only Alan Lomax and Shirley Collins, but also Peggy Seeger, the daughter of a pair of radical American academic musicologists. Courageously, Peggy had gone to the Moscow Youth Festival at the same time that her half-brother Pete was being persecuted for his political beliefs; while in the notably easier atmosphere of post-war Britain, Pete Seeger,

Lyttleton and Bert Lloyd were happy to be elected vice-presidents of the Workers' Music Association.

Apparently, the first regular venue for MacColl's group was the Scots Hoose, Cambridge Circus. Ballads and Blues, as the club was called, began in 1953, and was managed by Bruce Dunnet (another CP member, who later managed Julie Felix, and had the distinction of turning down the Rolling Stones). Pubs were ideal for this kind of entertainment in Britain because of the handy refreshment and the relatively relaxed licensing laws, which permitted under-age people to enter all pub rooms except those which had their own bar. (In the USA, the situation was notably different; and this accounts for the way in which the 'folk' movement there was largely a coffee bar institution, though it's true that coffee houses were also used in Britain, not least because of the availability of soft drugs, and the absence of licensing hours or strict control over personal and interpersonal behaviour.) Gradually, not only a network of clubs was built up, chiefly at first in London, but also a cadre of singers. First at Ballads and Blues, then at MacColl's Singer's Club and at Les Cousins, the core of the singers who were to form the backbone of the 1960s club movement was gradually formed: the embryo Young Tradition, Davy Graham, Bert Jansch, John Rembourn, Roy Harper, Al Stewart, Jackson C. Frank, Sandy Denny, then Louis Killen, Anne Briggs, Ian Campbell and Donovan Leitch, many of whom came out of the provinces to the 'crash pad' at Somali Road, Hampstead, in the later 1950s, went to the clubs, imbibed the songs, and went out as missionaries not only for the art but also to a lesser extent for the politics of the London coterie.[7]

What is highly significant, ideologically, though we can note only the ripples on the public surface of events, is the way in which the club movement underwent apparently major upheavals around 1960-1, just as it was about to become a national phenomenon. As early as 1957, *Sing* carried an advert for the breakaway *New Reasoner* journal, run by Edward Thompson and John Saville, two of the leaders of what had been the chief non-Stalinist faction inside the CPGB. Right through the later 1950s, and into the 1960s, *Sing* supported all those movements and pressure groups which fitted in with its liberal-socialist aims, including CND and the Anti-Apartheid Movement. Inside the relatively tiny folk fraternity, tensions spilled over in the second half of 1961. MacColl broke away from Malcolm Nixon and the Ballads and Blues Association to form the Singer's Club jointly with *Sing* magazine. At one level, evidently, the break was with Stalinism; but it was also, and significantly, a break with commercialism:

It was necessary to rescue a large number of young people, all of whom have the right instincts, from those influences that have appeared on the folk scene during the past two or three years — influences that are doing their best to debase the meaning of folk song. The only notes that some people care about are bank notes.[8]

Evidently, Bert Lloyd and Dominic Behan had withdrawn from the commercialized pub and coffee house clubs over this period, and MacColl and Peggy Seeger had sung more in North America than in Britain. (*Sing* itself had not appeared for over a year before this issue, and when it did it was distributed by Collett's Record Shop, another of the cultural institutions which formed part of the London left-wing network.) But what was publicized as a series of 'disagreements over artistic policy' clearly had much deeper roots. MacColl wrote that he was 'scared' when he saw the blatant commercialism of some of the British clubs, just as he was dismayed at the way in which audiences got sung down to. On the other hand, and ironically, by setting up a club which would give 'top traditional singers a platform where they will be protected from the ravages of the commercial machine', MacColl and company were in continuous danger of being seduced by another form of elitism, the kind which I believe permeates the 'Radio Ballads' for BBC radio, and which saturates the attitudes of people like Lloyd and MacColl towards a songwriter like Bob Dylan. The irony is all the deeper when we take into account the way in which Lloyd and MacColl, above all, seem to have cornered the market for 'folk' broadcasting right through the fifties and sixties, just as they dominated the recording of 'folk' songs at Topic Records (of which Lloyd is Artistic Director).

Apparently, the ructions in the London clubs continued into 1962, by which time the club movement had spread out into England and Scotland. In September 1961, there were perhaps forty-five clubs. By May 1962, *Sing* counted over eighty. Coming from Liverpool, Tony Davis of the Spinners noted 'the constant bitterness and division between the various singers, promoters and writers' in the capital; but his objectivity must be set in context. He was writing in the Spinners' own magazine, *Spin*, begun in October 1961, and his group's attitude towards commercialism was notably less acrid than that of a Lloyd or a MacColl. The Spinners, like the High Level Ranters, and indeed most of the personnel of the 1960s club movement, were not proletarian in origin or in lifestyle. They were not averse to making money; and they were much more tolerant of people like Bob Dylan than Eric Winter and company at *Sing* could ever bring themselves to be. In the pages of

Spin, there is an uneasy combination of frank commercialism (on a small scale) with a touching idealism. For example, one issue proclaims that the Spinners would sing free and pay their own expenses to encourage new clubs, though it is hard not to suspect that at least half an eye was open to the prospects of a full-time career on the club circuit, given that the movement could be sustained through its early years.[9] Inevitably, perhaps, the burgeoning of the folk club movement in the middle and later 1960s produced temptations for even the most purist singers. When Lloyd and MacColl collaborated with Cambridge graduate Charles Parker on the innovatory 'Radio Ballads', they found work for many of the Somali Road fraternity. At Topic, Lloyd saw to it that many of these same people contributed to compilation LPs on general themes, like *The Iron Muse* and *Farewell Nancy*, and from there they were able to go out to Birmingham say (like Ian Campbell), or to Tyneside (like Louis Killen), start their own clubs, and thus foster the growth of other clubs in neighbouring towns and cities. Drawing an audience from this network, the more successful performers could be asked by Topic to produce full LPs of their own material, some of it new and some of it 'traditional'.

In other areas, this same audience influenced radio producers and programmers into encouraging Lloyd and MacColl to write series on 'folk' song and lore, often at first for the Third Programme, but then even for the less prestigious channels, and eventually for television. Associated with the clubs were the early folk festivals, many of which got underway in the early 1960s, as did a number of newer folk magazines, like *Folk Music* (begun in 1963 and owned by K.F. Dallas Ltd), *Ballads and Songs*, and *Folk Scene* (both 1964). Over the years, the political edge was in many areas lost altogether. Typically, the Spinners' first *Spin* editorial set itself apart from *Sing*, and from the caucus which gave the folk movement life:

We try not to use our singing to put over any particular school of political propaganda. We keep social songs to the basic humanitarian issues – the bomb, peace, apartheid and so on. Too many folk singers grind political axes.[10]

This was the tendency which triumphed as the 1960s progressed, and which to some extent sucked in even Lloyd and MacColl.

By mid 1963, Topic was producing twelve-inch LPs once again, after a period of eighteen months of EPs. In less than a year, the company had produced its one-hundredth record. The ganglion which supported Topic also began to support the first major festivals, like that at Sidmouth in 1964; and, in turn, those festivals gave work (and cash) to visiting lecturers and performers. Instead of relying on WEA lecturing, or on freelance journalism, people like Bert Lloyd could now look to the once-despised commercial 'folk' institutions for a considerable slice of their income. If 1961 marked the early crises, in many ways, 1964 seems to have been the 'folk' watershed. If *Spin* had grown from 200 to 2000 between 1961 and 1964, by early 1965 it had a print order (and a new offset litho presentation, partly paid for by increased commercial advertising) of over 5000, a circulation which by then formed less than half of the folk magazine audience. Clearly, the rapprochement between the recording industry and elements in the 'folk scene' before the discovery of the Beatles was based on hard-headed market analysis.[11]

By 1967, MacColl had produced perhaps a hundred LPs of his own material and of 'traditional' songs. His fees for performances in clubs topped £50, plus expenses and high-grade accommodation for both himself and Peggy Seeger. On the other hand, in the mid 1960s Bert Lloyd was to be floated an Arts Council grant to help feed his family on top of material support from the Workers' Music Association and the publishers, Lawrence & Wishart, while he prepared *Folk Song in England*, a work based on *The Singing Englishman*, but much less sure of itself than the earlier text, and almost wholly devoid of theoretical discussion. In fact, it is clear that Lloyd saw himself by this time as following largely in the tradition of Cecil Sharp, whose 'principles' had gone a long way to forming the official definition of 'folksong' as promulgated by the International Folk Music Council in 1954. In other words, *Folk Song in England* represented a gain in terms of empirical scholarship, but a retreat in terms of its ideological core, even allowing a generous margin for Lloyd's tactical attempts to head-off Cold Warriors in the English Folk Dance and Song Society. MacColl, meanwhile, spent a considerable amount of time training singers, both at the Singers Club, and at more select gatherings of people (including the embryo Critics group), so as to carry on his methods and techniques. In public, MacColl made no serious theoretical contribution; but, fortunately, some of his training sessions were surreptitiously recorded.

We have already seen something of how, in London and the rest of Britain, the commercial road was taken by many of the performers and the clubs. From being non-profit-making bodies, held together by a group of regular singers who sang for pleasure, the clubs moved from pub backrooms to lounges. Entrance charges were winched up. 'Guest' singers came to dominate the entertainment every month, then every fortnight. To pay the fees of the semi-professionals and full-time professionals, more cash had to be brought in – by raffles, higher entrance charges, or whatever. In fact, once the profit motive had inserted a finger, it soon drove in the whole fist. The movement went sour. Landlords began to ask well-known singers to form clubs: running a club came to be regarded more as a bread-and-butter affair, a useful addition to income, rather than as a pleasant leisure-time activity. Not that there was anything surprising in this tendency: after all, the early British concert hall went just the same way, before it was transformed into music hall.[12] But what did stick in the craw were the pretensions of those who wanted to hang on to the radical elements in the folk club movement, while at the same time screwing the punters for all they were worth.

It became possible, in the later 1960s if not before, for a large group of 'folk' performers to make a comfortable living out of their singing and playing. Many – particularly of the earliest converts – retained vestiges of the ideological connections with working-class industrial culture; but they found that, just as they began to move away from their class of origin, so did their audience, until the singers were effectively retailing a nostalgic and deformed version of industrial culture to members of the aspiring working class and the petty bourgeoisie. For those who moved fully and openly into showbiz, like Steeleye Span, such criticism is inappropriate. But for those others who set up in business, say, as professional 'Geordies' – or 'Lankies', 'Brummies', 'Yorkies', or whatever – and whose entire act was a caricature of working-class culture, this writer at least has only contempt. The history of working-class culture is littered with people who exploit the resources of that culture for the benefit of their 'betters'. So, if some famous contemporary folk groups see their business in much the same way as any other pop artists, who run their own club (but can't always turn up if a more lucrative gig is available wlsewhere), who change record labels at will, who record LPs of songs largely rehashed from earlier group productions, then perhaps they're more to be pitied than blamed. Their connection with working-class culture is, in any case, minimal. Where the connection does exist, it now depends on school-teachers – remove the teachers from the revival, or from the folk club movement, and both would collapse overnight – or weekend, 'back-to-the-roots' former proletarians.

The fate of Bill Leader's record company is almost symbolic. Leader left Topic because of the label's refusal to encourage up-and-coming singers, or to issue songs and music from the twentieth century 'folk' heroes and heroines. Leader felt that the older, 'traditional' performers deserved to be made available to a wider audience; yet Topic's policy on new performers was highly restrictive. For a time, all went well. Some well-known performers, like the High Level Ranters, switched from Topic to Leader Records. But the 1973 oil crisis almost put Leader out of business. Because oil was in short supply, and because vinyl is made from oil products, the major companies who supplied Leader with unpressed discs simply cut off his quota. There's no point in bleating about this sort of commercial 'accident'. Even before the crisis, Leader had been at the mercy of pressing and distribution networks, and the whim of people like the Ranters who helped support the ambitious programme of 'traditional' releases. The Ranters now record for Topic.

Traditionally, mini-capitalist enterprises have had to become more and more commercially oriented, or run the risk of going bust. Leader Records was simply one amongst many, including institutions created on more democratic lines, like, say, the Tyneside Concert Hall.[13] It was probably inevitable, given the self-employed status of the revival's founders, that commercialism should triumph. It was also inevitable that the audience for folk performers should therefore become more and more middle class, more 'respectable'. Not that there was a lack of resistance from the genuinely non-commercial performers, the people who did it for pleasure or, at most, for a few drinks. But *they* suffered from an almost total lack of purposeful organization. The EFDSS lorded it over the clubs, which effectively kept the London institution going. Dance was given preference to song, by the EFDSS, and the same old bunch of London-based people continued to dominate the crumbling institution. Attempts were indeed made to set up an organization in opposition to the EFDSS, but, ironically, the cadre that was necessary could not be found, in part because of the split over commercialism. As a consequence, even in the late 1970s, the old guard and their proteges continue to control most festivals, the EFDSS, the access to the BBC, the lecture circuits, the American connections (chiefly, now, with universities, so respectable have folk-life studies become there), and the access to print. We badly need a full analytical history of the second folksong revival, just as we need a detailed account of the practices, assumptions and attitudes of the leading figures within the revival, particularly as regards their connections with the ideology of the first revival. Critical biographies of Bert Lloyd and Ewan MacColl are long overdue. Somebody ought to set about producing a history of the folk club and festival movement. The EFDSS could bear some dispassionate scrutiny, as could Topic Records, the Workers' Music Association, and the various folk magazines. Above all, perhaps, we need to be able to evaluate the 'folk' oriented editorial and scholarly critical work of the last thirty years, in terms of its ideological tendencies, so as to be sure what is worth saving for the reconstruction of working-class British culture.[14]

10 Songs of pitmen and pitwork

Is it possible to discover which songs amongst the thousands of texts labelled 'folksongs' genuinely were popular in origin and transmission? Is the evidence available? What criteria are appropriate? Does it matter if particular texts have come down to us through the heads and hands of middle-class, or even ruling-class, people? How can we attempt to penetrate the mediating influences of even the most careful folklorist? Is there any meaningful sense in which we can reconstruct song culture as it existed in former times, as part of the reconstruction of pre-industrial or working-class culture as a whole? Or are we bound to end up with a distorted picture? These are some of the most important questions which we have to try to answer if we are seriously interested in adding a historical dimension to the study of popular song, or in adding a broader cultural dimension to the study of history. We will not be able to answer them all satisfactorily here, but it will be possible to indicate some of the secondary problems which crop up, and to show some ways of tackling them, given the present state of research. What I propose to do is examine a series of songs written around a particular theme — coal and coal work, pits and pitmen — which have been taken to represent the point of view of workers in the industry over a long period of time. Any selection of theme, or of particular texts within a theme, will necessarily be arbitrary, will be another example of mediation. That is inevitable. This is why I have chosen to use songs from the north-east of England, a region whose pre-industrial and working-class culture has been studied more than any other in the British Isles. In this way, the reader will be better able to decode any secondary mediations which may occur.[1]

'The Collier's Rant' (lyrics on page 160)

This is the earliest-known song to concern itself fully with coal work in England, and it has generally been accepted as a 'folksong', as being genuinely popular in origin and in transmission.[2] As it happens, there

The Collier's Rant

As me and my marrow was ganning to work,
We met with the devil, it was in the dark;
I up with my pick, it being in the neit,
I knock'd off his horns, likewise his club feet.
  Follow the horses, Johnny my lad oh!
  Follow them through, my canny lad oh!
  Follow the horses, Johnny my lad oh!
  Oh lad ly away, canny lad oh!

As me and my marrow was putting the tram,
The lowe it went out, and my marrow went wrang;
You would have laughed had you seen the gam,
The devil gat my marrow, but I gat the tram,
  Follow the horses, etc.

Oh! marrow, oh! marrow, what dost thou think?
I've broken my bottle and spilt a' my drink;
I lost a' my shin-splints among the great stanes,
Draw me t' the shaft, it's time to gan hame.
  Follow the horses, etc.

Oh! marrow, oh! marrow, where hast thou been?
Driving the drift from the low seam,
Driving the drift from the low seam:
Had up the lowe lad, deil stop out thy een!
  Follow the horses, etc.

Oh! marrow, oh! marrow, this is wor pay week,
We'll get penny loaves and drink to our beek;
And we'll fill up our bumper and round it shall go,
Follow the horses, Johnny lad oh!
  Follow the horses, etc.

There is my horse, and there is my tram;
Twee horns full of greese will make her to gang;
There is my hoggars, likewise my half shoon,
And smash my heart, marrow, my putting's a' done.
  Follow the horses, Johnny my lad oh!
  Follow them through my canny lad oh!

Follow the horses, Johnny my lad oh!
Oh lad ly away, canny lad oh!

Anonymous, composed before 1793.
Source: John Bell (ed.), *Rhymes of Northern Bards* (1812; reprint 1971,
Newcastle: Frank Graham), p. 35. There are amended versions of this song,
probably the least inaccurate being in *Along the Coally Tyne*, LP Topic 12T189
(1962 and later reissues).

are doubts about the first criterion, and the second deserves to be
carefully examined. The first-known printed text of the song appears in
Joseph Ritson's *Northumberland Garland*, published in 1793. Ritson
was an antiquarian who worked as a lawyer in London, though he had
been born and brought up in Stockton, County Durham.[3] He was a
friend of William Shield, who wrote patriotic ballad operas, and who
also hailed from the north-east.[4] What we know of Ritson's scholarship indicates that he was vastly more accurate in transcribing and
editing material from oral culture than, say, his contemporary Bishop
Percy, whose *Reliques of Ancient Poetry* contained rewritten texts,
prefabricated texts, and so on.[5] After Ritson's death, a London
publisher reissued the *Garland* as part of a collection of Ritson's booklets
of song texts; but unfortunately, some of the contents of this 1810
edition were doctored.[6] When we next find the song in print is in John
Bell's *Rhymes of Northern Bards*, published in 1812, a compilation
put together as much from commercial as from antiquarian motives.[7]
Only after that did John Marshall publish the piece as part of a cheaper
song-book, some time in the 1810s, and then again in 1827.[8] It was
1834 before the song again saw the light of day in print, this time in Sir
Cuthbert Sharp's *Bishoprick Garland*, a deliberately quaint antiquarian
jumble of songs, verse and scraps of legend. From Sharp we learn that
the song used to be sung with 'marvellous effect' by a 'Mr W. S. of
Picktree', who used on it 'his powerful voice and genuine humour'.[9]
In the 1840s, we hear that a blind church organist from London
(another ex-patriot north-easterner, called Topliff) would use the piece
as part of his concert tours in his native region. William Brockie recalls
that it was 'a rare treat to hear Topliff sing' the *Rant*, not least, perhaps,
because he charged his audience a shilling a head, and held his concerts
in the long-room of genteel inns.[10]

With the possible exception of Marshall's song-book, this is indeed
a curious publishing pedigree for a 'folk' or popular song. Granted
that, by and large, songs had then to be collected by one kind or

another of antiquarian, how justified are we in querying this mode of transmission? How many knights (outside of irony) would refer to a working man as 'Mr' in the 1830s? How many industrial (let alone agricultural) workers in the 1840s would pay a shilling to hear some old songs in select company? And in the absence of any other evidence of oral transmission, don't we have to be all the more careful in ascribing popular origin to such a text? So far as is known, the song never appeared on any broadside in the north-east, and only once in one of the many cheap song-books aimed at a *working-class* audience, Marshall's 'songster'. Even John Marshall's 1827 publication was largely aimed at the better-off, as indeed were Davison's *Tyneside Songster* (1840), Fordyce's *Newcastle Songster* (1842), Robson's *Bards of the Tyne* (1849), and the late nineteenth-century works of Crawhall, *A Beuk o' Newcassel Sangs* (1888)[11], Allan, *Tyneside Songs* (1891).[12] and Stokoe, *Songs and Ballads of Northern England* (1893),[13] in all of which *The Collier's Rant* appeared in one form or another. To a greater or lesser degree, these collections were the product of regional patriotism – chauvinism, even – and were put together by members of the petty bourgeoisie for the delectation of their own class and their 'betters'.[14] What is particularly interesting is that the song did not appear in Bruce and Stokoe's *Northumberland Garland*[15] of 1882, an out-and-out collection of 'folksong' which formed one of the bases for the first folksong revival. Neither did the *Rant* appear in Catchside–Warrington's *Tyneside Songs* in the 1910s and 1920s, for all that these cheap song-books were aimed at the piano-owning labour aristocracy as well as at the clerks and shopkeepers of Tyneside. When we next encounter a printed version of the song it is in A.L. Lloyd's collections of 1952, *Come All Ye Bold Miners* and *Coaldust Ballads* (published by the Communist Party-linked firm of Lawrence & Wishart, and the Workers' Music Association, respectively). Ewan MacColl printed a version two years later, in *The Shuttle and Cage*, also published by the WMA; and then the piece took on a new lease of life in the folk club movement.

Bert Lloyd's *Come All Ye Bold Miners* is still referred to as 'the Bible' by some of the older north-east folk entertainers, notably by Johnny Handle of the High Level Ranters, who was originally inspired to write fresh songs by Lloyd's book. But what is crucial is Lloyd's admission there that in this century the *Rant* was 'learned from print and kept for formal occasions',[16] even by working pitmen:

only yesterday, when the mines were taken out of private hands, and the blue-and-white N.C.B. flag was run up, massed choirs of north-eastern miners roared out the Rant in salute.[17]

Presumably, the skilled and white-collar workers who composed the bulk of the folk club audiences were prepared to accept Lloyd's judgment about matters of authenticity. Certainly, after the song passed on to a Topic record (sung by Louis Killen) in 1962,[18] and gained some currency, it soon became possible for Lloyd to present an apparently consensus view of the piece, as he did in 1967, in *Folk Song in England*. Apparently, the song had become 'already so old' by Ritson's time, that 'its words had become corrupted and its story hardly coherent'. Yet some of its 'old epic force' remained visible to a perceptive folklorist, for all the 'burlesque'.[19] In other words, the song had been absorbed into an up-dated, left-sounding version of the 'folksong consensus'; and what didn't fit in with this perspective was written off as corruption, edited out of the Ritson text, or simply ignored.

As it happens, *The Collier's Rant* makes perfect sense as it stands in Ritson's 1793 song-book, given a little understanding of north-east worker's culture in the last quarter of the eighteenth century. As Sharp indicated in 1834, the piece as we now have it was *intended* to be funny. It was also intended to be a vehicle for full-lunged bragging, as the title indicates unambiguously. However, why we laugh, and what we laugh at, depends on our attitude towards working pitmen; because the whole story of the song tells of the pressures of pitwork under an early piece-rate system, and of the consequences for the pitmen's working relationships. After the 1760s, and above all during the industrial boom which was produced by the war-time economy of the 1790s, London demanded vastly increased imports of coal. The north-east coal owners had a virtual monopoly of that trade, and to meet the demand they began sinking new pits as well as reopening old, often dangerous workings. To chivvy the men, piece-rate systems were encouraged, and so relations between 'marrows' (or mates) were put under strain. The men had, as yet, no trade union: their solidarity was very much of hit-or-miss variety, and they were much less powerful than the Tyneside and Wearside keelmen. In part, this was the result of not working in large groups, and of being spread across an ever-widening coalfield. But within pit communities, wherever they might be in relation to the major towns, there was a fierce community spirit which dated in some cases from the previous century. This, crudely, is the context within which the *Rant* can make sense.[20]

As ever, the drive to increase production while minimizing capital investment was fulfilled at the expense of the workers. Pitmen, working in pairs as 'marrows', would drive each other on to greater effort, irrespective of safety, health or any other hazard, including mythological ones like the Devil. So, in spite of the superficial light-heartedness of the song —

You would have laughed had you seen the gam
The devil gat my marrow, but I gat the tram

— it is abundantly clear that the tram of hewn coal is more important to the man who hewed it than his mate's safety. Or so a straight reading of the text would suggest. But the reality of the marrow's working life was that the hewer had to help train the putter, first in the skills of shifting trams full of coal along difficult roadways, and then, gradually, in the techniques and skills of cutting coal. In this way, the putter worked his way up in the pit, from door boy, to putter, to half-marrow to full-blown hewer. He had to prove his worth (literally) to his more experienced marrow, even though frustrations would creep into the working relationships all the time. Some inexperienced boys and young men would be unable to keep the tram on the road especially before the introduction of wheeled trams in the 1770s, and of iron plates in the 1790s, and would fall by the wayside. Others would always be ready with 'Twee horns full of greese' to make the putting easier, and could cope without having to drag the hewer away from the face. This master-apprentice relation is, then, the kernel of the song.

Both men needed each other. No matter how clumsy the putter, the hewer needed him to get his coal to bank, so as to be paid. It was the hewer's responsibility (and in his interest) to sort out his marrow — to exhort him, chastise him if need be, and to break him into the work discipline that was essential to their job. And this gives us the clue to the tone of the song: it *parodies* the exclamations, excuses, frustrations and accidents of the inexperienced putter, at the same time as it illustrates clearly the mutually exploitative nature of their work. The whole song is underpinned by the repeated drive to 'follow ... follow ... follow ...', to get back to the face with empty tubs. If the putter must complain to make him feel better, and if learning the job meant learning to exploit yourself efficiently, so be it. So, they both swear, they both keep up their spirits with thoughts of the fortnightly pay week binge, and they both use the Devil as a handy butt (or threat) for their aggression and frustration. In its structure and content, then, the *Rant* articulates the feelings of the pitmen, their attitude towards the work, themselves and each other.

Of course, this analysis begs the question of popularity of origin or of use. Messrs. W.S. and Toplif could well have burlesqued what to them as non-pitmen, seemed grotesquely funny about the pitmen's trials and tribulations. The self-conscious 'phonetic' orthography of the printed versions would support this view. Who would *need* to have the 'dialect' written down but those who did not use it; and who would need to get their songs from printed sources? If the song came from this kind of culture, we would have to interpret it as an example of *cultural* exploitation, paralleling the economic exploitation on which the security of the petty bourgeoisie undoubtedly rested. In other words, the undeniable verve of the song — its raciness of metre and of idiom — would indicate a deliberate burlesquing of the 'habits and manners' of the 'terrible and savage pitmen'. On the other hand, the song may indeed have been of popular origin, and may have been taken up by the W.S.s and Topliffs to be used in this patronizing way, while it continued to exist in pit-village culture, performing quite another function. The truth is that the song can be taken both ways: for lack of firmer evidence, its status as a popular song is problematical.

Assuming popular origin and transmission (at least in part), *The Collier's Rant* can be taken to indicate an awareness on the part of working pitmen of their own exploitation, and the part they played in it, *vis à vis* each other. It also shows an understanding of the real relations of pitmen to the means of production — to the pit, the trams, and so on — which can be faced only by a bravado which, in the end, convinces no one, least of all the pitmen themselves. Hence the *need* for the Pay Saturday drinking session. There was no way in which pitwork in the late eighteenth century could be made bearable, by the exertions of the men, at any rate, short of organized solidarity and action. That this was the direction in which some men's thoughts were tending is indicated by the suppressed anger which runs through the song, an anger which might be vented in imprecations at the putter, but which is really the product of the work situation in which both men reluctantly find themselves, and which brings both of them to the end of their tethers at moments of crisis. In a sense, only the swearing and the blow-out prevent more violent and concerted forms of action. They are, if you like, safety valves. In the end, of course, the pressure burst through those valves, especially in the post-war economic depression of the late 1810s, as coal owners went on the offensive against the men's wage levels and conditions of work, trying to screw them further down. It is a matter of recorded history that the pitmen came to understand what they could do to change the degrading circumstances of their work; and that, after 150 years of struggle, they managed to wrest control of the pits from the hands of the coal owners. If *The Collier's Rant* was genuinely popular in origin, and if its attitudes were at all typical of 1760s, 1770s or 1780s north-east pitmen, we are justified in saying that the song indicates an early phase of the transition to full class-consciousness, of the making of the north-east working class.

'A New Song' (lyrics on page 167)[21]

Bert Lloyd helped to republicize this song, under the title of *The Coal Owner and the Pitman's Wife*.[22] Unfortunately, the version promulgated by Lloyd shows how cavalierly even the better folklorists can behave towards genuinely popular or working-class texts; and thus how difficult it can be to retrieve materials from working-class culture in their least mediated form. Fortunately, we still have the manuscript of *A New Song*, in the Picton Library, Liverpool, as well as an early broadside version, under the title of *The Old Woman and the Coal-Owner*, where the grammar of the manuscript is touched up so as to conform to ordinary practice. But it has been Lloyd's text which has permeated the folk club movement and the second revival, not the original 1840s texts; so it is important to examine how that amended text got into circulation.

The Coal Owner and the Pitman's Wife* appeared in Lloyd's 1952 compilation, *Come All Ye Bold Miners*, as 'communicated by J.S. Bell of Whiston, Lancs'.[23] From Ewan MacColl, in 1958, we learn that Mr Bell was a coal-face driller from Prescot, a 'studious Lancashire miner'.[24] But whether the mangling was done by Mr Bell (accidentally or otherwise) or by the professional folklorist hardly matters; not least because Lloyd's whole book is in large measure an arbitrary and unscientific selection. As we have already noted Lloyd's collection grew out of a competition sponsored by the National Coal Board as part of its contribution to the 1951 Festival of Britain. Prizes were offered in the NCB magazine, *Coal*, 'for those songs judged to be the best "finds"', and Lloyd did the judging. Perhaps inevitably, given his predilections and the state of research, several distortions were built-in. Lloyd included parodies of pit-village culture done by town tradesmen for the amusement of their own kind;[25] and he patronized the early Tyneside concert hall writers and singers, even though people like George Ridley and Ned Corvan were working-class in origin, worked

A New Song

A dialogue I'll tell you as true as my life
Between a coal owner and a poor pitman's wife
As she was a travelling all on the high way
She met a coal owner and this she did say
She met a coal owner and to him she said
Sir to beg on you I am not affraid:
    down hey derry down. *

Then where do you come from the owner he cries
I come from h—l the old woman replies
If you come from h—l come tell me right plain
How you contrived to get out again *

Aye the way ah gat out the truth ah will tell
They are turning the poor folk all out of h—l
This is [to] make room for the rich wicked race
For thare is a great number of them in that place *

And the number's not known sir that is in that place
And they chiefly consist of the rich wicked race
And the coal owners is the next in command
To arrive into h—l as I understand *

How know you the owners is next in command
How div ah naw ye shall understand
Ah hard the old devil say when ah cam out
The coal owners all had reciv'd their rout *

Then how does the old devil behave in that place
O sir he is cruel to the rich wicked race
He's far more uncrueler than you can suppose
Wye even a mad bull with a ring thro his nose *

Good woman says he I must bid you farewell
You give me a dismal account about h—l
If this be all true that you say unto me
I'll go home and with my poor men I'll agree *

If you be a coal owner, sir take my advice
Agree with your men and given them their ful price
For if you do not ah naw very well
You'll be in great danger of going to h–l *

For all ye coal owners great fortunes has made
By those Jovel men that work's in the coal trade
How can you think for to prosper or thrive
For wanting to starve your poor workman alive *

So all ye gay gentlemen thats got riche in store
Take my advice and be good to the poor
And if ye do this all things will gan well
Perhaps it will save ye for gannin to h–l *

So now the poor pitman may join heart and hand
For when their of work all trade's at a stand
Yon town of Newcastle all cry out amain
O since the pits were at work once again *

It's now to conclude little more I've to say
I was turned out of my house on the 13 of May
But it's now to conclude and I'll finish my song
I hope you'll relive me and let me carry on *

* *Chorus*

Words by William Hornsby, Shotton Moor, Co. Durham, 1844.
Source: Picton Library, Liverpool. *A History of the Coal Trade* (MSS etc). For
various cobbled, patched and 'improved' versions, see A.L. Lloyd, *Folk Song in
England* (Lawrence & Wishart, 1967), p. 344, where the song is given the title *The
Coal Owner and the Pitman's Wife*, and, on record, the mangled versions given by
Ewan MacColl on *Steam Whistle Ballads*, Topic 12T104 (1958 and later reissues),
and by the High Level Ranters in *The Bonnie Pit Laddie*, Topic 12TS271/2 (1975).
In the 1978 edition of Lloyd's *Come All Ye Bold Miners*, earlier liberties with
the text are corrected, but by no means all of them.

in an institution made and used by working-class people, and were
accepted there.[26] Even less surprisingly, given the ideological
dominance of the Sharp-based 'folksong' consensus, Lloyd's analysis of
his retitled version of *A New Song* is notably awry.

In Lloyd's mature view, the song seems to be put together in the form of a 'medieval French *débat pastoral*', and is a 'witty caricature of the lyric of former times'. Its tone, apparently, is wryly humorous, but with 'a smile that shows strong teeth', indicating something like class-conscious militancy.[27] As it happens, misplaced erudition and wish-fulfilling fantasy combine to blur the function of the song in the great pitmen's strike of 1844. Even from the limited evidence transmitted to us it is possible to be much more precise about the making and using of *A New Song*, especially after the appearance in 1968 of Brian Ripley and Ray Challinor's book on *The Miner's Association.*[28] True, we can't be certain who William Hornsby was, even though Lloyd assumes with Mr Bell that he was a working pitman.[29] Certainly, he wrote more than one song, and he came from Shotton Moor. His spelling in the manuscripts is usually unambiguous, his handwriting fairly neat; and his habit of using the eighteenth-century 's' might be taken to indicate that he was an older man, moderately well educated in childhood (or in an adult Sunday School class, or even self-taught). Like most working-class people who were literate in the 1840s, he had a preference for biblical syntax, largely because of the use of that text in teaching, and, of course, the close connection between militancy, literacy and nonconformist religious observance. So, Hornsby could have been a hewer, or even a minor colliery official. He was a trade unionist, of course, and he may well have been one of the lay preachers in the primitive Methodist church. These so-called Ranters were, many of them, high up in the union hierarchy, and were, as a consequence, amongst the first to be evicted from their tied cottages by the coal owners. Certainly, it was the Ranters who got the blame for putting together many of the strike songs;[30] but, ironically, it was precisely the Ranters who pressed for strike action *without resort to violence.* They were the 'moral force' cadre which dominated the union leadership.

There are many songs like *A New Song* in the pages of the men's union paper, the *Miner's Advocate*. Others again appear in manuscript or broadside form in various library collections of strike material.[31] What characterizes these 'official' pieces is their gradually increasing pessimism, quietism, and other-worldly fatalism, as the four-month strike neared its end.[32] From the song itself, we learn that it was designed to be used by men on the tramp, to collect money from sympathizers in other parts of the north; and that its singer is meant to be one of the very first to be evicted.[33] The song's tone may well have been kept muted and uncontroversial so as to alienate as few potential contributors as possible; but even allowing for that cosmetic operation, it is impossible to discover anything in the song which smacks of militancy.

As it stands, in manuscript and on the broadside, the song's overriding atmosphere is one of despair and defeat. The whole scenario is the product of a wish-fulfilling fantasy — that Lord Londonderry, the coal owner's 'shop steward', could be won to humanity by a moral argument. In reality, Londonderry refused even to meet the pitmen's leaders. What chance, then, of a sudden conversion on the highway by a ghostly Old Woman? But the fact remains that only a systematic attempt to escape from reality was possible for those who refused to contemplate forms of direct action which might involve violence. The song, in effect, articulates their ideological impotence, their inability to see a solution to this-worldly oppression, and their need to defer gratification to the next. So, while the Old Woman retains some vestiges of dignity (in spite of the habit of deference) she remains *dead*. Her only bargaining counter is the threat of vengeance after death for Lord Firedamp, in a very physical hell. Moral verities were in no way going to deter a man who used his own judicial power to close down outdoor relief for strikers' families at the work houses, who threatened sympathetic shopkeepers with bankruptcy, or who imported troops to help win a trade dispute. Londonderry managed even to ignore the protests of people of his own class, when they objected to the use of blackmail, coercion and legalized violence in a civil matter.[34] In other words, you do not realistically expect to beat coal owners with hell-fire-and-damnation preaching. If the likes of Hornby did choose to believe that you could, they were either supremely naive, or, at worst, cowardly and disingenuous. In either case, the limits of trade union consciousness of the non-violent kind had clearly been reached. All the singer can see is the next town, the next performance, the next copper collection. If he was representative, then the north-east pitmen were indeed in a cleft stick.

As it happens, there is evidence to suggest that the writer and singers of *A New Song* were by no means representative of rank-and-file pitmen. Whatever may have been the case amongst the men's union leaders — and there is a strong circumstantial case to identify this piece precisely with the Ranter elite — there is little evidence to suggest that working pitmen and their families subscribed to the quietism and fatalism of Hornsby and his kind. So, while the latter might control the union's *Advocate* newspaper, the 'official' broadsides, and the union purse strings, there was a reversion to more effective forms of direct action on the part of the more militant pit-village communities, notably in south-east Northumberland and north Durham. What is beyond doubt is that the victory of 'immoral force' in 1844 and cured many pitworkers and urban Tynesiders of religion for good and all.[35] In this sense, we can reasonably infer that Hornsby's song represents the internal contradictions of the 'moral force' ideology, as brought to a head by a defeated struggle. In no meaningful way does it represent the level of class-consciousness that was developing amongst rank-and-file pitworkers.

'The Blackleg Miners' (lyrics on page 172)

According to Bert Lloyd's *Come All Ye Bold Miners*, this song was first collected from Mr W. Sampey of Bishop Auckland, County Durham in 1949.[36] In *Coaldust Ballads* (published the same year, and compiled by Lloyd from his recent NCB collection), we are told that it was collected in 1951.[37] The two texts are remarkably dissimilar, even allowing for the fact that the later booklet aimed to 'give the best of these songs renewed life by publishing arranged versions which can be performed'.[38] On the 1958 Topic LP, *The Iron Muse*, the text had taken on a distinctly 'Geordie' flavour even in the printed version, and it was this 'phoneticized' version which appeared in *Folk Song in England* in 1967, as collected in County Durham in 1949 and 1952![39] Each text differs from all the others. Whole verses disappear from one version, and then reappear in later ones. Only Bert Lloyd is in a position to sort out this muddle. All we can do, here, is to assume that he has transmitted the contents of the song accurately in the fuller texts, adding and subtracting nothing of significance, and to try to situate those texts in the matrix of north-east working-class culture.

Though the song was current in the 1880s, and seems to have travelled across the Atlantic (and then, perhaps, back) in one form or another, the events which Lloyd's texts describe can be dated with some certainty as having taken place at the end of the great strike of 1844.[40] The pit villages of south-east Northumberland had been strongholds of working-class radicalism since at least 1819;[41] and we know from a strike broadside of 1831, *'The First Drest Man of Seghill'*, that putting trade union solidarity into song was well established amongst workers in that district.[42] (Incidentally, Lloyd is known to have changed that title, too.)[43] The methods of disciplining erring brethren (notably imported Welsh blacklegs) mentioned in *The Blackleg Miners* are known to have been employed around Seaton Delavel, Cramlington and Seghill, once the 1844 strike went down to defeat.[44] So, even if the texts we have now were put together or transcribed at a much later

The Blackleg Miners

It's in the evenin after dark
When a blackleg miner creeps te work
With his moleskin pants and dorty shirt
There goes the blackleg miner.

He'll take his picks an' down he goes
Te hew the coal that lies below
But there's not a woman in this town row
Will look at a blackleg miner.

Now, divvent gan near the Delaval mine
Across the way they stretch a line
Te catch the throat an' break the spine
Of the dorty blackleg miners.

An' Seghill is a terrible place
They rub wet clay in a blackleg's face
An' around the heap they run a foot race
Te catch the blackleg miner.

They take yer duds an' tools as well
An' hoy them doon the pit of hell
Down ye go an' fare ye well
Ye dorty blackleg miner.

So join the union while ye may
Don't wait till yer dyin' day
'Cause that may not be far away
Ye dorty blackleg miner!

Anonymous, composed before the 1880s and likely during the great strike of north-east pitmen in 1844.
Source: The Iron Muse, LP Topic 12T86 (1956 and later reissues).

date, we can be sure that the sentiments expressed, and even some of the details, were by no means peculiar to the 1880s or later.

As it stands, the song signals complete dissatisfaction with 'moral force' methods, and with a leadership who allowed sixteen or eighteen weeks of suffering to be wasted. Though a strike had been won in 1831 by the Ranter leaders, they were helped enormously then by a tactical alliance with middle-class parliamentary reformers, who needed them to blackmail the ruling class, and by a surprise attack.[45] The defeat of 1832 stemmed in large measure from a lack of both advantages: the owners were expecting another struggle and were prepared, while the reformers had no further use for the pitmen once they had themselves been enfranchised.[46] In the 1844 strike, the men were pretty much on their own, there being no working-class organization to support them, given that the keelmen had been largely replaced by coal-drops. Of course, they were met with systematic attrition. So, while William Hornsby and the 'moderate' (that is, right-wing) Ranters caved in, and wrote fatalist songs, the author of *The Blackleg Miners* must have come from one of the ideologically more advanced pit communities, where fully class-conscious radicalism – likely, with Chartist affiliations – had developed. This was the form of consciousness which went to create the 'red pits' of the early twentieth century, in which a song like *The Blackleg Miners* always found a welcome.[47]

Whether in 1972, 1974 or 1844, solidarity cannot always be achieved through intellectual persuasion. Sometimes discipline has to be enforced by a pit community in less subtle ways, even retrospectively. So, in the last few weeks of the 1844 struggle a song like this would function both as a rallying call to strikers, their families and friends, and at the same time as a sung warning to actual or potential class traitors.

'The Durham Strike' (lyrics on page 174)

Tommy Armstrong, the writer of this song, was born in north-west Durham in 1848. By 1857, at the age of nine, he was working down the pit.[48] During the 1860s, as a teenager, he took part in the variety entertainments known as *soirées* at the local village institutes, to which came the concert hall stars of urban Tyneside – George Ridley, Joe Wilson, and, probably, Ned Corvan.[49] As a young man, in the 1870s, Armstrong ran his own concert party. (By this time the town professionals no longer travelled the country circuits, but stuck to the larger music halls in the major towns and cities.) Armstrong wrote and sang his own songs, and had them printed on slips of paper, to be sold to help supplement his pitman's wages – often, for beer money. Later on, he was called upon to write for his trade union, so close did he remain to the culture of the pit villages; and by the time of the great struggles of

The Durham Strike

In our Durham County, I am sorry for to say
That hunger and starvation is increasing every day;
For the want of food and coals we know not what to do,
But with your kind assistance, we will stand the struggle through.
I need not state the reason why we have been brought so low,
The masters have behaved unkind, which everyone will know;
Because we won't lie down and let them treat us as they like,
To punish us they've stopt their pits and caused the present strike.

   Chorus
May every Durham colliery owner that is in the fault,
Receive nine lashes with the rod, then be rubbed with salt,
May his back end be thick with boils, so that he cannot sit,
And never burst until the wheels go round at every pit.

The pulley wheels have ceased to move, which went so swift around,
The horses and the ponies too are brought from underground;
Our work is taken from us now, they care not if we die,
For they can eat the best of food, and drink the best when dry.
The miner, and his partner too, each morning have to roam
To seek for bread to feed the little hungry ones at home;
The flour barrel is empty now, their true and faithful friend,
Which makes the thousands wish today the strike was at an end.

   Chorus

We have done our very best as honest working men,
To let the pits commence again we've offered to them "ten".
The offer they will not accept, they firmly do demand
Thirteen and a half per cent or let their collieries stand.
Let them stand, or let them lie, to do with them as they choose,
To give them thirteen and a half, we ever shall refuse.
They're always willing to receive, but not inclined to give,
Very soon they won't allow a working man to live.

   Chorus

With tyranny and capital they never seem content,
Unless they are endeavouring to take from us per cent;

If it was due what they request, we willingly would grant;
We know it's not, therefore we cannot give them what they want.
The miners of Northumberland we shall for ever praise,
For being so kind in helping us those tyrannising days;
We thank the other counties too, that have been doing the same,
For every man who reads will know that we are not to blame.

Chorus

Words by Tommy Armstrong, 1892.
Source: Song Book containing 25 Popular songs of the late Thomas Armstrong,
3rd ed. (1930). This songbook is reprinted with some amendments, in Tom
Gillfellon, *Tommy Armstrong Sings* (Newcastle: Frank Graham, 1971). There
are more seriously amended versions on record, the least reprehensible of which
is on the High Level Ranters, *The Bonnie Pit Laddie*, Topic 2-12TS271/2 (1975).

the 1890s, Tommy Armstrong was the recognized pitmen's union bard
in County Durham.[50]

In the third edition of his *25 Popular Songs*, published in 1930 and
edited by his son, the song in question is called *The Durham Strike*.
In *Come All Ye Bold Miners*, in 1952, and even in 1978, Lloyd titles
the song *The Durham Lock-Out*. He also changes Armstrong's favourite
tune, *Castles in the Air*, a variant of *The Ball o'Kirriemuir*, and replaces
it with the maudlin *Come All Ye Tramps and Hawkers*, thus con-
verting what had been a song with a smart cutting edge into one with a
self-pitying tone. What's more, whereas Armstrong used the most
stinging stanza as a chorus, Lloyd simply uses it as another verse.[51]
Two years afterwards, in 1954, Ewan MacColl missed out the chorus
completely from the text in *The Shuttle and Cage*; and by the time of
Lloyd's *Folk Song in England*, in 1967, what had been a spirited chorus
had been relegated to last verse but one.[52] It wasn't until 1971 that
Armstrong's words were republished; and even now Lloyd's tune still
holds sway in the folk clubs. Lloyd's version of this song is quite
different to Armstrong's. The folklorist's tune *makes* some of the
phrasing sound awkward, whereas Armstrong's helps give punch and
vigour even to the least happy constructions, not least because of
the swing that the original tune demands. Whereas Lloyd's song is a
lament, Armstrong's is a *threat*. What in Lloyd's hands sounds like a
barrel-organ whine — drab, mechanical and fatalistic — becomes, using
Armstrong's version, a rousingly defiant, even optimistic song, ending
on a high crowing note.[54]

The Durham Strike was written in May 1892, by a man who was at the heart of the struggle. The pitmen had refused to work at wages offered by the owners, some 10 per cent below what they had been getting. In other words, they struck and *then* they were locked out. (The coal owners later jacked up their demand to a 13.5 per cent cut.) Undeterred, the union set about supporting its members, and part of the effort, as ever, went into producing song propaganda for sale to sympathizers in other working-class communities. Hence Armstrong's piece, and hence in part its relatively muted anger. So organized were the pitmen, and so improved the general state of organization amongst the north-east working class, that the raw anger of *The Blackleg Miners* was neither appropriate nor necessary. Similarly, whereas in the 1844 strike the union men's resentment and action had been directed against traitors from *within* the working class, by the 1890s it was possible to assume a high level of discipline inside the ranks, and to direct anger at the *real* enemy, the 'They' and the 'Them' of Armstrong's song. True, the outlook of the song is what we would now term 'economist' — 'If it was due, what they request, we willingly would grant' — but then, such is the point of view of many trade union officials almost ninety years later. Besides, the men's propaganda had to avoid treading on too many ideological toes, in order to isolate the coal owners, and to collect money.

On the other hand, that biting chorus pulls no punches:

May every Durham colliery owner that is in the fault,
Receive nine lashes with the rod, then be rubbed with salt;
May his back end be thick with boils, so that he cannot sit,
And never burst until the wheels go round at every pit.

The jaunty tune does not signal defeatism. The muted criticism and almost Old Testament curses of the chorus are offered as the best *publicizable* account of the struggle from the men's point of view, given the state of class consciousness in the working community at large, and *not* that amongst the pitmen. If there is any 'infirm' grasp of the realities of class struggle in Armstrong's song — if he is in some ways pre-socialist — then at least he was no worse than almost all the major literary figures of his time, most of whom did not have much experience of trades unionism or of pitwork.[55] Besides, it is irrational to look for class-conscious militancy in a song designed to help collect strike funds. Armstrong's song did its work, expressing the pitmen's determination to refuse to accept the 13½ per cent reduction that the owners later demanded. On the other hand, because of the lack of a genuine *class* organization — the very reason for *The Durham Strike* — the Durham pitmen were forced to accept a 10 per cent cut in pay. So, whatever we may think about the politics of the song, we have to accept that it did represent the views of the north-east pitmen for whom it was written, and amongst whom it still circulates — that it was and is a 'popular' song, a working-class song, as much as any best-seller.

'Farewell to the Monty' (lyrics on page 178)

John Pandrich (stage name, Johnny Handle) was born in Wallsend in 1935. His father was a schoolteacher of Scottish descent, and his mother came from a Durham mining family. As a child, Handle learned to play several instruments; and by 1953 he had formed his own jazz band. He left school at 17, in 1952, and trained to become an underground surveyor in the pits:[56]

His main musical interest was formerly in jazz, and as a folk-singer he began with a repertoire of blues and American songs, gradually going over to British, especially northeastern material, including his own songs. These were inspired by a study of A.L. Lloyd's *Come All Ye Bold Miners* and other collections of mining songs.[57]

In 1957 or 1958 he helped Louis Killen form the Newcastle Folk Song and Ballad Club; and around 1960 he left the pits to retrain as a schoolteacher. It was at this period that he wrote the songs on which his later fame rests, notably *Farewell to the Monty*. Currently he is the most vociferous member of the High Level Ranters, who run their own club in Newcastle, and have made several LPs, as soloists and as a group, as well as having long been leading performers at clubs, dances, festivals and on radio and television. Teachers to a person, the Ranters have exercised considerable influence on the whole club movement in the north-east.

It is ironic that the song inspired by the published results of an NCB competition should concern itself with a colliery — the Montague, West Denton — which had been shut down as uneconomic by the nationalized industry. Characteristically, Handle does not see the irony. His song is thoroughly sentimental, fatalistic. It seeks to describe the colliery in a kind of anthropomorphic way — 'the pit's done its best' — as though generations of working miners hadn't struggled with the coal. Though the song is allegedly written from the standpoint of the men — 'we' and 'us' — it's difficult to escape the feeling that the colliery workforce are being in some way patronized. A nameless coal-face worker has words put into his mouth; and when rumours of pit closure start flying, Handle

Farewell to the Monty

For many lang years now the pit's done its best,
And sets have rolled oot of flats, north, east and west;
And aal o' the rumours that closin' was due,
Now they've aal been put down, for alas, it is true.

A meetin' wa held te discuss the affair,
And the manager said tiv us, right then and there,
We'll have one last go before this pit is done,
For to show a good profit on each single ton.

But though profits were made, through the stocks pilin' high,
The Coal Board decided this pit has to die,
And as output gans doon we get transferred away,
Te pits te the south for the rest of wor days.

Aa've worked in the Fanpit, and aa've cut in the seam,
In the Newbiggin Beaumont since aa was thorteen;
Aa've worked at the sections and in the Main Coal,
For it's hot down the Monty, she's a dorty black hole.

So farewell te ye, Monty, aa knaa yar roads well,
And yar work it's been good, but yar work it's been hell.
Na mair te yar dorty owld heap will aa come,
For yar workin' is finished and yar life it is run.

Words by Johnny Handle, music by Johnny Handle and Louis Killen, 1959.
Source: High Level Ranters in *The Bonnie Pit Laddie*, Topic 2-12T271/2 (1975).

implies that the men were quite content to identify with the aims of management. Any pitman over 30 who had worked there since he left school would have known that most of the same bosses were there before and after vesting day, and that they still spoke the same language:

We'll have one last go before this pit is done
For to show a good profit on each single ton.

The language of profitability, in a market still predominantly in the control of private capitalism, and for which nationalized industries simply provided cheap fuel, goods or services, is meant to have permeated the thoughts of a body of men who knew the problems of the Monty, but who also knew that closure would radically alter their working lives. Men who for generations had fought to get the pits into public ownership were said to be ready to buckle down and be exploited in the name of state capitalism.

At best, this is a curious scenario, and it gets curiouser the more we look at the ideological and factual content of the song. The men worked, made a profit, and still have the pit shut down, all, apparently, without a murmur of dissatisfaction, except for a grumble or two about being transferred away to 'Robens's Promised Land' in Yorkshire or Nottingham, or, at least, to the big coastal collieries of Durham and south-east Northumberland. To any listener aware of the events of 1972 and 1974, even in the politically backward north-east coalfield, such fatalism must seem improbable. *Farewell to the Monty* chooses not to examine the possibility that the men were less than content at being exploited, sold out, bullied, betrayed and then physically shipped off. Instead, it bears all the hallmarks of the kind of 'public relations' job so popular with so-called progressive management, especially those formerly working-class kids who got on (and out) into a secure white-collar job, and who could look upon manual workers' troubles all the more dispassionately.

It would be interesting to know whether this song was sung in 1959 in or around the Montague colliery – in the working-men's clubs or pubs, say – or whether its performance was restricted to the folk clubs, whose audience, precisely, was (and still is) largely of the labour aristocrat or white-collar variety. Typically, the early folk clubs had a predominantly Labourist outlook, leftish in talk, rightish in action, best summed up by the pitman's epigram, 'They vote Labour and work Tory.' The relationship between a siɔger/songwriter like Handle and such an audience was close indeed, especially with the mystique of shamateurism that prevailed. (Though cash payment out front was frowned upon, free drinks and 'exes' were common enough from the start.) And though the singers in the first north-east folk clubs sang songs *about* working miners – wrote new ones even – it was the case that the clubs were not formed in pit villages, by and large, but in large towns and cities such as Stockton, Middlesbrough and Newcastle. Miners did not compose the majority or even a significant minority of the audiences, or of the band of performers. Instead, it was left to actual or aspiring members of the petty bourgeoisie to dominate the clubs; and it was for them that songs like *Farewell to the Monty* were most appropriate.

What could the shutting down of an apparently difficult pit mean to *that* audience? If men were being released from the discomfort and dangers of an old colliery, were they not most of them going to work in other pits? To a working pitman, however, 'rationalization' often felt like what it was, hidden unemployment. All those saccharine labels used by management to disguise bitter pills — 'mobility, 'flexibility', and so on — might be taken for granted by bank clerks, schoolteachers and highly skilled tradesmen; but the pit communities had much more to lose than did the inmates of suburbia. There was a *good* side to pit-work, and to living in a pit village (even if it was on the edge of a city), which the folk club audience had either rejected or had never known. On the other hand, in the beery comfort of the folk clubs, Pandrich's song performed the ritual function of a spiritual return to the roots.

If you don't have to contemplate facing up to pitwork, and if you feel that the main problems of exploitation in the industry have been overcome by so-called nationalization, then there's a satisfying possibility of identifying with the victims of the horrors and the trades unionism of *earlier* generations. In a sense, songs like *Farewell to the Monty* functioned perfectly as vicarious spiritual regeneration, while the real miners were held at a safe distance. Besides, if the wild 'red' pitmen had succumbed — if they too had little control over their work and their destiny — it was easier for punier mortals wearing white collars or white coats to reassure themselves that we were all undignified together. So, romanticism, nostalgia, sentiment and tokenism were happily blended in Handle's song. One self-appointed, highly visible, would-be spokesperson could offer to set into song only the warmness of Montague pitmen for their old pit, for the *consumption* of others. What chance Handle for Arthur Scargill's bard? Even the question is ridiculous.

'The Big Hewer' (lyrics on page 181)

Ewan MacColl (real name, Jimmy Miller) we have already met. From the first he was an excellent singer, an able songwriter, and well established at the heart of the Second Revival. It was probably inevitable then, that MacColl should have been called upon by a BBC radio producer called Charles Parker to put together a new kind of documentary programme — the 'Radio Ballads' as it came to be termed — in the late 1950s and early 1960s. The first programme was commissioned in 1957, and was based on the use of the portable tape recorder, then just coming into vogue. Bert Lloyd was closely involved from the first, as were several of the Les Cousins group of performers.

The Big Hewer

Down in the dirt and darkness I was born, Go Down!
Out of the hard, black coal-face I was torn, Go Down!
Kicked on the world and the earth split open,
Crawled through a crack where the rock was broken,
Burrowed a hole, away in the coal, Go Down!

In a cradle of coal in the darkness I was laid, Go Down!
Down in the dirt and darkness I was raised, Go Down!
Cut me teeth on a five-foot timber,
Held up the roof with me little finger,
Started me time, away in the mine, Go Down!

On the day that I was born, I was six-foot tall, Go Down!
And the very next day I learned the way to haul, Go Down!
On the third day worked at bord-and-pillar,
Worked on the fourth as a long-wall filler,
Gettin' me steam up, hewing the seam, Go Down!

I'm the son of the son of the son of a collier's son, Go Down!
Coal dust flows in the veins where the blood should run, Go Down!
Five steel ribs and an iron backbone,
Teeth that can bite through rock and blackstone,
Workin' me time, away in the mine, Go Down!

Three hundred years I hewed at the coal by hand, Go Down!
In the pits of Durham and east Northumberland, Go Down!
Been gassed and burned and blown asunder,
Buried more times than I can number,
Diggin' a hole, away in the coal, Go Down!

I've scrabbled and picked at the face where the roof is low, Go Down!
Crawled in the seams where only a mole could go, Go Down!
In the thin-cut seams I've ripped and reddied,
Where even the rats are born bow-legged,
Diggin' a hole, away in the coal, Go Down!

I've worked in the Hutton, the Plessey, the Brockwell Seam, Go Down!
The Bensham, the Busty, the Beaumont, the Marshall Green, Go Down!
Lain on me back in the old Three-Quarter,

Up to the chin in stinking water,
Hewin' a hole, away in the coal, Go Down!

Out of the dirt and darkness I was born, Go Down!
Out of the hard, black coal-face I was torn, Go Down!
Lived in the shade of the high pit heap,
I'm still down there where the seams are deep,
But diggin' a hole, away in the coal, Go Down!

Words and music by Peggy Seeger and Ewan MacColl, 1961. Reproduced by kind
permission of Harmony Music Ltd.©Harmony Music Ltd.
Source: The World of Ewan MacColl and Peggy Seeger, LP Argo SPA-A102 (1970);
see also *Ewan MacColl – Peggy Seeger Songbook* (New York: Oak Publications,
1963); and the version interspersed throughout *The Big Hewer* radio ballad
available on a record, Argo RG 538.;

Originally, tape recorders had been used in a totally mechanical way,
to get

source material for an eventual script, with perhaps occasional direct
quotes from tape to substantiate a documentised sequence or to give
'local flavour'.[58]

The assumption was that most people in the streets and on park benches
were inarticulate, and probably moronic. What came to be termed 'vox
pop' was a self-fulfilling prophecy; and so even Parker and MacColl
were surprised at the quality of speech they were to get from working
men and women, quite without benefit of help from left-wing intellectuals and professional media persons. All the same, and so as to make
themselves not entirely redundant, the two men changed their idea of
producing a 'formal, studio-performed folk cantata'.[59] Instead, they
chose to use highly edited sequences of actuality tape, suitably whittled
and winnowed, as part of the very structure of their studio-performed
jazz/folk cantata. The result was a series of programmes celebrating the
'worker as hero' (rarely as heroine), in which they romanticized, over-
elaborated, indulged stylistic whims, and generally intellectualized and
mediated the taped material given to them by workers. *The Ballad of
John Axon* was their first production, but it was *The Big Hewer* which
represents the settled position of Parker and MacColl as 'socialist
artists'.

Their attitude towards the men and women who gave them the
interviews, and towards the interviews themselves, was almost entirely

instrumental. As privileged mediators, Parker and MacColl set out to 'fit' this novel kind of raw material into their own preconceptions about working-class life, work and culture:

It quickly became apparent to us, that the only way to *deal* adequately with the miner was to *make* him an epic figure; a daunting prospect until we realised that the men themselves were giving us the *means* to do just this. Wherever we went we heard stories . . . and among these tales we began to discern a figure of the archetypal miner, the Big Hewer . . . the collective expression of the miner's pride in his work and his true place in society. [my italics] [60]

It would be silly to deny that what the 'Radio Ballads' achieved was far and away the best thing produced on BBC radio up to that date (and, possibly, after it), from the point of view of documentary programmes about working-class people. On the other hand, it would be even more silly to place the programmes beyond criticism from a socialist position, not least because of the ways in which Parker and MacColl foisted their version of the Big Hewer myth on to working miners as a whole, and at the same time quite ignored the culturally and economically determined reasons for the production of the myth in the first place.

The 'Big Hewer' seems to have a history stretching back at least to the 1840s, in the north-east at any rate.[61] Certainly, whatever the coalfield, such a mythical figure – or a mythified real pitman – was developed well before nationalization in 1946. But it never seems to have occurred to Parker and MacColl that the mythical figure might have been a *deliberate* and *grotesque caricature* of the self-exploitative worker, the man who filled more tubs, dug more coal and worked more hours than any other. In pit culture, such a caricature would function in more than one way, depending on the context. To 'insiders' who shared the Big Hewer mentality, doubtless it would serve as a symbol of pride and virility. To other insiders – those who could see past the prowess and the pay packet – the myth would be both a self-mocking caricature, and an ideological stick with which to satirize men who, effectively, undercut piece-work rates, and so worked against the men's common interest and their union organization. (Limitation of production had been one of the earliest weapons to be used by pitmen.)[62] To 'outsiders', not excluding Parker and MacColl, likely the Big Hewer would be used as a symbol of masculine prowess (and so, by implication, a challenge), and also as a defensive screen to ward off criticism of what has always been a *degrading* and dangerous job. For all their technical and artistic sophistication, Parker and MacColl seem to have been incapable of coming to terms with working-class culture on its terms. They had a 'socialist-realist' prescription, they had access to the media, and they were going to *make* 'the miner' an 'epic figure' whether he liked it or not, in the manner of the real-life Russian hero, Stakhanov.

The cortex of the hour-long programme called 'The Big Hewer' was the song of the same name. In it, MacColl aggregated the various prodigious feats and mythical characteristics, and puts the resulting script into the mouth of the Myth himself, as impersonated by MacColl the singer. For all its self-deprecating manner, the song is a hymn to the horrors and the degradation of pitwork over the centuries. Taken cold, without the fine tune and the jaunty singing style, the text comes across as unselfconsciously moronic:

I've scrabbled and picked at the face where the roof is low, Go Down!
Crawled in the seams where only a mole could go, Go Down!
In the thin-cut seams I've ripped and reddied
Where even the rats are born bow-legged
Diggin' a hole, away in the coal, Go Down!

It has been argued that MacColl is simply restating the miner's own self-parody, that it is over-earnest breast-beating and almost patronizing to ask what happens to men's limbs in seams where rats have bow-legs. The song and the tales are simply expressions of the miner's self-mocking bravado. But then, what kind of a job is it which makes such a myth *necessary*? Just how much is that insistent 'Go Down!' of a refrain an echo of the material pressures which drive young men down the pits, and how much is it an exhortation, like the Coal Board's 1970s campaign slogan, 'It's a Man's Life in Mining'? Significantly, when Parker was faced by a girl student from a Barnsley mining family with the accusation that he was 'glorifying a shitty job', he had no reply. How could he? Men will feel ashamed at their own exploitation, whether they are paid £140 a week or not; and it is hardly the job of socialist intellectuals to shore up a self-image which mystifies the realities of pitwork. After all, the NCB pays advertising consultants to do that.

The closer we look, the more *The Big Hewer* is seen to reinforce the worst aspects of mining community bravado and solidarity. The whole text is ambivalent:

I'm the son of the son of the son of a collier's son, Go Down!
Coal dust flows in the veins where the blood should run, Go Down!

In the strict sense, and without meaning to be, the song is a parody of the pitmen's *self*-parody. What working miners use to fend off the full meaning of their own shitty job, MacColl and Parker have erected into a monolithic Myth. Of course, even in any future socialist state — certainly in the Eastern Bloc countries, which call themselves socialist — coal will have to go on being dug; but why should such work be the exclusive property of full-time pitmen, and why should not open-cast mining and automatic underground mining take over from flesh and blood workers more and more? Then again, what would be the role of intellectuals and media professionals in a genuinely socialist state? Would they be able to maintain the radical chic of being *avant-garde*, or would they, like the state, wither away as a social group? What happens to reformers when there is nothing to reform? Such questions are inevitably raised by the ambivalence of *The Big Hewer*. Like *Farewell to the Monty*, but in a much more fundamental way, MacColl's song and Parker's programme illustrate one of the key contradictions of petty-bourgeois radicalism, the recognition that society needs to be changed, and the simultaneous retreat from revolutionary politics.

'Close the Coalhouse Door' (lyrics on page 186)

Alex Glasgow's father worked for some years as a Gateshead pitman. Alex went to the local grammar school, and then to university, but for him, getting on did not mean getting out — out of Gateshead, or out of the commitment to working-class culture and politics. Musically, he followed the traditional post-war route, into the school choir, and then into a group of young singers who toured Tyneside, before going to Leeds, where he would sing and play at parties. After university he went to Germany, as an assistant English teacher; and he managed to get some recording work for educational programmes at Radio Bremen, so as to eke out his pay. This was in the mid 1950s, when Elvis Presley was coming to be known in Europe; and Glasgow once parodied the American singer's characteristic performance style to relieve the boring job of getting sound balance in the studio. The producer liked the parody, and recalling that he had taken the precaution of tape recording a well-known Hamburg band and its singer separately, some time before, asked the Englishman to sing the words over the band's version of a standard German song; a recording contract was made, Glasgow's song went to number 4 in the German Hit Parade, and was soon followed by another hit single. At this point — it being Christmas — Glasgow returned to Tyneside, losing his wallet on the way. In order to raise some cash he arranged to be interviewed on the BBC Home Service in

Close the Coalhouse Door

Close the coalhouse door, lad,
There's blood inside:
Blood from broken hands and feet,
Blood that's dried on pit-black meat,
Blood from hearts that know no beat;
Close the coalhouse door, lad,
There's blood inside.

Close the coalhouse door, lad,
There's bones inside:
Mangled, splintered piles of bones,
Buried 'neath a mile of stones,
Not a soul to hear the groans;
Close the coalhouse door, lad,
There's bones inside.

Close the coalhouse door, lad,
There's bairns inside:
Bairns that had no time to hide,
Bairns that saw the blackness slide,
Bairns beneath the mountainside;
Close the coalhouse door, lad,
There's bairns inside.

Close the coalhouse door, lad,
And stay outside:
Geordie's standin' at the dole,
And Mrs Jackson, like a fool,
Complains about the price of coal;
Close the coalhouse door, lad,
There's blood inside,
There's bones inside,
There's bairns inside,
So stay outside.

Words and music by Alex Glasgow 1968. ©1970 by Robbins Music Corp Ltd, 138-140 Charing Cross Road, London WC2.
Source: Songs of Alex Glasgow (LP Mawson & Wareham Music, Newcastle, MWM 1006, 1973). For its place in the play by Alan Plater, see *Close the Coalhouse Door* (Methuen, 1969); and for the full score, *Alex Glasgow: an anthology* (Robbins Music, 1971).

Newcastle, and from that initial contact came the opportunity to work as a freelance radio journalist.

In the late 1950s a programme called 'Voice of the People' (later changed to 'Voice of the North') was pioneering a new approach to radio journalism, using the new miniature tape recorders:

The tape-recorder was just beginning to be used for talking to people on park benches . . . but nobody was using it on a day-to-day basis.[63]

The consensus in the industry was still that 'You didn't talk to the ordinary man in the street about anything' because he was held to be 'inarticulate and rather stupid'.[64] Glasgow and his colleagues simply ignored the consensus, and gave regular access to radio to the thoughts, beliefs and attitudes of working men and women in north-east England. Unlike Parker and MacColl, however, the mediation was not the result of imposing a preconceived pattern on to working-class culture. Gradually, items from *Voice of the People* were fed into the national network, and began to appear on Jack DeManio's 'Today' programme. When Glasgow took to writing topical songs, at the instigation of his colleagues, they too were beamed to London for the national network; and eventually Glasgow was requested to produce songs directly for 'Today' at very short notice. He was well aware of the licence he was being allowed:

I liked it best when I was actually doing musical editorials. I was getting on comment that was not allowed any other way.[65]

His openly partisan songs gave news items a framework and a cutting edge quite at odds with the BBC's officially 'objective' ideology; but it wasn't until 1968, with his collaboration in the production of the stage-play, *Close the Coalhouse Door*, that Glasgow came to regard himself as more of a songwriter than a journalist. Only in such a context was it possible to do consistently, and at some length, what he liked doing best:

telling people back their own stories with my gloss on them, with my eyes . . . to make them more aware of the system they're in, who they are, what they are.[66]

Of course, the problems of being a committed socialist songwriter (or artist, or intellectual of any variety) are not magically solved by having working-class 'credentials'. The status of such people remains problematical in a class-based society. Crucially, what differentiates Glasgow from most other songwriters is his determined freelance status.

When the phone stops ringing, of course, there are problems. There have been times when it looked as though a more orthodox job was inevitable. But Glasgow has been sustained by his own talent and by a developing network of left-wing and radical artists, media professionals and members of what he terms the 'liberal bourgeoisie', as well as by a sizeable body of working-class militants. As a consequence, he has been able (so far) to keep himself remarkably free of the clutches of commercialism. If a BBC producer baulked at the words of a song he had chosen to sing, then Glasgow would not appear. If a folk club audience refused to allow him to sing his songs amidst quietness, then he would not come back. In this way, Glasgow is not on the market for a fee in the same way as a Handle or a MacColl. Hence the ridiculous amount of time which elapsed before his first LP, characteristically titled *Songs of Alex Glasgow*, was made available. He had to have complete control over the songs to be used, the number of musicians, the studio, the arrangements, the record sleeve, the lot, before he would get involved in the tacky commercial side of music. With this kind of autonomy, Glasgow is in no danger of retiring to the Bahamas, and he and his family have suffered frequently from spasms of financial insecurity. But he *is* able to do what almost all other major songwriters and singers cannot do: *speak his own mind*.

While he has put up with the frustrations brought about by a principled attitude towards commercialism, Glasgow also rejects the 'protest' mode, not simply because it has been appropriated in large measure by the commercial music industry, but because putting your conscience on your sleeve makes it too easy to be dismissed, however sincere you might be:

There's a Don McLean song, which is obviously, it seems to me, an early one. He's saying, what a terrible world this is, and the poor, and the rich, and it's disgusting, it's *absolutely disgusting*, that things should go on like this. And what he's telling you is what he thinks, and, yeah, yeah, you're quite right mate. Hem. Let's have the next track . . . .[67]

What Glasgow does is to efface his own personality as much as possible, in performance — deadpan face, 'correct' singing voice, spare guitar accompaniment more often than not, even a dark casual suit, in the best working-class traditions of being 'smart' at formal occasions. He places an enormous barb at the end of each song, digging into the listener's brain, niggling and irritating the unconverted, demanding attention from the most inveterate, liberal or armchair/taproom 'socialist'. More often than not the barb goes deeper in because of the relatively straight build-up which precedes it, softening up the audience, leading them into the ideological trap. There is no easy way to dismiss a Glasgow song. Even the most self-indulgent ones have a sharpness or a poignancy which compare favourably with the work of most contemporary British or North American songwriters.

Because of his open political commitment to working-class socialist politics, Alex Glasgow can do what very few other songwriters would dare do: he can criticize what he sees as reactionary traits *from inside* the working class. To him, the working class is no romantic, fetishized abstraction, somehow out there. The class is composed of individuals, not all of whom are heroes or heroines. Nor are those creations of the organized working class, the Trade Union Congress and the Labour Party, the twin seats of Righteousness. Like any other class, the working class has its traitors, its careerists, its lumpen elements; and above all else Glasgow aims his songs at the enemy within, the weeds and parasites of the labour movement. Next on his list is the set of 'commonsense' contradictions in social life, the elements of bourgeois ideology which have penetrated working-class culture. Only rarely does he hit the easy targets — the Queen, the RSPCA, populist Tories, Labour MPs.

The contrast with the work of Handle and MacColl is strikingly obvious in a song like Glasgow's *Close the Coalhouse Door*. While the folk singers lament a shut pit and glorify a degrading job, this son of a pitman takes it as read that the only good pit is a dead one:

Close the coalhouse door, lad
There's blood inside
There's bones inside
There's bairns inside
So stay outside.

When 'Mrs Jackson' complains about 'the price of coal' (a phrase that was the song's first title), she is unambiguously labelled as a *fool* for her blinkered ignorance. Glasgow puts her and her kind in their place, as would any other member of a pitworker's family. Also characteristic of genuine working-class culture is the way in which the song's real pathos is in no way self-indulgent. If anything, the pain and horror are understated. Though families were decimated, children sent down pits, and countless thousands maimed in Britain's coal industry, Glasgow sees pitworkers not as heroes but as *victims*. It isn't sentiment or nostalgia which underpins this song, but a restrained *anger*. And whatever might be the cultural losses — the warmth of the pit-village people, the comradeship of the mine — the only real solution for the price that pitmen and their families have paid for other people's coal, other people's comfort and profit, is to close the coalhouse doors for good, and the pits which supply them. Better the loss of the tight-knit community, which was in any case the product of a kind of siege mentality, better the stringencies of being on the dole, than the loss of more lives.

By writing and singing such songs — in clubs, on the radio or television, at concerts, or for workers occupying a factory — Glasgow has established a relationship with organized workers that is solid and based on mutual understanding and respect. Until relatively recently he has had to content himself with a small regular audience: but since the success of the play *Coalhouse*, then of Glasgow's own play about Joe Wilson, the Tyneside concert hall singer of the 1860s and 1870s, he has managed to establish himself quite firmly in the north-east as both songwriter and playwright. When *Coalhouse* was re-run at Newcastle University Theatre, the members of Ashington Working Men's Club (largely miners) booked every seat for one of the performances. Though *Joe Lives* started in a studio theatre, its very success forced a reluctant management to move it to the main auditorium. Though he may once have sung at a one night stand in South Wales to a handful of people, he is now in demand for large-scale Anti Nazi League concerts up and down the country. The phone rings more regularly than it did: Alex Glasgow's problem, now, is to resist commercial blandishments on a much larger scale than ever before. But because of the consistent work put in by him (and dozens of others like him) it seems more than likely that he and they will be able to survive.

Part Three
Approaches

11 Song and history

We have already seen some analysis of the problems of using so-called folksongs as material for historical study. What can be done on a larger canvas, as part of the study of the making of the north-east working class, can be seen in the present writer's forthcoming *Hammer and Hand*. For present purposes, we can usefully examine another cultural 'thread', the songs made and used in Lancashire over the period of the Industrial Revolution. We will meet much the same kinds of problems as we did in our study of pitmen and pitwork, but we will be less able to solve them simply because the research has yet to be done on Lancashire popular/working-class culture in any systematic way. Apart from the largely unexplored bodies of broadside songs in Preston Library, Cambridge University Library, and elsewhere, we are left with Harland and Wilkinson's *Ballads and Songs of Lancashire*, the work of the 'dialect' poets, the occasional piece collected by people like Lloyd and MacColl, and the repertoires of contemporary singers like Harry Boardman, the Oldham Tinkers, Bernard Wrigley and Mike Harding, most of whom owe an enormous debt to the collecting and research work of one man, Paul Graney. The resistance to theory, and to the systematic research work which theory demands, is still one of the leading characteristics of 'folklorists', amateur and professional alike; so if the following account provides more questions than answers, suggests more than it affirms, it is hoped that the reader will be encouraged to do the groundwork which might produce answers to those questions.

Working people in industrial Lancashire seem to have been better at producing poetry than song. And while there does appear to have been a considerable overlap in the audiences for recitations and song, especially in the middle and later nineteenth century, in pre-industrial times we can be fairly certain that song, especially broadside song, was the dominant literary form current amongst working people, above all in the towns. One of the earliest broadside successes was *Jone O' Grinfilt's Ramble* (lyrics on page 194), a piece known to have been a major popular 'hit' in the early 1790s, and one which might have

Jone O'Grinfilt's Ramble

Says Jone to his woife on a whot summer's day,
"Aw'm resolvt i' Grinfilt no lunger to stay;
For aw'll goo to Owdham os fast os aw can,
So fare thee weel Grinfilt, an' fare thee weel Nan;
    For a sodger aw'll be, an' brave Owdham aw'll see,
    An' aw'll ha'e a battle wi' th' French."

"Dear Jone", said eawr Nan, un' hoo bitterly cried,
"Wilt be one o' th' foote, or theaw meons for t' ride?"
"Ods eawns! wench, aw'll ride oather ass or a mule,
Ere aw'll keawr i' Grinfilt os black os th' owd dule,
    Booath clemmin', un' starvin', un' never a fardin',
    It 'ud welly drive ony mon mad."

"Ay, Jone, sin' we coom i' Grinfilt for t' dwell.
Wey'n had mony a bare meal, aw con vara weel tell."
"Bare meal, ecod! ay, that aw vara weel know,
There's bin two days this wick 'ot wey'n had nowt at o';
    Aw'm vara near sided, afore aw'll abide it,
    Aw'll feight oather Spanish or French."

Then says my Noant Marget, "Ah! Jone, theaw'rt so whot,
Aw'd ne'er go to Owdham, boh i' Englond aw'd stop."
"It matters nowt, Madge, for to Owdham aw'll goo,
Aw'st ne'er clem to deeoth, both sumbry (somebody) shall know:
    Furst Frenchmon aw find, aw'll tell him meh mind,
    Un' if he'll naw feight, he shall run."

Then deawn th' broo aw coom, for weh livent at top,
Aw thowt aw'd raich Owdham ere ever aw stop;
Ecod! heaw they staret when aw getten to th' Mumps,
Meh own hat i' my hont, un' meh clogs full o' stumps;
    Boh aw soon towd 'um, aw're gooin' to Owdham,
    Un' aw'd ha'e a battle wi' th' French.

Aw kept eendway thro' th' lone, un' to Owdham aw went,
Aw ax'd a recruit if they'd made up their keawnt?
"Nowe, nowe, honest lad" (for he tawked like a king),
"Goo wi' meh thro' th' street, un' thee aw will bring

Wheere, if theaw'rt willin', theaw may ha'e a shillin'."
Ecod! aw thowt this wuz rare news.

He browt meh to th' pleck, where they measurn their height,
Un' if they bin reight, there's nowt said abeawt weight;
Aw ratched me un' stretch'd meh, un' never did flinch:
Says th' mon, "Aw believe theawr't meh lad to an inch."
Aw thowt this'll do; aw'st ha'e guineas enoo'.
Ecod! Owdham, brave Owdham for me.

So fare thee weel, Grinfilt, a soger aw'm made:
Aw getten new shoon, un' a rare cockade;
Aw'll feight for Owd England os hard os aw con,
Oather French, Dutch, or Spanish, to me it's o' one;
Aw'll mak' 'em to stare, like a new started hare,
Un' aw'll tell 'em fro' Owdham aw coom.

Source: J. Harland and T.T. Wilkinson, *Ballads and Songs of Lancashire* (Manchester, 1882), p. 162. For a song version, see The Critics Group LP, *Waterloo–Peterloo*, Argo DA86 (1968).

dated from an earlier period. According to Harland and Wilkinson, 'more copies' of this song 'have been sold among the rural population of Lancashire than of any other known song.' Samuel Bamford recalled that

The song took amazingly. It was war time; volunteering was all in vogue then; and he remembers standing at the bottom of Miller Street, in Manchester, with a cockade in his hat, and viewing with surprise the almost rage with which the very indifferent verses were purchased by a crowd that stood around a little old-fashioned fellow, with a withered leg, who, leaning on a crutch, with a countenance full of quaint humour, and a speech of the perfect dialect of the county, sang the song, and collected the halfpence as quickly as he could distribute it.[1]

This broadside singer was later questioned as to the authorship of the song, and claimed that it was composed

by Joseph Lees, a weaver residing at Glodwick, near Oldham, and himself – Joseph Coupe – who at the time of its composition was a barber, tooth-drawer, blood-letter, warper, spinner, carder, twiner, stubber, and rhymester, residing at Oldham. He said they were both in a terrible predicament, without drink, or money to procure any, after having been drinking all night. They had been at Manchester to see the

play, and were returning to Oldham the day following; when, in order
to raise the wind, they agreed to compose a song, to be sung at certain
public-houses on the road where they supposed it would be likely to
take, and procure them what they wanted, the means for prolonging
their dissipation. A storm came on, and they sheltered under a hedge,
and the first verse of the song was composed by him [Coupe] in that
situation. Lees composed the next verse; and they continued composing
verse and verse until the song was finished as afterwards printed. But
it took them three days to complete it. They then 'put it i' th' press;'
and he said, 'We met ha' bin worth mony a hunthert peawnd, iv widdin
ha' sense to ta' care o' th' brass.'[2]

Popularity of origin and of reception is, therefore, clear. The broadside
printers of the later eighteenth century were an essential component of
urban, literate culture, producing children's books, schoolbooks, and
chapbooks for working people in town and country alike.[3] Sometimes,
it is true, they were called into service in the interests of the well-to-do,
especially at election times; but if Joseph Coupe's testimony is even
close to the truth it indicates that such was the most likely provenance
of a song like *Jone O'Grinfilt's Ramble*.

To gain acceptance with a Manchester street audience, in pubs on
the Oldham Road, and amongst 'the rural population of Lancashire',
this song must have articulated feelings and values which lay at the
heart of working people's culture. And the kernel of the song is the
economic necessity which drives a 'country' worker like Jone into an
army still reliant on batches of pressed men, convicted and unconvicted
criminals. If we paid attention to the observations of well-heeled
outsiders, we would remain ignorant of the plight of people who
(for all the possible poetic licence) languished in misery like Jone and
Nan.[4] On the other hand, working people *would* recognize the reality
which underpinned Jone's existence:

Booath clemmin', un' starvin', un' never a fardin',
It 'ud welly drive ony mon mad.

The two days without food, the inability to meet the weight require-
ments demanded by King's Regulations (and the fact that no recruiting
sergeant could afford to implement them to the letter if he wanted to
make up his quota in Oldham), the getting of not only a shilling but
'new shoon' – these apparently gratuitous details lie at the heart of the
song's potency. True, Jone is allowed to present himself as an impres-
sionable young man, with a fancy for trivia like the 'rare cockade'.
True, also, he appears to have been sucked in by the promise of booty
and 'guineas enoo' '. But underneath the uniform of this apparently
mindless, flag-waving, Frenchman-hating 'yokel' is the overridingly self-

conscious determination that 'Aw'st ne'er clem to deeoth, both sumbry [somebody] shall know . . . .'

Jone is a survivor:

Aw'll feight for Owd Englond os hard os aw con,
Oather French, Dutch, or Spanish, to me it's o' one —

who is prepared to put himself into uniform, and to take what he can get, so as to come back to 'brave Owdham' in better fettle.

Even better evidence than the existence of large broadside sales for the song's genuine popularity is the way in which *Jone O'Grinfilt's Ramble* entered South Lancashire workers' culture, and was developed into all but mythical status by sequel after sequel.[5] In just such a manner was the figure of 'Bob Cranky' — the allegedly archetypal pitman — argued over in the north-east.[6] The point was that both Jone and Bob were figures who represented some aspects of weavers and pitmen; but whereas Bob was the creation of a bunch of petty bourgeois song-writers in Newcastle social clubs, and in some measure symbolized the fear and resentment of such people at the temporary affluence and vitality of their pit-village cousins,[7] Jone seems to have been closer to the hearts of workers in town and country, whatever the satirical intentions of Lees and Coupe, and however reassuring the song might have been to the self-esteem of the educated and better-off, those who *needed* the 'dialect' written down for them (Lees is supposed to have been a schoolteacher). Besides, it was not to be long before the production and dissemination of songs about Jone were turned to good purpose by self-consciously working-class writers, singers and audiences, after what appears to have been a false start by jacobins.[8]

From this brief analysis of one song we can generate several areas of research. Before John Foster's careful study of Oldham industry and politics we had remarkably little systematic research available on the workers' culture of pre-industrial and early industrial Lancashire. Even now, we know all too little about the informal and formal institutional culture of the embryo working-class in this part of England — about the broadside and chapbook printers, the amateur and professional entertainers in town and country, the pubs, the fairs, the race-meetings, or about the pattern of leisure time activity. Foster has shown the wealth of material which exists. Perhaps we will eventually find as much as we know to be available for north-east England. Now, individual researchers are beginning to produce studies on which to build a systematic analysis of the struggles in the labour movement. What is lacking, however, outside the work of Edward Thompson and John Foster, is a *synthesizing* study of popular and working-class culture in general in this vitally important industrial region. So far, characteristically, only the later 'dialect' poets have been studied at all thoroughly, chiefly by academics concerned with literature, or by folklorists.[9] Historians have fought shy of the very real problems of tackling literary evidence alongside population figures or units of production, and tend to consign verse and song to the position of a chapter heading or a footnote, thereby missing the opportunity of helping reconstruct the totality of working-class culture or pre-industrial worker's culture.

If we move on to *The Bury New Loom* (lyrics on page 199), however, we can begin to sketch in some of the detail surrounding the transitional culture of an industrializing economy, and to make better founded assumptions about the ways in which that culture was being changed, about how the industrialization was being perceived and felt by the majority of people *on the receiving end*. Bert Lloyd tells us that the song was 'first printed on a broadside by Swindells of Manchester in 1804, and subsequently reissued over and over again by Shelmerdine'.[10] We do not know of any author, but we can be sure that repeated reprinting indicates at the very least some penetration of the working-class audience, and this at a time when the handloom weaving trade had begun to be racked by periodic crises, but had not yet entered the long, slow decline that characterized the post-war years. On the other hand, the discipline of the factory bell is not far off ' at Bolton I must be by noon'[11] – and the use of technical terms from the loom indicates not just a playfulness or a new-fangledness on the part of the singer, but something like a fetishistic attitude towards the machinery.[12] Taken one way, the song is pure male fantasy, an elaborate 'dirty joke';[13] taken another, it is the product of insecurity, sung by a stationary weaver who has lost whatever mobility he might once have had, in the mixed economy that preceded the widespread use of handlooms in the Lancashire towns and villages.

Of course, *The Bury New Loom* comes from a long line of pre-industrial songs which celebrate sexuality in terms of the tools of a trade. But what separates this song from, say *A Blacksmith Courted Me*,[14] is that the object of the song is not the phallic 'hammer' of the man, but an apparently precocious young woman who is described totally in terms of an extended mechanical metaphor. It is as though the (presumably male) singer were having a love affair with the loom itself, fantasizing himself 'out' of his immobility. By extension the ineluctable rhythm of the loom – particularly if the weaver has to work under the pressure of cutthroat piece-rates – may be taken as symbolic of an insatiable sexual appetite; and, no matter how clever the use of the loom image, we have to remember that, underlying the

The Bury New Loom

As I walked between Bolton and Bury, 'twas on a moonshiny night,
I met with a buxom young weaver whose company gave me delight.
She says: Young fellow, come tell me if your level and rule are in tune.
Come, give me an answer correct, can you get up and square my new loom?

I said: My dear lassie, believe me, I am a good joiner by trade,
And many a good loom and shuttle before in my time I have made.
Your short lams and jacks and long lams I quickly put them in tune.
My rule is now in good order to get up and square up a new loom.

She took me and showed me her loom, the down on her warp did appear.
The lam jacks and healds put in motion, I levelled her loom to a hair.
My shuttle ran well in her lathe, my tread it worked up and down,
My level stood close to her breast-bone, the time I was squaring her loom.

The cords of my lam jacks and treadles at length they began to give way.
The bobbin I had in my shuttle, the weft in it no longer would stay.
Her lathe it went bang to and fro, my main treadle it still kept in tune.
My pickers went nicketty-nack all the time I was reiving her loom.

My shuttle it still kept in motion, her lams she worked well up and down.
The weight in her rods they did tremble; she said she would weave a new gown.
My strength now began for to fail me. I said: It's now right to a hair.
She turned up her eyes and said: Tommy, my loom you have got pretty square.

But when her foreloom post she let go, it flew out of order again.
She cried: Bring your rule and your level and help me to square it again.
I said: My dear lassie, I'm sorry, at Bolton I must be by noon,
But when that I come back this way, I will square up your jerry hand-loom.

Source: Lloyd, *Folk Song in England* (1967), p. 320; see also *Deep Lancashire*
LP Topic 12T188 (1968).

whole encounter, is an essentially mechanistic mentality. From the joke of the first exchange, through the tortuous verses, to the man's final ejaculation, the whole story is one of a jocular reduction of man and woman alike to mere instrumentality. Above all, the woman remains unsatisfied, and the man feels strongly his own inadequacy. The humour can so easily go sour, like contemporary jokes about itinerant plumbers, milkmen or gasmen; and we are left to ponder whether the song is the product of most men's loss of autonomy at work (transformed into an even more sensitive area of human activity), or whether, simply, it is a tap-room story made into verse. Until we know more about who bought and used the song, or who wrote it and why, we cannot be sure which set of attitudes predominated.

With *Hand Loom v Power Loom* (lyrics on page 201), however, we have entered the period of factory building and factory work with a vengeance.[15] Its likely author was John Grimshaw, nick-named 'Common', who lived at Gorton near Manchester, and it probably dates from the early 1810s, when steam-driven factories were something of a novelty. It wasn't until the years of post-war depression, and especially the 1820s, that weaving was beginning to become predominantly mechanized. So the tone of this song is a mixture of fatalism — 'they're going to weave by steam' — and of resistance. Technical problems with weaving technology prevented its wholesale application in factories. Added to this was the ability of continental workers to drive down the piece-rate prices of handloom weavers in Lancashire using machine-spun thread.[16] Certainly, we can feel the pinch in this song, as the handloom weaver begins to recognize the unequalness of the contest between handloom and power-loom, and turns to face the new working and social relations brought about by the factory system. Time discipline, job specialization, and a whole set of minute regulations governing the speed, quality and method of work were the consequence of relatively capital-intensive enterprise. From a position of some auto-nomy, the handloom weaver has to adapt to one of all but complete subjection to the capitalist's system. No longer does he own and control the means of production. No longer can he decide when to work and when to relax. No longer is he able to take positive pride in his work. Instead, he works for wages on another man's machine; goes to work in a mill perhaps miles from his home in order to support his family: and is obliged to look on his work in an almost purely negative way by the fines, and by the system of overlookers, the lackeys of 'the master'.

It is impossible to underestimate the psychological and social (as well as economic) upheaval that this form of industrialization brought about. In its own tentative way, *Hand Loom v Power Loom* illustrates how these changes were perceived from just outside the factory gate. There is already, a strong feeling of resentment, of Us and Them; and there is an ambivalence about the final verse which cannot be discounted:

So, come all you cotton weavers, you must rise up very soon,
For you must work in factories from morning until noon:
You musn't walk in your garden for two or three hours a-day,
For you must stand at their command, and keep your shuttles in play.

Hand Loom v Power Loom

Come all you cotton weavers, your looms you may pull down;
You must get employed in factories, in country or in town,
For our cotton masters have found out a wonderful new scheme,
These calico goods now wove by hand they're going to weave by steam.

In comes the gruff o'erlooker, or the master will attend;
It's "You must find another shop, or quickly you must mend;
For such work as this will never do; so now I'll tell you plain,
We must have good pincop-spinning, or we ne'er can weave by steam."

There's sow-makers and dressers and some are making warps;
These poor pincop-spinners they must mind their flats and sharps,
For if an end slips under, as sometimes perchance it may,
They'll daub you down in black and white, and you've a shilling to pay.

In comes the surly winder, her cops they are all marr'd:
"They are all snarls, and soft, bad ends; for I've roved off many a yard;
I'm sure I'll tell the master, or the joss, when he comes in:"
They'll daub you down, and you must pay; – so money comes rolling in.

The weavers' turn will next come on, for they must not escape,
To enlarge the masters' fortunes they are fined in every shape.
For thin places, or bad edges, a go, or else a float,
They'll daub you down, and you must pay threepence, or else a groat.

If you go into a loom-shop, where there's three or four pair of looms,
They all are standing empty, incumbrances of the rooms;
And if you ask the reason why, the old mother will tell you plain,
"My daughters have forsaken them, and gone to weave by steam."

So come all you cotton-weavers, you must rise up very soon,
For you must work in factories from morning until noon:
You mustn't walk in your garden for two or three hours a-day,
For you must stand at their command, and keep your shuttles in play.

Source: Harland and Wilkinson, p. 188. See also The Critics Group LP, *Waterloo-Peterloo*, Argo DA86 (1968).

The factory, after all, is seen as a prison: 'The weavers' turn will next come on, for they must not escape.' Gruffness and surliness, threats and tale-telling, these are singled out as the chief characteristics of the experience of factory work. It is both possible and necessary to identify those who side with the owner, in order to survive; for when all that a person has to sell is his or her labour-power, and the capitalist owns not only the yarn but the loom too, any bargain is necessarily one-sided: '"You must find another shop, or quickly you must mend . . . ." ' On the other hand, particularly at the outset, what responses other than verbal resentment and behind-hand muttering were possible in this situation, especially in a trade where collective organization had been limited, and in a country where political oppression was becoming rife? Does that 'rise up' mean, simply, get out of bed; or is it deliberately ambiguous, a cautious call to unionize − or even to insurrection? Is the sense of Us and Them mature enough to signify *class* consciousness, or is the song intended to function as a safety valve for frustrations and humiliation? Clearly, its significance and function amongst working weavers would depend entirely on who sang it, when and where, and on the response of other workers. But at the very least we can get from the song a strong sense of the weavers' understanding of their own alienated labour. If the song had any acceptance in the working communities of Gorton, Oldham or Bolton, we can say with some assurance that a section at least of the embryo working class had come to face up to their own subjection, recognized the broader effects of the de-skilling of their work, and so knew the task that lay ahead for themselves and their community at large, economically and politically.

Jone O' Grinfilt Junior (lyrics on page 203) indicates how the hand-loom weaver's lot had worsened dramatically after 1815, and how, too, working men had appropriated the 'Jone' of earlier, less sympathetic songs, so as to express more directly their own views.[17] Interestingly, this reappropriation of 'Jone' was much too strong meat for liberal apologists like Mrs Gaskell, later in the century;[18] and Harland and Wilkinson could not resist a pious comment on the alleged improvidence of the weavers in times of prosperity:

. . . just after the battle of Waterloo, when times were bad . . . hand-loom weavers' wages fell from about £3 to a guinea or 25s a week − i.e. for three or four days' work, for then weavers could seldom be induced to work on Monday, Tuesday, or often on Wednesday, these days being devoted to recreations produced with high wages.[19]

But whereas, in the north-east, the good years of 1800-4 had given rise to the satirical 'Bob Cranky' figure, in Lancashire, a decade later, the archetypal 'Jone O' Grinfilt' had given birth to offspring of a much more proletarian kind. In the post-war economic crises, as under-

Jone O'Grinfilt Junior

Aw'm a poor cotton-wayver, as money a one knaws,
Aw've nowt t'ate i' the 'heawse, un' aw've worn eawt my cloas,
You'd hardly gie sixpence fur o'aw've got on,
Meh clogs ur' booath baws'n, un' stockings aw've none;
 Yo'd think it wur hard, to be sent into th'ward
 To clem un' do best 'ot yo' con.

Eawr parish-church pa'son's kept tellin' us lung,
We'st see better toimes, if aw'd but howd my tung;
Aw've howden my tung, till aw con hardly draw breoth
Aw think i' my heart he meons t' clem me to deoth:
 Aw knaw he lives weel, we' backbitin' the de'il,
 Bur he never pick'd o'er in his loife.

Wey tooart on six week, thinkin' aich day wur th'last,
Wey tarried un'shifted, till neaw wey're quite fast;
Wey liv't upo' nettles, whoile nettles were good,
Un' Wayterloo porritch wur' th' best o' us food;
 Aw'm tellin' yo' true, aw con foind foak enoo,
 Thot're livin' no better nur me.

Neaw, owd Bill o' Dan's sent bailies one day,
Fur t' shop scoar aw'd ow'd him, 'ot aw couldn't pay;
Bur he're just to lat, fur owd Bill o' Bent,
Had sent tit un'cart, un'ta'en t' goods fur t' rent;
 They laft nowt bur a stoo' 'ot're seeots for two:
 Un' on it keawrt Karget un' me.

The bailies sceawlt reawnd os sly os a meawse,
When they seedn o' things wur ta'en eawt o' the heawse;
Un t' one says to th' tother, "O's gone, theaw may see."
Aw said "Never fret lads, you're welcome ta'e me."
 They made no moor ado, bur nipt up th' owd stoo',
 Un' wey booath leeten swack upon th' flags.

Aw geet howd o' eawr Marget, for hoo're strucken sick,
Hoo said, hoo'd ne'er had sich a bang sin' hoo're wick,
The bailies sceawrt off, wi' th' owd stoo' on their back,
Un they wouldn't ha'e caret if they'd brokken her neck.
 They'rn so mad at own Bent, 'cos he'd ta'en goods fur rent,
 Till they'rn ready to flee us alive.

Aw said to eawr Marget, as wey lien upon th' floor,
"Wey ne'er shall be lower i' this wo'ald, aw'm sure,
Fur if wey mun alter, aw'm sure wey mun mend,
Fur aw think i' my heart wey're booath at fur end,
*   Fur mayt wey han none, nur no looms to wayve on,*
*   Ecod! th' looms are as well lost as fun".*

My piece wur cheeont off, un' aw took it him back;
Aw hardly durst spake, mester looked so black:
He said, "Yo're o'erpaid last toime 'ot you coom."
Aw said, "If awr'wur', 'twui wi' wayving beawt loom;
*   Un i' t' moind 'ot aw'm in, aw'st ne'er pick e'er again,*
*   For aw've wooven mysel' to th' fur end."*

So aw coom eawt o' th' wareheawse, un' laft him chew that,
When aw thowt 'ot o' things, aw're so vext that aw swat;
Fur to think aw mun warch, to keep him un' o' th' set,
O' th' days o' my loife, un' then dee i' the'r debt:
*   But aw'll give o'er this trade, un work wi' a spade,*
*   Or goo un' break stone upo' th' road.*

Eawr Marget declares, if hoo'd clooas to put on,
Hoo'd go up to Lunnun to see the great mon;
Un' if thins did no' awter, when theere hoo had been,
Hoo says hoo'd begin, un' feight blood up to th' e'en,
*   Hoo's nout agen th' king, bur hoo loikes a fair thing,*
*   Un' hoo says hoo con tell when hoo's hurt.*

Source: Harland and Wilkinson, p. 169. For a related text, see *The Iron Muse*
LP Topic 12T86 (1956 and later reissues).

employment became a curse rather than a blessing, and as factory
wages came to dominate household finances (at least, for those who
were not weavers), the communities of handloom weavers came to be
driven into a long-drawn-out phase of self-exploitation which was to
end with the extinction of their trade. This song is a sardonic account
of the misery of the process, combined with a residual pride, and a
determination to hang on to the status of the self-employed as long as
humanly possible, bailiffs notwithstanding.

Though it was printed by Harland and Wilkinson in a 'phonetic'
version, the song was said to have been 'taken down from the singing
of an old hand-loom weaver at Droylesden', and, like *Hand-Loom v*

Power-Loom, need not have been *composed* in 'dialect'.[20] On the other hand, both songs show that handloom weavers had come to recognize what they were up against, whether in the form of overlookers or bailiffs, parsons or masters. The connections between their degradation and the economic system which led to it are seen clearly enough:

Fur to think aw mun warch, to keep him un' o' th' set,
O' th' days o' my loife, un' then dee i' the'r debt:
   But aw'll give o'er this trade, un work wi' a spade,
   Or goo un' break stone upo' th' road.

What is more (and though the text is ambiguous), it seems that Jone's wife is prepared to reject not only the screwing-down of the putter-out, but the factory too, and, if need be, the established order of society:

Eawr Marget declares, if hoo'd clooas to put on,
Hoo'd go up to Lunnun to see the great mon;
Un' if things did no' awter, when theere hoo had been,
Hoo says hoo'd begin, un' feight blood up to th' e'en,
   Hoo's nout agen th' king, bur hoo loikes a fair thing,
   Un' hoo says hoo con tell when hoo's hurt.

The choice was now so stark — the factory or the workhouse — and the differences so minimal, that even the breaking of stone in the open air is preferred to the miseries of the mill.[21] Doubtless, this 'very popular song'[22] would function as a safety valve too, amongst those who were not really all that sorry that they had no 'clooas to put on' to present themselves at court. But Harland and Wilkinson also tell us that 'the three last lines have become "household words" in industrial Lancashire',[23] showing that the logic of Marget's solution was largely supported by many workers in the post-war Radical agitation.[24]

Most of the Radical propaganda in the north-west seems to have been published in the forms of placards, banners, leaflets, pamphlets and books. If there was a body of overtly political song from the period 1815-1830, it seems to have been badly preserved. For example, only a fragment of a song about the Peterloo massacre is now extant:

With Henry Hunt we'll go, we'll go,
   With Henry Hunt we'll go;
We'll raise the cap of liberty,
   In spite of Nadin Joe.[25]

Hunt was one of the middle-class Radical orators; Nadin was Deputy Constable of Manchester; and the 'cap of liberty' raised by the supporters of the former was like a red rag to the shopkeepers in

Nadin's yeoman cavalry, with all the associations of revolutionary France that it carried. Verses — even sets of verses — have been 'discovered' since Harland and Wilkinson's time; but most of them bear unmistakable marks of recent composition. All we can glean from the original fragment is that it was probably written by a member of the liberal petty bourgeoisie, or by a worker who had imbibed the ideology of that class. Certainly, it expresses great confidence in Hunt's leadership; yet it is a matter of recorded history how the likes of Hunt built their movement on the backs of workers, only to ditch them once they had secured the vote for the property-owning minority. In a sense, whereas 'Eawr Marget' in *Jone O' Grinfilt Junior* may be taken to speak for the strong solution, her weaver husband, and the proletarian singers of this chorus, seem to articulate the retreat into respectable agitation, religious nonconformity and 'moral force' ideology in general, as though we were being given an account of an ideological crisis as it might have taken place in the working community, even within one household.[26] But then what with the holes in the antiquarian records, and the mediations of the antiquarians and the folklorists, not to mention those of contemporary folk entertainers, we have a considerable amount of work to do of a straightforwardly scholarly nature before we can be at all sure that the nuances we think we can see in a particular text were there from the beginning. Sometimes, the best we can do is to decode the mediations from text to text, in an effort to situate the mediators, and we have to accept that the search for an 'original' text will remain problematical.[27]

As recent research on north-east popular culture has shown, above all in the editing work of John Bell and Thomas Allan,[28] it would be thoroughly foolish to believe that people like Harland and Wilkinson have given us a representative selection of popular songs that were available to them. Even so, the inclusion of a piece like *The Hand-Loom Weavers' Lament* (lyrics on page 207) indicates that there was a much more strident element in embryo working-class culture, and one which was too obvious to be ignored, particularly during the 1820s, before the major period of Chartism.[29] It is as though Jone O' Grinfilt had carried his analysis of the new economic order just that bit further. His God is now much more the Old Testament God of battles and retribution; and the tone of his song is much more ambivalent, alternating between honest indignation and outright threats. Marget, if you like, was winning the argument:

The Hand-Loom Weavers' Lament

You gentlemen and tradesmen, that ride about at will,
Look down on these poor people; it's enough to make you crill;
Look down on these poor people, as you ride up and down,
I think there is a God above will bring your pride quite down.
  Chorus:
  You tyrants of England, your race may soon be run,
  You may be brought unto account for what you've sorely done.

You pull down our wages, shamefully to tell;
You go into the markets, and say you cannot sell;
And when that we do ask you when these bad times will mend,
You quickly give an answer, "When the wars are at an end."

When we look on our poor children, it grieves our hearts full sore,
Their clothing it is worn to rags, while we can get no more,
With little in their bellies, they to their work must go,
Whilst yours do dress as manky as monkeys in a show.

You go to church on Sundays, I'm sure it's nought but pride,
There can be no religion where humanity's thrown aside;
If there be a place in heaven, as there is in the Exchange,
Our poor souls must not come near there; like lost sheep they must range.

With the choicest of strong dainties your tables overspread,
With good ale and strong brandy, to make your faces red;
You call'd a set of visitors – it is your whole delight –
And you lay your heads together to make our faces white.

You say that Bonyparty he's been the spoil of all,
And that we have got reason to pray for his downfall;
Now Bonyparty's dead and gone, and it is plainly shown
That we have bigger tyrants in Boneys of our own.

And now, my lads, for to conclude, it's time to make an end;
Let's see if we can form a plan that these bad times may mend;
Then give us our old prices, as we have had before,
And we can live in happiness, and rub off the old score.

Source: Harland and Wilkinson, p. 193. See also *Deep Lancashire* LP Topic
12T188 (1968).

You gentleman and tradesmen, that ride about at will,
Look down on these poor people; it's enough to make you crill;
Look down on these poor people, as you ride up and down,
I think there is a God above will bring your pride quite down.
     You tyrants of England, your race may soon be run,
     You may be brought unto account for what you've sorely done.

The whole public face of capitalism is seen to be shot through with
hypocrisy. First they blamed the war, then Bonaparte in person; but
the handloom weavers are no longer to be duped:

Now Bonyparty's dead and gone, and it is plainly shown
That we have bigger tyrants in Boneys of our own.

But then, on the brink of the strong solution of open class conflict,
the song draws back into a form of wish-fulfilling fantasy. The weaver
asks for 'our old prices', and promises to 'live in happiness, and rub off
the old score'. True, there seems to be less real confidence in a conversion of cut-throat capitalists than we saw in William Hornsby's *New
Song*; but there is still the appeal to the masters' better nature, the hope
of moral conversion. However understandable the song's wish to draw
back from class warfare, we have to admit, with benefit of hindsight,
that as a solution to the logic of industrialization and capital concentration, the *Lament* is strikingly inane.

     We could say that this song illustrates the last vestiges of ideological
delusion on the part of miserable workers, the tenaciousness of ideas
of Reason and Christianity in the face of *laissez-faire* ideology. The
best that the singer can hope for is that the 'bad times' will 'mend',
rather like the weather, presumably, thus enabling those who were
visibly 'tyrants' to undergo spiritual regeneration, and to stop a system
which profited the few at the same time as it pinched and made white
the faces of the majority. In a real sense, then, this song illustrates
the dilemma faced by intelligent workers who saw their economic
and social life crumbling before their eyes, piecemeal, perhaps over a
period as long as thirty years. But if we choose to point up their con-

fusion, we have to remember that no real political solution to their problems was available until the Chartists began to establish a genuinely working-class movement, and that even then (in the absence of a fully worked-out theory of capitalism and its antidote, revolutionary socialism) the culture and ideology of the labour movement and working class was to remain riddled with internal contradictions.

The later history of Lancashire song and verse illustrates the general tenacity of the ideological confusion of the early nineteenth century. *The Shurat Weaver's Song*, written by Samuel Laycock, in the 1860s implores the Yankees to stop blockading the southern cotton ports, so that Lancashire weavers can get back to using better quality raw material, even though this would mean that slavery of a more obvious kind would continue in America.[30] Similarly, Benjamin Brierley's *Weaver of Wellbrook* seems to rejoice in the class system (lyrics on page 210), and disguises mindless conservatism in a thick layer of pawky humour, and thoroughly irrational self-congratulation.[31] Martha Vicinus has begun the analysis of the culture of these later writers, most of whom (in the north-west at any rate) came to be distanced from the realities of the shop floor, and one way or another parted company with working-class consciousness.[32] In the north-east, by way of a parallel, Joseph Skipsey followed one of the available routes out of the pit, and was caught up and patronized by middle-class literateurs.[33] There, too, Thomas Burt followed the formal political path out of the working class, into Parliament, and then on to the Privy Council as a respected Liberal.[34] The trajectories of such men, when they are mapped out by research, will help compose a history and a pathology of the ideology of 'getting on' and getting out. About the culture and achievements of working-class people inside the working-class community, of course, such an analysis will tell us little enough, and that only by negation.

The Weaver of Wellbrook

Yo gentlemen o with you heawnds an' yor parks,
    Yo may gamble an' sport till yo dee;
Bo a quiet heawse nook, – a good wife an' a book,
    Is mooar to the likins o' me-e.

    Wi' mi pickers an' pins,
    An' mi wellers to th' shins;
Mi linderins, shuttle, and yealdhook;
    Mi treddles an' sticks,
    Mi weight-ropes an' bricks;
What a life! said the wayver o' Wellbrook.

Aw care no' for titles, nor heawses, nor lond;
    Owd Jones' a name fittin' for me;
An' gie me a thatch wi' a wooden dur latch,
    An' six feet o' greawnd when aw de-e. Etc.

Some folk liken t' stuff their owd wallets wi' mayte,
    Till they're as reawnt an' as brawsen as frogs;
Bo for me – aw'm content when aw've paid deawnt mi rent,
    Wi' ennof t'keep mi up i' mi clogs-ogs. Etc.

An' ther some are too idle to use ther own feet,
    An' mun keawr an' stroddle i' th' lone:
Bo when aw'm wheelt or carried – it'll be to get berried,
    An' then Dicky-up wi' Owd Jone-one. Etc.

Yo may turn up yor noses at me an' th' owd dame,
    An' thrutch us like dogs agen th' wo;
Bo as lung's aw con nayger aw'll ne'er be a beggar,
    So aw care no' a cuss for yo-o. Etc.

Then Margit, turn reawnd that owd hum-a-drum wheel,
    An' mi shuttle shall fly like a bird;
An' when aw no lunger can use hont or finger,
    They'n say – while aw could do aw did-id. Etc.

Words by B. Brierley.
Source: Harland and Wilkinson, p. 447. See also *New Voices* LP Topic 12T125
(1965).

12 Commitment

The committed artist is in an invidious position in capitalist society, unless his commitment is to the system, and to his own success within it. Above all, the radical songwriter and singer who genuinely wants to use the transmission channels provided by the commercial music industry has more problems than most. The single record has been made into a consumable article. Styles, which once were regulated by the industry so as to maximize return on investment, are now turned over much more rapidly. The commercially appropriated aspects of punk rock (though not the cultural roots from which it sprang) have to some extent been taken up and processed in less than two years. The industry operates on the basis of short-lived, volume-selling records: in Britain in 1976, 50 single records accounted for 25 per cent of sales, and 100 accounted for over one-third, out of a total of 3152 released! Of course, to some extent what has happened in the mid and late 1970s reflects the thrashing about of the commercial exploiters for another bread-and-butter trade; and the response of the music press (not to mention the other media) to the alignment of, say, the Tom Robinson Band and Sham 69 with a movement like the Anti Nazi League, shows up the time-worn contradiction at the heart of the industry. They want to make money by using radical rhetoric; but when radicalism oversteps their mark, and becomes politically committed (for whatever motives), a distinct uneasiness rumbles through EMI, the BBC and IPC.

Doubtless, the corporate executives will be reassuring themselves that the built-in obsolescence of singles will bring about the taming of punk. Yet more and more bands are doing gigs for Rock against Racism: the Sex Pistols are still getting their records banned from the BBC; and there are real signs of an attempt to set up politically aligned, non-commercial networks of live music. It will be interesting to see whether the impetus given to this movement is maintained in conjunction with political issues other than the fight against racism and fascism, or whether we are witnessing the honeymoon period of 'radical chic' amongst groups who are primarily interested in getting rich. What is noticeable is the complete absence from RAR concerts of established groups; and though individual 'folk'-style singers have been in evidence in the indoor ANL concerts — notably Ewan MacColl, Mike Harding and Alex Glasgow — the outdoor events have been predominantly punk and reggae oriented, and the audience has been overwhelmingly working class.

Compared to this particular late 1970s phenomenon, the solo efforts of a JohnLennon or a Bob Dylan (in Britain at any rate) pale into the background. Seemingly, Lennon recognizes his own dilemma. His first solo LP after the break-up of the Beatles, *John Lennon and the Plastic Ono Band*, offers to be honest, and is intended to be listened to with respect. It is not the kind of LP aimed at chart success, but it still reached number 11 in Britain in early 1971 and in the USA it had an advance order in excess of 2,500,000. Its audience, perhaps inevitably, was predominantly a student-oriented one, not least because it was put together by a former art student, and one who had some connections with the working class. This is why Lennon expressed his aim in writing a song like *Give Peace a Chance* in terms of an earlier generation of radical dissent:

. . . in me secret heart I wanted to write something that would take over 'We Shall Overcome'. I don't know why. Maybe because that was the one they always sang. I thought why doesn't somebody write one for the people now, you know, that's what my job is, our job is, to write for the people now, the songs that they go and sing on the buses even, and not just love songs. I had the same kind of hope for 'Working Class Hero'. I know it's a different concept, but I feel as though . . . I think it's a revolutionary song.[2]

To get to this position Lennon had had to go through Beatlemania, marry Yoko Ono, and get treatment from Dr Arthur Janov, whose *Primal Scream* therapy was in vogue in California: 'The dream is over. It's just the same only I'm thirty and a lot of people have got long hair, that's all . . . .'[3] On the other hand, Lennon was not unaware that any record he made would go through the same music industry matrix on its way to millions of ears. What does he do with this power of access, this relative autonomy?

Lennon's LP is a continuation of his therapy, not excluding the 'Mother, mother, mother' mantra recommended by Janov. Ironically, it comes from a man who publicly rejects 'intellectualism', who believed that the future of rock 'n' roll is

Whatever we make it. If we want to go bullshitting off into intellectualism with rock and roll, we are going to get bullshitting rock
intellectualism. If we want real rock and roll, it's up to all of us to
create it and stop being hyped by, you know, revolutionary image and
long hair. We've got to get over that bit. That's what cutting hair is
about.[4]

Of course, by cutting hair Lennon has accepted the rules of the
intellectual 'game', he is trapped by his own anti-intellectualism into
being intellectualist. The contradiction is compounded by the 'commonsense' attitude of working-class British people towards intellectuals in
general, and towards theory in particular. The product, inevitably, is
bullshitting anti-intellectualism. *Working Class Hero* (lyrics on page
214) best illustrates Lennon's confusion, especially because of his
express intention of trying to intervene, musically, in contemporary
politics. The whole LP could have been entitled *No*, so fierce is the
rejection of a wide range of intellectual and cultural 'solutions'. And if
this rejection brings on paranoia, as do the 'freaks on the phone', then
it is not surprising that 'reality' seems to be just 'Yoko and me'. On the
other hand, superstar Lennon is honest enough to feel the guilt and
the responsibilities of his position, without using the music industry
as an excuse for self-indulgence.

If *Working Class Hero* is a 'revolutionary song', in what ways is it
subversive of the established order? Its very title expresses the dilemma
of the successful popular songwriter and singer. In what way is Lennon,
for example, a hero *of* that class? How can you be a hero in any meaningful way without identifying wholeheartedly with that class; and
doesn't that mean that you have to have lived the class experience fully
enough to understand it? Put crudely, Lennon's working-class credentials
are dubious — grammar school, art college — however serious his
intention to write *for* 'the people'. In a minor way, it is symptomatic
that his 'Scouse' accent came as a surprise to his father: 'He spoke
lovely English. When I heard his scouse accent years later I was sure it
must be a gimmick.'[5] But then, because he was one of those who had
the give-away 'twenty odd years' of formal education, it is hardly
surprising that this song should come out of, and be popular in, that
stratum of college-educated young people in Britain and the USA
who were on their way out of the working class. Its form of consciousness is radical nonconformist *and* petty bourgeois: its attitudes remain
unclarified and confused by anxiety; it's one of those 'bits' that we
have to 'get over' if we're to be socialised into a culture and an ideology

Working Class Hero

As soon as you're born they make you feel small
By giving you no time instead of it all
Till the pain is so big you feel nothing at all
A workin' class hero is somethin' to be
A workin' class hero is somethin' to be

They hurt you at home and they hit you at school
They hate you if you're clever and they despise a fool
Till you're so fucking* crazy you can't follow their rules
A workin' class hero is somethin' to be
A workin' class hero is somethin' to be

When they've tortured and scared you for twenty odd years
Then they expect you to pick a career
When you can't really function you're so full of fear
A workin' class hero is somethin' to be
A workin' class hero is somethin' to be

Keep you doped with religion and sex and TV
And you tnink you're so clever and classless and free
But you're still fucking* peasants as far as I can see
A workin' class hero is somethin' to be
A workin' class hero is somethin' to be

There's room at the top they are telling you still
But first you must learn how to smile as you kill
If you want to be like the folks on the hill
A workin' class hero is somethin' to be
A workin' class hero is somethin' to be

If you want to be a hero well just follow me
If you want to be a hero well just follow me

* Word sung on record, but an asterisk replaced it in the lyrics on the inside
record sleeve with accompanying note: 'Omitted at the insistence of EMI'.

Words and music by John Lennon. ©1970 Northern Songs Limited for the
world. Reproduced by kind permission of ATV Music Limited.
Source: John Lennon, *Plastic Ono Band LP*, Apple Records PCS 7124 (1970).

which will leave the economic and social structure of capitalist society largely unchanged. One general conclusion remains unchallenged, then, by the solo John Lennon. If, on the one hand, post-Beatles youth culture forced bourgeois ideology to retreat on matters like the family and 'decency', on the other hand property relations and the power of the market had become perhaps even stronger in the process.[6] It wasn't that Lennon didn't recognize this:

. . . there has been a change and we are a bit freer and all that, but it's the same game, nothing's really changed. They're doing exactly the same things, selling arms to South Africa, killing blacks on the street, people are living in fucking poverty with rats crawling over them, it's the same. It just makes you puke.[7]

Now, Lennon knows that puking is not enough. His contribution is to market his own anxieties amongst those other people who 'pick a career' rather than *get a job*, and who are undergoing (or have undergone) the painful transition from aspirational working-class consciousness to what is a slightly hip form of petty bourgeois individualism.

Of course, Lennon is by no means happy about the situation he finds himself in. He recognizes that he has been duped by his own aspirations, and wants to forewarn others. Time and again he comes back to that increasingly sardonic refrain, 'A working class hero is something to be'. Yet the tone of the song and of the LP, is that he feels more like a victim than a hero. Heroes suffer, go through 'head changes', feel pain everywhere. Who is responsible for the pain? Of course, the people who put him in that position — the position he once wanted and still shows no sign of giving up — the buyers of records and the music industry, *they* are to blame. So Lennon patronizes, confuses, labels, gets generally aggressive and inchoate, and then lets the 'sound' take the weight of the meaning, puts all the responsibility on to the shoulders of the listener. In the last analysis, *Working Class Hero* articulates confusion and contradictions rather than solves them, right from the first line: 'As soon as you're born they make you feel small.' Lennon cannot tell 'you' from 'they', never knows which 'side' he can be on, any more than Dylan, and so wants to reject the notions of sides, blurring the focus into an almost total paranoia:

They hurt you at home and they hit you at school
They hate you if you're clever and they despise a fool,

until it's impossible to differentiate parents from teachers from bosses from 'Them'. Everybody is 'Them' to Lennon — either a torturer, a scarer, a smiler or a killer — except, of course, 'Yoko and me'. Seen from this intellectual foetal position, no solutions seem to be available, and that means that he is driven back on to his own guilt.

About the working class whose hero he is alleged to be, Lennon can tell us nothing. They are 'Them', too. His introversion and alienation are products of his inability to make contact, even with the record-buying public. In trying to foist his own lack of commitment on to the working class, all Lennon succeeds in doing is to project his own inability to cope, his own uncomfortable disillusion. He wants social change on a plate: he is not prepared to fight for it, to jeopardize his own career. According to an employee of his financial manager, it is Lennon who 'watches TV twenty-three hours a day'.[8] What he criticizes in others he cannot see in himself. So, while we may sympathize with his predicament, recognize his anguish, and welcome his attempt at honesty, in the end we have to say that songs like *Working Class Hero*, or *Power to the People*, or *Give Peace a Chance* remain part of John Lennon's therapy, and function as public confession of guilt, all the way to the bank. If this self-image is shared by many students, if the song touches them too closely for comfort, and if a challenge to it seems like a challenge to them, all well and good.

Compared to Lennon's transparency, Bob Dylan's apparent attempts at intervention are complex indeed. Dylan's double-sided single, *George Jackson* (lyrics on page 217), released in 1971, was his first 'protest' song since the early 1960s. On first hearing the acoustic side comes across as a simple, straightforward, didactic personal statement, as a conscious taking of sides over the killing in prison of the black political activist, allegedly while trying to escape. The music, as with Lennon's LP, is downgraded deliberately on the acoustic version; but in the 'Big Band' version on the other side the whole song has its sharper edges smoothed away completely, as though Dylan was embarrassed by having issued a record which sounded as though he really meant what he said. When we come to examine what he does say, we have to recognize that his embarrassment was unnecessary.

George Jackson divided society into two groups, the Innocent and the Guilty. He believed ever more firmly in 'sides', especially after his treatment at the hands of the police, the courts and the prison system.[9] In Dylan's hands, this polarization is systematically blurred over, so as to shore up the idea of there being no sides to *be* on. He tries to convert Jackson's Us and Them into a false dualism, Us and Us, with a bit of Them in each of us. By so doing he seeks not only to shore up his

George Jackson

I woke up this mornin'
There were tears in my bed
They killed a man I really loved
They shot him through the head

Lord lord they cut George Jackson down
Lord lord they laid him in the ground

They sent him off to prison
For a seventy dollar robbery
They closed the door behind him
And they threw away the key

Lord lord they cut George Jackson down
Lord lord they laid him in the ground

He wouldn't take shit from no-one
He wouldn't bow down or kneel
Th' authorities they hated him
Because he was just too real

Lord lord they cut George Jackson down
Lord lord they laid him in the ground

Th' prison guards they cursed him
As they watched him from above
But they were frightened of his power
They were scared of his love

Lord lord they cut George Jackson down
Lord lord they laid him in the ground

Sometimes I think this whole world
Is one big prison yard
Some of us are prisoners
The rest of us are guards

Lord lord they cut George Jackson down
Lord lord they laid him in the ground

soggy humanitarianism and 'objectivity', but also the ideology of bourgeois individualism from which his own position ultimately derives. Of course, Dylan shows up yet again the contradictions in his position and in the dominant ideology. On the one hand he 'really loved' this class-conscious revolutionary, as an individual human being; and on the other hand, 'prisoners' and 'guards' are all part of 'us', the human race, one big happy family, all in it together, and so on. At one and the same time, then, Dylan verbally criticizes and gives support to the system which guarantees his own economic security, and which took George Jackson's life. In trying to make a personal intervention after the killing, to let his audience know that he really cares, to help sustain an ailing radical aura, Dylan personalizes and then blurs a political issue which George Jackson knew was a collective, class problem, and one which could be solved only by revolutionary means.

It is ironic, then, that the BBC banned this record. (It doesn't take much: a word like 'shit' will usually suffice.) Partly as a consequence, it does not figure in the charts. Had they realized that, under the rhetoric of seeming to celebrate the life of a black American militant, Dylan was on their side in helping mystify political issues, doubtless they would not have worried so much about embarrassing Britain's NATO ally. Had they noted that Dylan was more than ever an LP-oriented songwriter and singer, with two recent number 1 LPs to his credit — LPs every bit as banal as other such hits — perhaps they would have recognized the man's confusion was working against the politics of Black Power.

George Jackson is a parody of the dead man's beliefs. Jackson's 'power' is juxtaposed with his 'love', implying that the one was a product of the other, and nothing to do with intellectual conviction about revolutionary struggle. In the end, Dylan's Jackson is a kind of *John Wesley Harding* caricature: the qualities which appeal to the songwriter are precisely the negative ones. Being 'real' — 'too real', even — means, in Dylan's way of seeing, not taking shit from anyone, not bowing down or kneeling. Jackson's power, apparently, is in his martyrdom. 'Real' heroes have to suffer to have any influence. The only solution is an individual solution. To parody Joe Hill, the great

Wobbly songwriter and socialist who was also framed and shot, Dylan seems to be declaiming, 'Don't waste time organizing: mourn'.[10] The tendency of his song is towards mysticism, and mysticism operates in the interests of the *status quo*.

While Lennon agonizes, Dylan restricts himself to one-off campaigns (at best) like that which involved *Hurricane*, and Paul McCartney produces the totally ingenuous *Give Ireland Back to the Irish*, there seems to be little hope of such superstars ever getting to grips with real social problems as songwriters and singers. They sometimes represent a dissident minority in the commercial entertainments industry, it is true, but they are not much more than that; and their effectiveness is bound to be minimized by the constraints imposed by commercial distribution, advertising and suchlike, even if they did clarify their position on fundamental ideological issues. But what else is there? Do we submit to being entertained by the purveyors of radical chic, and get our politics outside of song? Do we pin our faith in the latest cult, the latest apparently 'deviant' youth cultural style – teds, rockers, mods, skins, punks – and run the risk of seeing that transformed and appropriated? Or do we adopt a lefter-than-thou attitude, and ostentatiously wash our hands, as so many left-wingers do? Do we go off into nationalistic 'folk', or into intellectualized 'jazz'? And is what's left simply fit only for pathological analysis? In reality, working-class men and women and kids will continue to take from commercial 'popular' music what they find exciting or of interest, as they have always done. They will reappropriate the vital components of rock 'n' roll, blues and soul. They will take what they want from the retailers, and if it's not to be had, they'll make it themselves. This, the positive side of working-class culture, has hardly begun to be studied.

While journalists and critics have tended to analyse their own attitudes towards singers, songwriters and musicians, what we have not got are systematic accounts of the reception and response to the artists by people other than intellectuals. We do not know, for example, all that much about the cultural 'moments' of *Rock around the Clock, Jailhouse Rock, Rock Island Line* or *Love Me Do*. Again, figures like Victor Sylvester are often patronized, but rarely, it seems to me, *explained*, any more than is the reception of *South Pacific, The King and I,* or *Tapestry*. The receiving end of commercial musical products is largely unexplored, apart from a few spiritual autobiographies. And though we are beginning to get accounts of some key cultural institutions – record companies, the BBC, and suchlike – our knowledge and understanding of the folk clubs, Topic Records, the Workers' Music Association — even, bless it, the English Folk Dance and Song Society — is minimal. Then again, we have few accounts of the values, methods and assumptions of key mediators. We know very little about Lew Grade, 'Colonel' Parker, or other entrepreneurs. In the 'folk' field, we do not have biographies of Bert Lloyd and Ewan MacColl, let alone Paul Graney or Harry Boardman. Social biographies of singers, songwriters and musicians can be counted on the fingers of one hand. While journalistic pastiches on certain aspects of song and music abound, we await a full history of the juke box, a detailed account of the technological history of records and record playing equipment. And while we have a lengthy survey of the American music industry, the British industry is badly served in this respect.[11]

The further back we go in the history and development of the musical culture of British and North American working people, the thinner the research gets. We have no systematic account of broadside and chapbook printers, at a national level.[12] The early 'folksong' collectors have gone largely unexamined in a critical sense.[13] Only one British region has been studied over any length of time, to show what the musical resources were, and what were made of them by working people.[14] In general, accounts of popular and working-class culture remain at an impressionistic level.[15] The research commitment for the next ten or fifteen years is needed to reconstruct working-class (and pre-industrial) history and culture as part of a joint enterprise. Only through decoding the mediators and their mediations, now and in the past, can we hope to come at anything like clear testimony. To do that work is to make an important commitment, too.

Appendix 1 Worldwide sales of individual songs and single records

Worldwide collective sales of record units,* in millions, to the end of 1975

White Christmas	135	I Want to Hold Your Hand	13+
Rudolph the Red-Nosed Reindeer	110	Paper Doll	12+
		Release Me	12+
Winter Wonderland	45+	Young Love	12
Santa Claus is Coming to Town	40+	Great Balls of Fire	11
The Third Man Theme	40	I Saw Mommy Kissing Santa Claus	11
Little Drummer Boy	25+		
The Prisoner's Song	25	Never on Sunday	10+
Rock Around the Clock	25	Tennessee Waltz	10+
It's Now or Never	20+	Till the End of Time	10+
Twist and Shout	14+	Love Is Blue	10

Worldwide sales of individual single records, in millions, to the end of 1975

Bing Crosby	White Christmas	30+
Bing Crosby	Silent Night/Adeste Fideles	30+
Bill Haley	Rock Around the Clock	22
Elvis Presley	It's Now or Never	20
Beatles	I Want to Hold Your Hand	12
George McRae	Rock Your Baby	11+
Mills Brothers	Paper Doll	11
Monkees	I'm a Believer	10
Procul Harum	A Whiter Shade of Pale	10
Roy Acuff	Wabash Cannonball	10
Middle of the Road	Chirpy, Chirpy, Cheep Cheep	10
Paul Anka	Diana	9
Elvis Presley	Hound Dog/Don't Be Cruel	9
Shocking Blue	Venus	8+
Gene Autry	Rudolph the Red-Nosed Reindeer	8+
Mary Hopkin	Those Were the Days	8
Georgie Fame	Bonnie and Clyde	7½+

Beatles	Hey Jude	7½+
Danyel Gerard	Butterfly	7
Royal Scots Dragoon Guards	Amazing Grace	7
Julie Rogers	The Wedding	7
Dawn	Knock Three Times	6½+
Vernon Dalhart (Victor)	The Prisoner's Song	6½
Beatles	Can't Buy Me Love	6+
Bing Crosby	Jingle Bells	6+
Mungo Jerry	In the Summertime	6+
Patti Page	Tennessee Waltz	6+
Simon & Garfunkel	Bridge over Troubled Water	6+
Harry Simeone Chorale	Little Drummer Boy	6+
Archies	Sugar, Sugar	6
Dawn	Tie a Yellow Ribbon	6
Neil Diamond	Cracklin' Rosie	6
New Seekers	I'd Like to Teach The World to Sing	6
Terry Jacks	Seasons in the Sun	6
Champs	Tequila	6
Jeannie C. Riley	Harper Valley P.T.A.	5½
David Seville & Chipmunks	Chipmunk Song	5½
Barry Sadler	Ballad of the Green Berets	5+
Beatles	She Loves You	5+
Engelbert Humperdinck	Release Me	5+
Elvis Presley	Surrender	5+
Jackson 5	I'll Be There	5+
Donny Osmond	Puppy Love	5+
ABBA	Waterloo	5+
Tom Jones	Delilah	5
Gene Autry	Silver-Haired Daddy	5
Tornadoes	Telstar	5
Bee Gees	Massachusetts	5
Gene Austin	My Blue Heaven	5
Nino Rosso	Il Silenzio	5
Mitch Miller	March from 'Bridge on the River Kwai'	5
1910 Fruitgum Co.	Simon Says	5
George Harrison	My Sweet Lord	5
Partridge Family	I Think I Love You	5
Three Dog Night	Joy to the World	5

Sources: L. Lowe, *Directory of Popular Music 1900-1965* (Droitwich: Peterson, 1975), p. 496; J. H. Chipman, *Index to Top-Hit Tunes 1900-1951* (Boston, n.d.), p. 141; J. Murrells, *The Book of Golden Discs* (Barrie & Jenkins, 1978), p. 395. See also A. Wilder, *American Popular Song* (New York: Oxford University Press, 1972), pp. 94, 115, 117, 425.

Appendix 2 Value of U S recorded music sales

Value of US recorded music sales, 1921-77

Year	($m)	Year	($m)
1921	106	1948	189
1922	92	1949	173
1923	79	1950	189
1924	68	1951	199
1925	59	1952	214
1926	70	1953	219
1927	70	1954	213
1928	73	1955	277
1929	75	1956	377
1930	46	1957	460
		1958	511
1931	18	1959	603
1932	11	1960	600
1933	6		
1934	7	1961	640
1935	9	1962	687
1936	11	1963	698
1937	13	1964	758
1938	26	1965	· 862
1939	44	1966	959
1940	48	1967	1173
		1968	1358
1941	51	1969	1586
1942	55	1970	1660
1943	66		
1944	66	1971	1744
1945	109	1972	1924
1946	218	1973	2017
1947	224	1974	2200

1975	2389
1976	2737
1977	3501

Source: BPI Yearbook 1977, p. 155; see also I. Whitcomb, *After the Ball* (Penguin, 1973), pp. 97, 100; and C. Gillett, *The Sound of the City* (Sphere, 1971), pp. 3, 368.

Value of US recorded music sales 1921-40

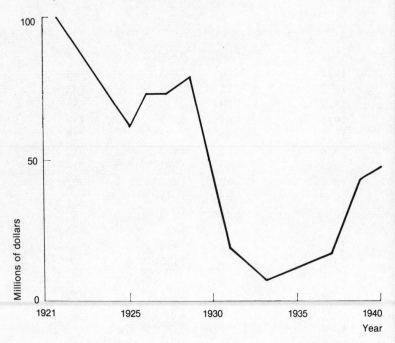

Value of US recorded music sales, 1940-77

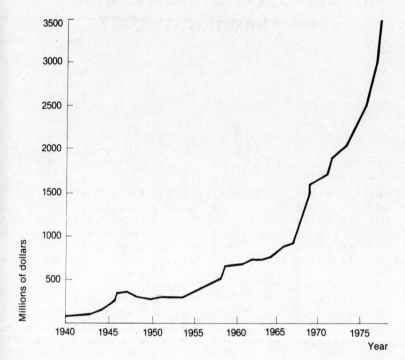

Appendix 3 The British recording business, 1955-77

Year	78s	45s	All singles	33s	cassettes and cartridges	All LPs	All records	All recordings	Unit recordings LPs, singles*	% yearly change	Value (£millions) at manufacturers retail prices	% yearly change
1955	46.3	4.6	50.9	9.0		9.0	59.9	59.9	95.9		9.1	
1956	47.5	6.9	54.4	12.1		12.1	66.5	66.5	114.9	19.8	11.2	23.0
1957	51.4	13.2	64.6	13.8		13.8	78.4	78.4	133.6	16.2	14.1	25.9
1958	28.3	27.5	55.8	15.6		15.6	71.4	71.4	133.8	0.02	13.8	−2.1
1959	8.1	43.2	51.3	15.4		15.4	66.7	66.7	128.3	−0.4	13.6	−1.4
1960	3.8	51.8	55.6	17.1		17.1	72.7	72.7	141.1	9.9	15.0	10.3
1961	2.2	54.8	57.0	19.4		19.4	76.4	76.4	154.0	9.1	16.0	6.7
1962	1.9	55.2	57.1	20.4		20.4	77.5	77.5	159.1	3.3	17.4	8.8
1963	1.9	61.3	63.2	22.3		22.3	85.5	85.5	174.7	9.8	21.8	25.3
1964	0.6	72.8	73.4	27.8		27.8	101.2	101.2	212.4	21.5	25.6	17.4
1965	0.5	61.8	62.3	31.5		31.5	93.8	93.8	219.8	3.5	25.5	−0.4
1966	0.4	51.2	51.6	33.3		33.3	84.9	84.9	218.1	−0.7	25.1	−1.6
1967	0.3	51.6	51.9	38.0	0.3	38.3	89.9	90.2	243.4	11.6	27.9	11.2
1968	0.2	49.2	49.4	49.2	0.3	49.5	98.6	98.9	296.9	22.0	30.1	7.9
1969	0.2	46.6	46.8	59.6	0.4	60.0	106.4	106.8	346.8	16.8	32.4	7.6
1970	0.1	47.0	47.1	65.9	1.0	66.9	113.0	114.0	381.6	10.0	39.3	21.3
1971		48.2	48.2	72.3	5.5	77.8	120.5	126.0	437.2	14.6	43.5	10.7
1972		52.9	52.9	84.5	10.9	95.4	137.4	148.3	529.9	21.2	65.9	51.5
1973		60.7	60.7	100.8	16.4	117.2	161.5	177.9	646.7	22.0	92.0	39.6
1974		68.3	68.3	105.6	24.5	130.1	173.9	198.4	718.8	11.1	115.6	25.7
1975		75.7	75.7	102.0	24.4	126.4	177.7	202.1	707.7	−1.5	141.0	18.0
1976		78.8	78.8	120.6	24.3	144.9	199.4	223.7	803.3	13.5		
1977		83.2	83.2	122.8	25.6	148.4	206.0	231.6	825.2	2.7		

* One LP is calculated here as being equal to 5 singles units.
Sources: BPI Yearbook 1978, passim; S. Frith, *The Sociology of Rock* (Constable, 1978), p. 102.
Note: All figures (except % yearly change) in millions.

Appendix 4 Worldwide sales of record units and LPs

Worldwide collective sales of record units,* in millions, to the end of 1975

Beatles	575	Led Zeppelin	84
Bing Crosby	400+	Creedence Clearwater Revival	80
Elvis Presley	350+	Freddy	80
Mantovani	300	Cliff Edwards	74
Herb Alpert	270	Eddie Arnold	70+
Elton John	252	Fats Domino	65+
James Last	240	Lettermen	65
Frank Sinatra	165	Glen Campbell	62+
Peter, Paul and Mary	160	ABBA	62
Rolling Stones	145	Grand Funk Railroad	62
Nat 'King' Cole	140	Beach Boys	60+
Andy Williams	135	Temptations	60+
Johnny Cash	130	Harry Belafonte	60+
Ferrante & Teicher	120	Andrews Sisters	60
Kingston Trio	112	Glenn Miller	60
Monkees	110	Patti Page	60
Mitch Miller	100+	Bill Cosby	60
Guy Lombardo	100	Barbra Streisand	60
Engelbert Humperdinck	100	Miracles	55
Tom Jones	100	Four Seasons	54
Supremes	100	Perry Como	50+
Ray Conniff	100	Pat Boone	50
Carole King	96+	James Brown	50
Roger Williams	90+	Benny Goodman	50
Frankie Laine	90+	Andre Kostalanetz	50
Simon & Garfunkel	90+	Lawrence Welk	50
Bill Haley	90	Stevie Wonder	50
Bert Kaempfert	90	Jackson 5	50
The Who	90	The Osmonds	50
Gene Austin	86		
Jose Feliciano	85+		

*Estimated: 1 LP = 6 units; 1 EP = 2 units

Source: J. Murrells, *The Book of Golden Discs* (Barrie & Jenkins, 1978), p. 384, adjusted in line with information found elsewhere.

Worldwide collective sales of LPs, in millions, to the end of 1975

Beatles	90+	Glen Campbell	10+
Mantovani	50+	Supremes	10+
Herb Alpert	45+	Harry Belafonte	10
Elton John	42+	Bill Cosby	10
James Last	40	Grand Funk Railroad	10
Elvis Presley	30+	Barbra Streisand	10
Frank Sinatra	25+	Nat 'King' Cole	8+
Peter, Paul & Mary	25	Emerson, Lake & Palmer	8+
Andy Williams	20+	Tom Jones	8+
Johnny Cash	20	Temptations	8+
Ferrante & Teicher	20	ABBA	8
Kingston Trio	18+	Neil Diamond	8
Carole King	16+	Rusty Warren	8
Mitch Miller	16+	John Denver	7+
Rolling Stones	15+	Charlie Pride	7+
Simon & Garfunkel	15+	Miracles	7
Chicago	15	Gene Pitney	6.5
Ray Conniff	15	Dean Martin	6+
Bert Kaempfert	15	Johnny Mathis	6+
Monkees	15	Partridge Family	6+
The Who	15	Three Dog Night	6+
Roger Williams	15	Mamas & Papas	6
Led Zeppelin	14	Vaughn Meader	5.5
Creedence Clearwater Revival	12+	Kermit Schaeffer	5
Beach Boys	10+		

Worldwide sales of individual LPs,* in millions, to the end of 1975

Soundtrack and original cast	The Sound of Music	17.5
Harry Simeone Chorale	Little Drummer Boy	14+
Bing Crosby	Merry Christmas	†
Carole King	Tapestry	13+
Soundtrack and original cast	South Pacific	11+
Soundtrack and original cast	West Side Story	10.5
Simon & Garfunkel	Bridge Over Troubled Water	10+
Soundtrack and original cast	My Fair Lady	9.5
Beatles	Abbey Road	9

*Records of same material with differing titles counted together.
Double and quadruple LPs counted as single LPs.
† Figure unknown, but said to be 'several millions'.

Sources: C. Gillett, *Rock File 2* (Panther, 1974); J. Murrells, *The Book of Golden Discs* (Barrie & Jenkins, 1978), pp. 384, 387; J. Murrells, *The Book of Golden Discs* (London: Guinness, 1966), pp. 405-6.

Soundtrack	Mary Poppins	7+
Elton John	Captain Fantastic	7
Elton John	Greatest Hits	7
Elton John	Goodbye Yellow Brick Road	7
Beatles	Sgt Pepper	7
Beatles	The Beatles DLP	6.5+
Beatles	Meet the Beatles	6.5
Original cast	Jesus Christ Superstar	6+
John Denver	Greatest Hits	6+
Vaughn Meader	The First Family	5.5+
ABBA	Greatest Hits	5.5+
Original cast	Hair	5+
Herb Alpert	Whipped Cream	5+
Mike Oldfield	Tubular Bells	5
The Who	Tommy DLP	5
Monkees	The Monkees	5
Monkees	More of the Monkees	5
Kermit Schaeffer	Radio Bloopers	4.75
Fleetwood Mac	Fleetwood Mac	4.5+
Led Zeppelin	Physical Graffiti	4.5+
(John Fitzgerald Kennedy)	A Memorial Album	4+
Led Zeppelin	Led Zeppelin 2	4+
ABBA	ABBA	4
Elton John	Rock of the Westies	4
Elton John	Caribou	4
Elton John	Don't Shoot Me	4
Soundtrack and original cast	Oklahoma	4
Beatles	Beatles for Sale	3.75+
John Denver	Windsong	3.5+
Beatles	Rubber Soul	3.5+
Santana	Santana	3.5+
Beatles	Let It Be	3.5+
Beatles	Hey Jude	3.5+
Allman Brothers	Brothers and Sisters	3.5+
Creedence Clearwater Revival	Cosmo's Factory	3.5+
Charlie Rich	Behind Closed Doors	3.5
Beatles	A Hard Day's Night	3.5
Rusty Warren	Knockers Up	3.5
George Harrison & Friends	Concert for Bangladesh	3+
Beatles	Magical Mystery Tour	3+
Led Zeppelin	Led Zeppelin 1	3+
George Harrison	Living in the Material World	3
Elvis Presley	Blue Hawaii	3
Carpenters	The Singles	3

ABBA	Waterloo	3
Mamas & Papas	If You Can Believe	3
John Denver	Back Home Again	3
Iron Butterfly	In a Gadda-Da-Vida	3
George Harrison	All Things Must Pass	3
Soundtrack and original cast	Fiddler on the Roof	3

Introduction

1 R. Goldstein, *The Poetry of Rock* (New York: Bantam, 1969), p. xi.

2 See J. Spriggs, 'Doing Eng. Lit.' in T. Pateman, *Counter Course* (Penguin, 1972), pp. 221-46.

3 See H. Braverman, *Labour and Monopoly Capitalism* (Monthly Review Press, 1974), *passim*.

4 See W. Reich, *The Mass Psychology of Fascism* (Penguin, 1975), *passim;* P. Foot, *Why You Should be a Socialist* (London: Socialist Workers Party, 1977), *passim*.

5 D. Harker, 'Cecil Sharp in Somerset: some conclusions', *Folk Music Journal* (1972), pp. 220-40; see also D. Harker, *Fakesong* (Pluto Press, forthcoming).

6 See J. Beerling, *Emperor Rosko's DJ Book* (Everest Books, 1976); G. Tremlett, *The Gary Glitter Story* (Futura, 1974).

7 See R. Williams, *Marxism and Literature* (Oxford University Press, 1977), pp. 1-7; T. Eagleton, *Criticism and Ideology* (New Left Books, 1976), pp. 21-42.

8 I. Birchall, 'The rhymes they are a-changing', *International Socialism* no. 23 (1965), p. 16.

9 R. Williams, *The Country and the City* (Chatto & Windus, 1973), *passim*.

10 T. Eagleton, *Criticism and Ideology, passim*.

11 E. P. Thompson, *The Making of the English Working Class* (Penguin, 1968), pp. 9-10.

12 K. Marx, Preface to *A Contribution to the Critique of Political Economy*, in K. Marx, *Selected Works* (Lawrence & Wishart, 1943), vol. 1, p. 356.

13 See E. P. Thompson, 'Review of *The Long Revolution*', *New Left Review*, May/June and July/August 1961.

14 M. Collins *et al.*, *The Big Red Song Book* (Pluto Press, 1977), pp. 56, 112.

15 E. P. Thompson, 'Review of *The Long Revolution*'.

16 See D. Harker, *Fakesong* (forthcoming).

17 T. Adorno, 'On popular music', *Studies in Philosophy and Social Science* (New York, 1941); T. Adorno, 'A social critique of radio music', *Kenyon Review*, vol. 7 (1944); see also A. Beckett, 'Popular music, basic assumptions and background', *New Left Review*, no. 39 (1966).

1 Electricity

1 J. Borwick, 'A century of recording', *Gramophone*, vol. 54, nos. 647 and 648 (April and May 1977), *passim*. See also J. Murrells, *The Book of Golden Discs* (Barrie & Jenkins, 1978), pp. 6, 12.

2 C. Gillett, *The Sound of the City* (Sphere, 1971), p. 4; Borwick, 'A century of recording', *passim;* C. Thompson, *The Complete Crosby* (W. H. Allen, 1978), pp. 15, 22-3.

3 Gillett, *The Sound of the City*, p. 3; Thompson, *The Complete Crosby*, pp. 27-8.

4 S. Spaeth, *A History of Popular Music in America* (London: Phoenix Books, 1960), p. 540; I. Whitcomb, *After the Ball* (Penguin, 1973), pp. 200-3. See also M. Wale, *Vox Pop* (Harrap, 1972), pp. 101-2; A. Shaw, *Sinatra* (Coronet, 1970), p. 58; V. Lynn, *Vocal Refrain* (Star Books, 1976), pp. 98, 123-4.

5 R. Williams, *Sing a Sad Song* (New York: Ballantine, 1973), p. 99; see also T. Palmer, *All You Need Is Love* (Futura, 1977), p. 185.

6 P. Guralnick, *Feel Like Going Home* New York: Outerbridge & Lazard, 1971), p. 50; Gillett, *The Sound of the City*, pp. 1, 15-16.

7 Whitcomb, *After the Ball*, p. 211; see also S. Chapple and R. Garofalo, *Rock'n'Roll Is Here to Pay* (Chicago: Nelson-Hall, 1977), p. 20.

8 B. Millar, *The Coasters* (Star Books, 1975), p. 19.

9 Williams, *Sing a Sad Song*, p. 126.

10 Gillett, *The Sound of the City*, p. 120.

11 G. Herman, *The Who* (Studio Vista, 1971), p. 52.

12 C. Keil, *Urban Blues* (London: University of Chicago Press, 1966), p. 70.

13 ibid.

14 L. Jones, *Blues People* (Jazz Book Club, 1966), p. 103.

15 S. Finkelstein, *Jazz: A People's Music* (1964), quoted in Jones, *Blues People* (Jazz Book Club, 1966), p. 25; see also K. Swanwick, *Popular Music and the Teacher* (Pergamon, 1968), pp. 1, 64; and W. Mellers, *Music in a New Found Land* (Barrie & Rockcliff, 1964),*passim*.

16 See. W. Reich, *The Mass Psychology of Fascism* (Penguin, 1975), *passim;* T. Adorno, 'On popular music', *Studies in Philosophy and Social Science* (New York, 1941), pp. 17-48; Palmer, *All You Need Is Love*, pp. 150, 153; Lynn, *Vocal Refrain*, p. 51.

17 Millar, *The Coasters*, pp. 119-20. See also G. Tremlett, *The Gary*

Glitter Story (Futura, 1974), p. 44; T. Hatch, *So You Want to Be in the Music Business* (Everest Books, 1976), p. 199; Chapple and Garofalo, *Rock'n'Roll Is Here to Pay*, p. 38.

18 Millar, *The Coasters*, pp. 43, 92-3; see also D. Laing, *Buddy Holly* (Studio Vista, 1971), p. 69; D. Morse, *Motown* (Studio Vista, 1971), pp. 14, 18; K. Townsend, 'From mono to multitrack', *Studio Sound* (August 1976), pp. 24-32.

19 H. Davies, *The Beatles* (Mayflower Books, 1969), p. 278. See also R. Greenfield, *A Journey Through America with the Rolling Stones* (Panther, 1975), p. 45; A. Shaw, *Rock Revolution* (Macmillan, 1969), p. 114; D. Laing, *The Sound of Our Time* (Sheed & Ward, 1969), p. 100; F. Newton, *The Jazz Scene* (Penguin, 1961), p. 20; J. J. Goldrosen, *Buddy Holly* (London: Charisma, 1975), p. 102; G. Tremlett, *The Who* (Futura, 1975), p. 90; G. Tremlett, *The Slade Story* (Futura, 1975), pp. 8, 12; C. S. Wren, *Johnny Cash* (Abacus, 1974), p. 129; S. Frith, *The Sociology of Rock* (Constable, 1978), p. 117.

20 W. Mellers, *Twilight of the Gods* (Faber, 1973), pp. 82-5. See also Laing, *The Sound of Our Time*, pp. 76, 78; Davies, *The Beatles*, p. 297; Gillett, *The Sound of the City*, p. 311; R. Mabey, *The Pop Process* (Hutchinson, 1969), p. 40.

21 C. Gillett and S. Frith, *Rock File 3* (Panther, 1975), p. 33; J. Beerling, *Emperor Rosko's DJ Book* (Everest Books, 1976), pp. 40-1; Chapple and Garofalo, *Rock'n'Roll Is Here to Pay*, pp. 104-5; Whitcomb, *After the Ball*, p. 216.

22 See Wale, *Vox Pop*, p. 258; Greenfield, *A Journey through America with the Rolling Stones*, pp. 29-30, 144 ff.

23 Shaw, *Sinatra*, pp. 13-14; cf. Palmer, *All You Need Is Love*, p. 23.

24 Whitcomb, *After The Ball*, p. 34; Palmer, *All You Need Is Love*, pp. 26, 35, 53.

25 Jones, *Blues People*, pp. 98, 101. See also Laing, *The Sound of Our Time*, pp. 3, 7; H. Braverman, *Labour and Monopoly Capital* (Monthly Review Press, 1974), pp. 146-50; Thompson, *The Complete Crosby*, pp. 24-5.

2   The average popular song

1 D. Laing, *The Sound of Our Time* (Sheed & Ward, 1969), p. 41; see also I. Whitcomb, *After the Ball* (Penguin, 1973), p. 97.

2 Whitcomb, *After the Ball*, p. 114.

3 ibid, p. 100.

4 A. Silver and R. Bruce, *How to Write and Sell a Hit Song* (New York: Prentice-Hall, 1939), pp. 19, 39; see also C. Gillett, *The Sound of the City* (Sphere, 1971), p. 299.

5 Silver and Bruce, *How to Write and Sell a Hit Song*, p. 20.

6 M. Wale, *Vox Pop* (Harrap, 1972), pp. 16, 17; R. Williams, *Sing*

a Sad Song (New York: Ballantine, 1973), p. 159. See also J. Eisen, *The Age of Rock 2* (New York: Vintage Books, 1970), p. 56; S. Chapple and R. Garofalo, *Rock'n'Roll Is Here to Pay* (Chicago: Nelson-Hall, 1977), pp. 47, 105, 196.

7 Silver and Bruce, *How to Write and Sell a Hit Song*, pp. 2, 32; see also T. Adorno, 'On popular music', *Studies in Philosophy and Social Science* (New York, 1941), pp. 19, 38, 40.

8 P. McCabe and D. Schonfield, *Apple to the Core* (Sphere, 1971), p. 79. See also T. Palmer, *All You Need Is Love* (Futura, 1977), p. 102; Chapple and Garofalo, *Rock'n'Roll Is Here to Pay*, p. 88; H. Braverman, *Labour and Monopoly Capital* (Monthly Review Press, 1974), *passim*; S. Frith, *The Sociology of Rock* (Constable, 1978), p. 83.

9 J. Murrells, *The Book of Golden Discs* (Barrie & Jenkins, 1978), p. 205; B. Holiday, *Lady Sings the Blues* (Abacus, 1975), p. 79.

10 J. Goldrosen, *Buddy Holly* (Charisma, 1975), pp. 25-8; J. Hopkins, *Elvis* (Abacus, 1974), pp. 26-7; A. Scaduto, *Bob Dylan* (Sphere, 1973), pp. 6-7.

11 Holiday, *Lady Sings the Blues*, p. 96; see also Palmer, *All You Need Is Love*, pp. 60, 82-3.

12 N. Cohn, *Awopbopaloobopalopbamboom* (Paladin, 1970), p. 15. See also Scaduto, *Bob Dylan*, p. 7; Gillett, *The Sound of the City*, p. 299.

13 Gillett, *The Sound of the City*, p. 46.

14 Whitcomb, *After the Ball*, p. 119.

15 S. Spaeth, *A History of Popular Music in America* (Phoenix Books, 1960), p. 532; Murrells, *The Book of Golden Discs*, p. 32.

16 Murrells, *The Book of Golden Discs*, p. 395.

17 A.L. Lloyd, *Folk Song in England* (Paladin, 1967), pp. 391-3.

18 M. Freedland, *Irving Berlin* (W. H. Allen, 1974), p. 140; C. Thompson, *The Complete Crosby* (W. H. Allen, 1978), pp. 95-6.

19 Freedland, *Irving Berlin*, p. 209.

20 N. Shapiro, *Popular Music* (New York: Adrian, 1965), vol. 2, p. 298.

21 L. Lowe, *Directory of Popular Music 1900-1965* (Droitwich: Peterson, 1975), p. 622.

22 See P. O'Flinn, *Them and Us in Literature* (Pluto Press, 1976), pp. 10-13.

23 J.H. Chipman, *Index to Top Hit Tunes* (Boston, n.d.), p. 143; Lowe, *Directory of Popular Music*, p. 345.

24 C. Gillett and S. Frith, *Rock File 3* (Panther, 1975), p. 204.

25 See M. Shaw, *Marxism and Social Science* (Pluto Press, 1975), *passim;* R. Hoggart, *The Uses of Literacy* (Penguin, 1957), *passim*.

3 Thank God for Elvis Presley?

1 C. Gillett, *The Sound of the City* (Sphere, 1971), pp. i-ii; see also T. Adorno, 'A social critique of radio music', *Kenyon Review,* vol. 7 (1944), pp. 208-17.

2 B. Millar, *The Drifters* (Studio Vista, 1971), p. 31; see also Gillett, *The Sound of the City,* p. 10.

3 Millar, *The Drifters,* p. 9.

4 C. Gillett, *Making Tracks* (Panther,1975), p. 39.

5 ibid; G. Herman, *The Who* (Studio Vista, 1971), p. 18.

6 Gillett, *The Sound of the City,* p. 59.

7 C. Gillett, *Rock File 2* (Panther, 1974), p. 41.

8 C. Keil, *Urban Blues* (London: University of Chicago Press, 1966), p. 81.

9 Gillett, *The Sound of the City,* p. 12.

10 Millar, *The Drifters,* p. 15.

11 ibid., pp. 15-16; see also S. Chapple and G. Garofalo, *Rock'n'Roll Is Here to Pay* (Chicago: Nelson-Hall, 1977), pp. 233-4, 246.

12 Millar, *The Drifters,* p. 9; see also Gillett, *The Sound of the City,* pp. 135-6.

13 B. Fong-Torres (ed.), *Rolling Stones Interviews 2* (New York: Warner, 1973), pp. 314-15. See also Millar, *The Drifters,* pp. 5, 61; B. Millar, *The Coasters* (Star Books, 1975), pp. 98, 112, 12.

14 I. Whitcomb, *After the Ball* (Penguin, 1973), pp. 102-3.

15 ibid, p. 199.

16 Gillett, *The Sound of the City,* pp. 9-10; see also R. Williams, *Sing a Sad Song* (New York: Ballantine, 1973), p. 118.

17 Gillett, *The Sound of the City,* pp. 1, 38; see also C. S. Wren, *Johnny Cash* (Abacus, 1974), p. 161.

18 Gillett, *The Sound of the City,* pp. 30-1; see also A. Silver and R. Bruce, *How to Write and Sell a Hit Song* (New York: Prentice-Hall, 1939), pp. 17-18.

19 Gillett, *The Sound of the City,* pp. 144, 298, 343; see also Chapple and Garofalo, *Rock'n'Roll Is Here to Pay,* p. 234; J. Murrells, *The Book of Golden Discs* (Barrie & Jenkins, 1978), p. 69.

20 C. Gillett and S. Frith, *Rock File 4* (Panther, 1976), pp. 186, 371.

21 Whitcomb, *After the Ball,* p. 226.

22 J. Hopkins, *Elvis* (Abacus, 1974), p. 47.

23 Gillett, *The Sound of the City,* p. 154.

24 Millar, *The Coasters,* p. 34.

25 Murrells, *The Book of Golden Discs,* p. 84; Gillett, *The Sound of the City,* p. 109.

26 Hopkins, *Elvis,* p. 56.

27 Hopkins, *Elvis,* pp. 46, 59; see also P. Guralnick, *Feel Like Going*

Home (New York: Outerbridge & Lazard, 1971), p. 139.

28 Williams, *Sing a Sad Song*, p. 59.

29 Williams, *Sing a Sad Song*, pp. 123-4; see also T. Palmer, *All You Need Is Love* (Futura, 1977), p. 186.

30 Hopkins, *Elvis*, p. 78.

31 Hopkins, *Elvis*, p. 89. See also Palmer, *All You Need Is Love*, p. 208, and Gillett, *The Sound of the City*, pp. 64-5.

32 Gillett, *The Sound of the City*, p. 162.

33 ibid., p. 151.

34 ibid., p. 195.

35 Hopkins, *Elvis*, p. 122. See also Wren, *Johnny Cash*, p. 10; C. Gillett and S. Frith, *Rock File 3* (Panther, 1975), p. 62; Williams, *Sing a Sad Song*, pp. 191-2.

36 N. Cohn, *Awopbopaloobopalopbamboom* (Paladin, 1970), p. 35.

37 Keil, *Urban Blues*, p. 165.

38 *Rolling Stone Interviews 1* (New York: Warner, 1971), p. 371.

39 ibid., p. 366.

40 Gillett, *The Sound of the City*, p. 66.

41 See J. Marks, *Mick Jagger* (Abacus, 1974), pp. 31-2.

42 Gillett, *The Sound of the City*, p. 37.

43 ibid.; see also C. Belz, *The Story of Rock* (New York: Oxford University Press, 1969), p. 40.

44 Chapple and Garofalo, *Rock'n'Roll Is Here to Pay*, p. 47.

45 See Cohn, *Awopbopaloobopalopbamboom*, *passim*.

46 Hopkins, *Elvis*, p. 199.

47 Murrells, *The Book of Golden Discs*, p. 395.

48 Whitcomb, *After the Ball*, pp. 4, 42. See also Palmer, *All You Need Is Love*, pp. 103, 113; S. Spaeth, *A History of Popular Music in America* (Phoenix Books, 1960), pp. 115, 117; Silver and Bruce, *How to Write and Sell a Hit Song*, p. 146; P. Leslie, *Fab* (MacGibbon & Kee, 1965), p. 37.

49 Belz, *The Story of Rock*, p. 53; see also, Whitcomb, *After the Ball*, p. 62.

50 See M. Kidron, *Western Capitalism Since the War* (Weidenfeld & Nicolson, 1970), *passim*.

51 Belz, *The Story of Rock*, p. 53.

52 Murrells, *The Book of Golden Discs*, p. 46.

53 Whitcomb, *After the Ball*, p. 101; D. Laing, *The Sound of our Time* (Sheed & Ward, 1969), p. 40.

54 Gillett, *The Sound of the City*, p. 51.

55 Belz, *The Story of Rock*, p. 53. See also J. Marks, *Rock and Other Four Letter Words* (New York: Bantam, 1968); Murrells, *The Book of Golden Discs*, p. 46; J. Borwick, 'A century of recording', *Gramophone*, vol. 54, nos. 647 and 648 (1977), p. 1762.

56 Belz, *The Story of Rock*, pp. 54-5.

57 A. Shaw, *Sinatra* (Coronet, 1970), p. 233; Chapple and Garofalo, *Rock'n'Roll Is Here to Pay*, p. 53; see also G. Melly, *Revolt into Style* (Penguin, 1972), p. 78.

58 Gillett, *The Sound of the City*, pp. 239-40; Chapple and Garofalo, *Rock'n'Roll Is Here to Pay*, pp. 51, 66, 247.

4   Taming jazz

1 A. Briggs, *A History of Broadcasting in the United Kingdom* (Oxford University Press, 1961–), vol. 1 (1961).

2 I. Whitcomb, *After the Ball* (Penguin, 1973), p. 170. See also, R. Williams, *The Long Revolution* (Penguin, 1961); V. Lynn, *Vocal Refrain* (Star Books, 1972), pp. 66, 81, 83.

3 HMSO, *Annual Abstract of Statistics* (1955-65).

4 B. Ferrier, *The Wonderful World of Cliff Richard* (Peter Davis, 1964), pp. 236-7. See also Lynn, *Vocal Refrain*, pp. 47-8, 50, 124-5; S. Frith, *The Sociology of Rock* (Constable, 1978), p. 126.

5 P. Leslie, *Fab* (MacGibbon & Kee, 1965), p. 46.

6 B. Jones, 'Pop goes the profit', *Youth Review*, no. 19 (1970), p. 10.

7 cf. Ferrier, *The Wonderful World of Cliff Richard*, p. 122.

8 Whitcomb, *After the Ball*, p. 178.

9 P. Flattery, *The Illustrated History of Pop* (London: Music Sales, 1973), pp. 6, 19.

10 H. Davies, *The Beatles* (Mayflower Books, 1969), p. 166. See also Townsend, 'From mono to multitrack', *Studio Sound* (August 1976), *passim*.

11 J. Young, *J.Y.* (Star Books, 1974), p. 96.

12 N. Cohn, *Awopbopaloobopalopbamboom* (Paladin, 1970), p. 61; see also G. Melly, *Revolt Into Style* (Penguin, 1972), p. 189.

13 cf. R. Mabey, *The Pop Process* (Hutchinson, 1969), p. 40; Young, *J.Y.*, p. 127, Whitcomb, *After the Ball*, p. 179.

14 HMSO, *Annual Abstract of Statistics* (1955-65).

15 C. Gillett and S. Frith, *Rock File 4* (Panther, 1976), pp. 186, 386.

16 Whitcomb, *After the Ball*, pp. 226-7.

17 R. Mabey, *Behind the Scene* (Penguin, 1968), p. 8.

18 K. Dallas, *Singers of an Empty Day* (Kahn & Averill, 1971), p. 47; see also Melly, *Revolt Into Style*, p. 30.

19 D. Johnson, *Beat Music* (Copenhagen: Wilhelm Hansen, 1969), p. 6.

20 Flattery, *The Illustrated History of Pop*, p. 21.

21 J. Kennedy, *Tommy Steele* (Corgi, 1959), p. 17; see also Townsend, 'From mono to multitrack', p. 25.

22 Kennedy, *Tommy Steele*, pp. 25, 29.

23 ibid., p. 53.

24 ibid., p. 88.

25 ibid., p. 156; see also D. Morse, *Motown* (Studio Vista, 1971), p. 10.

26 HMSO, *Annual Abstract of Statistics;* see also M. Abrams, *The Teenage Consumer* (Press Exchange, 1959), pp. 16-17.

27 C. Gillett, *The Sound of the City* (Sphere, 1971), p. 297.

28 Ferrier, *The Wonderful World of Cliff Richard, passim;* see also Melly *Revolt into Style,* pp. 55-6.

29 D. Laing, *The Sound of Our Time* (Sheed & Ward, 1969), p. 27; see also C. Parker, 'Pop song: the manipulated ritual' (unpublished paper, 1973), p. 4.

5   Happy little rockers

1 See N. Cohn, *Awopbopaloobopalopbamboom* (Paladin, 1970), *passim.*

2 C. Gillett and S. Frith, *Rock File 4* (Panther, 1976), p. 201.

3 D. Laing, *Buddy Holly* (Studio Vista, 1971), p. 45; J. J. Goldrosen, *Buddy Holly* (Charisma, 1975), p. 147.

4 J. Marks, *Mick Jagger* (Abacus, 1974), p. 56.

5 J. Eisen (ed.), *Age of Rock 2* (New York: Vintage Books, 1970), p. 110.

6 M. Abrams, *The Teenage Consumer* (Press Exchange, 1959), pp. 5-10.

7 ibid., pp. 13-14.

8 P. Rock and S. Cohen, 'The Teddy Boy', in V. Bogdanor and R. Skideslsky (eds.), *The Age of Affluence* (Macmillan, 1970), p. 309.

9 Goldrosen, *Buddy Holly,* p. 221.

10 R. Mabey, *The Pop Process* (Hutchinson, 1969), p. 48.

11 C. Gillett, *The Sound of the City* (Sphere, 1971), p. 299.

12 Rock and Cohen, 'The Teddy Boy', p. 289.

13 Abrams, *The Teenage Consumer,* p. 3.

14 P. Flattery, *The Illustrated History of Pop* (Music Sales, 1973), p. 71.

15 C. May and I. Phillips, *British Beat* (Socion Books, n.d.), *passim;* see also A. Scaduto, *Mick Jagger* (Mayflower Books, 1975), pp. 44-6, 49-50.

16 Gillett, *The Sound of the City,* pp. 300, 301.

17 ibid., p. 293; P. Leslie and B. Gwynn-Jones, *The Book of Bilk* (MacGibbon & Kee, 1963), *passim.*

18 B. Fong-Torres (ed.), *Rolling Stone Interviews 2* (New York: Warner, 1973), p. 228; see also Scaduto, *Mick Jagger,* pp. 51, 66.

19 G. Tremlett, *The Who* (Futura, 1975), p. 14.

20 Mabey, *The Pop Process,* p. 62.

21 P. Harris, *When Pirates Ruled the Waves* (Impulse, 1968), *passim.*

22 ibid.; see also R. Williams, *The Long Revolution* (Penguin, 1961), *passim.*

23 B. Jones, 'Pop goes the profit', *Youth Review,* no. 19 (1970), p. 10; see also J. Beerling, *Emperor Rosko's DJ Book* (Everest Books, 1976), p. 95.

24 Mabey, *The Pop Process,* p. 116.

25 T. Palmer, *Born Under a Bad Sign* (William Kimber, 1970), p. 12; see also C. Gillett and S. Frith, *Rock File 3* (Panther, 1975), p. 39.

26 HMSO, *Annual Abstract of Statistics* (1960-70); S. Frith, *The Sociology of Rock* (Constable, 1978), p. 211n.

27 M. Gray, *Song and Dance Man* (Hart-Davis, 1972), p. 112.

28 J. Wenner, *Lennon Remembers* (Penguin, 1972), p. 182.

29 See S. Chapple and R. Garofalo, *Rock'n'Roll Is Here to Pay* (Chicago: Nelson-Hall, 1977), p. 70.

30 See E. Cleaver, *Soul on Ice* (Cape, 1969), p. 197.

31 G. Melly, *Revolt Into Style* (Penguin, 1972), *passim.*

6   Their music or ours?

1 *British Companies in the music trade* (Jordan & Sons Surveys Limited, 1977), *passim;* C. Gillett and S. Frith, *Rock File 3* (Panther, 1975), p. 49.

2 M. Wale, *Vox Pop* (Harrap, 1972), p. 9.

3 ibid., p. 94; see also B. Ferrier, *The Wonderful World of Cliff Richard* (Peter Davis, 1964), p. 107; *Guardian*, 11 July 1979, p. 16, and 5 October 1979, p. 18.

4 Ferrier, *The Wonderful World of Cliff Richard,* pp. 105-6.

5 ibid., p. 107.

6 ibid.

7 Wale, *Vox Pop,* p. 95; S. Frith, *The Sociology of Rock* (Constable, 1978), pp. 114-15, 117.

8 J. Eisen, *The Age of Rock 2* (New York: Vintage Books, 1970), p. 128; see also S. Chapple and R. Garofalo, *Rock'n'Roll is Here to Pay* (Chicago: Nelson-Hall, 1977), pp. 190, 193, 219-24.

9 S. Shemel and M. W. Krasilovsky, *This Business of Music* (New York: Watson-Guptill, 1971), p. xviii.

10 R. Gleason, *The Jefferson Airplane* (New York: Ballantine, 1971), p. 67.

11 Shemel and Krasilovsky, *This Business of Music,* p. xvii; see also S. Chapple and R. Garofalo, *Rock'n'Roll is Here to Pay,* pp. 95, 97.

12 J. Murrells, *The Golden Book of Discs* (Barrie & Jenkins, 1978), p. 7; see also Shemel and Krasilovsky, *This Business of Music,* p. xvii; C. Belz, *The Story of Rock* (New York: Oxford University Press, 1972), p. 114; Frith, *The Sociology of Rock,* p. 9.

13 Chapple and Garofolo, *Rock'n'Roll is Here to Pay*, p. 49; K. Dallas, *Singers of an Empty Day* (Kahn & Averill, 1971), p. 35. See also A. Shaw, *Sinatra* (Coronet, 1970), pp. 280-1.

14 Shaw, *Sinatra*, p. 319.

15 C. Gillett, *Making Tracks* (Panther, 1975), p. 214; see also D. Walley, *No Commercial Potential: the Saga of Frank Zappa and the Mothers of Invention* (New York: Dutton, 1972), p. 116; Chapple and Garofolo, *Rock'n'Roll is Here to Pay*, pp. 40, 83-5, 92-3, 126, 187, 197, 203-5, 213; C. Thompson, *The Complete Crosby* (W. H. Allen, 1978), pp. 50, 82, 90, 99-101, 132, 204, 258.

16 T. Palmer, *Born Under a Bad Sign* (William Kimber, 1970), p. 15.

17 ibid., pp. 15-16.

18 Frith, *The Sociology of Rock*, pp. 114-5; G. Tremlett, *The Paul McCartney Story* (Futura, 1975), pp. 8-9.

19 G. Herman, *The Who* (Studio Vista, 1971), p. 54; see also G. Melly, *Revolt Into Style* (Penguin, 1972), p. 171.

20 H. Edgington, *Abba* (Magnum Books, 1977), p. 135.

21 ibid., pp. 149-50.

22 ibid., p. 135.

23 ibid., p. 87.

24 Palmer, *Born Under a Bad Sign*, pp. 12-13; D. Short, *Englebert Humperdinck* (New English Library, 1972), p. 34.

25 C. Gillett, *Rock File 2* (Panther, 1974), pp. 7, 28-9, 32. See also J. Eisen, *The Age of Rock* (New York: Vintage Books, 1969), p. 196; Frith, *The Sociology of Rock*, pp. 222-3.

26 P. Leslie, *Fab* (MacGibbon & Kee, 1965), p. 49-50; Murrells, *The Book of Golden Discs*, p. 52.

27 R. Mabey, *Behind the Scene* (Penguin, 1968), p. 11.

28 T. Cash (ed.), *Anatomy of Pop* (BBC Publications, 1970), p. 27; see also G. Tremlett, *10 CC* (Futura, 1976), p. 111.

29 C. Gillett and S. Frith, *Rock File 4* (Panther, 1976), pp. 58-63. See also P. C. Luce, *The Stones* (Howard Baker, 1970), p. 42; Frith, *The Sociology of Rock*, p. 95; *BPI Yearbooks*.

30 See J. Young, *J.Y.: the autobiography of Jimmy Young* (Star Books, 1974), p. 100; Wale, *Vox Pop*, pp. 236-7; G. Tremlett, *The Who* (Futura, 1975), p. 46; Tremlett, *10 CC*, pp. 33, 65; Frith, *The Sociology of Rock*, p. 90.

31 C. Gillett and S. Frith, *Rock File 3* (Panther, 1975), p. 39; see also J. Beerling, *Emperor Rosko's DJ Book* (Everest, 1976), p. 42.

32 Gillett and Frith, *Rock File 3*, p. 41.

33 ibid., p. 38.

34 ibid., pp. 43-4. See also R. Greenfield, *A Journey Through America with the Rolling Stones* (Panther, 1975), p. 32; Beerling, *Emperor Rosko's DJ Book*, pp. 99-100; Chapple and Garofalo, *Rock 'n' Roll is Here to Pay*, pp. 100-2.

35 Chapple and Garofalo, *Rock 'n' Roll is Here to Pay,* pp. 155-6; Belz, *The Story of Rock,* p. 117.

36 Wale, *Vox Pop,* p. 266; Chapple and Garofalo, *Rock 'n' Roll is Here to Pay,* pp. 166-9, 183, 227, 229.

37 D. Laing, *The Sound of Our Time* (Sheed & Ward, 1969), p. 27.

38 C. Gillett, *Rock File 1* (New English Library, 1972), pp. 11-14.

39 HMSO Annual Abstract of Statistics (1958-78); Gillett, *Rock File 1, passim.* See also Mabey, *Behind the Scene,* pp. 34-5; Wale, *Vox Pop,* p. 130.

40 Murrells, *The Book of Golden Discs,* pp. 155, 171.

41 Gillett, *Rock File 1,* pp. 126-7; Leslie, *Fab,* p. 93; J. Hopkins, *Elvis* (Abacus, 1974), p. 317.

42 Gillett, *Rock File 1,* pp. 11-12, 76-7.

43 ibid., *passim.*

7   Counter-culture

1 B. Fong-Torres (ed.), *Rolling Stone Interviews 2* (New York: Warner, 1972), p. 292.

2 R. Greenfield, *A Journey Through America with the Rolling Stones* (Panther, 1974), p. 55.

3 A. Scaduto, *Mick Jagger* (Mayflower, 1974), p. 254.

4 Fong-Torres, *Rolling Stone Interviews 2,* pp. 287-8; see also S. Chapple and R. Garofalo, *Rock 'n' Roll is Here to Pay* (Chicago: Nelson-Hall, 1977), p. 128.

5 R. Neville, *Playpower* (Paladin, 1970), p. 75.

6 J. Eisen, *The Age of Rock* (New York: Vintage Books, 1969), p. xii.

7 J. Eisen, *The Age of Rock 2* (New York: Vintage Books, 1970), p. 170.

8 C. Gillett, *Making Tracks* (Panther, 1975), pp. 57-8.

9 A. Shaw, *Sinatra* (Coronet, 1970), p. 67, 304.

10 H. Davies, *The Beatles* (Mayflower, 1969), p. 371; P. Leslie, *Fab* (MacGibbon & Kee, 1965), p. 34.

11 B. Holiday, *Lady Sings the Blues* (Abacus, 1973), p. 163; see also Chapple and Garofalo, *Rock 'n' Roll is Here to Pay,* p. 236.

12 C. Keil, *Urban Blues* (London: Chicago University Press, 1966), pp. 82, 86; *Rolling Stone Interviews 1* (New York: Warner, 1971), p. 182. See also T. Palmer, *All You Need Is Love* (Futura, 1977), pp. 30-1.

13 Keil, *Urban Blues,* p. 88; Chapple and Garofalo, *Rock 'n' Roll is Here to Pay,* pp. 260, 263.

14 Gillett, *Making Tracks,* pp. 102, 169-70.

15 Keil, *Urban Blues,* p. 79.

16 Gillett, *Making Tracks,* p. 102.

17 M. Wale, *Vox Pop* (Harrap, 1972), pp. 114-5.

18 Gillett, *Making Tracks*, p. 28.

19 B. Millar, *The Coasters* (Star Books, 1975), p. 68.

20 C. Gillett, *The Sound of the City* (Sphere, 1971), pp. 11n, 121.

21 Gillett, *The Sound of the City*, p. 121.

22 M. Gray, *Song and Dance Man* (Hart-Davis, 1972), p. 109.

23 Keil, *Urban Blues*, p. 78.

24 Gillett, *The Sound of the City*, p. 341.

25 Keil, *Urban Blues*, p. 78

26 Eisen, *The Age of Rock 2*, p. 170.

27 D. Laing, *The Electric Muse* (Methuen, 1975), p. 65.

28 Neville, *Playpower*, p. 26n.

29 R. Mabey, *The Pop Process* (Hutchinson, 1969), p. 103.

30 Wale, *Vox Pop*, p. 10; R. Gleason, *The Jefferson Airplane* (New York: Ballantine, 1969), p. 91.

31 Wale, *Vox Pop*, pp. 12-13; see also G. Tremlett, *The Slade* (Futura, 1975), p. 10.

32 Eisen, *The Age of Rock 2*, p. 61; see also, N. Cohn, *Awopbopaloobopalopbamboom* (Paladin, 1970), p. 217; Chapple and Garofalo, *Rock'n'Roll is Here to Pay*, p. 158-65; *The Sociology of Rock* Constable, 1978), p. 145.

33 M. Friedman, *Janis Joplin* (Star Books, 1975), p. 91.

34 S. Sarlin, *Turn It Up* (Coronet, 1975), p. 183.

35 ibid., p. 184.

36 Keil, *Urban Blues*, pp. 86-7; see also Chapple and Garofalo, *Rock'n'Roll is Here to Pay*, pp. 62, 116.

37 Gleason, *The Jefferson Airplane*, pp. 10, 25, 46; Chapple and Garofalo, *Rock'n'Roll is Here to Pay*, pp. 113-14, 117-18, 121. See also Palmer, *All You Need Is Love*, p. 149.

38 See P. McCabe and R. D. Schonfield, *Apple to the Core* (Sphere, 1971); R. DiLello, *The Longest Cocktail Party* (Charisma, 1973), pp. 7, 125, 139, 140, 199; Davies, *The Beatles*; G. Tremlett, *10 CC* (Futura, 1976), pp. 78, 111.

8 Which side can you be on?

1 A. Scaduto, *Bob Dylan* (Sphere Books, 1973), p. 15.

2 ibid., p. 9.

3 ibid., p. 23; R. S. Denisoff, 'Protest movements', *Sociological Quarterly*, vol. 9 (Spring, 1968), p. 232.

4 T. Thompson, *Positively Main Street* (New York: Caward McCann, 1971), p. 28.

5 Denisoff, 'Protest movements', p. 232; see also M. Collins, D. Harker and G. White, *The Big Red Song Book* (Pluto Press, 1977), *passim*.

6 W. Guthrie, *Born to Win* (New York: Macmillan, 1965), p. 13.

7 Denisoff 'Protest movements', p. 231*n*.

8 ibid., p. 232.

9 ibid., p. 232.

10 B. Sarlin, *Turn It Up* (Coronet, 1975), p. 18.

11 T. Palmer, *All You Need Is Love* (Futura, 1977), p. 200.

12 Scaduto, *Bob Dylan*, p. 27.

13 J. Eisen, *The Age of Rock* (New York: Vintage Books, 1969), p. 97.

14 Scaduto, *Bob Dylan*, p. 6.

15 ibid., pp. 6-7.

16 ibid., p. 25.

17 ibid., p. 27.

18 ibid., p. 41; see also A. Scaduto, *Mick Jagger* (Mayflower, 1974), p, 86.

19 Scaduto, *Bob Dylan* p. 54; see also D. Myrus, *Ballads, Blues and the Big Beat* (Macmillan, 1966), *passim*.

20 Thompson, *Positively Main Street*, p. 100.

21 Scaduto, *Bob Dylan*, p. 45.

22 Denisoff, 'Protest movements', p. 241.

23 ibid., p. 242.

24 Eisen, *The Age of Rock*, p. 210.

25 Scaduto, *Bob Dylan*, p. 32.

26 ibid., p. 66; see also D. Myrus, *Ballads, Blues and the Big Beat*, *passim*.

27 Scaduto, *Bob Dylan*, pp. 115, 118, 146.

28 ibid., pp. 94-5.

29 ibid., pp. 105, 110, 137.

30 ibid., p. 111.

31 ibid., p. 140.

32 P. Willis, 'Pop music and youth cultural groups in Birmingham' (unpublished Ph.D thesis, University of Birmingham, 1972), *passim*.

33 R. Goldstein, *The Poetry of Rock* (New York: Bantam, 1969), p. 6; see also G. Tremlett, *The Gary Glitter Story* (Futura, 1974), pp. 70-1.

34 D. Laing *et al.*, *The Electric Muse* (Methuen, 1975), p. 41.

35 See Sarlin, *Turn It Up*, p. 70.

36 Scaduto, *Bob Dylan*, p. 218.

37 ibid., p. 180.

38 ibid., pp. 180, 223.

39 M. Gray, *Song and Dance Man* (Hart-Davis, 1972), p. 26.

40 ibid., p. 171; see also T. Eagleton, *Exiles and Emigres* (Chatto & Windus, 1970), pp. 138-78.

41 B. Fong-Torres (ed.), *Rolling Stone Interviews 2* (New York: Bantam, 1973), p. 14.

42 Scaduto, *Bob Dylan,* p. 188.

43 ibid., p. 212; see also A. Shaw, *Sinatra* (Coronet, 1970), p. 344.

44 cf. W. Guthrie, *Born to Win* (New York: Macmillan, 1965), *passim.*

45 See R. Williams, *The English Novel from Dickens to Lawrence* (Chatto & Windus, 1970), pp. 28-59.

46 Gray, *Song and Dance Man,* p. 61.

47 ibid., p. 181.

48 ibid., p. 7.

49 Scaduto, *Bob Dylan,* p. 248.

50 Gray, *Song and Dance Man,* p. 37.

51 See ibid., p. 214.

9   Fakesong

1 D. Harker, *Fakesong* (Pluto Press), forthcoming.

2 See A.L. Lloyd, *Folk Song in England* (Lawrence & Wishart, 1967), p. 5.

3 D. Harker, 'Cecil Sharp in Somerset: some conclusions', *Folk Music Journal,* 1972, pp. 220-40.

4 C. J. Sharp, *English Folk-Song: Some Conclusions* (Simpkin, 1907), pp. 135-6.

5 See E. J. Hobsbawm, *Labouring Men* (Weidenfeld & Nicholson, 1964), p. 263; K. Marx, *Selected Works* (Lawrence & Wishart, 1943), vol. 1, pp. 235-6.

6 See J. Nuttall, *Bomb Culture* (Paladin, 1970), pp. 40-41; see also J. Boyd, 'Trends in youth culture', *Marxism Today,* December 1973, p. 378.

7 D. Laing *et al., The Electric Muse* (Methuen, 1975), pp. 86-91.

8 *Sing,* August 1961, p. 65.

9 *Spin,* October/November 1962; see also *Sing,* August 1962.

10 *Spin,* October 1961.

11 ibid., vol. 3, no. 1, and *Folk Scene,* February 1965.

12 See D. Harker, 'Popular song and working-class consciousness in north-east England' (unpublished Ph.D thesis, University of Cambridge, 1976).

13 See D. Harker, *Hammer and Hand* (Frank Graham, forthcoming).

14 D. Harker, *Fakesong,* passim.

10   Songs of pitmen and pitwork

1 D. Harker, 'Popular song and working-class consciousness in north-east England', unpublished Ph.D thesis, University of Cambridge, 1976; cf. R. Colls, *The Collier's Rant* (Croom Helm, 1977), passim.

2 A.L. Lloyd, *Folk Song in England* (Lawrence & Wishart, 1967), p. 336.

3 B.H. Bronson, *Joseph Ritson: Scholar-at-Arms* (University of California Press, 1938).

4 R. Welford, *Men of Mark 'Twixt Tune and Tweed* (Newcastle: Walter Scott, 1895), vol. 3, pp. 390-4.

5 See B. H. Bronson, *Joseph Ritson: Scholar-at-Arms.*

6 See J. Ritson, *Northern Garlands* (R. Triphook, 1810; reprinted 1973).

7 See D. Harker, 'John Bell, the Great Collector', in J. Bell (ed.), *Rhymes of Northern Bards* (Frank Graham, 1971), p. ix.

8 J. Marshall, *Newcastle Songster*, Part 2, n.d.; see also F.M. Thomson, *Newcastle Chapbooks* (Oriel Press, 1969), p. 62.

9 C. Sharp, *The Bishoprick Garland* (Nichols, Baldwin & Craddock, 1834), pp. 52-3.

10 Poster and Local Biographical Cuttings, Newcastle Central Library.

11 Reprinted 1965: Newcastle; Frank Graham.

12 See D. Harker, 'Thomas Allen and "Tyneside Song" ', in T. Allen (ed.), *Tyneside Songs* (Frank Graham, 1972).

13 Reprinted 1973: Newcastle; Frank Graham.

14 See D. Harker, *Hammer and Hand* (Frank Graham, forthcoming).

15 Reprinted 1965: University of Pennsylvania; Folklore Associates.

16 A. L. Lloyd, *Come All Ye Bold Miners* (Lawrence & Wishart, 1952), p. 19.

17 ibid., p. 17.

18 See *Along the Coally Tyne* LP (1962).

19 Lloyd, *Folk Song in England,* p. 336.

20 Harker, *Hammer and Hand;* see also T. S. Ashton and J. Sykes, *The Coal Industry of the Eighteenth Century* (Manchester University Press, 1929).

21 See D. Harker, *Songs of the north-east Pitmen's Strikes 1831-1844* (Frank Graham, forthcoming).

22 Lloyd, *Come All Ye Bold Miners,* p. 93.

23 ibid., p. 137.

24 *Steam Whistle Ballads* LP (1958).

25 Lloyd, *Come All Ye Bold Miners,* pp. 9, 28, 32; see also Colls, *The Collier's Rant, passim.*

26 Harker, *Hammer and Hand;* see also D. Harker, *George Ridley* (Frank Graham, 1973); D. Harker, *Ned Corvan*, (Frank Graham, forthcoming).

27 Lloyd, *Folk Song in England,* p. 344.

28 See Harker, *Hammer and Hand*; see also Colls, *The Collier's Rant.*

29 Lloyd, *Come All Ye Bold Miners,* p. 137.

30 Bell Mining Collection, North of England Institute of Mining Engineers, Newcastle.

31 Newcastle Central Reference Library, Wigan Central Library.

32 Harker, *Hammer and Hand*.

33 Bell Mining Collection, North of England Institute of Mining Engineers.

34 R. Fynes, *The Miners of Northumberland and Durham* (SR Publications, 1971), pp. 83, 88, 98-9; cf. R. Challinor and B. Ripley, *The Miners Association* (Lawrence & Wishart, 1968); K. Marx and F. Engels, *On Britain* (Lawrence & Wishart, 1953), p. 292.

35 Harker, *Hammer and Hand*.

36 Lloyd, *Come All Ye Bold Miners*, p. 137.

37 A. L. Lloyd, *Coaldust Ballads* (Lawrence & Wishart, 1952), p. 40.

38 ibid., p. ii.

39 Lloyd, *Folk Song in England*, pp. 385-6, 421.

40 Lloyd, *Come All Ye Bold Miners*, p. 137; cf. M. Vicinus, *The Industrial Muse* (Croom Helm, 1974); Harker, *Hammer and Hand*.

41 *Address of the Reformers of Fawdon*, 1819 (reprinted 1969); cf. Harker, *Hammer and Hand*.

42 John Bell and Robert White Broadside Collection, Newcastle University Library.

43 Lloyd, *Come All Ye Bold Miners*, p. 91; Lloyd, *Folk Song in England*, p. 339.

44 Harker, *Hammer and Hand*.

45 ibid.

46 ibid.

47 D. Douglass, *Pit Life in County Durham* (History Workshop, 1972)

48 T. Gilfellon, *Tommy Armstrong Sings* (Frank Graham, 1971).

49 Harker, *Hammer and Hand*.

50 Gilfellon, *Tommy Armstrong Sings*.

51 Lloyd, *Come All Ye Bold Miners*, pp. 101, 137; E. MacColl, *Shuttle and Cage* (Workers Music Association, 1954), p. 14.

52 Lloyd, *Folk Song in England*, pp. 380-1.

53 See D. Craig, *The Real Foundations* (Chatto & Windus, 1973), p. 82.

54 See *Tommy Armstrong of Tyneside* LP (n.d.).

55 See Craig, *The Real Foundations*, pp. 82, 85-6, 91.

56 *Spin*, vol. 3, no. 3; see also Lloyd, *Folk Song in England*, p. 397.

57 *Along the Coally Tyne* LP (1962).

58 C. Parker, 'John Axon and the Radio Ballad', *The Ballad of John Axon* LP (1965).

59 ibid.

60 C. Parker, *The Big Hewer* LP (1967); see also C. Parker, 'Pop song: the manipulated ritual', unpublished paper, 1973.

61 *The Monthly Chronicle of Lore and Legend* (Newcastle, May 1887), p. 111.

62 Harker, *Hammer and Hand*.

63 Interview with Dave Harker, Gateshead (1975).

64 ibid.
65 ibid.
66 ibid.
67 ibid.

11 Song and history

1 J. Harland and T. T. Wilkinson, *Ballads and Songs of Lancashire* (Manchester: John Heywood, 1882), p. 162.

2 ibid., pp. 163-4.

3 See D. Harker, *Hammer and Hand* (Frank Graham, forthcoming).

4 cf. J. Foster, *Class Struggle and the Industrial Revolution* (Metheun, 1977), p. 8; E. P. Thompson, *The Making of the English Working Class* (Penguin, 1968), pp. 323-4; A.L. Lloyd, *Folk Song in England* (Lawrence & Wishart, 1967), p. 322.

5 See Harland and Wilkinson, *Ballads and Songs of Lancashire*, pp. 167-74.

6 See Harker, *Hammer and Hand*.

7 See R. Colls, *The Collier's Rant* (Croom Helm, 1977).

8 Harland and Wilkinson, *Ballads and Songs of Lancashire*, p. 164; cf. M. Vicinus, *The Industrial Muse* (Croom Helm, 1974), pp. 48-51.

9 See Lloyd, *Folk Song in England*; Vicinus, *The Industrial Muse*.

10 Lloyd, *Folk Song in England*, p. 320.

11 See. E. P. Thompson, 'Time, work-discipline and industrial capitalism', *Past and Present*, no. 38 (December 1967), pp. 56-97.

12 See Vicinus, *The Industrial Muse*, pp. 40-4.

13 See G. Legman, *The Rationale of the Dirty Joke* (Panther, 1972), *passim*.

14 See S. Sedley, *The Seeds of Love* (Essex Music Ltd, 1967), p. 169.

15 Harland and Wilkinson, *Ballads and Songs of Lancashire*, p. 188; cf. Vicinus, *The Industrial Muse*, pp. 45-7.

16 Foster, *Class Struggle and the Industrial Revolution*, pp. 21, 79.

17 Harland and Wilkinson, *Ballads and Songs of Lancashire*, p. 169; see also Lloyd, *Folk Song in England*, pp. 323-4; Vicinus, *The Industrial Muse*, pp. 49-51.

18 See E. Gaskell, *Mary Barton* (Everyman, 1965), pp. 32-3; R. Williams, *Culture and Society* (Penguin, 1961), pp. 99-103.

19 Harland and Wilkinson, *Ballads and Songs of Lancashire*, p. 169.

20 ibid.

21 See Vicinus, *The Industrial Muse*, pp. 58-9.

22 Harland and Wilkinson, *Ballads and Songs of Lancashire*, p. 169.

23 ibid. p. 172.

24 Thompson, *The Making of the English Working Class*.

25 Harland and Wilkinson, *Ballads and Songs of Lancashire*, p. 195.

26 Thompson, *The Making of the English Working Class*; see also

Harker, *Hammer and Hand.*

27 See Lloyd, *Folk Song in England,* pp. 324-6.

28 D. Harker, 'John Bell, the Great Collector', in J. Bell (ed.), *Rhymes of Northern Bards* (Frank Graham, 1971); D. Harker, 'Thomas Allan and "Tyneside Song" ', in T. Allan (ed.), *Tyneside Songs* (Frank Graham, 1972).

29 Harland and Wilkinson, *Ballads and Songs of Lancashire,* p. 193.

30 ibid., p. 506.

31 ibid., p. 447; see also Vicinus, *The Industrial Muse,* p. 53.

32 Vicinus, *The Industrial Muse.*

33 R. Spence Watson, *Joseph Skipsey* (T. Fisher Unwin, 1909), passim.

34 T. Burt, *From Pitman to Privy Counsellor,* 1924; see also S. Bamford, *Passages in the Life of a Radical,* 1844 (reprinted MacGibbon & Kee, 1967).

12   Commitment

1 *BPI Yearbook,* 1977, pp. 216-18; S. Frith, *Sociology of Rock* (Constable, 1978), p. 75.

2 J. Murrells, *The Book of Golden Discs* (Barrie & Jenkins, 1978), p. 282; J. Wenner, *Lennon Remembers* (Penguin, 1972), p. 110.

3 ibid., p. 12.

4 ibid., p. 100.

5 H. Davies, *The Beatles* (Mayflower, 1969), p. 8.

6 R. Merton, 'Comment', *New Left Review,* no. 59 (January/ February 1970).

7 Wenner, *Lennon Remembers,* p. 12.

8 P. McCabe and R. D. Schonfield, *Apple to the Core* (Sphere, 1971), p. 143.

9 G. Jackson, *Soledad Brother* (Penguin, 1971).

10 M. Collins, D. Harker and G. White, *The Big Red Song Book* (Pluto Press, 1977), p. 55.

11 See J. Krivine, *Juke Box Saturday Night* (New English Library, 1977); S. Chapple and R. Garofalo, *Rock'n'Roll is Here to Pay* (Chicago: Nelson-Hall, 1977).

12 See L. Shepard, *The Broadside Ballad* (Herbert Jenkins, 1962); L. Shepard, *The History of Street Literature* (David & Charles, 1973); D. Harker, *Hammer and Hand* (Frank Graham, forthcoming).

13 D. Harker, 'Cecil Sharp in Somerset: some conclusions', *Folk Music Journal,* 1972.

14 Harker, *Hammer and Hand.*

15 A. L. Lloyd, *Folk Song in England* (Lawrence & Wishart, 1967); R. Hoggart, *The Use of Literacy* (Penguin, 1957); C. MacInnes, *Sweet Saturday Night* (Panther, 1967).

Bibliography

When I planned this bibliography I thought there might be a hundred or so relevant books and articles; but as I worked through the *British National Bibliography* and the *American Subject Index of Books in Print*, the thing grew alarmingly from draft to draft. Very early on, it was clear that I would not be able to read all the titles. Some were out of print, or available only in the USA. Others might be picked up in second-hand bookshops, but most of them have not been worth opening. All the same, I've included all the titles I've encountered, and to save others trouble and pain I've decided to adopt a rating system for those I've read.

Three asterisks (***) indicate a title which is vital to any serious student of popular song. Two asterisks (**) indicates a piece which ought to be in any college or large public library where study on this topic will be carried on. One asterisk indicates that an item is of marginal interest or significance. No asterisks is intended to indicate material of interest only to the student of parasitic literature. Those texts which have not been read (for whatever reason), have a dagger (†); and related texts commended to me on the subject of 'jazz' are marked with two daggers (††).

Why include what Bryn Jones calls 'the plethora of largely emphemeral literary production which lives off pop music'? Well, if antiquarians of the eighteenth and nineteenth century had done their work properly in this line, we would have found the reconstruction of working-class and pre-industrial workers' culture a lot easier. Besides, these texts represent part of the body of literary production from which people can and do choose. If we are seriously concerned with the totality of working-class culture, we have to take account of the good and bad together.

There was a particular difficulty in trying to categorize works for this bibliography. First to be rejected was the division by so-called 'kinds' of music and song. Terms like 'jazz', 'rock 'n' roll' and 'folk' remain highly vague, and tend to confuse rather than clarify. Next to go was the idea of simply listing entries alphabetically, by author, because the size of the list would make the bibliography almost unusable. So, I have decided to arrange entries in nine categories, some of which are necessarily selective, while others aim to be as exhaustive as possible.

General cultural theory (page 252) contains all those works which the
   present writer has found to be useful or stimulating in the discussion of approaches to, and models of, cultural practice in general.
Criticism of cultural practice (page 254) includes pieces which analyse
   the cultural practice of particular social groups, up to and including
   nations, on the basis of an explicit (or implicit) set of theoretical
   assumptions.
Surveys of music, song and society (page 258) contains all those other
   pieces which concern themselves less systematically (and, usually
   more impressionistically) with the relations between music, song and
   social groups.
(Auto)biography (page 263), *Institutions and technology* (page 272)
   and *Critical theory* (page 276) will be self-explanatory.
Critical practice (page 276) contains items which apply particular
   cultural theories to songs or bodies of songs, working 'out' from
   analysis of song 'into' more general social analysis.
Reference (page 279) includes those works which embody significant
   quantities of usable factual information.
Miscellaneous (page 282) is simply a bag in which to put all those items
   which do not fit elsewhere.

Two further points have to be made. I do not attempt to list titles
of song collections, except in rare instances, where material is referred
to in the main body of the text. For individual songs, the reader is
referred to the *BBC Songs Catalogue*, and to publishers' catalogues.
Secondly, I have not included the titles of periodicals, annuals and
suchlike. Otherwise, while I do not suppose that my chosen headings
are ideal, or that the entries are ideally complete — not least because
some of the titles I have not read will be in the wrong sections — I
hope that the bibliography will have its own kind of consistency. In
order to make it all the more usable, the publishers have agreed to
leave some space at the end, so that the reader can insert new or newly
discovered items.

My largest debt for the bibliography is to the Librarian and staff of
the old John Dalton Library, and of the new Central Library,
Manchester Polytechnic. Particularly, I would like to single out Ian,
Theresa, Jean and Brenda, not least for their forbearance and dogged
good humour in the face of curious requests for even curiouser books
and articles. Thanks, too, to Les Berry and Tony Stimson, for their
help in recommending books on 'jazz', and to Ian Winship of Newcastle
Polytechnic Library, for his continuing help with bibliographical
matters.

By the time this book appears, the bibliography will be a year out of date. This is inevitable. But I hope that the sections primarily concerned with song, singers and music institutions will be largely complete up to the end of 1978.

General cultural theory

*** Baxandall, Lee, and Morawski, Stefan (eds.), *Marx/Engels on Literature and Art*, New York: International General, 1974

Bigsby, C.W.E. (ed.), *Approaches to Popular Culture*, London: Edward Arnold, 1976 (Mainly retreats)

Boyd, John, 'Discussion contribution on trends in youth culture', *Marxism Today*, December 1973 (Determinist)

† Braun, D.Duane, *Toward a Theory of Popular Culture: The Sociology and History of American Music and Dance 1920-1968*, Ann Arbor, Michigan: University of Michigan Press, 1969

** Braverman, Harry, *Labour and Monopoly Capitalism: The Degradation of Work in the Twentieth Century*, London: Monthly Review Press, 1974

** Clarke, John, 'Subcultural symbolism: reconceptualising "Youth cultures" ', unpublished MA thesis, University of Birmingham, 1975

*** Clarke, John and Jefferson, Tony, 'Working class youth cultures', Centre for Contemporary Cultural Studies, University of Birmingham, University of Birmingham, stencilled paper no. 14 (1973)

*** Clarke, John and Jefferson, Tony, 'Working youth cultures', Centre for Contemporary Cultural Studies, University of Birmingham, stencilled paper no. 18 (1973)

*** Clarke, John, *et al.*, 'Subcultures, cultures and class', *Working Papers in Cultural Studies* no. 7/8 (1975), republished by Hutchinson as *Resistance Through Rituals*.

** Clarke, John, *et al.*, *Working Class Culture*, London: Hutchinson, 1979

* Cockburn, Alexander (ed.), *Student Power: Problems, Diagnosis, Action*, Harmondsworth: Penguin, 1969

* Corrigan, Paul and Frith, Simon, 'The politics of youth culture', *Working Papers in Cultural Studies* no. 7/8 (1975)

** Dale, Roger, *et al.*, *Schooling and Capitalism: A Sociological Reader*, London: Routledge & Kegan Paul/Open University, 1976

* Eagleton, Terry, *Criticism and Ideology*, London: New Left Books, 1976

* Enzensberger, Hans Magnus, *Raids and Reconstructions: Essays in Politics, Crime and Culture*, London: Pluto Press, 1976

* Goldman, Lucien, 'The sociology of literature: status and problems of method', *International Social Science Journal*, vol. 19, no. 4 (1967)
* Gramsci, A., *Prison Notebooks*, London: Lawrence & Wishart, 1973
*** Hall, Stuart, and Jefferson Tony, (eds.), *Resistance Through Rituals*, London: Hutchinson, 1976
** Hall, Stuart and Whannel, Paddy, *The Popular Arts*, London: Hutchinson, 1964 (one of the first serious surveys: each chapter deserves to form the basis of a series in the 1980s)
** Harker, Dave, *Fakesong*, London: Pluto Press (forthcoming)
** Hoggart, Richard, *The Uses of Literacy*, Harmondsworth: Penguin, 1957 (The academic ice-breaker: reads like a disjointed novel)
* Hunt, Alan (ed.), *Class and class structure*, London: Lawrence & Wishart, 1977
* Jackson, Brian and Marsden, Dennis, *Education and the Working Class*, Harmondsworth: Penguin, 1969
  Johnstone, J. and Katz, E., 'Youth and popular music: a study in the sociology of taste', *American Journal of Sociology*, vol. 62, (May 1957)
*** Jones, Bryn, 'The politics of popular culture', Centre for Contemporary Cultural Studies, University of Birmingham, stencilled paper no. 12 (n.d.)
* Kidron, Michael, *Western Capitalism Since the War*, London: Weidenfield & Nicolson, 1968
** Kidron, Michael, *Capitalism and Theory*, London: Pluto Press, 1974
* Leavis, Frank Raymond, *Mass Civilisation and Minority Culture*, London: Chatto & Windus, 1930 (For 'and' read 'or')
** Legman, Gershon, *The Rationale of the Dirty Joke*, London: Panther, 1972
** Lenin, V.I., *On Literature and Art*, Moscow: Progress Publishers, 1970
* Lifshitz, Mikhail, *The Philosophy of Art of Karl Marx*, London: Pluto Press, 1973
* Loewenthal, Leo, *Literature, Popular Culture and Society*, New York: Spectrum Books, 1961
*** Marx, Karl, *Selected Works*, London: Lawrence & Wishart, 1943
*** Marx, Karl, *Capital*, London: Lawrence & Wishart, 1974
** Murdock, Graham, and Golding, Peter, 'For a political economy of mass communications', in *Socialist Register 1973*, London: Merlin, 1974
† Murdock, Graham, and Golding, Peter, 'Capitalism, communications and class relations', in J. Curran *et al.*, *Mass Communications and Society*, London: Edward Arnold/Open University, 1977
** Parkin, Frank, *Class Inequality and Political Order*, St Albans: Paladin, 1972
* Pateman, Trevor (ed.), *Counter Course: A Handbook for Course*

Criticism, Harmondsworth: Penguin, 1972

** Reich, Wilhelm, *The Mass Psychology of Fascism*, Harmondsworth: Penguin, 1975

* Rosenburg, Bernard, and White, David Manning, *Mass Culture: The Popular Arts in America*, New York: Free Press, 1964

† Rosenberg, Bernard, and White, David Manning, *Mass Culture Revisited*, New York: Van Nostrand Reinhold, 1971

* Sartre, Jean Paul, *Search for a Method*, New York: Vintage Books, 1968

* Sharp, Cecil James, *English Folk Song: Some Conclusions*, London: Simpkin, 1907 (Of pathological interest only)

Thompson, Denys (ed.), *Discrimination and Popular Culture*, Harmondsworth: Penguin, 1964 (Leavisite: for 'and' read 'or')

** Thompson, Edward, P., *The Poverty of Theory*, London: Merlin, 1978

*** Trotsky, Leon, *Literature and Revolution*, Ann Arbor, Michigan: University of Michigan Press, 1960 (A theoretical analysis still un-challenged by bourgeois critics)

** Williams, Raymond, *Culture and Society*, Harmondsworth: Penguin, 1958 (Hardly anything on pre-industrial or workers' culture)

** Williams, Raymond, *The Long Revolution*, Harmondsworth: Penguin, 1961 (Essentially reformist)

* Williams, Raymond, *Communications*, Harmondsworth: Penguin, 1970

** Williams, Raymond, 'Base and superstructure in marxist cultural theory', in *New Left Review*, no. 82, (Nov./Dec. 1973) (The first clear sign of Williams's rapprochement with marxism)

* Williams, Raymond, *Television: Technology and Cultural Form*, London: Fontana, 1974

*** Williams, Raymond, *Keywords*, London: Fontana, 1976 (A vital glossary, but one which poses rather than solves problems)

* Williams, Raymond, *Marxism and Literature*, London: Oxford University Press, 1977 (Very disappointing)

*** *Working Papers in Cultural Studies*, Centre for Contemporary Cultural Studies, University of Birmingham, spring 1971 to date, now published by Hutchinson. *WPCS* no. 7/8 has been republished as *Resistance Through Rituals*; *WPCS* no. 10 has been republished as *On Ideology*.
(Worth four stars: the best journal in Britain dealing with popular/working-class cultural theory and practice)

Criticism of cultural practice

† Aitken, Jonathan, *The Young Meteors*, London: Secker & Warburg, 1967

Allsop, Kenneth, 'Pop goes Young Woodley', in Richard Mabey (ed.),

Class, London: Blond & Briggs, 1967 (Silly)

†† Barzun, Jacques, *Music in American Life*, New York: Doubleday, 1958

Bicat, Anthony, 'Fifties children: sixties people', in V. Bogdanor and R. Skidelsky (eds.), *The Age of Affluence*, London: Macmillan, 1970

†† Blesh, R., *Shining Trumpets*, London: Cassell, 1958

†† Boulton, David, *Jazz in Britain*, London: W.H. Allen, 1958

† Chalker, Bryan, *Country Music*, London: Phoebus, 1976

* Charters, Samuel Barclay, *The Country Blues*, London: Michael Joseph, 1960

** Clarke, John, 'Skinheads and the study of youth culture', Centre for Contemporary Studies, University of Birmingham, stencilled paper no. 23 (n.d.)

** Clarke, John, 'The skinheads and the magical recovery of community', *Working Papers in Cultural Studies* no. 7/8 (1975)

*** Cohen, Stanley, *Folk Devils and Moral Panics*, London: Paladin, 1973

* Cohen, Stanley, and Young, Jock, *The manufacture of the news: deviance, social problems and the mass media*, London: Constable, 1973

* Corrigan, Paul, 'Doing nothin' ' *Working Papers in Cultural Studies* no. 7/8 (1975)

Denisoff, R. Serge, 'Protest movements: class consciousness and the propaganda song', *Sociological Quarterly*, vol. 9 (spring 1968)

* Denisoff, R. Serge, *Great Day Coming: Folk Music and the American Left*, Urbana, Illinois: University of Illinois Press, 1971 (McCarthyism fifteen years on)

** Douglas, Dave, *Pit Life in County Durham*, Oxford: Ruskin History Workshop, 1972

** Douglas, Dave, *Pit Talk in County Durham*, Oxford: Ruskin History Workshop, 1973

** Dyer, Richard, 'The meaning of Tom Jones', *Working Papers in Cultural Studies*, no. 1 (1971)

* Dyer, Richard, 'Social values of entertainment and show business', Centre for Contemporary Studies, University of Birmingham, stencilled paper no. 36 (1975)

* Eisen, Jonathan (ed.), *The Age of Rock*, New York: Vintage Books, 1969 (Good in parts)

Eisen, Jonathan, *Sights and Sounds of the American Cultural Revolution: The Age of Rock 2*, New York: Vintage Books, 1970 (Not good in parts)

Eisen, Jonathan, *Twenty-Minute Fandangoes and Forever Changes: A Rock Bazaar*, New York: Random House, 1971 (Worse)

†† Ellis, Royston, *The Big Beat Scene*, London: Four Square, 1961

Fabian, Jenny, and Byrne, Johnny, *Groupie*, London: Mayflower, 1970

** Fletcher, Colin, 'Beat gangs on Merseyside', in Timothy Raison (ed.), *Youth in New Society*, London: Hart-Davis, 1966

†† Fox, Charles, *Jazz in Perspective*, London: BBC Publications, 1969

** Fyvel, T.R., *The Insecure Offenders: Rebellious Youth in the Welfare State*, Harmondsworth: Penguin, 1963

* Gardner, Carl (ed.), *Media, politics and culture*: a socialist view, London: Macmillan, 1979

† Gosling, Ray, *Sum Total*, London: Faber, 1962

** Hall, Stuart, 'The hippies: an American "moment" ', Centre for Contemporary Cultural Studies, University of Birmingham, stencilled paper no. 16 (1968)

* Harker, Dave, 'Cecil Sharp in Somerset', *Folk Music Journal*, 1972, pp. 220-40.

** Harker, Dave, *The Songs of the North-East Pitmen's Strikes 1831-1844*, Newcastle: Frank Graham (forthcoming)

** Harker, Dave, *Hammer and Hand: A People's History of Tyne and Wear to 1850*, Newcastle: Frank Graham (forthcoming)

** Hebdige, Dick, 'The Style of the mods', Centre for Contemporary Cultural Studies, University of Birmingham, stencilled paper no. 20 (1974)

** Hebdige, Dick, 'The meaning of mod', Centre for Contemporary Cultural Studies, University of Birmingham, stencilled paper no. 25 (1975)

† Hedgepeth, W., *The Alternative Communal Life in New America*, New York: Macmillan, 1970

†† Hentoff, Nat, *The Jazz Life*, London: Hamish Hamilton, 1964

†† Hentoff, Nat, and McCarthy, Albert J., *Jazz*, New York: Holt, Rinehart, 1959

†† Hodeir, André, *Jazz: Its Evolution and Essence*, London: Secker & Warburg, 1966

† Hodenfield, Chris, *Rock '70*, London: Pyramid Books, 1970

** Ingham, Roger, *et al.*, *Football Hooliganism*, London: Inter-Action Imprint, 1978

Jasper, Tony, *Jesus in a Pop Culture*, London: Fontana, 1975 (Unbelievable)

** Jefferson, Tony, 'The Teds — a political resurrection', Centre for Contemporary Cultural Studies, University of Birmingham, stencilled paper no. 22 (1973)

** Jones, Leroi, *Blues People*, London: Jazz Book Club, 1966

† Keyes, Tom, *All Night Stand*, New York: Ballantine, 1970

† Kofsky, Frank, *Black Nationalism and the Revolution in Music*, New York: Pathfinder Press, 1970

Laurie, Peter, *Teenage Revolution*, London: Blond & Briggs, 1965

* Lawrence, David Herbert, *Phoenix*, London: Heinemann, 1936

† Leaf, David, *The Beach Boys and the California Myth*, New York: Grosset & Dunlap, 1978

Leslie, Peter, *Fab: The Anatomy of a Phenomenon*, London: MacGibbon & Kee, 1965

**MacInnes, Colin, *England, Half English*, Harmondsworth: Penguin, 1966

** MacInnes, Colin, *Absolute Beginners*, London: Panther, 1972

Marks, J., *Rock and Other Four Letter Words*, New York: Bantam, 1968

** Melly, George, *Revolt into Style*, Harmondsworth: Penguin, 1972 (Already a historical document in its own right).

†† Mezzrow, Mezz, *Really the Blues*, London: Transworld, 1961

† Murdock, Graham, and McCron, Robin, 'Scoobies, skins and contemporary pop', *New Society*, 29 March 1973

† (Music Educators National Conference), *Youth Music*, Reston, Virginia: Music Educators, 1969

* Neville, Richard, *Playpower*, London: Paladin, 1970 (The Underground coming up to die)

* Nolan, Tom, 'Groupies: a story of our times', in Jonathan Eisen (ed.), *The Age of Rock*, New York: Vintage, 1969

* Nuttall, Jeff, *Bomb Culture*, London: Paladin, 1970

† O'Toole, J., *Watts and Woodstock*, New York: Holt, Rinehart, 1973

† Peatman, John, 'Radio and popular music', in P.F. Lazarfield and F.N. Stanton (eds.), *Radio Research 1942-3*, New York: Duell Sloan & Pierce, 1944

* Raison, Timothy, *Youth in New Society*, London: Hart-Davis, 1966

* Roberts, Brian, 'Parents and youth cultures', Centre for Contemporary Studies, University of Birmingham, stencilled paper no. 28 (1973)

† Robinson, Richard and Zwerling, Andy, *The Rock Scene*, New York: Pyramid, 1971

** Rock, Paul, and Cohen, Stanley, 'The teddy boy' in V. Bogdanor and R. Skidelsky (eds.), *The Age of Affluence*, London: Macmillan, 1970

* Rubin, Jerry, *Do It!*, London: Simon & Schuster, 1970

Sandford, Jeremy, *Synthetic Fun*, Harmondsworth: Penguin, 1967

† Seeger, Peter, 'Whatever happened to singing in the unions?', *Sing Out*, May 1965

† Simmons, J., and Windgrad, B., *It's Happening: A Portrait of the Youth Scene Today*, Santa Barbara, California: Marc Laird Publications, 1966

†† Simon, George, *The Big Bands*, New York: Macmillan, 1969

Swanwick, Keith, *Popular Music and the Teacher*, London: Pergamon, 1968 (Or, How to Cure Kids for Life)

Taylor, Ken, *Rock Generation*, Melbourne, Australia: Sun Books, 1970

† Vassal, Jacques, *Electric Children: Roots & Branches of Modern*

Folkrock, New York: Taplinger, 1976

* Williams, Raymond, *The Country and the City*, London: Chatto & Windus, 1973

** Willis, Paul, 'Pop music and youth cultural groups in Birmingham', unpublished Ph.D thesis, University of Birmingham, 1972 (A ground-breaking study)

** Willis, Paul, 'The cultural meaning of drug use', *Working Papers in Cultural Studies* no. 7/8 (1975)

*** Willis, Paul, *Learning to Labour: How Working Class Kids Get Working Class Jobs*, Farnborough: Saxon House, 1977

*** Willis, Paul, *Profane Culture*, London: Routledge & Kegan Paul, 1978

† Wilson, Jane, 'Teenagers', in *Len Deighton's London Dossier*, Harmondsworth: Penguin, 1967

Surveys of music, song and society

† Barnes, Ken, *Twenty Years of Pop*, London: Kenneth Mason, 1973

** Beckett, Alan, 'Mapping pop', *New Left Review*, no. 54 (spring 1969)

* Belz, Carl, *The Story of Rock*, New York: Oxford University Press, 1972

† Benson, Dennis C., *The Rock Generation*, Nashville, Tennessee: Abingdon, 1976

†† Berendt, J., *The New Jazz Book*, London: Jazz Book Club, 1965

** Birchall, Ian, 'The decline and fall of rhythm and blues', in Jonathan Eisen (ed.), *The Age of Rock*, New York: Vintage Books, 1969

* Bird, Brian, *Skiffle*, London: Robert Hale, 1958 (The only book there is)

† Blair, Dike, and Anscomb, Elizabeth, *Punk: Punk Rock, Style, Stance, People, Stars*, New York: Urizen, 1978

† Boeckman, Charles, *And the Beat Goes On: A History of Pop Music in America*, Washington D.C.: Luce, 1972

† Boot, Adrian, and Thomas, Michael, *Jamaica: Babylon on a Thin Wire*, New York: Schocken, 1977

† Boston, Virginia, *Punk Rock*, New York: Penguin, 1978

† Broven, John, *Walking to New Orleans*, Bexhill, Kent: Blues Unlimited, 1974

* Burchill, Julie, and Parsons, Tony, *'The Boy looked at Johnny'; the obituary of rock and roll*, London: Pluto Press, 1978

† Burt, Rob, and North, Patsy, *West Coast Story*, London: Hamlyn, 1977

† Bygrave, Mike, *Rock*, New York: Watts, 1978

†† Carr, Ian, *Music Outside: Contemporary Jazz in Britain*, London: Latimer, 1973

†† Chase, Gilbert, *America's Music*, New York: McGraw Hill, 1967

† Clarke, Dick, and Robinson, Richard, *Rock, Roll and Remember*, New York: Harmony, 1978

Cohn, Nik, *I Am Still the Greatest Says Johnny Angelo*, London: Secker & Warburg, 1967

** Cohn, Nik, *Awopbopaloobopalopbamboom*, London: Paladin, 1970 (A total ego-trip; self-consistent, and almost a self-mockery. Useful as a historical document in its own right – a spiritual autobiography)

† Cohn, Nik, *Rock Dreams*, New York: CBS Publications, Popular Library, 1974

†† Collier, Graham, *Inside Jazz*, London: Quartet Books, 1973

* Colls, Robert, *The Collier's Rant*, London: Croom Helm, 1977 (Wrong about many historical matters, but useful in parts)

†Coon, Caroline, *Nineteen Eighty-Eight: The New Wave Punk Rock Explosion*, New York: Hawthorn, 1978

† Cummings, Tony, *The Sound of Philadelphia*, London: Eyre Methuen, 1975

† Dachs, David, *Anything Goes: The World of Pop Music*, Indianapolis, Indiana: Bobbs-Merrill, 1964

† Dachs, David, *Inside Pop Number 2*, New York: Scholastic Book Services, 1970

† Dachs, David, *American Pop*, New York: Scholastic Book Services, 1974

†† Dance, Stanley, *Jazz Era: The Forties*, London: MacGibbon & Kee, 1961

† Davis, Julie (ed.), *Punk*, London: Millington, 1977

† Dexter, Dave, *Playback*, New York: Watson-Guptill, 1976

† Doney, Malcolm, *Summer in the City: rock music and way of life*, Berkhamsted: Lion Publishing, 1978

† Dunson, Josh, 'Freedom Singing Gathering in the Heart of Dixie', *Sing Out*, September 1964

† Dunson, Josh, *Freedom in the Air: Song Movements of the '60s*, New York: International Publishers, 1965

† Ewen, David, *Panorama of American Popular Music*, Englewood Cliffs, New Jersey: Prentice-Hall, 1957

† Ewen, David, *History of Popular Music*, London: Constable, 1961

† Ewen, David, *American Popular Songs from the Revolutionary Wars to the Present*, New York: Random, 1966

† Ewen, David, *All the Years of American Popular Music*, Englewood Cliffs, New Jersey: Prentice-Hall, 1977

† Farren, Mick, and Snow, George, *Rock 'n' Roll Circus,* Reading, Mass.: Addison-Wesley Publishers, 1978

†† Finkelstein, Sidney, *Jazz: A People's Music*, London: Jazz Book Club, 1964

Flattery, Paul, *The Illustrated History of Pop*, London: Music Sales, 1973

† Fleischer, Leonore, *Joni Mitchell*, New York: Book Sales, 1976

† Ford, Larry, 'Geographic factors in the origin, evolution and diffusion of rock and roll music' *The Journal of Geography*, vol. 70, no. 18 (November 1971)

† Freeman, Larry G., *Melodies Linger On*, Watkins Glen, N.Y.: Century House, 1951

† Fuld, James, J., *American Popular Music 1775-1950*, Philadelphia: Musical Americana, 1956

† Gabree, John, *The World of Rock*, Greenwich, Connecticut: Fireweed Publications, 1968

* Gammond, Peter, *Scott Joplin and the Ragtime Era*, London: Abacus, 1975

† Gilbert, Douglas, *Lost Chords: The Diverting History of American Popular Songs*, New York: Cooper Square, 1971

*** Gillett, Charlie, *The Sound of the City*, London: Sphere, 1971 (Very useful for factual information — a bit loose on cultural analysis)

† Goodman, Benny, and Kolodin, Irving, *Kingdom of Swing*, New York: Ungar, 1961

† Grissim, John, *Country Music: White Man's Blues*, New York: Paperback Library, 1970

† Groom, Bob, *The Blues Revival*, London: Studio Vista, 1971

† Grossman, Loyd, *A Social History of Rock Music: From the Greasers to the Glitter Rock*, New York: McKay, 1976

† Hamburger, Robert, and Stern, Susan, *The Thirties*, New York: Music Sales, 1975

** Harker, David, 'Popular song and working-class consciousness in north-east England', unpublished Ph.D thesis, University of Cambridge, 1976

† Hemphill, Paul, *The Nashville Sound: Bright Lights and Country Music*, New York: Ballantine, 1975

† Hennessy, V., *Punk: we're all in the gutter*, London: Quartet, 1978

† Hollingworth, B., *Songs of the People: Lancashire Dialect Poetry of the Industrial Revolution*, Manchester: Manchester University Press, 1977

† Hopkins, Jerry, *The Rock Story*, New York: Signet, 1970

† Jahn, Mike, *Rock: A Social History of the Music, 1945-1972*, New York: Quadrangle, 1973

† Jahn, Mike, *Rock: From Elvis Presley to the Rolling Stones*, New York: Time Books, 1973

† Jekyll, W., *Jamaican Song and Story*, London: Constable, 1966

Johnson, Derek, *Beat Music*, Copenhagen: Wilhelm Hansen, 1969

†† Jones, Leroi, *Black Music*, London: MacGibbon & Kee, 1969

** Laing, Dave, *The Sound of Our Time*, London: Sheed & Ward, 1969 (The best analysis of British music in the 1960s)

* Laing, Dave, *et al.*, *The Electric Muse*, London: Eyre Methuen, 1975

† Lang, Paul H., *One Hundred Years of Music in America*, New York: Schirmer, 1961

* Lee, Edward, *Music of the People*, London: Barrie & Jenkins, 1970

† Leiber, Jerry, and Stoller, Mike, *Baby, That Was Rock & Roll*, New York: Harcourt Brace, 1978

† Lennon, Cynthia, *A Twist of Lennon*, London: Star Books, 1978

†† Leonard, Neil, *Jazz and the White American; The Acceptance of a New Art Form*, London: Jazz Book Club, 1964

† Levy, Lester S., *Give Me Yesterday: American History in Song 1890-1920*, Norman, Oklahoma: University of Oklahoma Press, 1975

** Lloyd, Albert Lancaster, *The Singing Englishman*, London: Workers' Music Association, 1944 (The first attempt to produce a serious analysis of 'folksong' in its historical context)

*** Lloyd, Albert Lancaster, *Folk Song in England,* London: Lawrence & Wishart, 1967 (The standard text, though theoretically evasive, and much less sure of itself than his earlier work)

† McCarthy, Albert, *The Dance Band Era*, London: Studio Vista, 1971

† Malone, Bill C., *Country Music USA*, Austin, Texas: University of Texas Press, 1969

* Marcus, Greil, *Mystery Train: Images of America in Rock 'n' Roll Music*, New York: Dutton, 1976

† Mattfield, Julius, *'Variety' Musical Cavalcade: Musical-Historical Review*, Englewood Cliffs, New Jersey: Prentice-Hall, 1962

May, Chris, *Rock 'n' Roll*, London: Socion Books, n.d.

May, Chris, and Phillips, Ian, *British Beat*, London: Socion Books, n.d.

* Mellers, Wilfred, *Music in a New Found Land*, London: Barrie & Rockcliff, 1964

† Miller William, *The World of Pop Music and Jazz*, London: Concordia, 1965

† Miron, Charles, *The Rock Jazz Revolution*, New York: Drake Publications, 1977

* Mooney, H.F., 'Popular music since the 1920s: the significance of shifting taste', in Jonathan Eisen (ed.), *The Age of Rock*, New York: Vintage Books, 1969

Morse, David, *Motown*, London: Studio Vista, 1971

† Nanry, Charles, *American Music: From Storyville to Woodstock*, New Brunswick, New Jersey: Transaction Books, 1975

† Oster, Harry, *Living Country Blues*, Detroit: Gale, 1969

Palmer, Tony, *Born Under a Bad Sign*, London: William Kimber, 1970

* Palmer, Tony, *All You Need Is Love*, London: Futura, 1977 (Flashy, and almost wholly derivative)

* Pearsall, Ronald, *Popular Music of the Twenties*, Newton Abbot: David & Charles, 1976

Pegg, Bob, *Folk*, London: Wildwood, 1976

† Pulling, Christopher, *They Were Singing, and What They Sang About*, London: Harrap, 1953

† Reid, Jan, *The Improbable Rise of Redneck Rock*, New York: Da Capo, 1977

† Roberts, John Storm, *Black Music of Two Worlds*, New York: Morrow, 1974

† Robinson, Richard, *Rock Revolution*, New York: CBS Publications, Popular Library, 1976

† Rublowsky, John, *Popular Music*, New York: Basic, 1967

†† Russell, Ross, *Jazz Style in Kansas City and the South West*, Berkeley, California: University of California Press, 1973

† Ruth, L., 'The scene', *English Journal* no. 62 (February 1973)

† Saxton, Martha, *The Fifties*, New York: Music Sales, 1975

† Saxton, Martha, *The Twenties*, New York: Music Sales, 1976

† Schafe, William J., *Rock Music: Where It's Been, What It Means, Where It's Going*, Minneapolis, Min.: Augsburg, 1972

† Schaumburg, Ron, *Growing Up With the Beatles*, New York: Harcourt Brace, 1976

* Shaw, Arnold, *The Rock Revolution*, London: Macmillan, 1969

† Shaw, Arnold, *World of Soul: The Black Contribution to Pop Music*, Chicago: Contemporary Books, 1970

† Shaw, Arnold, *The Rockin' Fifties: The Decade That Transformed the Pop Music Scene*, New York: Hawthorn, 1975

† Shelton, Robert, and Goldblatt, B., *Country Music Story*, Indianapolis, Indiana: Bobbs-Merrill, 1966

** Shepard, Leslie, *The Broadside Ballad*, London: Herbert Jenkins, 1962 (Good for factual material – weak on ideas)

** Shepard, Leslie, *The History of Street Literature*, Newton Abbot: David & Charles, 1973 (Ditto)

† *Sociology and History of Popular American Music and Dance 1920-1968*, Ann Arbor, Michigan: University of Michigan Press, n.d.

* Spaeth, Sigmund, *A History of Popular Music in America*, London: Phoenix, 1960 (More a chronology than a history)

†† Stearns, Marshall, *The Story of Jazz*, London: Muller, 1958

† Stevenson, Ronald, *Western Music*, London: Kahn & Averill, 1971

† Trow, Mike, *The Pulse of '64: The Mersey Beat*, New York: Vantage, 1978

† Van de Horst, Brian, *Rock Music*, New York: Watts, 1973

*** Whitcomb, Ian, *After the Ball: Pop Music from Rag to Rock*, Harmondsworth: Penguin, 1973. Perhaps the best overall survey of post-war pop

* Whitcomb, Ian, *Tin Pan Alley: A Pictorial History 1919-1939*, London: Wildwood House/EMI Publishing, 1975

† White, John I., *Git Along Little Dogies: Songs & Songmakers of the American West*, Urbana, Illinois: University of Illinois Press, 1975

* Wilder, Alec, *American Popular Song: The Great Innovators 1900-1950*, New York: Oxford University Press, 1972

†† Williams, Martin, *Jazz Panorama*, London: Jazz Book Club, 1965

† Witmark, Isidore, and Golder, Isaac, *From Ragtime to Swingtime*, New York: Da Capo, 1975

† Wolman, Baron, *Festival: The Book of American Music Celebrations*, New York: Macmillan, 1970

† Wootton, Richard, *Honky tonkin': a guide to music USA*, London: Wootton, 1978

† Yorke, Ritchie, *The History of Rock 'n' Roll* New York: Methuen 1976

(Auto)biography

** Albertson, Chris, *Bessie, Empress of the Blues*, London: Abacus, 1975

Alexander, Robert, *Bob Dylan: an illustrated history*, London: Elm Tree Books, 1978

† Anderton, Barrie, *Sonny Boy: The World of Al Jolson*, London: Jupiter, 1975

† Barlow, Roy, *The Elvis Presley Encyclopaedia*, A. Hand, 41 Derby Road, Heanor, Derbyshire, 1964

† Barnes, Ken, *Sinatra and the Great Song Stylists*, Shepperton: Ian Allan, 1972

† Barnes, Ken, *The Beach Boys: A Biography in Words & Pictures*, New York: Barnes & Noble, 1976

† Barnes, Ken, *The Bee Gees: The authorized biography*, London: Octopus, 1979

† Berman, Connie, *The Dolly Parton Scrapbook*, New York: Grosset & Dunlap, 1978

† Berman, Connie, *The Shaun Cassidy Scrapbook*, New York: Grosset & Dunlap, 1978

†† Berton, Ralph, *Remembering Bix*, London: W.H. Allen, 1974

* Braun, Michael, *Love Me Do*, Harmondsworth: Penguin, 1964 (The first Beatles book of any significance)

* Bronson, Bertrand Harris, *Joseph Ritson: Scholar-at-Arms*, Berkeley, California: University of California Press, 1938

** Broonzy, William, *Big Bill Blues: William Broonzy's Story as told to Yannick Bruynoghe*, London: Cassell, 1955

† Buckle, Philip, *All Elvis: An Unofficial Biography of the 'King of Discs'*, London: Daily Mirror, 1962

Burt, Robert, *The Beatles: The Fabulous Story of John, Paul, George and Ringo*, London: Octopus, 1975

† Burton, Peter, *Rod Stewart: a Life on the Town*, London: New English Library, 1977

Carr, Roy, and Tyler, Tony, *The Beatles: An Illustrated Record*, London: New English Library, 1975

† Carr, Roy, *Fleetwood Mac: Rumours N' Fax*, New York: Harmony, 1978

Caserta, Peggy, *Going Down With Janis*, London: Futura, 1975

* Cash, Johnny, *Man in Black*, London: Hodder & Stoughton, 1975

† Charles, Ray, and Ritz, David, *Brother Ray: Ray Charles' own story*, London: Macdonald and Jane's, 1979

* Charters, Samuel Barclay, *The Legacy of the Blues: A Glimpse into the Art and the Lives of Twelve Great Bluesmen: An Informal Study*, London: Calder & Boyars, 1975

† Chilton, John, *Billie's Blues: A Survey of Billie Holiday's Career 1933-1959*, London: Quartet Books, 1975

† Claire, Vivian, *David Bowie*, New York: Music Sales, 1977

† (Clapton), *Eric Clapton: 461 Ocean Boulevard*, New York: Peer-Southern, 1975

† Clooney, Rosemary, and Strait, Raymond, *This For Remembrance*, London: Robson, 1978

† Cohen, Mitchell S., *Carole King: A Biography in Words & Pictures*, New York: Barnes & Noble, 1976

† Cole, Bill, *John Coltrane*, London: Macmillan, 1978

† Cole, Maria, *Nat King Cole: An Intimate Biography*, London: W.H. Allen, 1972

† Colin, Syd, *Al Bowly*, London: Elm Tree Books, 1979

† Cooper, Alice, *Me, Alice: The Autobiography of Alice Cooper*, New York: Putnam, 1976

† Cowan, Philip, *Behind the Beatles Songs*, London: Polyantric Press, 1978

† Cromelin, Richard, *Rod Stewart: A Biography in Words & Pictures*, New York: Barnes and Noble, 1976

† Dachs, David, *John Denver*, New York: Pyramid, 1976

† (Daily Mirror), *Meet the Monkees*, London: Daily Mirror, 1967

Dalton, David, *The Rolling Stones: An Unauthorised Biography*, London: Star Books, 1975

Dalton, David, *Janis: Janis Joplin*, London: Calder, 1972

** Davies, Hunter, *The Beatles*, London: Mayflower, 1978 ('It was bullshit', according to John Lennon, but it's the fullest biography available)

† Demorest, Steve, *Alice Cooper*, New York: CBS Publications, Popular Library, 1974

† Douglas, David, *Presenting David Bowie*, New York: Pinnacle Books, 1975

† Dragonwagon, Crescent, *Stevie Wonder*, New York: Music Sales, 1977

† Dufrechou, Carole, *Neil Young*, New York: Music Sales, 1978

† Dunleavy, Steve, *Elvis: What Happened*, New York, Ballantine, 1977

Dunn, Paul, *The Osmonds*, London: W.H. Allen, 1975

* Edgington, Harry and Himmelstrand, Peter, *Abba*, London: Magnum Books, 1978 (Engagingly honest about market calculations)

† Edwards, Audrey and Wohl, Gary, *The Picture Life of Stevie Wonder*, New York: Watts, 1977

† Eldred, Patricia M., *Diana Ross*, Mankato, Minnesota: Creative Educational Society, 1975

† Eliot, Marc, *Death of a Rebel: Phil, Ochs and a Small Circle of Friends*, New York: Doubleday, 1979

** Ellington, Duke, *Music is my Mistress*, London: W.H. Allen, 1974

† Elsner, Constanze, *Stevie Wonder*, New York: CBS Publications, Popular Library, 1978

† *Elvis Lives!*, London: Galaxy, 1978

† *Elvis Presley 1935-1977 – a tribute to the King*, West Midlands: Wednesbury, 1977

* Epstein, Brian, *A Cellarful of Noise*, London: Souvenir Press, 1964 (Written by Derek Taylor)

† Ewen, David, *Men of Popular Music*, New York: Arno, 1972

† Ewen, David, *Great Men of American Popular Song*, Englewood Cliffs, New Jersey: Prentice-Hall, 1972

† Faith, Adam, *Poor Me*, London: Souvenir Press, 1961

† Farren, Mick, and Marchbank, Pearce (eds.) *Elvis in his own words*, London: Omnibus, 1977

† Fawcett, Anthony, *John Lennon, one day at a time*, London: New English Library, 1977

† Feather, Leonard, *From Satchmo to Miles*, London: Quartet Books, 1974

Ferrier, Bob, *The Wonderful World of Cliff Richard*, London: Peter Davis, 1964

† Fox Cumming, Ray, *Stevie Wonder*, London: Mondabrook Books, 1977

† Frank, Alan, *Sinatra*, London: Hamlyn, 1978

* Freedland, Michael, *Irving Berlin*, London: W.H. Allen, 1974

* Freedland, Michael, *Al Jolson*, London: Abacus, 1975

† Freedland, Michael, *Sophie: The Sophie Tucker Story*, London: Woburn Press, 1978

† Freedland, Michael, *Jerome Kern*, London: Robson, 1978

* Friedman, Myra, *Buried Alive: the Story of Janis Joplin*, London:

Star Books, 1975

† Gallo, Armando, *Genesis: the evolution of a rock band,* London: Sidgwick & Jackson, 1978

Gambaccini, Paul, *Elton John and Bernie Taupin,* London: Star Books, 1975

† Gambaccini, Paul, *Paul McCartney in his own words,* London: Omnibus, 1976

† Gehman, Richard, *Elvis Presley: Hero or Heel?,* London: L. Miller & Sons, 1957

† Gill, Brendan, *Cole: a Biographical Essay,* London: Michael Joseph, 1972

†† Gitler, Ira, *Jazz Masters of the Forties,* London: Macmillan, 1975

* Gleason, Ralph, *The Jefferson Airplane and the San Francisco Sound,* New York: Ballantine, 1971

† Golden, Bruce, *The Beach Boys: Southern California Pastoral,* Hollywood, California: Borgo Press, 1976

* Goldrosen, John J., *Buddy Holly, His Life and Music,* London: Charisma, 1975

Golumb, David, and Jasper, Tony, *The Bay City Rollers Scrapbook,* London: Queen Anne Press, 1975

† Goodman, Pete, *Our Own Story by the Rolling Stones,* London: Transworld, 1964

† Graham, Samuel, *Fleetwood Mac: The Authorized History,* New York: Warner, 1978

† *Grand Funk,* New York: Peer-Southern, 1975

† Gray, Andy, *Great Pop Stars,* London: Hamlyn, 1973

† Gray, Andy, *Great Country Music Stars,* London: Hamlyn, 1975

†† Green, Benny, *The Reluctant Art,* London: MacGibbon & Kee, 1962

†† Green, Benny, *Drums in my Ears,* London: Davis-Poynter, 1973

† Greene, Myrna, *You Gotta Have Heart: The Eddie Fisher Story,* New York: Eriksson, 1978

* Greenfield, Robert, *A Journey Through America with the Rolling Stones,* St Albans: Panther, 1975

† Gregory, James, *The Elvis Presley Story,* Leicester: Thorpe and Porter, 1960

† Gross, Michael and Plant, Robert, *Led Zeppelin,* New York: CBS Publications, Popular Library, 1975

† Gross, Michael, *Bob Dylan: Illustrated History,* London: Elm Tree Books, 1978

** Guthrie, Woody, *Born to Win,* New York: Macmillan, 1965

*** Guthrie, Woody, *Bound for Glory,* London: Picador, 1974

* Guthrie, Woody, *Seeds of Man,* New York: Dutton, 1976

† Hallowel, John, *Inside Creedence,* London: Bantam, 1971

† Hamblett, Charles, *Here are the Beatles*, London: New English Library, 1964

† Hand, Albert, *The Elvis Presley Pocket Handbook*, Heanor, Derbyshire, A. Hand, 1961

† Hand, Albert, *Elvis Special*, Manchester: World Distribution, 1968/9/70

* Handy, W.C., *Father of the Blues*, London: Jazz Book Club, 1961

Harbinson, W.A., *Elvis Presley: an Illustrated Biography*, London: Michael Joseph, 1975

** Harker, David, 'John Bell, the Great Collector', in John Bell (ed.), *Rhymes of Northern Bards*, Newcastle: Frank Graham, 1971

** Harker, David, 'Thomas Allan and "Tyneside Song" ', in Thomas Allan (ed.), *Tyneside Songs*, Newcastle: Frank Graham, 1972

* Harker, David, *George Ridley*, Newcastle: Frank Graham, 1973

* Harker, David, *Ned Corvan*, Newcastle: Frank Graham, (forthcoming)

† Harris, Jet, and Ellis, Royston, *Driftin' with Cliff Richard: The Inside Story of What Really Happens on Tour*, London: Charles Buchan, 1959

Harrison, Hank, *The Grateful Dead*, London: Star Books, 1975

† Hart, Dorothy, *Thou Swell, Thou Witty: the life and lyrics of Lorenz Hart*, London: Elm Tree Books, 1978

Haskins, James, *The Story of Stevie Wonder*, London: Panther, 1978

** Hentoff, Nat, and Shapiro, N., *Hear Me Talkin' To Ya*, London: Jazz Book Club, 1962

* Herman, Gary, *The Who*, London' Studio Vista, 1971

*** Holiday, Billie, and Dufty, William, *Lady Sings the Blues*, London: Abacus, 1975

† Holmes, Robert, *The Three Loves of Elvis Presley*, London: Hulton Press, 1959

† Home, Robin Douglas, *Sinatra*, London: Michael Joseph, 1962

*** Hopkins, Jerry, *Elvis*, London: Abacus, 1974 (Just about the most workpersonlike pop biography there is)

† Hudson, James A., *The Osmond Brothers*, New York: Scholastic Book Services, 1974

** Hunter, Ian, *Diary of a Rock 'n' Roll Star*, St Albans: Panther, 1974 (Seemingly the most honest account of a US tour)

† Jacobs, David, *Pick of the Pop Stars*, Nottingham: Palmer, 1962

* Jacobs, David, *Jacobs' Ladder*, London: Peter Davies, 1963 (Interesting on the post-war armed forces broadcasting mafia)

† Jacobs, Linda, *Stevie Wonder: Sunshine in the Shadows*, St Paul, Minn.: EMC Publications, 1976

† Janson, John S., *Helen Shapiro, Pop Princess*, London: New English Library, 1963

† Jay, Dave, *Jolsonography*, Bournemouth: Barrie Anderton, 1974

† John, Elton, *Elton: It's a Little Bit Funny*, New York: Viking Press, 1977

* Jones, Max, and Chilton, John, *Louis: The Louis Armstrong Story 1900-1971*, St Albans: Mayflower, 1975

Jones, Peter, *Tom Jones*, London: Arthur Baker, 1970 (Dire — possibly the worst pop biography there is)

† Jones, Peter, *Elvis*, London: Octopus Books, 1976

† Kahn, E.J., *The Voice: The Story of an American Phenomenon*, New York: Harper & Row, 1947

† Kasak, Richard, *Jim Croce: His Life and Music*, Secaucus, New Jersey: Derbibooks, 1975

† Katz, Susan, *Frampton!*, New York: Harcourt Brace, 1978

** Kennedy, John, *Tommy Steele*, London: Corgi, 1959 (One of the most revealing of the star fabrication biographies)

Knight, Curtis, *Jimi: An Intimate Biography*, London: Star Books, 1975

† Kooper, Al, and Edmonds, Ben, *Backstage Passes: Rock 'n' Roll Life in the Sixties*, Briarcliff Manor, N.Y.: Stein & Day, 1977

* Laing, Dave, *Buddy Holly*, London: Studio Vista, 1971

† Larkin, Rochelle, *The Beatles — Yesterday, Today, Tomorrow*, London: Scholastic Book Service, 1977

† Lauder, Sir Harry, *Roamin' in the Gloamin*, Wakefield: EP, 1976

Leigh, Spencer, *Paul Simon: Now and Then*, Liverpool: Raven Books, 1973

Leslie, Peter, and Gwynn-Jones, Patrick, *The Book of Bilk*, London: MacGibbon & Kee, 1963

† Levy, Alan, *Operation Elvis*, London: Consul, 1962

† Lindvall, Marianne, *Abba: the ultimate pop group*, London: Souvenir, 1977

** Lomax, Alan, *Mister Jelly Roll*, London: University of California Press, 1973

Luce, Philip C., *The Stones*, London: Howard Baker, 1970

† Lydon, Michael, *Rock Folk: Portraits from the Rock 'n' Roll Pantheon*, New York: Dell, 1973

† Lynn, Loretta, and Vecsey, George, *Coal Miner's Daughter*, London: Panther, 1979

* Lynn, Vera, *Vocal Refrain: An Autobiography*, London: Star Books, 1976

† Lyttleton, Humphrey, *Take It From The Top*, London: Robson Books, 1975

† McGreane, Meagon, *On Stage with John Denver*, Sacramento, California: Creative Editions, 1975

McGregor, Craig, *Bob Dylan: A Retrospective*, London: Angus & Robertson, 1973

† McKnight, Connor, and Silver, Caroline, *The Who*, New York: Scholastic Book Services, 1974

Mander, Margaret, *Suzi Quatro*, London: Futura, 1976

† Mann, May, *Elvis and the Colonel*, London: Drake, 1975

† Manning, Steve, *The Jacksons*, New York: Bobbs-Merrill, 1976

Marks, J., *Mick Jagger*, London: Abacus, 1974

† Marsh, Dave, *Bruce Springsteen: Born to Run*, New York: Pocket Books, 1976

† Marsh, Dave, *Paul Simon*, New York: Music Sales, 1978

† Martin, James, *John Denver, Rock Mountain Wonderboy*, London: Everest, 1977

† Marx, Samuel, and Clayton, Jan, *Rodgers and Hart: Bewitched, Bothered and Bedevilled*, New York: Putnam, 1976

† Mathis, Sharon B., *Ray Charles*, New York: T.Y. Crowell, 1973

† Melhuish, Martin, *The Bachman-Turner Overdrive Biography*, New York: Two Continents, 1976

* Melly, George, *Owning Up*, London: Penguin, 1970

† Michaels, Ross, *George Harrison*, New York: Music Sales, 1977

† Miles, Barry, *The Beatles in their own words*, London: Omnibus Press, 1978

† Miles, Barry, *Bob Dylan in his own words*, London: Omnibus Press, 1978

* Millar, Bill, *The Drifters*, London: Studio Vista, 1971

** Millar, Bill, *The Coasters*, London: Star Books, 1975

** Mingus, Charles, *Beneath the Underdog*, Harmondsworth: Penguin, 1975

† Morse, Ann, *Olivia Newton-John*, Mankato, Minnesota: Creative Educational Society, 1976

† Morse, Ann, *Barry Manilow*, Mankato, Minnesota: Creative Educational Society, 1978

† Morse, Charles and Ann, *Jackson Five*, Mankato, Minnesota: Creative Educational Society, 1974

† Munshower, Suzanne, *The Bee Gees*, New York: Music Sales, 1978

† Mylett, Howard, *Led Zeppelin*, St Albans: Panther, 1976

† Nash, Bruce M., *The Elvis Presley Quizbook*, New York: Warner, 1978

† Newman, Gerald, and Bivona, Joe, *Elton John*, New York: New American Library, 1976

† Nobbs, George, *The Wireless Stars*, Norwich: Wensum Books, 1972

† Nolan, Frederick, *The Sound of their Music: the Story of Rodgers & Hammerstein*, London: Dent, 1978

† Nolan, Tom, *The Allman Brothers Band: A Biography in Words and Pictures*, New York: Barnes & Noble, 1976

† Nolan, Tom, *The Sex Pistols File*, London: Omnibus, 1978

† Orloff, Katherine, *Rock 'n' Roll Women*, Los Angeles: Nash, 1974

† O'Shea, Mary, *Chicago*, Sacramento, California: Creative Editions, 1975

† Pascall, Jeremy, *Paul McCartney & Wings*, London: Hamlyn, 1977

† Pascall, Jeremy, *The Rolling Stones*, London: Hamlyn, 1977

† Pascall, Jeremy, and Burt, Rob, *The Stars and Superstars of Black Music*, London: Phoebus, 1977

Paton, T., *The Bay City Rollers*, London: Everest, 1975

Peers, Donald, *Pathway*, London: Warner Laurie, 1951

† Pennebaker, D.A., *Don't Look Back*, New York: Ballantine, 1968

† (Photoplay), *Elvis Presley: His Complete Life Story*, USA: Illustrated Publications, 1956

Pidgeon, John, *Slade in Flame*, London: Panther, 1975

† Pidgeon, John, *Eric Clapton*, London: Panther, 1976

†Pidgeon, John, *Rod Stewart and the Changing 'Faces'*, London: Panther, 1976

† Pleasants, Henry, *The Great American Popular Singer*, London: Gollancz, 1974

† Pollock, Bruce, *In Their Own Words: Lyrics and Lyricists*, New York: Macmillan, 1975

† Previn, Dory, *Midnight Baby: An Autobiography*, London: Corgi, 1978

† Pryce, Larry, *Queen*, London: Star Books, 1976

† Pryce, Larry, *The Bee Gees*, St Albans: Panther, 1979

† Race, Steve, *Musician at Large*, London: Methuen, 1979

†† Ramsay, F., and Smith, C., *Jazzmen*, New York: Harcourt Brace, 1939

* Randall, Allan, and Seaton, Ray, *George Formby*, London: W.H. Allen, 1974

† Ribakov, S., and Ribakov, B., *Folk Rock: the Bob Dylan Story*, New York: Dell, 1966

† Richard, Cliff, *It's Great to be Young*, London: Souvenir Press, 1960

† Richard, Cliff, *Me and My Shadows*, London: Daily Mirror, 1961

† Richard, Cliff, *The Illustrated 'Which One's Cliff'*, Sevenoaks: Hodder & Stoughton, 1978

† Ridgway, John, *The Sinatrafile*, Birmingham: John Ridgway Books, 1978

† Rinzler, Alan, *Bob Dylan: An Illustrated Record*, New York: Harmony, 1978

† Robeson, Paul, *Here I Stand*, Boston, Mass.: Beacon Press, 1971

† (Rochdale Museum), *Our Gracie*, Rochdale: Rochdale Museum, 1978

† Rodgers, Richard, *Musical Stages: An Autobiography*, New York: Random House, 1975

†† Rooney, James, *Bossmen: Bill Monroe and Muddy*, New York: Dial, 1971

** Scaduto, Anthony, *Bob Dylan*, London: Sphere Books, 1973 (For all its faults, the best there is)

* Scaduto, Anthony, *Mick Jagger*, St Albans: Mayflower, 1975

† Schwartz, Charles, *Cole Porter*, London: W.H. Allen, 1978

† Scott, Ronnie, *Some of my best friends are blues*, London: W.H. Allen, 1979

† Seeger, Pete, *The Incompleat Folksinger*, New York: Simon & Schuster, n.d.

** Shaw, Arnold, *Sinatra*, London: Coronet Books, 1970

† Shaw, Greg, *Elton John: A Biography in Words and Pictures*, New York: Barnes & Noble, 1976

† Shearlaw, John, *Status Quo*, London: Sidgwick & Jackson, 1979

† Shepherd, Billy, *The True Story of the Beatles*, London: Beat Publications, 1964

Short, Don, *Englebert Humperdinck: the Authorised Biography*, London: New English Library, 1972

†† Simon, George, *Glen Miller*, London: W.H. Allen, 1974

† Slaughter, Todd, *Elvis Presley*, London: Star Books, 1977

Somma, Robert, *No One Waved Good-Bye*, New York: Outerbridge & Dienstfray, 1971

† Sonin, Ray, *The Johnnie Ray Story*, London: Horace Marshall, 1955

†† Spellman, A.B., *Four Lives in the Be-Bop Business*, London: MacGibbon & Kee, 1967

Stein, Cathi, *Elton John*, London: Futura, 1975

† Stein, Jeff, and Johnston, Chris, *The Who*, New York: Stein & Day, 1973

†† Stewart, Rex, *Jazz Masters of the Thirties*, London: Macmillan, 1973

† Tatham, Dick, and Jasper, Tony, *Elton John*, London: Octopus, 1976

Taylor, Derek, *As Time Goes By*, London: Abacus, 1974

† Taylor, Paula, *Elton John*, Mankato, Minnesota: Creative Educational Society, 1975

† Taylor, Paula, *One Stage with the Jackson Five*, Mankato, Minnesota: Creative Educational Society, 1975

† Taylor, Paula, *Carole King*, Mankato, Minnesota: Creative Educational Society, 1976

† Thomas, Bob, *The One and Only Bing*, London: Michael Joseph, 1977

* Thompson, Charles, *The Complete Crosby*, London: W.H. Allen, 1978

* Thompson, Toby, *Positively Main Street*, New York: Caward

McCann, 1971

† Tobler, John, *The Beach Boys*, London: Hamlyn, 1977

Tremlett, George, *The Gary Glitter Story*, London: Futura, 1974

Tremlett, George, *The David Essex Story*, London: Futura, 1974

Tremlett, George, *The Osmond Story*, London: Futura, 1974

Tremlett, George, *The Rolling Stones Story*, London: Futura, 1974

Tremlett, George, *The Cliff Richard Story*, London: Futura, 1975

Tremlett, George, *The Marc Bolan Story*, London: Futura, 1975

Tremlett, George, *The Paul McCartney Story*, London: Futura, 1975

Tremlett, George, *The Slade Story*, London: Futura, 1975

Tremlett, George, *The Who*, London: Futura, 1975

Tremlett, George, *The John Lennon Story*, London: Futura, 1976

Tremlett, George, *Slik*, London: Futura, 1976

† Turner, Steve, and Davis, John, *A Decade of the Who*, London: Elm Tree Books, 1977

† Vaughan, Frankie, *The Frankie Vaughan Story*, London: Penrow, 1957

† Vermorel, Fred, and Vermorel, Judy, *The Sex Pistols: the Inside Story*, London: Star Books, 1978

* Walley, David, *No Commercial Potential: the Saga of Frank Zappa and the Mothers of Invention*, New York: Dutton, 1972

† Waterman, I., *Keith Moon: life and death of a rock legend*, London: Arrow, 1979

† Welch, Chris, *Hendrix: a Biography*, London: Ocean Books, 1972

** Wenner, Jan, *Lennon Remembers*, Harmondsworth: Penguin, 1972

Williams, Richard, *Out of His Head: The Sound of Phil Spector*, London: Abacus, 1974

* Williams, Roger, *Sing a Sad Song, The Life of Hank Williams*, New York: Ballantine, 1973

† Wilson, Beth P., *Stevie Wonder*, New York: Putnam, 1978

† Wilson, Earl, *Sinatra*, London: Star Books, 1978

† Winter, David, *New Singer, New Song: The Cliff Richard Story*, London: Hodder & Stoughton, 1967

† Wooding, Dan, *I Thought Terry Dene was Dead*, London: Coverdale House, 1974

† Wooding, Dan, *Rick Wakeman: the caped crusader*, London: Hale, 1978

* Wren, Christopher S., *Johnny Cash: Winners Got Scars Too*, London: Abacus, 1974

† Wyn, Hefin, *Doedd ned yn besco dam*, Wales: Penygroes, n.d.

† Yancey, Becky, *My Life with Elvis*, London: W.H. Allen, 1977

† Yorke, Ritchie, *The Led Zeppelin Biography*, New York: Two Continents, 1976

Young, Jimmy, *J.Y.: the Autobiography of Jimmy Young*, London: Star Books, 1974

Institutions and technology

† Ackerman, Paul, and Zhito, Lee, *The Complete Report of the First International Music Industry Conference*, New York: Billboard Publications, 1969

† Archer, Gleason L., *History of Radio to 1926*, New York: The American Historical Company, 1938

† Barnouw, Eric, *History of Broadcasting in the United States*, New York: Oxford University Press, 1966

† Bart, Teddy, *Inside Music City USA*, Nashville, Tennessee: Aurora Publications, 1970

Beerling, Johnny, *Emperor Rosko's DJ Book*, London: Everest, 1976

† *EMI: the Many Worlds of Music*, New York: EMI, 1969

* Borwick, John, 'A century of recording', *Gramophone*, vol. 54, nos. 647 and 648 (April and May 1977)

** Briggs, Asa, *History of Broadcasting in the United Kingdom*, London: Oxford University Press, 1961, 1965, 1970, 1979

** (British Phonographic Industries), *BPI Yearbooks*, London: BPI, 1976 to date

† Busby, Roy, *British Music Hall*, London: Paul Elek, 1976

† Cable, Michael, *The Pop Industry Inside Out*, London: W.H. Allen, 1977

Cash, Tony (ed.), *Anatomy of Pop*, London: BBC Publications, 1970

*** Chapple, Steve, and Garofalo, Reebee, *Rock 'n' Roll Is Here To Pay: The History & Politics of the Music Industry,* Chicago: Nelson-Hall, 1977 (The fullest and most serious study of the economics of the American industry)

† Chavez, Carlos, *Toward a New Music: Music & Electricity*, New York: Da Capo, 1975

† Cheshire, D.F., *Music Hall in Britain*, Rutherford, N.J.: Fairleigh Dickinson, 1974

** Clarke, John, 'Framing the arts: the role of cultural institutions', Centre for Contemporary Cultural Studies, stencilled paper no. 32 (1975)

† David, Clive, and Willwerth, James, *Clive: Inside the Record Business*, New York: Morrow, 1974

* Denisoff, R. Serge, *Solid Gold: The Popular Record Industry,* Brunswick, N.J.: Transaction, 1975

Dilello, Richard, *The Longest Cocktail Party*, London: Charisma, 1973

† Doncaster, Pat, *Discland, a Panorama of the Fabulous World of the Gramophone Record*, London: Daily Mirror, 1956

† (Economist Intelligence Unit), *Retail Business*, no. 23, 1960, 479-86; no. 74, 1964, 49-53; no. 98, 1966, 20-32; no. 159, 1971, 18-34; no. 200, 1974, 37-46; no. 242, 1978, 33-41.

† Ewen, David, *The Life and Death of Tin Pan Alley*, New York: Funk

& Wagnall, 1964

* Escott, Colin, and Hawkins, Martin, *Catalyst: the Sun Records Story*, London: Aquarius Books, 1975

† Faulkner, Robert R., *Hollywood Studio Musicians: their Work and Careers in the Record Industry*, Chicago: Aldine, 1971

† Fisher, W., *One Hundred Years of Music Publishing in the US*, New York: Gordon, n.d.

† Gelatt, Roland, *The Fabulous Phonograph*, London: Cassell, 1956

** Gillett, Charlie, *Making Tracks: Atlantic Record Company*, St Albans: Panther, 1975 (The best study of a single company: should be the first of a series)

† Goldberg, I., *Tin Pan Alley*, New York: Ungar, 1961

† Griffin, Alistair, *On the Scene at the Cavern*, London: Hamish Hamilton, 1964

† Harris, Herby and Farrar, Lucien, *How to Make Money in Music: A Guidebook for Success in Today's Music Business*, New York: Arco, 1977

Harris, Paul, *When Pirates Ruled the Waves*, London: Impulse, 1968

Harris, Paul, *Broadcasting from the High Seas: the History of Offshore Radio in Europe*, Edinburgh: Harris, 1977

† Head, Sydney, *Broadcasting in America*, Boston: Houghton-Mifflin, 1956

† Hill Leslie, 'An insight into the finances of the record industry', *Three Banks Review*, no. 118 (June 1978)

† Hirsch, P., *The Structure of the Popular Music Industry*, Ann Arbor, Michigan: University of Michigan Press, 1969

† (The Hollies), *How to Run a Beat Group*, London: Daily Mirror, 1964

† Hopkins, Jerry, *Festivals! The book of American Music Celebrations*, New York: Macmillan, 1970

† Hudson, James, *Fillmore: East and West*, New York: Scholastic Book Services, 1972

† Jenkins, J., and Smith J., *Electric Music*, Newton Abbot: David & Charles, 1975

* Jones, Bryn, 'Pop goes the profit', *Youth Review*, no. 19 (1970)

† (Jordan Dataquest Ltd.), *British Companies in the Music Trade*, London: Jordan Dataquest, 1977

† Kealy, E.R., 'The real rock revolution: sound mixers, social inequality, and the aesthetics of popular music production', unpublished Ph.D thesis, Northwestern University, Illinois, 1974

** Lane, Basil, '75 years of magnetic recording', *Wireless World*, vol. 81, nos. 1471-1475 (March-July 1975)

† Leadbitter, Mike, *From the Bayou*, Bexhill-on-Sea: Blues Unlimited, 1970

* Lees, Gene, 'Nashville: the sounds and symbols', in Jonathen Eisen (ed.), *The Age of Rock*, New York: Vintage Books, 1969

† Luthe, Heinz Otto, 'Recorded music and the record industry', *International Social Science Journal*, vol. 20, no. 4 (1968)

* Mabey, Richard, *Behind the Scene,* Harmondsworth: Penguin, 1968

** Mabey, Richard, *The Pop Process*, London: Hutchinson, 1969

McCabe, Peter and Schonfield, Robert D., *Apple to the Core*, London: Sphere, 1971

* Mander, Raymond, *The British Music Hall*, New York: International Publications Service, 1975

† Marcuse, Maxwell F., *Tin Pan Alley in Gaslight*, Watkins Glen, N.Y.: Century House, n.d.

** Mellor, G.J., *Northern Music Hall*, Newcastle: Frank Graham, 1970 (The only book-length account of British Music Hall outside London)

† Murdoch, Graham, and Golding, Peter, 'Beyond monopoly — mass communications in an age of conglomerates', in P. Beharrell (ed.), *Trade Unions and the Media*, London: Macmillan, 1977

† *The Music Industry: Markets and methods for the seventies*, New York: Billboard, 1970

** Newton, Francis, *The Jazz Scene*, Harmondsworth: Penguin, 1961 (The standard survey, badly in need of a sequel)

* Nolan, Tom, 'Underground radio', in Jonathan Eisen (ed.), *The Age of Rock*, New York: Vintage Books, 1969

† Peterson, Richard A., and Berger, David, 'Entrepreneurship in organisations: evidence from the popular music industry', *Administrative Science Quarterly*, vol. 16, no. 1 (1971)

† Reid, Oliver, and Welch, Walter, *From Tin Foil to Stereo*, Indianapolis, Indiana: Bobbs-Merrill, 1959

† Rogers, Eddie, *Tin Pan Alley*, London: Hale, 1964

† Rowland, John Venmore, *Radio Caroline*, London: Landmark Press, 1967

† Rust, Brian, *The Dance Bands*, Shepperton: Ian Allan, 1972

† Rust, Brian, 'The development of the recording industry', *Gramophone*, vol 54, nos. 647 and 648 (April and May 1977)

† Sadler, Barry, *Everything You Want to Know About the Record Industry*, Nashville, Tenn.: Aurora, 1978

† Schiffman, Jack, *Uptown — The Story of Harlem's Apollo Theatre*, New York: Cowles, 1971

† Schiller, Herbert, *Mass Communications and American Empire*, Boston: Beacon Press, 1971

* Shearer, Harry, 'Captain Pimplecream's fiendish plot', in Jonathan Eisen (ed.), *The Age of Rock*, New York: Vintage Books, 1969

** Shemel, Sidney, and Krasilovsky, M. William, *This Business of Music*, New York: Watson-Guptill, 1971

† Skues, Keith, *Radio Onederland*, London: Landmark Press, 1968

† Stokes, Geoffrey, *Star-Making Machinery: The Oddyssey of an Album*, Indianapolis, Indiana: Bobbs-Merrill, 1976

† Stokes, Geoffrey, *Star-Making Machinery: Inside the Business of Rock 'n' Roll*, New York: Random House, 1977

* Townsend, Ken, 'From mono to multitrack', *Studio Sound*, no. 24-32 (August 1976)

** Wale, Michael, *Vox Pop*, London: Harrap, 1972

† Wise, Herbert A., *Professional Rock and Roll*, London: Macmillan, 1968

† Wood, L.G., 'The growth and development of the recording industry', *Journal of the Royal Society of Arts*, vol. 119 (Sept 1971)

Critical theory: song and music

** Adorno, T., 'On popular music', *Studies in Philosophy and Social Science*, New York: 1941

* Adorno, T., 'A social critique of radio music', *Kenyon Review*, vol. 7, (1944)

† Adorno, T., *Introduction to the Sociology of Music*, New York: Seabury Press, 1976

† Bobbit, Richard *Harmonic Technique in the Rock Idiom*, Belmont, California: Wadsworth, 1976

* Chester, Andrew, 'For a rock aesthetic', *New Left Review*, nos. 59 and 62, (1970)

†† Dankworth, Avril, *Jazz: an Introduction to the Musical Basis*, London: Oxford University Press, 1968

Denisoff, R. Serge, and Levine, M.H., 'The one-dimensional approach to popular music', *Journal of Popular Culture*, vol. 4, no. 4 (1971)

† Denisoff, R. Serge, and Peterson, Richard A., *Sounds of Social Change*, San Francisco, California: Rand, n.d.

* Flood-Page, M., and Fowler, Pete, 'Writing about rock', *Working Papers in Cultural Studies*, no. 2 (spring 1972)

** Frith, Simon, *The Sociology of Rock*, London: Constable, 1978 (Some useful factual information, but weak on cultural analysis)

† Guthrie, Woody, 'People's songs', *The Worker* (USA), 13 March 1946

Hayakawa, S.I., 'Popular songs versus the facts of life', in B. Rosenberg and D.M. White (eds.), *Mass Culture*, New York: Free Press, 1964

† Hirsch, Paul, 'Sociological approaches to the pop music phenomenon', *American Behavioural Scientist*, vol. 14, no. 3 (1971)

* Horton, Donald, 'The dialogue of courtship and marriage in popular songs', *American Journal of Sociology*, vol. 62 (1962)

Kaplan, Arlene, 'A study of folksinging in a mass society', *Sociologue*, vol. 5, no. 19 (1955) (Real Cold War stuff)

† Kees, Weldon, 'Muskrat Ramble: popular and unpopular music',

Partisan Review, vol. 15, no. 5 (May 1948)

† Lomax, Alan, 'Musical style and social context', *American Anthropologist*, no. 57 (1959)

* Lomax, Alan, 'Song structure and social structure', *Ethnology*, no. 1 (1962)

Meltzer, R., *The Aesthetics of Rock*, New York: Something Else Press, 1970

†† Ostransky, Leroy, *The Anatomy of Jazz*, Westport, Conn.: Greenwood, 1973

* Parker, Charles, 'Pop song: the manipulated ritual', unpublished paper, 1973

† Peterson, Richard A., and Berger, David, 'Cycles in symbol production: the case of popular music', *American Sociological Review*, vol. 40 (1975)

* Reisman, David, 'Listening to popular music', in B. Rosenberg and D.M. White (eds.), *Mass Culture*, New York: Free Press, 1964

†† Schuller, Gunther, *Early Jazz, Its Roots and Musical Development*, London: Oxford University Press, 1968

† Seeger, Peter, 'People's songs and singers', *New Masses* (USA) 16 July 1964

† Shepherd, John, *et al.*, *Whose Music? A Sociology of Musical Languages*, London: Latimer, 1977

†† Williams, Martin, *The Art of Jazz*, London: Jazz Book Club, 1962

*** Willis, Paul, 'Symbolism and practice: a theory for the social meaning of pop music', Centre for Contemporary Cultural Studies, University of Birmingham, stencilled paper no. 13 (n.d.)

Critical practice: song and music

†† Balliett, Whitney, *The Sound of Surprise*, Harmondsworth: Penguin, 1963

†† Balliett, Whitney, *Such Sweet Thunder*, London: MacDonald, 1968

* Beckett, Alan, 'Popular music, basic assumptions and background', *New Left Review*, no. 39 (Sept/Oct 1966)

** Beckett, Alan, 'Stones', *New Left Review*, no. 47 (Jan/Feb 1968)

† Bennett, H.S. 'Other people's music', unpublished Ph.D thesis, Northwestern University, Illinois, 1972

** Birchall, Ian, 'The Rhymes They Are A-Changing', *International Socialism*, no. 23

Bowen, Meirion, 'Musical developments in pop', in Tony Cash (ed.), *Anatomy of Pop*, London: BBC Publications, 1970

† Bruchac, Joseph, *The Poetry of Pop*, Paradise, California: Dustbooks, 1973

† Buckle, Philip, *Top Twenty*, London: New English Library, 1963 and 1965

† Buckle, Philip, *The Year's Top Twenty*, London: Mayflower, 1964

Carey, James T., 'Changing courtship patterns in popular song', *American Journal of Sociology*, vol. 74 (1969)

* Chambers, Iain, 'A strategy for living: black music and white sub-cultures', *Working Papers in Cultural Studies*, no. 7/8 (1975)

Charters, Samuel, *The Poetry of the Blues*, New York: Oak, 1963

* Christgau, Robert, 'Rock lyrics are poetry (maybe)', in Jonathan Eisen (ed.), *The Age of Rock*, New York: Vintage Books, 1969

† Clark, Sam, 'Freedom songs and the folk process', *Sing Out*, Feb/Mar 1964

* Cole, Peter, 'Lyrics in Pop', in Tony Cash (ed.), *The Anatomy of Pop*, London: BBC Publications, 1970

† Cook, Bruce, *Listen to the Blues*, London: Robson Books, 1975

Dallas, Karl, *Singers of an Empty Day*, London: Kahn & Averill, 1971

Denisoff, R. Serge, 'Songs of persuasion: a sociological analysis of urban propaganda songs', *Journal of American Folklore*, vol. 79 (1966)

Denisoff, R. Serge, 'The popular protest song: the case of "Eve of Destruction" ', *Public Opinion Quarterly*, Spring 1971, pp. 117-22

* Fong-Torres, Ben, *The 'Rolling Stone' Rock 'n' Roll Reader*, New York: Bantam, 1974

† Freeman, Larry G., *Melodies Linger On*, Watkins Glen, N.Y.: Century House, 1951

† Garland, Phil, *The Sound of Soul*, Chicago: Regnery, 1969

* Goldstein, Richard, *The Poetry of Rock*, New York: Bantam, 1969 (Several complete lyrics)

* Goldstein, Richard, *The Poetry of Soul*, New York: Bantam, 1971 (Ditto)

Gray, Michael, *Song and Dance Man*, London: Hart-Davis MacGibbon, 1972

** Hebdige, Dick, 'Reggae, rastas and rudies: style and the subversion of the form', Centre for Contemporary Cultural Studies, University of Birmingham, stencilled paper no. 24

Hoare, Ian, *et al.*, *The Soul Book*, London: Methuen, 1975

†† Horricks, R., and Morgan B., *Modern Jazz Development Since 1939*, London: Gollancz, 1956

Hughes, Donald, 'Recorded music', in Denys Thompson (ed.), *Discrimination and Popular Culture*, Harmondsworth: Penguin, 1964

Jaspers, Tony, *Understanding Pop*, London: SCM Press, 1972

*** Keil, Charles, *Urban Blues*, London: Chicago University Press, 1966

* Landau, Jon, 'A whiter shade of black', in Jonathan Eisen (ed.), *The Age of Rock*, New York: Vintage Books, 1969

** MacInnes, Colin, *Sweet Saturday Night*, London: Panther, 1967
(The best account of the cultural significance of Music Hall songs)

†† McRae, Barny, *The Jazz Cataclysm*, London: Dent, 1967

† Marcus, Greil, *Rock and Roll Will Stand*, New York: Beacon Press, 1969

† Mellers, Wilfred, *Caliban Reborn*, London: Gollancz, 1968

* Mellers, Wilfred, *Twilight of the Gods: the Beatles in Retrospect*, London: Faber, 1973

** Middleton, Richard, *Pop Music and the Blues*, London: Gollancz, 1968

** Merton, Richard, 'Comment', *New Left Review*, no. 47 (Jan./Feb. 1968) and no. 59 (Jan./Feb. 1970)

* Myrus, Donald, *Ballads, Blues and the Big Beat*, London: Macmillan, 1966

† Noebel, David A., *Communism, Hypnotism and the Beatles, an Analysis of the Communist Use of Music – the Communist Master Music Plan*, Tulsa: Christian Crusade Publications, 1965

†† Oliver, Paul, *Blues Fell this Morning* London: Cassell, 1960

†† Oliver, Paul, *Conversations with the Blues*, London: Cassell, 1965

†† Oliver, Paul, *Screening the Blues*, New York: Cassell, 1968

† Oster, Harry, *Living Country Blues*, Detroit: Gale, 1969

* Parsons, Michael, 'Rolling Stones', *New Left Review*, no. 49 (May/June 1968)

Parsons, Michael, 'Vanilla fudge', *The Listener*, 3 January 1969

† Paxton, Tom, 'Folk rot', *Sing Out*, vol. 15 (January 1966)

† Peck, I., *The New Sound/Yes*, New York: Four Winds Press, 1966

* Rorem, Ned, 'The music of the Beatles', in Jonathan Eisen (ed.), *The Age of Rock*, New York: Vintage Books, 1969

† Rosenstone, Robert A., 'The times they are a-changing', *Annals*, vol. 381, (March 1969)

† Rublowsky, John, *Popular Music*, New York: Basic, 1967

* Sarlin, Bob, *Turn it up! (I can't hear the words)*, London: Coronet, 1975

† Seeger, Peter, 'You Can't Write Down Freedom Songs', *Sing Out*, July 1965

† Walton, Ortiz, *Music: Black, White and Blue*, New York: Pocket Books, 1970

Reference

† Alex, Peter, *Who's Who in Pop Radio*, London, New English Library, 1966

† *Alphabeat: Who's Who in Pop*, London: Century 21 Publishers, 1969

** *Annual Abstract of Statistics*, London: HMSO, Central Statistical Office

† Armitage, Andrew D., and Tudor, Dean, *Annual Index to Popular Music Record Reviews*, Metuchen, N.J.: Scarecrow Press, 1973, 1974, 1976

† Baggelaar, Kristen, and Milton, Donald, *The Folk Music Encylopaedia* London: Omnibus, 1976

** (BBC), *Songs Catalogue*, London: BBC Publications, 1966

†† Berg., I., and Yeomans, I., *An A to Z 'Who's Who' of the British Traditional Jazz Scene*, Slough: Foulsham, n.d.

† Blacklock, Robert, *Which Song and When: a Handbook of Selected Song Titles from 1880-1974*, Edinburgh: Bandparts Music Stores, 1975

Boyd, John, *Select Bibliography on Youth*, London: Marx Memorial Library, Quarterly Bulletin, Oct./Dec. 1972

† Brown, Len, and Friedrich, Gary, *Encyclopedia of Rock and Roll*, New York: Tower, 1970

† Brown, Len, and Friedrich, Gary, *So You Think You Know Rock and Roll*, New York: Tower, 1970

† Brown, Len, and Friedrich, Gary, *Encyclopedia of Country and Western Music*, New York: Tower, 1971

† Burton, Jack, *Index of American Popular Song*, Watkins Glen, N.J.: Century House, n.d.

† Burton, Jack, *Blue Book of Tin Pan Alley*, Watkins Glen, N.J.: Century House, n.d.

† Chilton, John, *Who's Who of Jazz*, London: Bloomsbury Bookshop, 1970

* Chipman, John H., *Index to Top-Hit Tunes 1900-1951*, Boston, Mass.: Branden, n.d.

† Colbert, W., *Who Wrote That Song: Popular Songs in America & Their Composers*, Brooklyn, N.J.: Revisionist Press, 1974

† Craig, Warren, *Sweet & Lowdown: America's Popular Song Writers*, Metuchen, N.J.: Scarecrow, 1978

† Dachs, David, *Encyclopedia of Pop/Rock*, New York: Scholastic Book Services, 1974

† Dellar, Fred, *et al.*, *The Illustrated Encyclopedia of Country Music*, London: Salamander, 1977

* Denisoff, R. Serge., *American Protest Songs of War and Peace. A Selected Bibliography and Discography*, Los Angeles: Centre for the Study of Armament and Disarmament, California State College, 1970

† Denisoff, R. Serge, *Songs of Protest, War and Peace: A Bibliography and Discography*, Santa Barbara, California: ABC-Clio, 1973

† Dichter, H., *Handbook of American Sheet Music*, West Orange, N.J.: Saifer, n.d.

† Engel, Lyle, *Popular Record Directory*, London: Muller, 1968

†† Feather, Leonard, *The Encyclopedia of Jazz*, New York: Horizon

Press, 1955

†† Feather, Leonard, *The Encyclopedia of Jazz in the 60's*, New York: Horizon Press, 1966

† Fredericks, Vic, *Who's Who in Rock 'n' Roll*, New York: Frederick Bell, 1958

† Gammond, Peter and Clayton, Peter, *A Guide to Popular Music*, Los Angeles: Phoenix House, 1960

† Gammond, Peter, and Clayton, Peter, *Dictionary of Popular Music*, St Clair Shores, Michigan: Scholarly, 1961

** Gillett, Charlie, *Rock File 1*, London: New English Library, 1972

*** Gillett, Charlie, *Rock File 2*, St Albans: Panther, 1974

** Gillett, Charlie, and Frith, Simon, *Rock File 3*, St Albans: Panther, 1975

*** Gillett, Charlie, and Frith, Simon, *Rock File 4*, St Albans: Panther, 1976

* Gillett, Charlie, and Frith, Simon, *Rock File 5*, London: Panther, 1978

† Gonzalez, Fernando L., *Disco-File: The Discographical Catalog of American Rock & Roll and Rhythm and Blues,* Flushing, N.Y.: Gonzalez, 1977

† Green, Stanley, *Encyclopedia of the Musical*, London: Cassell, 1977

* *Guinness Book of British Hit Singles*, London: Guinness Superlatives 1977

†† Haselgrove, J.R., and Kennington, D., *Reader's Guide to Books on Jazz*, London: London Library Association, 1965

† Havlice, P.P., *Popular Song Index*, Metuchen, N.J.: Scarecrow Press, 1976

† Havlice, P.P., *Popular Song Index: First Supplement*, Metuchen, N.J.: Scarecrow Press, 1978

† Hurst, Walter E., *The Music Industry Book: How to Make Money in the Music Industry*, Hollywood: Seven Arts, 1963

* Jasper, Tony, *20 Years of British Record Charts 1955-1975*, London: Futura, 1979

** Jones, Bryn, 'A bibliography of rock', *Working Papers in Cultural Studies*, no. 2, 1972

† Jones, R.M. 'Popular Music: a survey of books', *Music Library Association Notes*, 30 December 1973

† Karshner, Roger, *The Music Machine*, Los Angeles: Nash, 1971

†† Kinkle, Roger D., *The Complete Encyclopedia of Popular Music and Jazz, 1900-50*, New Rochelle, N.Y.: Arlington House, 1974

† *Legal & Business Problems of the Record Industry 1978 Course Handbook*, New York: Practising Law Institute, 1978

** Logan, Nick, and Finnis, Rob, *The New Musical Express Book of Rock*, London: Star Books, 1975

† Logan, Nick, and Woffinden, Bob, *The Illustrated New Musical*

Express Book of Rock, London: Salamander, 1978

† Lowe, Leslie, *Directory of Popular Music, 1900-1965*, Droitwich: Peterson Publishing, 1975

†† Markewitch, Leese, *Bibliography of Jazz and Pop Tunes Sharing the Chord Progressions of Other Compositions*, New York: Markewitch, 1970

† Meggett, Joan M., *Music periodical literature: an annotated bibliography of indexes and bibliographies*, Metuchen, N.J.: Scarecrow Press, 1978

* Murrells, Joseph, *The 'Daily Mail' Book of Golden Discs*, London: Guinness, 1966

* Murrells, Joseph, *The 'Daily Mail' Book of Golden Discs*, London: Guiness, 1966

** Murrells, Joseph, *The Book of Golden Discs*, London: Barrie & Jenkins, 1974; 2nd ed., 1978

† Naha, Ed. (ed.), *Lillian Roxin's Rock Encyclopedia*, New York: Grosset & Dunlap, 1978

† Nite, Norm N., *The Illustrated Encyclopedia of Rock 'n' Roll*, New York: T Y Crowell, 1978

† Noyce, John L., and Skinner, Alise, *Rock Music Index*, Brighton: Noyce, 1977

† Nugent, Stephen, and Gillett, Charlie, *Rock Almanac: Top Twenty American and British Singers and Albums of the 50s, 60s and 70s*, New York: Doubleday, 1978

†† Postgate, John, *A Plain Man's Guide to Jazz*, London: Hanover Books, 1956

† Rohde, H.K., *The Gold of Rock and Roll, 1955-1967*, New York: Arbor House, 1970

† *Rolling Stone Illustrated History of Rock and Roll*, New York: Random House, 1976

* Roxon, Lillian, *Rock Encyclopedia*, New York: Grosset & Dunlap, 1970

† Rust, Brian, *The American Dance Band Discography 1917-1942*, New Rochelle, N.Y.: Arlington House, 1976

† Rust, Brian, and Debus, Allen G., *The Complete Entertainment Discography From the mid 1897 to 1942*, New Rochelle, N.J.: Arlington House, 1973

† Shapiro, Nat, *Popular Music, an Annotated Index of American Popular Songs*, New York: Adrian, 1964-1975

† Shestack, Melvin, *Country Music Encyclopedia*, New York: T.Y. Crowell, 1974

† Soderbergh, Peter A., *Seventy-Eight RPM & Price Guide*, Desmoines, Iowa: Wallace-Homestead, 1977

† (Songwriters' Guild of Great Britain), *60 Years of British Hits 1907-*

1968, London, Songwriters' Guild, 1968

† Stambler, Irwin, *Encyclopedia of Popular Music*, New York; St Martin's Press, 1965

† Stambler, Irwin and Landon, Grelun, *Encyclopedia of Folk, Country and Western Music*, New York, St Martin's Press, 1969

† Stecheson, Anne, and Stecheson, Anthony, *Classified Song Directory*, Cedar Knolls, N.J.: Wehman, 1961

† Stecheson, Anne, and Stecheson, Anthony, *Stecheson Classified Song Directory*, New York: Criterion Music, 1967

* Thompson, F.M., *Newcastle Chapbooks in Newcastle University Library*, Newcastle: Oriel Press, 1969

† Tudor, Dean and Tudor, Nancy, *Popular Music Periodicals Index 1973, 1974, 1975*, Metuchen, N.J.: Scarecrow Press, 1974, 1975, 1976

† Tudor, Dean, Biesenthal, Linda, and Tudor, Nancy, *Annual Index to popular music record reviews 1976*, Metuchen, N.J.: Scarecrow Press, 1977

† Whitburn, Joel, *Record Research 1955-1971*, Menomenee Falls, Wisconsin: 1972

† Whitburn, Joel, *Rhythm and Blues*, Menomenee Falls, Wisconsin: 1973

† Wilks, Max, *They're Playing Our Song: From Jerome Kern to Stephen Sondheim – the Stories Behind the Words and Music of Two Generations*, London: W.H. Allen, 1974

Wood, Graham *An A-Z of Rock and Roll*, London: Studio Vista, 1971

Miscellaneous

** Abrams, M., *The Teenage Consumer*, London: Press Exchange, 1959

† Adler, Bill, *Love Letters to the Beatles*, London: Blond & Briggs, 1964

† Allan, Jon, *The Rock Trivia Quizbook*, New York: Drake, 1976

** Allan, Thomas, *Tyneside Songs*, Newcastle, 1891 (reprinted 1972)

† Anderton, Craig, *Home Recording for Musicians*, Saratoga, N.Y.: Guitar Player Books, 1978

* Armstrong, Thomas, *Song Book Containing 25 popular songs of the late Thomas Armstrong*, Chester-le-Street: Noel Wilson, 1930

* Baez, Joan, *Daybreak*, London: MacGibbon & Kee, 1970

† Barker, Tony, *Music Hall Records*, London: Tony Barker, 1978

† Barnes, Richard and Townsend, Pete, *The Story of Tommy*, Twickenham: Eel Pie Publishing, 1977

** (Beatles) *The Beatles Lyrics Complete*, London: Futura, 1974

** Bell, John, *Rhymes of Northern Bards*, Newcastle, 1812, (reprinted 1971)

† Berk, Lee, *Legal Protection for the Creative Musician*, Boston: Berklee Press, 1970

† *Best of Pop and Rock*, New York: Peer-Southern, 1975

† Blackford, Andy, *Disco Dancing Tonight: Clubs, Dances, Fashion, Music*, London: Octopus Books, 1979

† Bloher, Arlo, *Rock*, Mahwah, N.J.: Troll Associates, 1976

† Bobbitt, Richard, *Harmonic Technique in the Rock Idiom*, Belmont, California; Wadsworth, 1976

† Boyce, Tommy, *How to Write a Hit Song & Sell It*, Hollywood, California: Wilshire, 1974

† Boye, Henry, *How to Make Money Selling the Songs You Write*, New York: Fell, 1975

† Brown, R., 'Popular music in an English secondary school', *American Behavioral Scientist*, vol. 14, no. 3 (1971)

** Bruce, J.C., and Stokoe, J., *Northumbrian Minstrelsy*, Newcastle, 1882 (reprinted 1965)

* Cable, Paul, *Bob Dylan: his unreleased recordings,* London: Scorpion Publications, 1978

* Catchside-Warrington, C.E., *Tyneside Songs*, vols. 1-4, Newcastle: J.G. Windows Ltd., 1911-1920

† Christgau, Robert, *Any Old Way You Choose It*, Baltimore: Penguin, 1974

** Cleaver, Eldridge, *Soul on Ice*, London: Cape, 1969

† Clews, Frank, *The Golden Disc*, London: Brown Watson, 1963

Cohen, Leonard, *Beautiful Losers*, London: Panther, 1972

† Colin, Sid, *And the Bands Played On*, London: Elm Tree Books, 1977

† Collier, James L., *Making Music for Money*, New York: Watts, 1976

*** Collins, Mal, *et al., The Big Red Song Book*, London: Pluto, 1977

† Coryell, Julia, and Friedman, Laura, *Jazz Rock Fusion*, New York: Delacourte, 1978

† Cowan, Philip, *Behind the Beatles Songs*, London: Polyantric Press, 1978

* Craig, David, *The Real Foundations*, London: Chatto & Windus, 1973

* Craig, David, and Heinemann, Margot, *Experiments in English Teaching*, London: Arnold, 1976

† Craig, Warren, *Sweet and Lowdown: America's Popular Song Writers*, Metuchen, N.J.: Scarecrow Press, 1978

* Crawhall, Joseph, *A Beuk o' Newcassel Sangs*, Newcastle: Mawson, Swann and Morgan, 1888 (reprinted 1965)

† Dachs, David, *Pop-Rock Questions & Answer Book*, New York: Scholastic Book Services, 1977

† Dalton, David and Kaye, Lenny, *Rock One Hundred*, New York: Grosset & Dunlap, 1976

* Davison, William, *Tyneside Songster*, Alnwick: Davison, 1840

† *The Dee Jay Book*, Milwaukee, Wisconsin: Purnell, 1969

† Dexter, Dave, *Playback*, New York: Watson-Guptill, 1976

† Dicks, Ted and Platz, Paul, eds., *Marc Bolan: a Tribute*, London: Springwood, 1978

† (Disc), *Pop Today*, London: Hamlyn, 1974

† Doney, Malcolm, *Summer in the City*, Berkhamstead: Lion, 1978

Dylan, Bob, *Tarantula*, St Albans: Panther, 1973

** Dylan, Bob, *Writings and Drawings*, St Albans: Panther, 1974

** (Dylan), *Bob Dylan Song Book*, London: Warner Brothers, n.d.

† Emerson, Lucy, *Gold Record*, New York: Fountain, 1978

† Ewen, David (ed.), *Songs of America: A Cavalcade of Popular Songs with Commentaries*, Westport, Conn.: Greenwood, 1978

* Fong-Torres, Ben, *The Rolling Stone Interviews vol. 2*, New York: Warner Books, 1973

*** Foot, Paul, *Why You Should Be A Socialist*, London: Socialist Workers Party, 1977 (In case you don't know)

* Fordyce, W., *Newcastle Songster*, Newcastle: Fordyce, 1842

† Frankel, Aaron, *Writing the Broadway Musical*, New York: Drama Books, 1977

† Gambaccini, Paul, *The Rock Critics' Choice: The Top 200 Albums*, New York: Music Sales, 1978

† Garcia, Jerry, *et al.*, *Garcia: A Signpost to New Space*, San Francisco: Straight Arrow, 197?

† Gelly, David, *The Facts about a Rock Group, Featuring Wings*, New York: Harmony, 1977

* Gilfellon, Tom, *Tommy Armstrong Sings*, Newcastle: Frank Graham, 1971

† Glaser, Hy, *How to Write Lyrics that Make Sense & Dollars*, Hicksville, N.Y.: Exposition, 1977

** Glasgow, Alex, *Alex Glasgow, An Anthology*, London: Robbins Music, 1971

† Gorman, Clem, *Backstage Rock*, London: Pan, 1978

† Green, Jonathan, *The Book of Rock Quotes*, New York: Music Sales, 1978

† Green, Stanley, *American Musical Shows*, London: Yoseloff, 1974

Greene, Bob, *Million Dollar Baby*, New York: New American Library, 1975

† Gross, Michael, *Rock Book no. 3: Robert Plant*, New York: CBS Publications, Popular Library, 1973

† (Guitar Player Editions), *Rock Guitarists*, Cupertino, California: GPI Books, n.d.

† (Guitar Player Editions), *Rock Guitarists vol. 2*, Cupertino, California: GPI Books, 1978

* Guralnick, Peter, *Feel Like Going Home*, New York: Outerbridge & Lazard, 1971

† Hale, Tony, *Pop Music Questions & Answers*, London, BBC Publi-

cations, 1977

† Harris, Herby, and Farrar, Lucien, *How to Make Money in Music: A Guidebook for Success in Today's Music Business*, New York: Arco, 1978

Harrison, Hank, *The Dead Book*, London: Link Books, 1973

† Harrison, Max, *et al.*, *Modern Jazz: The Essential Records*, London: Aquarius Books, 1978

† Haskins, J., and Benson, K., *The Stevie Wonder Scrapbook*, London: Cassell, 1979

Hatch, Tony, *So You Want to be in the Music Business*, London: Everest Books, 1976

† Henderson, Bill, *How to Run Your Own Rock & Roll Band*, New York: CBS Publications, Popular Library, 1977

† Herscher, Lou, *Successful Songwriting*, Sherman Oaks, California: Solo, 1966

† Hipgnosis, *Hands Across the Water: Wings Tour USA*, Danbury, New Hampshire: Reed Books, 1978

* *History of Music Machines*, New York: Drake, 1975

† Hoggard, Stuart, and Shields, Jim, *Bob Dylan, an illustrated discography*, Oxford: Transmedia Press, 1978

† Hudson, Jan, *The Sex and Savagery of Hells Angels*, New York: New American Library, 1967

† Hutchinson, Larry, *Rock and Roll Songwriters' Handbook*

† *The Illustrated Rock Almanac*, London: Paddington Press, 1977

† Jackson, Arthur, *The World of Big Bands*, Newton Abbot: David & Charles, 1977

† Jahn, Mike, *How to Make a Hit Record*, Scarsdale, N.Y.: Bradbury Press, 1976

* Janov, Arthur, *The Primal Scream*, London: Sphere, 1973

Jasper, Tony, *Simply Pop*, London: Queen Anne Press, 1975

Jenkinson, Phillip, and Warner, Alan, *Celluloid Rock*, London: Lorimer, 1975

** Kerouac, Jack, *On the Road*, London: Panther, 1961

† Klinn, Maurice, *Pop Quiz Book*, New York: Warner, 1976

† Klamkin, Marian, *Old Street Music: A Pictorial History*, New York: Hawthorn, 1975

* *Knockin' On Dylan's Door*, London: Dempsey Cassell, 1975

† Krivine, J., *Juke Box Saturday Night*, London: New English Library, 1977

† Landau, Jon, *It's Too Late to Stop Now: A Rock & Roll Journal*, San Francisco: Straight Arrow, n.d.

† Lecky, Zip, and Benyon, Tony, *How T'Make it as a Rock Star*, London: IPC, 1977

† Leibovitz, Annie, *Shooting Stars: The Rolling Stone Book of*

Portraits San Francisco: Straight Arrow, n.d.

* Leitch, Michael, *Popular Songs in English 1939-1945*, London: Wise Publications, 1975

Lennon, John, *Spaniard in the Works*, London: Cape, 1965

Lennon, John, *In His Own Write*, London: Cape, 1968

† Lerner, Alan Jay, *The Street Where I Live*, London: Hodder & Stoughton, 1978

† Leslie, David, *Two Left Feet*, London: Pan, 1963

† Levy, Lester, *Grace Notes in American History. Popular Sheet Music from 1820-1900*, Chicago: University of Chicago Press, 1967

† Lindsay, Martin, *Teach Yourself Songwriting*, New York: Dover, n.d.

† McCartney, Linda, *Linda's Pictures*, New York: Knopf, 1976

** MacColl, Ewan, and Seeger, Peggy, *Ewan MacColl-Peggy Seeger Songbook*, New York: Oak, 1963

† Makos, Christopher, *White Trash*, New York: Stonehill, 1977

† Marchbank, Pearce, and Marchbank, Miles, *The Illustrated Rock Almanac*, New York: Paddington, 1977

* Marshall, John, *A Collection of Original Local Songs*, Newcastle: Marshall, 1819

* Marshall, John, *A Collection of Songs, Comic, Satirical and Descriptive, chiefly in the Newcastle dialect*, Newcastle: Marshall, 1827

† Maxwell, John, *The Greatest Billy Cotton Band Show*, London: Jupiter Press, 1977

† (Melody Maker), *Rock Life*, London: Hamlyn, n.d.

† Merriam, Alan, *The Anthropology of Music*, Evanston, Illinois: Northwestern University Press, 1964

† *Mersey Beat: the Beginnings of the Beatles*, London: Omnibus, 1978

† Meyer, Hazel, *The Gold in Tin Pan Alley*, Westport, Conn.: Greenwood, 1977

† Murdock, Graham, and Phelps, Graham, *Mass Media and the Secondary School*, London: Macmillan, 1973

† Myron, Charles, *Rock Gold*, New York: Drake, 1977

† Nicholl, Don, *Jack Jackson's Record Round-Up*, London: Parrish, 1955

† Nite, Norm N., *Rock On*, New York: CBS Publications, Popular Library, 1977

† O'Donnell, Jim, *The Rock Book*, New York: Pinnacle Books, 1975

*** O'Flinn, Paul, *Them and Us in Literature*, London: Pluto Press, 1976

† Otis, Johnny, *Listen to the Lambs*, New York: Norton, 1968

† Pascall, Jeremy, *The Illustrated History of Rock Music*, London: Hamlyn, 1978

† Passman, Arnold, *Dee Jays*, New York: Macmillan, 1971

** Pearsall, Ronald, *Victorian Popular Music*, Newton Abbot: David & Charles, 1973

** Pearsall, Ronald, *Edwardian Popular Music*, Newton Abbot: David & Charles, 1975

Peelaert, Guy, and Cohn, Nik, *Rock Dreams,* London: Pan, 1974

* Percy, Thomas, *Reliques of Ancient Poetry*, London: 1765

Petrie, Gavin, *Pop Today*, London: Hamlyn, 1974

Petrie, Gavin, *Black Music*, London: Hamlyn, 1974

Petrie, Gavin, *Rock Life*, London: Hamlyn, 1975

† Pincus, Lee, *The Songwriters' Success Manual*, New York: Music Press, 1976

** Plater, Alan, *Close the Coalhouse Door*, London: Methuen, 1975

† (Playboy Editors), *Playboy's Music Scene*, Chicago: Playboy, 1973

† Pollock, Bruce, *In Their Own Words: Lyrics and Lyricists 1955-74*, New York: Macmillan, 1975

† Pollock, Bruce, and Wagman, John, *The Face of Rock & Roll*, New York: Holt, Rinehart, 1978

† Powell, Aubrey, *Wings Tour USA*, Limpsfield, Surrey: Paper Tiger, 1978

† Propes, Steven, *Those Oldies but Goodies: A Guide to 50's and 60's Record Collecting*, Radnor, Penn.: Chilton, 1975

† Quirin, Jim, and Cohen, Barry, *Rock 100 1976/7/8*, Covington, Louisiana: Chartmasters, 1976, 1977, 1978

† Quirin, Jim, and Cohen, Barry, *Supplement to Rock 100*, Covington, Louisiana: Chartmasters, 1976

† Rachlin, Harvey, *The Songwriters' Handbook*, New York: Funk & Wagnall, 1977

† *Readers Digest Treasury of Best Loved Songs*, New York: Norton, 1972

† Richard, Cliff, *Top Pops*, London: Daily Mirror, 1963

* Ritson, Joseph, *The Northumberland Garland*, Newcastle: Hall & Elliot, 1793

* Ritson, Joseph, *Northern Garlands*, London: Triphook, 1810

* Robson, Joseph Philip, *Songs of the Bards of the Tyne*, Newcastle: P. France & Co., 1849

** (Rolling Stone), *The Rolling Stone Interviews vol 1*, New York: Warner, 1971

† (Rolling Stone), *The Rolling Stone Record Review No. 2*, New York: Pocket Books, 1974

* (Rolling Stones), *The Rolling Stones Anthology: One and Two*, New York, Peer-Southern, 1975

† Rowe, Mike, *Chicago Breakdown*, London: Eddison Press, 1973

* Scanlon, Paul, *Reporting: the Rolling Stone Style*, New York: Doubleday, n.d.

† Schaffner, N., *The Beatles forever*, Harrisburg, Pennsylvania: Stackpole, 1977

† Sharp, Cuthbert, *The Bishoprick Garland*, London: Nichols, Baldwin & Cradock, 1834

** Shaw, Martin, *Marxism and Social Science*, London: Pluto Press, 1975

† Shepard, Sam, *Rolling Thunder Logbook*, Harmondsworth: Penguin, 1978

* Silver, Abner, and Bruce, Robert, *How to Write and Sell a Hit Song*, Englewood Cliffs, N.J.: Prentice-Hall, 1939

† Sotkin, Marc, *The Official Rock 'n' Roll Trivia Quizbook*, nos. 1 and 2, New York: New American Library (1977 and 1978)

Soul, Pop, Rock, Stars, Superstars: Story of Pop, London: Octopus, 1974

† Spitz, Robert S., *The Making of Superstars: the Artists and Executives of the Rock Music World*, New York: Doubleday, 1978

Stewart, Ed., *'Stewpot' Stewart's Book of Pop*, London: Pan, 1973

* Stokoe, John and Reay, Samuel, *Songs and Ballads of Northern England*, Newcastle: Walter Scott, 1893 (reprinted 1974)

† Storemen, Win., *Jazz Piano: Ragtime to Rock Jazz*, New York: Arco, 1975

† Straw Dog, *Improving Rock Guitar*, New York: Schirmer Books, 1975

** Thompson, Edward P., 'Time, work-discipline and industrial capitalism', *Past & Present*, 38 (December 1967)

*** Thompson, Edward P., *The Making of the English Working Class*, Harmondsworth: Penguin, 1968

† Tobler, John, *Pop Quest*, London: ITV Books/Arrow, 1978

†† Ulanov, Barry, *A Handbook of Jazz*, London: Hutchinson, 1958

† Ulsan, Michael and Solomon, Bruce, *The Rock 'n' Roll Trivia Book*, New York: Simon & Schuster, 1978

* Vulliamy, G., and Lee, D., *Pop Music in School*, Cambridge: Cambridge University Press, 1976

† Walker, Jerry L., *Pop Rock Lyrics*, vols. 1-3, New York: Scholastic Book Services, 1971

† Walker, Jerry L., *Pop/Rock Songs of the Earth*, New York: Scholastic Book Services, 1972

† White, Mark, *Observer's Book of Big Bands*, London: Warne, 1978

† Whitfield, Jane, *Songwriters Rhyming Dictionary*, Hollywood, California: Wilshire, 1974

† Wilbur, L. Perry, *How to Write Songs that Sell*, Chicago: Contemporary Books, 1977

† Williams, Allan, and Marshall, William, *The Men Who Gave the Beatles Away*, London: Elm Tree Books, 1975

† Williams, John R., *This Was Your Hit Parade 1935-1950*, USA: Courier Gazette, 1973

Wolfe, Tom, *The Kandy-Kolored Tangerine Flake Streamline Baby*, London: Mayflower, 1968

Wolfe, Tom, *The Mid-Atlantic Man*, London: Weidenfeld & Nicolson, 1969

* Wolfe, Tom, *The Electric Kool-Acid Test*, London: Weidenfeld & Nicolson, 1969

† Young, Jean, and Young, Jim, *Succeeding in the Big World of Music*, Boston, Mass.: Brown and Company, 1978

** Young, Jock, *The Drugtakers: the Social Meaning of Drug Use*, London: Paladin, 1971

† Zadan, Craig, *Sondheim & Co.*, New York: Macmillan, 1974

(Zigzag), *The Road to Rock: A Zigzag Book of Interviews*, London: Charisma Books, 1974

Index